Praise for Alex Kovacs

"Kovacs puts one man's mind at war with the machinations of a whole world with considerable subtlety, intellectual ambition and wit."—Juliet Jacques, *New Statesman*

"Kovacs' novel . . . demonstrates that imaginative agitation can incite versions of reality that are more mindful and just."—Zach Savich, *Iowa Review*

"He displays a genuine knack for approaching the quotidian with a keen theoretical and essayistic eye."—Walter Gordon, full-stop.net

"The quality of the writing is enviable."—Sue Magee, *Bookbag*

"Alex Kovacs draws on the weight of meaning that paper can bear in the arts."—Laura Harris, *The Fourdrinier*

Other books by Alex Kovacs

The Currency of Paper

T0051665

Deep Vellum | Dalkey Archive Press
3000 Commerce Street
Dallas, Texas 75226
www.dalkeyarchive.com

Support for this publication has been provided in part by grants from the National Endowment for the Arts, the Texas Commission on the Arts, the City of Dallas Office of Arts and Culture, the Communities Foundation of Texas, and the Addy Foundation.

Paperback ISBN: 9781628975024
Ebook ISBN: 9781628975277
LCCN: 2024012067

Cover design by Matthew Avery
Interior design by Anuj Mathur
Printed in the United States of America

Images used on the cover include:
Via Unsplash: "person on a running horse," Lee Pigott (pappigo); "human face with paint," Daniel Apodaca (danielapodaca96); "sunken ship," Olga ga (olgaga); "yellow green and red floral print cards," Viva Luna Studios; "white polar bear in close up photography," Hans-Jurgen Mager (hansjurgen007); "city skyline under gray cloudy sky during daytime," Loïc Fürhoff (imagoiq) Via iStock: "Young black man in set of purple tracksuit stock photo," danielkrol Via WikiMedia Commons: "Diagram of Tissue Page 87.jpg," Alvin Davison

Alex Kovacs

SEXOLOGY

DALKEY ARCHIVE PRESS

Dallas, TX / Rochester, NY

Contents

Part Two: "Going Out into The World"

PART ONE:

Our Curious Origins

1.

Mother

I have spent much of my life being scared of my Mother.

When she was a child, Mother would devote long periods of time to destroying things. She liked to incinerate ants with piercing white rays of sunlight directed through a magnifying glass. During her adolescence, she began to enjoy breaking off the wing mirrors of cars with a crowbar after nightfall. She had done this solely for the illicit thrill that the act gave her. Sometimes she would share anecdotes of these occasions, shocking and en-thralling us with her accounts. She was a gifted storyteller and loved to have us as her doting audience, waiting for every last word to emerge from her like loyal courtiers. We took her excesses wholly for granted, knowing no alternative, and it was many years until we realized that her candid manner represented an unusual method of parenting.

A large part of the anxiety that she generated within me was due to her enormous imaginative capabilities. When playing the part of storyteller she could convince all of her children that we were occupying any location at all, as her narrations roamed across a multitude of differing spaces and situations. Bidding us to close our eyes, Mother would commence her descriptions of visual scenes, of mansions or tenements, of marketplaces or town squares, settings she had visited and those she had not, although she would always maintain that she had seen everything of which she spoke. I began to have my doubts about the veracity of this claim shortly after puberty began, even if I didn't voice these thoughts to anyone else at the time.

Every night when we were growing up she would burn sandalwood-scented incense and offer us plates heaped with currants and clementines. Once we were settled in our bedsheets, our whispered communiqués calling back and forth across our bedrooms as thinly as possible, we would stay expectantly awake, whilst we waited to hear Mother embarking on her often nightly journey of great shuddering orgasms, turbulent noises that would resound and echo throughout the house, causing wine glasses in the kitchen to vibrate against each other and form little tinkling sounds. Her ecstatic moans were also sometimes punctuated with the bitter slashing sounds of a whip, although that depended on who she was with that night, as her lengthy acts of commingling could be with one or another of her considerable catalogue of lovers.

She would often tell us that she felt tired of the burden of womanhood, that she would have preferred to have been born with male physiology and characteristics. Before any of her children had entered the world, there was a period in which she had taken on the appearance of a man, attempting to disguise herself thoroughly in that way on a daily basis. During that time she would often wear a brown derby, with a nearly matching camel-coloured suit, her outfit finished with the flourish of a white silk handkerchief spilling from her breast pocket. However, this sort of look was only destined to last for a brief time. She soon began to feel a strong attachment to her femininity and came to a point where she formally renounced all aspirations to a masculine identity.

Whilst she was a man she had enjoyed employing a gruff

voice, as well as "typically male" actions like placing a toothpick in the corner of her mouth or spending afternoons lurking inside betting shops. Being a man for a while had apparently, perhaps paradoxically, brought her closer to her femininity, made her appreciate the body and mind that she *did* possess. In particular, she became fascinated with her body's capacity for conceiving and bringing forth children, as well as with the many possibilities for conception available to her. At the age of twenty-four she felt she had lost time for potential child rearing, resolving there and then to make more of an effort in this direction. Procreation was to become a self-confessed addiction for her and in all she would give birth to ten children.

In descending order of first appearance these children were called: Ag, Lucinda, Flo, Rebecca, Gerard, Eliza, Barnaby, Billy, Lilly, and Matty (Me). After a number of years Mother was to become gainfully employed as a professional sexologist.

She enjoyed creating many occasional and disposable personas with us. In a spirit of full collaboration she would help us to invent new names, histories, pastimes, ages, wardrobes, aspirations. Retrospectively, I can see how, as with so many of her activities, this was supposed to be liberating, when often it seemed to wind up being terrifying, at least to me. At the time she had a clear set of responses to combat accusations like this from her children, often stating clearly to us that despite its extraordinary beauty, existence could be an overwhelming, disquieting fact, and that our venturing towards some ideal of freedom was therefore bound to involve aspects which would frighten us. We accepted this, just as we accepted the wisdom and truth of just about every single utterance that she made.

She liked to teach us certain blatant untruths that I still feel incredibly resentful over. Memories of her presenting certain statements as incontestable facts resound in my mind like fragments of bad, jarring music. She told us that in Thailand, ironically, no one wears ties. She claimed that the moon was constructed with human labour. That clean air was a commodity regulated by the government. In what was perhaps her worst lie, she told us that if we ate a large enough number of broad beans we could be immunized from certain fatal diseases, such as cancer. I now find it curious to consider her motives behind this genuinely mischievous behaviour. Did she never stop herself to consider the harm she might be doing us? Later, she would say that she had invented these outrages to "surprise" us when we were older. But after years of these intermittent surprises, after I had passed my thirtieth birthday, I confronted her one evening with great uncontrolled wrath, and we launched into the first of a series of long shouting duels, which would often end in long silences.

In fact Mother was a self-diagnosed manic-depressive. My feeling is that she had once *decided* to be a manic-depressive and had also resolved to remain one. When she entered a negative phase it was terrifying for anyone to encounter her. She might spend hours with her face buried in her hands, sobbing uncontrollably. Any attempt on the part of her children to relieve her misery was liable to be met with confusion. She might shout at us, or tell us to leave her alone, or she might simply form indistinct sounds representative of misery. Nevertheless, she never blamed her children for her episodes of unhappiness, it was always the wider social sphere. Our great consolation during her low periods was that we knew the current episode would be over by the following day, because, without failure, they always were.

Whilst we were growing up, her many histrionic fits would alternate with smothering, wholly maternal episodes of hugging and attention-giving. These were occasions which we certainly preferred, but which could be, in their own way, just as intimidating. Her affections were so unhindered that it sometimes felt as if she was imposing herself upon us with both the physical enormity of her hugs, as well as the psychological weight of her out-of-control emotional hyperbole. Nevertheless, despite my occasional wincing, I did enjoy being crushed by her embraces, even as I might emit a series of squeaks, as she thrust my face into the substantial expanse of her shoulders, which resembled those of a wrestler.

Mother always intended to be encouraging. Only rarely would she criticize any of our actions, and only then because she genuinely believed that this might aid our improvement as human citizens. Whenever possible she liked to garland us with praise, even if we had accomplished only the most minimal endeavour, be it successfully tying our shoelaces for the first time, or winning a backstroke race at a swimming gala. When we grew older she liked to praise any sign of excess or rebellion she could detect within us, regardless of our intentions. Of course we played up to this, trying to win her affections however we could, using any means necessary to please her, acting like faithful adherents to a sect seeking solemn approval from our leader.

Mother would dress in eccentric outfits every day that I ever knew her. She never needed a wedding to attend. Her wardrobe was a parade of polychrome: shades of fuchsia, aquamarine, emerald, canary-yellow, velveteen-purple, poinsettia-red. She liked to live in the pretence that the house was a tropical environment, that the glowering skies of England did not exist. Different personalities would take her over, sometimes residing for months at a time, and it was often confusing to figure out which one needed to be appealed to. For a while she was fond of wearing a large, black tricorne hat and dispensing wisdom with the haughty tone of a mayor. On a Wednesday afternoon she might be seen tiptoeing around the living room in our family home in Highgate, barefoot, wearing a pink tulle dress, extending her arms in the air to accompany the music which often reverberated solely within the confines of her own head. Indeed, my strongest images of Mother during my younger years are all of her dressed in luridly coloured outfits, engaged in bouts of dancing. Careening across the house, she would form improbable shapes on the floor, before jumping up to break out into gyrations, whirling and swaggering into ramshackle configurations of limbs. Whenever possible she would draw anyone nearby towards her, urging them to join in, attempting to encourage every last person to dance with her, in whatever form they wished to, seizing them by the hand or the hip, trying to get them to align themselves with her chaos of unrestrained parading. "Come on Matty, my sweetheart! Come and dance with me!" She might call out. Despite my shyness, I was always glad when I did.

2.

Father

My Father was a millionaire who had inherited his fortune by having been fortuitously born into a zip manufacturing dynasty. He possessed few direct links to the machinations of industry, electing instead to shrewdly place a series of servile henchmen throughout the physical confines of his grandfather's sprawling empire, ranging from mineshaft entrances to factory floors to office unit desk spaces. At every last location in this elaborate network a series of exclusively masculine individuals could be observed, neatly marshalling stacks of papers imprinted with black rows of statistics. Many of the more senior of these men were in the habit of secretly procuring things such as their remote island properties or weekend escapes to Monte Carlo. This and a multitude of similar actions were achieved through the use of forgotten bank accounts that functioned as secret economic annexes. Whenever necessary, they would bark statements like vociferous hounds into telephones or faces, so that their authority might be known and feared.

After separating from Mother, it became rare for Father to bestow his presence upon us at all. Essentially he was absent almost every single day of my life. Often vulgarly indifferent to the needs and sufferings of others, Father dedicated most of his time to maximizing the privileges and joys of ownership. Nevertheless, it must be said, he always provided us with vast, lavish gifts, and sums of money.

He would begin each working day at around noon, sat in an armchair, garbed in his maroon silk dressing gown emblazoned with roaring yellow lions, feet snugly encased in felt slippers, his standard attire for holding a conference with the assistants he was on most intimate terms with. These figures, in contrast to Father, were all required to endure the entire meeting standing up, whilst always wearing well-laundered black suits, an appearance which was deemed necessary largely in order to provide a stark contrast with Father's, so causing an unequivocal representation of the precise dynamics of their power relations in the form of a daily visual tableau, an image which was generally only viewed by those contributing to its formation.

On two or three occasions, when I was still a child, I was permitted to observe this everyday summoning of secretarial fawning, an experience that I would never be capable of forgetting, which in later years would lodge itself in my mind as an aberration of self-indulgent gimmickry, made all the worse by my consanguineous associations with the man sat before me. Even as a child, when I could only instinctively sense the wrongness of many acts, this behaviour made me feel deeply uneasy, and during my adolescence I made a conscious vow to never attempt to even slightly emulate this kind of behaviour.

I was always destined to possess a special bond with my youngest sister Lilly, because we were the only two of the siblings who had been brought forth by the same source of spermatozoa, and we were also the two youngest of the entire clan. There was often a sense of the two of us sharing some species of nearly unspoken conspiratorial knowledge capable of causing ruptures in the lives of anyone who ventured too close to us. We both despised our father but were nevertheless fascinated by him, somewhat against our better judgement.

Usually, whenever anyone was looking for us at home, they would first go to see if we were hiding in the attic together and playing one of the variety of games we had invented inside what we named "The Fortress," a construction which we had built out of flattened cardboard boxes, ones that had once held clusters of red cherries and which still bore bright-coloured images of that fruit on their sides. We often liked to pretend that we were trapped inside a city which was under siege. Surveying the terrain with a pair of binoculars, we would spend hours taking turns diligently observing the stairs, watching out for the possible arrival of enemies. When behind our blockade, we would go on reconnaissance missions, cautiously creeping through the territories of the house, attending to all behaviours and visual data we encountered, then returning to the refuge of The Fortress, where we would give breathless, though wholly serious and comprehensive reports of all that we had encountered, which might result in new directives or the formation of difficult decisions that had to be made impulsively. Terrified of the explosions constantly rending the skies, and of the rumbling of tanks in the streets below us, we would lie huddled in each other's arms, falling into little episodes of sleep, during which time Lilly would often emit long, perfectly translucent strings of dribble that fell onto my neck.

In Father's absences, which sometimes lasted for years on end without so much as one of his scrawled notes arriving in the post, he would, at erratic intervals, send the two of us elaborate, beribboned crates of toys. These often arrived without formal explanation and were usually sent from distant locations, places we assumed he must have been visiting at the time. When these arrived we would apishly hack them open as quickly as we could, submerging our fingers into the cache of riches that lay within, pulling out figurines with outlandish faces, or enigmatic contraptions that neither we nor Mother knew the correct names for.

I do distinctly remember one occasion on which I found myself alone with Father during my childhood, a rare example of Lilly's absence during one of these meetings. This took place inside one of Father's many offices when I was only six years old. He used this as an opportunity to speak with me "man to man" as it were.

"Do you know what you want to do with your life yet?" He asked me in a scary voice that held a great deal and felt very serious and of major consequence.

"No, I don't," I said in a small, cracked voice.

"Well, I must say, I believe in a young man like you possessing some ambitions from the earliest age possible. I believe they're a very good, very healthy thing for a young man to have going around in his head . . . Do you happen to have any ambitions?"

"No," I said, truthfully, after attempting to give this some genuine thought.

"What kind of things do you like to do?"

I thought about this for a while and let my eyes scan around the room as I did so. There were many rows of red leather-bound books with gold lettering on their spines. Between some of these was the marble bust of a man whose name I was destined to never get to know.

"I like eating ice cream," I said, finally.

"Ah ha. Ice cream."

He pondered this information for a while, placing the fingers of both hands together whilst he did so, which was one of his habits when deep in thought. "Yes, I do believe the age of ice cream will come to an end at some point . . ."

I didn't know how to respond to that either, so I stared at him with a certain amount of fear, maintaining my silence. Eventually, Father spoke again:

"Well, my son, let me give you some advice. As soon as you possibly can, I would recommend that you seize hold of ambitions. That you begin to dream any dreams for your life that you might come to possess. And then research. You will need to do research into how you might make these dreams come true. You will need to discover what it will be necessary for you to do, in order to make these dreams become realities. So. Bearing that in mind, I would suggest that you should go straightaway and give these ideas some thought. Ambitions my son. That's the key word here. Ambitions."

I never did pay any attention to any of that. When I think of him now Father appears to me as a human busily caricaturing the features and mannerisms of a shiftless puppet rodent who had somehow acquired a monocle and a velvet smoking jacket. His greyish skin looked possessed with a kind of moral distemper that had come to dominate his physiology. He occupied a lean, bony frame that was suitable for acts of acquisitive lunging and clawing. Within his darting eyes you could see feverish stratagems for domination appearing, thoughts that seemed almost touchable. He was fond of both bigotry and cigars, of secretly winking at his children in an effort to make them feel that a significant and private interaction had occurred between us. This was the confidence trick of an emotional racketeer, of a man who wished to somehow veil each of his imminent departures in a hollow gesture of fake camaraderie. What felt even more infuriating was that every time he performed this trick, it was a wholly successful act, his winks becoming one image which we clung onto in his absence as flimsy evidence that he actually cared about us, when all of the available facts pointed to the contrary.

With Father chronically absent, I took to inventing him, fabricating an unreal figure, someone whose mind contained far more plentiful quantities of intellect and imagination than his actually did. Faced with a general paucity of details about someone, you are free to invent them yourself, and if you are writing the history of your own Father you are bound to make him heroic, nuanced, and charismatic, someone who has been, at least in their own way, victorious. I would gaze at the few photographs of him which I possessed and would endow his figure, his suits and stances, with the attributes of iconography. Eventually I realized what foolish assumptions I had been making about him. I came to feel that he was merely a vain, empty socialite; the kind of man who insisted that a martini always be present in his hand, a grin always etched onto his mouth like a necessary additional feature foolishly tacked on to him at the last moment.

Once I began to reach some form of adult awareness he diminished in my reckoning to the point that I dismissed him altogether and simply tried to forget him. Amongst the few photographs of him I had to hand there was one in which his pose involved his mouth creating a wide "O" shape, whilst he pretended to scratch his armpits; doubtless this was all in an effort to be jovial, but I suddenly felt I had been spawned by a buffoon.

In the final analysis, I feel that Father could never really bring himself to believe in anything whatsoever. Politics was a source of interminable boredom to him, as was any form of learning or artistry. Had he wished to, he could, of course, have attended university, but he never did. I have often wondered what Mother saw in him. Why, in fact, had she chosen to have children with him on two separate occasions? Did she do this merely for the sake of financial comfort? I assume that there must have been some kind of meaningful rapport existing between them, as they lived within the confines of the same house for close to two and a half years. (Father was then dismissed shortly after I was born.) It may well be that Mother disliked every last second of this arrangement as it unfolded, but when questioned on the issue she always denied this. "He was a man who possessed an instinct for being alive," she would say, in pretence, most likely, perhaps in order to cover up her extraordinary skills of extortion, which were largely muffled and hidden from view. In her sexological writings she frequently stated that as humans we ought to explore the potential of erotic attraction with every last consenting individual that we encounter in adulthood. Her attempts to practice this belief led her to some very curious life choices and I would certainly propose that her marrying Father was the most curious of all of them. Perhaps her relationship with him involved a significant quantity of self-deception as well.

Father was also a constant wanderer, given over to undertaking flamboyant journeys often lasting for long periods. These included his drifting across the skyscapes above Europe inside a zeppelin and his inscrutable voyage down the length of the Mississippi inside a bulbous, inflatable yellow rubber dinghy. These excursions might take place on a whim, and it was particularly dangerous if someone at a dinner party made a suggestion or a dare to him, as he was then liable to commence boarding a succession of vehicles the following day that would lead him to a further series of locations that were unknown to him, commencing another episode of his travels.

Father once spent an entire year having a yacht prepared in order to embark upon a long, rambling journey across the world's oceans. The yacht, pristinely new and covered in an inevitable sheen of white, stood in the docks of Southampton for the whole year awaiting its owner. For months, packages and deliveries would arrive on a nearly daily basis, with a constant crowd of men in overalls heaving large examples of antique furnishings and a vast assortment of other artefacts onto the boat. Waiting staff arrayed in waistcoats and black bowties began to lodge on board. Extensive supplies of brand new nautical equipment were hoarded on the vessel, including examples of every possibly useful object, regardless of whether it was actually required or not. Wallpaper bearing a specially commissioned design by a Norwegian graphic designer, was plastered across the walls, with a motif of anchors and coils of rope repeated across a turquoise background.

The yacht continued to stand in the harbour, waiting for Father to board it, with the assembled crew and serving staff all becoming more restless day by day, until eventually Father seemed to become entwined in more pressing concerns and finally the yacht was depopulated, its denizens motioned to leave. It was destined to lie empty and forlorn, with most of its contents still present for the best part of a decade, until Father suddenly remembered its existence and sold it to the owner of a safari park who he had met at a cocktail party one evening in Kuala Lumpur.

When I was twelve years old Father disappeared altogether and I was destined to never see him again.

3.

My Siblings

From as early as I can remember, I believed my presence was unwanted by the majority of my siblings. It was as if by the very acts of breathing and moving, I was trespassing within a dominion where only others held the right of sovereignty. My older siblings constituted a group so numerically large that I felt as if I had been forced into a great surging torrent of humanity. From the beginning I was bombarded by the clamour of human needs, egotisms, preferences, rivalries, voices. Arguments were often a daily occurrence in our household, sometimes seeming as ubiquitous as air. For my part, I never thought that I possessed the status required to launch into a didactic defence of my own point of view, be it an opinion on a model railway set, or, later, one related to the ethics of democratic governance. It was simply evident that beside my seniors I was their clear hierarchical inferior, someone who was worthy of contempt. Later, I would come to accept that these feelings were in fact partly a consequence of my own acute neuroticism, but that didn't make the experience of them any easier to cope with at the time.

The Elder Set (Ag, Lucinda, and Flo)

Ag, Lucinda, and Flo, being the three oldest, formed a natural triumvirate. In time they would become known to everyone as "The Elder Set," a name of their own coinage, which they used frequently, a clear upsurge of pride being embedded in their voices whenever they did so. At times they resembled a group of female lieutenants, commandeering events whenever they thought it was necessary, paying considerable attention to hygienic routines each evening after Mother had retired, and always ensuring that everyone fulfilled their quota of chores. The Elder Set's group identity often manifested itself in a shared sense of superiority and entitlement, a factor of the household which could be terrifying to me in its many ramifications.

They would share absolutely everything, from make-up supplies to burgeoning aesthetic opinions, and could frequently be seen exchanging sentences into each other's ears in conspiratorial murmurs, like spies operating within the realm of teenagers. These secret communications would frequently be followed shortly afterwards with joyous, knowing peals of laughter, affirming that their underhand knowledge had become reciprocal.

If I was not performing as they wanted a younger brother to, any of them was liable to clamp their hands upon my body, guiding my shoulders and fingers into the positions that they approved of. "Not like that Matty," was a continual refrain applied by all of them during my earliest years. I was their cherubic, rosy-cheeked creature to manipulate as they wanted, their surrogate child to practice their mothering skills on, a child who never possessed the confidence to turn on them and question their authority.

Even in a household taken up with libertarian attitudes, they were permitted a number of freedoms that the younger children were not. For example, we looked on with furious envy as we saw them being allowed to come home at any hour, to attend indie concerts, and to bring boyfriends home and have sex with them. In an unforgivable series of actions, Mother once let The Elder Set be entirely responsible for choosing our family holiday destinations for three years in a row. Because the rest of us were repeatedly denied a voice in this matter, we, the younger siblings, proceeded to complain our way through an interminable series of European hotel lobbies, gift shops, and beach cafés.

One issue which became a particular grudge for Lilly and me, was that from an early age The Elder Set were allowed to cook their own meals, which was something that we longed to do, doubtless only because we couldn't. Tucked into woollen blankets inside The Fortress, we would dream aloud, longing for the elaborate dishes we might prepare in the future, and for many other imagined freedoms that we did not possess. We became particularly fixated on the possibility of eating blancmange every night, something that we had only eaten once before, at a friend's house, and which despite our pleading Mother repeatedly denied us.

Lucinda was only the second oldest of the siblings, but acted as if she was in fact the most senior. She was certainly the bossiest and most demanding. Occasionally she would summon me into her bedroom for a confrontation with officialdom, taking harsh stances that Mother never did and which Lucinda therefore felt she ought to implement herself. Enthroned in her armchair, her long legs crossed in imitation of an adult, I would sit at Lucinda's feet, considerably smaller in stature, my thick-framed plastic spectacles held together with masking tape, always in the act of nodding or apologizing. She was a full eleven years older than me, whilst also being very tall for her age, so she struck me as being a towering giant, as someone who belonged to a different category to the rest of the siblings. Often in fact she appeared more obviously adult than Mother, who was always something of a fantasist.

"How do you feel about what you've done?" Lucinda demanded.

"What have I done?"

"You know what you've done," she asserted.

"I don't."

"Disturbing Mummy when she was busy with her work."

"I wanted her to help me with my scarecrow drawings," I pleaded.

"You do realize that you mustn't disturb Mummy when she's doing certain things, don't you?"

"Yes," I agreed.

"There are a few things you need to understand about how this household works Matty," she began, "there are various boundaries which you mustn't cross because they disturb the privacy of others. There are some things that you shouldn't say to other people. You really shouldn't, for example, only talk about yourself and what you want. You need to begin to form some moral considerations towards other people and the sooner you start to do that the better."

She paused so that I might feel the weight of the room's silence and her gaze falling strongly upon me.

"Do I make myself clear?"

She didn't.

"Yes," I said.

"Very well, you can go back and join Lilly and continue with your scarecrow drawings now."

"Thank you," I said.

Rebecca

Rebecca was someone who I could always rely on for support and amiable company. Too young to be considered worthy of The Elder Set, Rebecca presented her own hectic, mirthful example in the household, being an ebulliently vocal individual, even amongst such an enormous group of voices clamouring for attention.

Plump, with wobbly arms and pockets of fat gathered around her form, Rebecca found her movements to be slightly impeded by her bulk, but this never seemed to stop her infectious sense of enthusiasm from carrying her onwards. In a gesture that saw her make a statement in favour of masculinity, she always kept her hair cropped short, and in her late teens always kept one side shaved close to the skin, a habit she took on in order to prove her affinity with certain lesbian lovers, who, to Mother's delight, Rebecca put at the centre of both her romantic and social worlds.

At first I didn't understand the causal connections between her haircut and her many sassy girlfriends, who would often be encouraged by Mother to sleep over in Rebecca's room, and could be heard giggling uncontrollably in the midst of the night. Doubtless because I loved Rebecca so much, I always enjoyed picking out that sound amongst the usual nocturnal rustlings which generally dominated the upper reaches of the house.

She would wear patchwork dresses she had sewn together herself whilst humming musical numbers from the 1930s that no one else was familiar with. She loved making her own badges, tiny luminescent windows of colour, which brightened her rucksacks and lapels. Her designs often involved porcupines— her favourite animal.

I remember Rebecca grabbing me to her chest in the garden and twirling the two of us around in rapid circles, until we were both dizzy and collapsing together on the lawn with flushed, roseate cheeks. Indeed I could always count on her for hugs of enormous duration, a tendency she had evidently inherited from Mother. Rebecca exuded a pleasantly mammalian, milky odour which seemed to be partly composed of items stolen from the kitchen.

She was fond of making videotapes consisting exclusively of adverts culled from television stations. These would be viewed again and again with impatient excitement, and I loved to sit beside her as this was occurring. Often she would fast-forward through adverts, always wishing to skip ahead in the hope of perhaps reaching some kernel of glory that might lie at the tape's heart. When she discovered an advert she wanted to watch she would put the remote control down and clap her hands together in delight.

"Look, Matty!" she would exclaim, "it's the dancing woman made out of butter!" and she would proceed to quote the script of the advert by heart as it unfolded, jumping up to mirror the dance actions of the butter woman, sometimes breaking into ballroom dancing with Mother if she happened to be present and falling into infectious laughter.

At one time Rebecca loved to routinely refer to herself in the third person. She always refused to explain why she did this exactly. Tickling was one of her favourite activities, and indeed subjects of conversation, and this remained so well into her adulthood. She liked to read encyclopedias and forgotten old reference books, reciting facts from them at the dinner table, eagerly declaring "It's a fact!" after she had finished on each occasion. She would send fan letters to quiz show hosts who she felt to be unfairly neglected. When she was fifteen she suddenly became fixated upon the cuisine of Kazakhstan, probably because no one else was.

Rebecca was also addicted to lying. She didn't do this in a selfish, deceitful way, as it was always well known to everyone that she was quite evidently lying about a large range of subjects. Her falsehoods involved a merging of the practice of lying with that of joke telling, a brand of social exhibitionism some in the family found tiresome after encountering it regularly over the course of many years, but which I personally never felt anything other than admiration for.

During another period Rebecca was fond of delivering ten-minute "presentations" to the family. These would appear with little to no prior warning. Suddenly she would be racing through the house, urgently conveying the fact of her imminent performance through her raised voice and the tender squeezing of arms. These were always brief one-woman affairs often involving costumes and props. Illustrative materials were provided in the guise of slide projections and A4 photocopied handouts that ended in tiny bibliographies of only three or four items. She would often use these occasions to make affectionate, ironic commentaries upon the goings on in the household, or she might deliver a miniature lecture about her reactions to the work of Frida Kahlo, or indeed on "the meaning of windows."

The Independent Republic of the Third Floor (Gerard, Eliza, and Barnaby)

When they were, respectively, 14 (Gerard), 13 (Eliza), and 12 (Barnaby), three members of the household declared that they had formed an independent state. This nation had its "centre" in the portion of the third floor occupied by these three siblings, but this state was not to be considered an entity solely defined by geography. They claimed that their state would continue to exist in any physical location whatsoever, depending entirely upon where any of its three citizens happened to be at that precise moment in time. Nevertheless they always insisted that it was a "place." The Parliament, which met once a week, was located in Gerard's room, whilst Eliza's room was the site of the Treasury, and Barnaby hosted the Foreign Office.

At the moment of the state's inception they drafted a constitution over the course of a weekend. A series of preliminary laws were rendered in looping calligraphic script on a number of scrolls of brown parchment paper, with elaborate and almost illegible signatures securing the veracity of all that was proclaimed upon the bottom of each page. By Sunday evening they had fashioned a flag from an old dishcloth and had composed a national anthem on a broken miniature Casio keyboard, which they sang for the whole family before dinner that night.

The Elder Set immediately kicked up a fuss, chairing a "public debate" on Monday evening, which saw them rejecting the Republic as a political entity, referring to it as "demoralizing" and "destructive to the necessary conditions of family life." They demanded the "stepping down" of the Republic, to ensure the reign of equality and democracy in the household, ending their speech with a call for a public vote, asking householders to openly declare whether the Republic should possess a right to exist. The Elder Set won this vote by six votes to five, but Mother overturned the vote saying that the Republic would be permitted to continue existing until the moment when all of its members were deceased.

Lucinda made what would later seem to me a genuinely pertinent point: namely that these three siblings were not in fact the sole occupants of the third floor, as Rebecca also had a room on that floor. It therefore seemed a little excessively territorial to claim the *entire* third floor of the house as their very own Republic. When responding to this issue the Republic claimed, in a highly prepared statement of the kind that the family would become extremely used to hearing, that their territory encompassed the bedrooms of the three citizens of the state, as well as the spaces of corridor immediately adjacent to their own bedrooms, but that it did not include those spaces which stood in front of Rebecca's bedroom or her bedroom itself. This having been established and approved by Mother, tensions gradually decreased over time.

By the end of the nation's inaugural weekend, crisscrossing lines of patriotic bunting had been set up in the hallway. A barricade of dining room chairs separated their portion of the floor from the rest. On top of one of them a brass handbell had been placed beside a typewritten note asking all visitors to: "Ring for the attentions of passport control." No one felt sure what might be permissible in this territory any longer. Personally I felt an enormous sense of trepidation looking on to the Republic. From the other side of the border I intuited that citizenship would almost certainly be denied me, and in any case, I did not feel brave enough to make an application for it.

In the following months and years the nation's three citizens often refused to speak as individuals, only issuing statements collectively, discourses that usually commenced with the words: "The Independent Republic of the Third Floor declares that . . ." To the general credit of the Republic, such statements were liable to be read out by any of its three citizens, this despite the fact that the general impetus behind most of them, ideologically and aesthetically speaking, was Gerard, who had possessed the original inspiration for the country's formation.

All three siblings possessed the same father, whilst all of the other siblings were the consequence of different paternities. This remained a largely unspoken element of the Republic's decision to create such a dramatic rift within the house, being a feature of family relations that no one wanted to mention at all, as it was something that secretly caused all of us confusion and pain in our different ways, often in a manner that was quite inchoate and lasted for years on end.

Billy

Billy was the least confused member of the family. He would simply do whatever pleased him, often selfishly disregarding anyone else and yet rarely receiving any punishment for his actions. Lacking the slightest enthusiasm for any form of cleaning, his hair was always greasy and matted, protruding outwards into wild tufts and angles, a state of affairs that seemingly could not be resolved, even with the aid of a brush, as Lucinda always discovered whenever she tried to apply one to his unkempt mane. Most of his clothes possessed some form of perforation, a consequence of his constant scaling of walls, fences, and trees. He always claimed to prefer his clothes in that state and would complain vehemently whenever anyone attempted to alter his opinion on the subject.

As he grew older, all of us worried more and more about Billy. He didn't seem capable of developing any sensible aspirations, or of controlling his manic urges. Like Mother in her youth he was fired up by the thrill of vandalism. Unlike most of the other siblings he had no interest whatsoever in education of any kind. In late adolescence he drifted towards the world of Rock 'n' Roll, often not returning home after a night out until noon the next day, when he would collapse into an exhausted sweating heap, sometimes remaining in bed for a further twenty hours.

During these years his voice became hoarse and grainy and (greatly at odds with everyone else in the family), he took to imitating the timbre and style of the speech of his friends, who were mostly working-class. A strong liking for whisky eventually made his voice sound permanently cracked. He often liked to deliberately avoid using many basic grammatical structures, making frequent gleeful errors with both tenses and prepositions, in order to show how little he cared about them.

He was both narcissistic and cruel towards anyone who did not share his lack of morality, chastising me for not sampling any of the many illicit substances which he was fond of both selling and socially circulating. Taunting me, he might try to tempt me into actually fighting him. For some reason he seemed to think it was his duty to make certain people feel as uncomfortable as possible.

Billy enjoyed screaming as loudly as he could. If he got bored of this, he liked to destroy any objects which entered his hands. Mother would often support him in this direction: "Let it out Billy, yes, Billy, let it out," she might say, patting him firmly with approval, as if he was a member of her livestock.

He liked to remain in the same clothes for some time without washing or changing, so his odour became highly recognizable. Traces of it were deposited in unexpected locations around the house, and it was possible to have clear foreknowledge of his arrival—for quite a few seconds before he actually appeared. Mother explained this as a natural episode of growing up, but eventually The Elder Set refused to accept this, and would bundle him, whilst yelling and writhing, into the bathtub, tearing off his clothes and assailing his body with flannels and bars of soap. Professing hatred of this, he always secretly enjoyed the conflict involved in the situation and would even sometimes instigate it deliberately.

During one period Billy began to emit a series of abstract noises, sounds that fell a long way short of cohering into recognizable verbal patterns, a habit which made him appear to be lacking in sanity. These were liable to be sounds of any variety, be they throat-centred growling variations, or high-pitched palettes of noises that you felt could have emerged from concealed items of machinery. When younger he would produce these noises in any location, being especially interested in disorientating strangers whenever given the chance. Lucinda would sternly admonish him for this, coming to physical blows with Mother over the issue, who felt that this was perhaps Billy's principal form of creative expression and should not be attacked. To settle the issue Mother challenged Lucinda to a wrestling match, a proposal which Lucinda responded to with hysterical shrieking:

"What sort of a fucking Mother are you anyway? Do you actually have any boundaries at all?"

"Probably not," said Mother, calmly, cocking her eyebrow.

Lilly

Before she turned thirteen years old, the age at which she decided to reject me, Lilly and I were almost inseparable, operating in our own expansive fantasy world of secret games and signals. We never let anyone else enter this domain, but it was populated with thousands of invisible beings, some of whom came to possess names and personalities, their precise motives usually resting out of reach, as if obscured behind an endless range of opaque screens.

Lilly, being older than me by two years, had been the first architect of this imaginative location, dragging me into it, wide-eyed and captivated, whilst I was still so naive and unschooled that I was incapable of telling the time by decoding the meaning of the placement of hands upon a clockface. She led me, stumbling, across the surfaces of alien planets, or into vast water kingdoms where citizens only paused on land for a few moments each month, before promptly returning to the aqueous depths which were seen as highly preferable.

When telling me about these things Lilly would command me to place my hands over my eyes, as she whispered her lengthy monologues to me, occasions on which I was teleported to a series of fictive places that came to possess the weight of the real. Whatever Lilly requested of me, I would willingly perform; as she always led me into hopeful places, I was always glad to be her accomplice.

We both loved to speculate about whether aliens existed and would dream of traversing intergalactic spaces. Late at night we would discuss where we believed the universe ended, how many planets it contained, and what proportion of those planets could sustain life-forms. We hardly knew anything about astronomy. During our first conversation of this sort we decided that we were both firm believers in the existence of aliens.

In those years we would invent many elaborate environments, purely through the act of speaking. For hours we might concentrate all of our energies on the invention of a town, agreeing upon its architectural landmarks, layout, and essential atmosphere, as well as compiling elaborate biographies of the persons who lived there. We were attentive to every last permutation that our imaginations revealed to us and would debate the likelihood of certain details, discussing whether certain elements did or didn't "fit" into our scheme. "No Matty," Lilly might state very matter-of-factly, "it wouldn't be like that, it would be much better if it was . . ." But we would never actually have very serious disputes over these issues. We soon learned to welcome the other's inventions.

For a number of years Lilly and I were the people that we each trusted the most. When confronted with the other siblings, or most other adults or outsiders, Lilly would often lapse into purely monosyllabic speech, deeply unsure of how to successfully represent herself to any gazing public. When things became too much in these situations her features would visibly redden and she would bury herself in Mother's shoulders, resembling a creature burrowing into the ground in order to evade the pervasive glare of light.

After reaching the age of thirteen she suddenly decided one day that she could no longer be unguarded with me. This arrived entirely without warning. She wasn't cruel towards me, or even overtly dismissive, but it suddenly seemed impossible for us to talk and invent things together as we used to. Now she would suddenly walk away from me, visiting other destinations in the house, making it known that she wanted to be alone. Frequently she would use the excuse of wanting to read books, which she claimed, quite plausibly, was an activity that had to be performed in solitude. She had entered another location to me, and from then onwards I would always be locked out of it.

4.

The Momentous Frantic Liberation Game

We lived in a very large house in Highgate with rooms that contained high, corniced ceilings and long staircases that seemed to sprawl endlessly upwards. Mother was in the habit of leaving little piles of books on almost every single step, maybe in order to encourage us to read, or perhaps just due to the relentless disorder of her private library. There were so many rooms that you frequently had to spend some minutes pacing around and calling out the name of whoever you were looking for before you located them.

On the final Friday of each month this unreal edifice became the stage for an elaborate family exercise, during which Mother would encourage us to withdraw from our imaginative inhibitions and celebrate our potential for unruliness. This occasion was known as "The Momentous Frantic Liberation Game," a name which Mother would write in green-coloured chalk on the kitchen blackboard, with that month's times for setting up, commencement, termination, and clearing up. Within these bounds most behaviours were deemed possible, as there were no rules to speak of and few clear goals to be attained. Firstly, all of the house's many fragile objects had to be cleared away and stored in the attic. Canvas sheets were draped across the remaining furnishings, walls, and surfaces. At the beginning of each game Mother would ring her handbell and exclaim: "Play has commenced!"

During the occasions when the game was played, manoeuvring through the thoroughfares of the house in a clear, linear fashion often became challenging. A cacophonous stampede of hollering, ululating children was liable to erupt at any moment. In such conditions, a room of ordinary dimensions and appearance might rapidly become an auditorium, a parliament, a museum, or a courthouse. As soon as enough members of the Elder Set had declared the direction a game was taking, it often would, indeed, unswervingly take that course. Rooms would come to possess a multiplicity of identities, a notion which Mother was eager to instill in us. She would always join in the game at the beginning, often insisting upon veneration, as she inhabited the bodies of a series of senior and eminent figures. This often saw her assuming a low, booming intonation, in order to imitate, enjoy, and mock the authority of a series of red-faced men who dwelt in late middle age.

A general dispersal of the siblings into a series of either single or double groupings was also a frequent occurrence. In this variant of the game each sibling or duo came to represent a small, densely populated island, each with its own customs and characteristics. The three hours of the game's duration would be taken up with acts of larking and cavorting, seeing many zany outpourings played out on a scale that most people never get to witness. In one room, tambourines might be beaten among individuals practicing discordant carousing, whilst elsewhere another family member might be spraying the front hall with tendrils of silly string, with another scrunching sheets of paper through an amplifier whilst sprawled underneath a gigantic layer of spontaneously arranged camouflage netting. One year, for some months, a life-size sugarcube igloo stood in the centre of the floor in the conservatory, which provided a good location for dashing in and out of during the game, usually when you had no particular purpose in mind. Lounging horizontally inside it was also recommendable.

When in a certain mood we might assume costumes or new identities, as rodeo cowboys, as sorcerers, as beauty pageant queens, as frogmen. The latter role appealed to me enormously and I would rush through the house slapping my flippers with exaggerated effort upon the hard tiles of the kitchen floor, my features snugly hidden behind my wetsuit and a black rubber eye mask, all the while puffing for enjoyment on an empty oxygen canister strapped to my back, which I lugged around the spaces of the house, enjoying the spectacle it was helping me to create.

As they got older the members of the Elder Set were generally anxious to demonstrate their good taste, displaying their creative abilities each month, in order to set an example for their younger siblings, to prove how much closer to maturity they were themselves. An ongoing battle was established between their considered aestheticism and our uncultivated acts of vandalism. Ag and Flo would often prepare elaborate, precocious examples of song and dance routines well in advance of each game session. One year they would always arrive wearing matching purple leotards, performing with twirling batons as they sang, forming precise geometrical patterns in tightly choreographed motions, actions that had been perfected during the previous weeks behind the locked door of Ag's bedroom.

Anarchy would always break out in a multitude of forms. I remember one of many comparable occasions from these games:

"Benevolent creatures! Hidden personalities!" Gerard was busy proclaiming. "You must come downwards and flourish around and within us! Know that you might dwell safely within the confines of our Living Room! That this can be your own home as well as ours!" he said loudly, in a grandiloquent voice, which betrayed a lack of absolute seriousness.

"What are you doing Gerard?" asked Flo.

"I'm invoking the muses, the deities hidden amongst us!" stated Gerard.

"Is that how you do that?" wondered Flo.

"Yes, it is!" said Gerard.

"Forget deities," said Rebecca. "You just need to know what day it is . . ."

"It's Friday," said Gerard, in a very matter of fact voice.

"I was just going to . . ." began Rebecca, but she was cut off by Barnaby who proceeded to softly, even affectionately, place the form of a rhubarb pie dripping with custard on to the empty canvas of her face.

Events proceeded rapidly towards a further level of illogical disintegration from there onwards. Such were the ways of our game.

When I was younger I could, at times, feel uneasy when we played like this, sensing that my actions were perceived as inferior when compared with those of the Elder Set. Mother wouldn't let any of her children actively participate until they were five years old, so prior to then I was merely a jealous observer, often running along at the margins of activities. It was extremely anxiety inducing for me when I finally became a debutant. I spent my first few games crying and clutching onto my Mother's legs, burying my head in the material of one of her cotton dresses, inhaling its odour in pursuit of the comfort it gave me.

Eventually I realized that no one really controlled this game, that indeed the entire purpose of it was to offer a space for self-expression, and at that moment (when I was eight years old), I began to enjoy adding precisely whichever goofy dissonances to our collective outpourings that I wanted to. It seems I had just needed a little encouragement, which as always, Mother had provided me with.

Usually one sibling would launch themselves upon the turntable near the beginning of each game, appropriating for a few moments the distant glamour of disc jockeys, providing us with a soundtrack selected from Mother's extensive and eclectic record collection. For a couple of years it was a constant challenge for me to get near the turntable at all, as my siblings were always encircling it like insects attracted by a lightbulb. Choosing what went on the turntable became a privilege always denied to me. Even if I ran towards it and reached the destination first I was usually shouldered away, made to feel guilty about my assuming a role that I could not adequately fulfil. It took Mother a while to realize what was going on in this regard, and when she did lend me her help, I found that all I ever wished to hear was the tune "Spanish Fly" by Herb Alpert and the Tijuana Brass, a song which everyone other than Mother and I hated. The entire household would repeatedly implore me to take it off, to play any other track whatsoever, but it was the music that induced the most joyousness within me. With Mother adjacent, safeguarding my position, I was liable to play this single song twenty or thirty times in a row, a practice which would continue for a number of years, until I, too, finally tired of it myself.

Despite the freedoms afforded us by the game, Mother did in fact subtly control us through the placement of her person at crucial moments, making her disapproval known if necessary, but mostly urging us onwards as she looked on or joined in with the general merriment and mayhem.

It was always very clear to us that we were not permitted to physically attack each other, that although it was possible to unleash fermented bean paste spatterings upon the walls, for example, any sort of physical violence was out of the question. Our antics always stopped short of actually being hazardous, probably through the subliminal, nearly hypnotic influence of Mother, whose presence could always be clearly detected, and was often somehow clearly palpable, even inside rooms from which she was entirely physically absent.

When I came to be a little older I became, for a time, more disturbed by this game. I recall Billy, his hair laden with drooping strands of tinned spaghetti, mingled with tomato sauce, as he busied himself with serenading a nude, bald, wax mannequin which he cradled in his arms, swooping down to the floor with her, before immediately raising her into the air, always clutching her tenderly like a dance partner, like his surrogate girlfriend, like the woman he would never come to possess, but dearly dreamed of. He exuded sweat and a feral intensity. There was a lunacy resident in his eyes that afternoon, the sight of which has never departed from me, providing me retrospectively with a sense that he had been allowed to stray too far from civility, that he had been profoundly misguided. It was the first time I had ever questioned the game, had ever pondered over its sensibleness.

Nevertheless, the game could take on an infinite variety of permutations and few of us ever wearied of playing it entirely. At any one time you might find Billy wrestling on the living room carpet with an inflatable alligator; Ag and Flo might be anointing each other with patterns of UV paint in order to adopt the faces of tree sprites; Gerard could on occasion be found wandering from room to room, reciting long lists of horse racing statistics from a newspaper held out in front of him; Lucinda, deliberately withdrawing from the game's atavistic tendencies, would often be found in her room profoundly absorbed in the reading of an antiquarian engineering manual, dreaming of building clock-towers and steamships; Eliza and Barnaby might be staring into each other's irises, attempting to exchange identities; Lilly could be flushed from sprinting through the garden, brandishing an iridescent whirligig; Rebecca might approach you and proclaim: "Watch me create a sparkling Universe!"

We would all gradually congregate in the kitchen when Mother commenced clanging her handbell declaring: "Come all ye! Come all ye! The Game is over! Dinner is served!"

5.

Education, Education, Education

Mother had radical beliefs about the nature of education, thinking of most schools as places that stunted genuine growth and imagination. She saw home schooling as the best way to implement her own ideas. Wishing for us to determine the direction of our learning ourselves, she would ask us what we would like to study and then collaborate with us in the creation of timetables and curricula.

At this time we possessed a deep belief in this ideology. Mother was exceptionally gifted at convincing us of the importance of embarking on the adventure of attaining knowledge, speaking frequently of our potential emancipation from the fetters of society, urging us onwards with promises of ideal days and the outlandish fulfilments of adulthood.

All of us were to be assembled every weekday morning in the kitchen for breakfast at eight thirty, and our schooling would unfailingly commence at nine, with Mother delivering a speech of relevance to the entire audience, a body of persons that included the whole household, with the occasional addition of one of Mother's lovers. When delivering these speeches she possessed the outrageous charisma of a cult leader, feeding herself on her illusions, whilst busily propagating them:

"You can be or do *anything*, any last thing that you want to achieve can be achieved, you just have to seize things whole, grasp things in their entirety . . ." she would assert, often adding improvised rhetorical flourishes as she spoke.

After these morning orations were finished we would then be split into four separate "classes," each group being based, primarily, in a different room. Membership of these cohorts was officially determined by age, but a subsidiary effect of this partitioning was that each cluster of siblings who studied together possessed the same Father.

Ag, Lucinda, and Flo were the children of Percival Evans; Rebecca and Billy were the children of Dagmar Polke; Barnaby, Eliza, and Gerard were the children of Stephen Millicent; whilst Lilly and I were the children of Reginald Humberholdt. We nevertheless all first thought of our identities as being defined by our particular age groups, partly because most of these men only turned up at the house occasionally, our own Father being the least likely to put in an appearance.

As we progressed through our years of education, my older siblings always seemed to occupy unreachable intellectual domains, separate from our own, places in which they would engage in conversations whose content I knew only through the conjecture of childish interpretations. These were dialogues that I was entirely left out of, exchanges that seemed so much more sophisticated than the ones I had with Mother and Lilly. Many of the older children seemed to start resembling adults by the time they were fifteen, but when it was finally my turn to be fifteen I seemed to have retained every last feature of my boyish simplicity and gullibility.

Mother always employed a small group of teaching assistants, who were all selected from amongst her postgraduate students at the university and whose faces changed with an alarming regularity. Generally, we didn't like being taught by these people as much as by Mother herself. They often didn't really seem to know quite what they were doing and they lacked Mother's many personal touches. We were often in the habit of moaning about them in a spirited way.

Even if Mother was present, we often learnt very little during our lessons because she would disappear to attend to the other children, or to do academic research in her study. This left us to play games with each other, or do things like complete dot-to-dot pictures under the table on our knees. These things were not strictly forbidden, but we nevertheless knew they were not really what Mother really wanted from us. Sometimes Lilly and I would sabotage the lesson, attacking Mother with tickling or water pistols. In any case she didn't seem to mind these interruptions, and in fact she would sometimes start them herself, once clownishly unleashing jets of whipped cream upon us, whilst she was engaged in delivering a particularly tedious and longwinded speech about some of the tactics involved in organic farming.

Whenever a subject appeared to be of interest to us, Mother would attempt to encourage our development by assailing us with books, exercises, games, and images, so that our curiosity was usually satisfied. When one year I showed a passing enthusiasm for the nation of Brazil, Mother rapidly attempted to kindle this by providing me with great stacks of material on the country, projecting hundreds of slides on the wall, and playing Samba records until I finally had to tell her that I was no longer interested in the country at all. But this did not quell her persistence for some months. Mother was always ready with encouragements of this kind, and in retrospect, it strikes me as one of the most touching aspects of her character.

Eventually I began to wonder if Mother actually planned out our education, as we seemed to follow the agreed upon curriculums only erratically. Often she would begin talking to us about one very clear, evidently significant subject, and before even a minute had elapsed, her mind would have skipped ahead to entirely different locations, her teaching breaking down into extended conversations about spaceships or elephants, in which digressions would take place within digressions. Early on in our educational history we learnt to prompt these circuitous verbal journeys, as we tended to prefer them to anything that struck us as being too redolent of more recognized forms of schoolwork. Nevertheless, Mother did demand that we pursue many of the compulsory elements found in ordinary schools, so we were destined to learn about trigonometry and ox bow lakes, although these subjects were presented to us in a haphazard manner, interspersed between topics that an outsider would find unexpected in an educational context.

When she saw that we had become restless, Mother would often break off lessons for the day, and we would leap upwards and depart, pursuing whatever odd notions our absorbent minds had developed at that particular moment, eagerly testing our new theories with data charts and graphs, or resuming an abandoned arm-wrestling tournament. Mother would frequently lecture us on the essential importance of play, telling us that it mattered just as much to adults as it did to children, but that adults usually eradicated it from their lives, in favour of a variety of breeds of sterility and silence.

Mother would be frank with us about the limits of her own knowledge and experience, telling us that most people pretended they possessed no ignorance whatsoever. To prove how many other branches of knowledge existed, Mother would regularly bring in a number of outsiders to speak to us about their own fields in a way that she said she was incapable of doing. These guest speakers possessed differing forms of specialist knowledge, ranging from an appreciation of the processes with which phosphate is extracted from the earth, to, on one occasion, a nightclub DJ, who described the banality of his weekly routine, as well as some of its perks. Inevitably, he played us some records as we formed a crescent of adulation on the floor around him. We were all deeply marked by the DJ's appearance and bearing—noting his beard, his fluorescent green bubble shades, their matching green tracksuit, as well as his green-and-white chequered bowling shoes. Rumours persisted among the siblings for some weeks afterwards that he was one of Mother's new lovers, but this proved to be unfounded, much to the disappointment of both Lilly and myself, who had wanted to visit his flat and play on his decks.

One memorable educational episode saw Mother acting as the custodian of a collectively crafted papier-mâché blue whale, rendered in accurate life-size dimensions with strips of newspaper, glue paste, paint, and meshes of chicken wire. Once completed it spent an entire summer living suspended from the ceiling of an extensive white canvas marquee that stretched across the entirety of the lawn in the back garden. During the brief periods when no one else was present I liked to circumambulate around the perimeter of this creature and imagine its marine existence, tracing my finger along its voluminous bulk, staring for protracted periods into its elaborately detailed jaws, its mouth permanently ajar, displaying spongy baleen plates lodged in exact rows, protruding outwards solidly before tapering into thin strands like fuzzy unkempt brush heads. These basked inside sepulchral pink expanses of gums which seemed capable of swallowing entire buildings.

Whilst we made the whale together Mother wanted us to explore our relationship with nature, by gaining a tactile intimacy with the physiology of the largest animal ever known on our planet. It took us four days to make, despite working all day. In the evenings, when our labours ceased, Mother would encourage us to lie horizontal on the floor of the darkened living room and listen to recordings of the sounds emitted by blue whales. During the afternoons she would regale us with many facts about the creatures, standing in the corner of the room, quoting long paragraphs from a variety of textual sources, whilst we tirelessly slathered glue paste and moulded our wire framework.

To celebrate the completion of the sculpture we held a party in the garden with a maritime dress code, in which Lilly and I wore pirate costumes involving eye patches and plastic scabbards, whilst The Elder Set all appeared as mermaids, and Mother ruled as the figure of Poseidon, complete with a fake grey beard and imposing antique trident. We sang sea shanties to the accompaniment of an accordion. Sailors handed out trays of canapés consisting of crustaceans and pickled octopus tentacles, garnished with sorrel leaves. A rowing boat stood upon the grass, containing a looped recording of an ocean sound effects tape pouring out through concealed speakers embedded somewhere within the boat's frame. Lilly and I sat inside it for hours, closing our eyes and managing to feel that we were actually traversing an enormous body of water.

One morning, when I was eleven and Lilly was thirteen, Mother projected a slide for us illustrating a typical female fashion model appropriated from a women's magazine, a figure who lay languorously splayed on a plastic lounge chair that stood on a pristine white sand beach fringed with coconut trees.

"What do you think about the way she's been photographed?" Mother asked us.

"She looks nice," I said.

"Does she?" asked Mother, employing a tone that betrayed moderate concern.

"She doesn't," I said.

"Why not?" she asked, with the dogged persistence of an elite detective.

"I don't know," I said.

"What do you think, Lilly?" asked Mother.

"I think she has a good look," said Lilly.

"Why?"

"I like her bikini and her sunglasses," she offered, her voice wavering a little insecurely as she did so.

"Do you think the photographer is using her body for his photograph?" asked Mother.

"Maybe," said Lilly.

"In what way?"

"Maybe he's looking at her body because he wants to own it?" suggested Lilly, her voice stumbling.

"Yes, I think some idea of ownership is part of what's going on here," said Mother, with some emphatic assurance. She launched into a longer explanation: "The photographer is using the woman by reducing her to the level of an image, so that she is no longer a full human being. He is doing this, partly to obtain money, because he knows that her image will give him that. He is also using her body to represent her, so that she does not show any of her actual individual personality. What kind of swimming costume is she wearing here, Matty?"

"A bikini," I said brightly, glad of the certainty of my knowledge.

"Why is she wearing a bikini, Matty?"

"Maybe because she's hot?"

"No," said Mother. "Perhaps we'll return to this subject another day . . ."

The image of the model always lingered in my mind after that. Over time the sense of guilt engendered by this lesson was considerable. As I continued to think about the photograph in the months and years ahead embarrassment rose inside me and became embedded within my mind, like some small ailment which always seems to refuse to leave your body entirely.

6.

An Assortment of Occurrences in the Household

For some years Flo used this Japanese drawing of a hot air balloon from 1787 to decorate the door of her room:

****

(One day Rebecca began to write down the definitions of a good many nouns that she happened to like inside a small pale blue spiral bound notebook):

caboodle (noun) the whole number or quantity of people or things in question

gutta-percha (noun) a hard, tough substance resembling rubber, obtained from certain Malaysian trees

lickspittle (noun) a person who behaves in a flattering or servile way to those in power

tankini (noun) a woman's two-piece swimsuit combining a top half styled like a tank top with a bikini bottom

yawp (noun) a harsh or hoarse cry or yelp

A day when a miscellany of abandoned objects was strewn across the stairs and corridors, all discarded and appearing neglected and forlorn, without owners, without spatial designation, long strands of white toilet paper extended into streamers, gleaming buttons cut away from garments for unknown reasons, left staring upwards from the carpets like brilliant-coloured eyes; a white paper tiara fashioned for satirical purposes, left behind after being thrown across the room and trampled over with heavy boots. There was the remaining odour of incense sticks which Mother would sometimes wave around the spaces of the house whilst singing, hoping to achieve the effect of calming proceedings as constituted at that moment. Lilly left alone with a tape recorder playing and replaying spools of tape which had captured voices a few hours beforehand.

****

(These statements were placed around the mirror of the bathroom on the Second Floor, sometimes alone and sometimes in unison):

LOOK CAREFULLY FOR ALL THE HIDDEN AVENUES

TOMORROW YOU WILL HAVE CHANGED BUT WILL YOU ACTUALLY NOTICE?

IS YOUR LEFT IRIS THE MOST UNEXPECTED PART OF YOU?

PERHAPS YOU SHOULD BECOME SOMEONE ELSE

TRY TO CHOOSE YOUR FACE FOR TODAY AS IF IT WERE A MASK

I DO NOT RECOMMEND AN EXCESS OF GLOWERING

At five in the afternoon. The House is being itself. Pale sunlight coating a desk. Mysteries of certain words spoken. Cat opens pink gums wide. Noisy shuffling of paper documents. Examination of an empty hand. Attaching postcards to white walls. The afternoon fades and lapses. Silent treading over strange memories. Shadows thrown by piano legs. The humming of kitchen machinery. Eliza brandishes an equestrian statuette. Rebecca swallows a hardboiled egg. Lilly dreams of an envelope. Billy hums a raucous tune. Scrabbling for a shopping list. The ebony jaws of tigers. Murmurs from under the stairwell. Observing visions of theatrical spectaculars. Mother signs a legal document. Gerard slides into a bathtub. Fanciful words emerge from mouths. Parameters of a poster outlined. Forgotten photographs uncovered from boxes.

****

Lucinda liked staring at images like this in her room, for hours on end, whilst she dreamt of making grand buildings and structures:

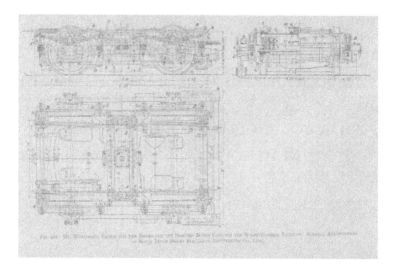

Lilly let herself in through the front door and traipsed into the hallway uncertainly, ignoring Gerard, Flo and Rebecca who she encountered there, and who in turn ignored her, busy as they were reading aloud from the script of an Edward Albee play. Passing them by, Lilly stepped into the Living Room, but found that Mother was sat there reading The Guardian and looking preoccupied. So Lilly then wandered into the kitchen hoping to find both avocados and some Graham crackers, but instead she found Lucinda sat alone at the table preparing taramasalata. After entering, Lucinda glared at her for a moment, as if she was an intruder, so silently Lilly took her leave of that room as well and then crept up the stairs towards her own room, where she intended to hide behind a locked door for some hours and work her way through a book of word puzzles.

****

Ag, wearing a white nightgown, standing still in the garden at night, holding a small red candle close to her.

Then there was the day that Flo once spent only reading the tiny stories left in the corners of local newspapers, the kind that only last for a sentence or two. An act she always forgot to repeat after rediscovering it. These were stories about hairdressers, goldfish bowls, irate motorists. At their best, these were entertaining to an unusual extent. In particular, she liked the sense of entire realities being contained within such tiny written discourses. Miniature realities without density or detail whose depictions disappeared almost at the same moment as they had commenced. She thought that this would probably very often be the only occasion on which certain people would find themselves amplified by the media. Some of these articles possessed the ability to cause eternal resentment or joy. They could never be taken back. All of this and more was fascinating to Flo that day and then she forgot about this subject again for quite a few years.

****

Bunches of bright-coloured cellophane intended for decorative purposes

Hand gestures responding to ordinary afternoon statements

Repeated drawings of fingers pointing towards the location of a spoon

Fake sea shanties invented after the onset of nightfall

Snacks concocted by Rebecca one afternoon in August

Occasions of attempted spying on the actions of neighbours through a telescope

Rebecca placed a copy of this image on the door of her room. It was a 19th Century drawing of a large, extinct marine reptile known as *ichthyosaurus quadriscissus*:

Ichthyosaurus quadriscissus.   Oberer Lias.

✦✦

Gerard once summoned us all to the Living Room in order to deliver the following speech:

"Is it possible that we have lived certain lives before this that are now unknown to us?

Perhaps we once sold fruit at a market stall in Tibet nearly a thousand years ago. Or could it be plausible, that in 1569, one of us was responsible for building a tower in a country estate, in Buckinghamshire, a building which was subsequently consumed by flames?

It could well be that I once spent many thousands of days being lowered into a salt mine, toiling there in darkness and exhaustion. It could also be the case that I didn't.

You will all come up with your own possibilities.

That is all for tonight Family, Thankyou."

Mother was born in 1942, Ag was born in 1966, Lucinda was born in 1967, Flo was born in 1968, Rebecca was born in 1970, Gerard was born in 1971, Eliza was born in 1972, Barnaby was born in 1973, Billy was born in 1975 and Lilly was born in 1976.

So now you know that about them too.

****

When he was fifteen, in a moment of rage, Billy covered practically all of the spaces of the white walls in his room with visual forms like this:

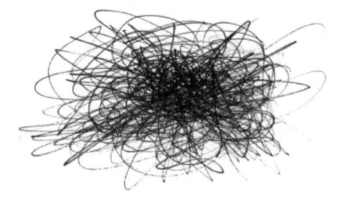

          teenage Ag

creeping through the hallway

                drunken, elated

      in a torn lace dress

           gazing into the eyes of figures related to her

    which appeared

in a daguerreotype that stared outwards from the wall

                    inside a brass frame

     and it was then

that she registered the presence of this image entirely

                   for the first time

✳✳

I might traipse downstairs in an ordinary way and suddenly see through Rebecca's open doorway an unexpected image which in fact she had composed expressly for any passing eyes presumably including my own and this involved statues of towers fabricated from coloured paper cones and twisted strands of wire all rising vertical and seeming to me then incredibly tall and improbable entities that suddenly existed when they had never previously been visible and amidst these forms Rebecca was thrusting out her arms and creating zigzag patterns with flickering finger twitchings and all of these were what she later called her "performance strategies" as we learnt after she had received a generous and heartfelt round of applause from the four of us who happened to have stood witnessing this peculiar occurrence.

7.

The Independent Republic
of the Third Floor

When a member of the household chose to cross the border and enter the Republic, particularly for the first time, a palpable sense of otherness immediately became discernible. Exactly where this feeling emanated from was unclear, but suddenly, once anyone stepped into their territory, you clearly felt that you were now present in another culture, one that possessed different customs and patterns of thought, a place where you were liable to experience a sense of either shock or delight, just as if you had travelled to a distant country of which you had no previous experience. Discordant music would spill from the Republic's three doorways, demarcating their air territory as effectively as if they had partitioned physical space.

All three citizens developed very similar aesthetic leanings, although Barnaby and Eliza were essentially in thrall to the ideas of Gerard. Through his leadership they discovered a liking for such things as the Sun Ra Arkestra, the painting of murals, and the riding of tricycles in cavalcade formation.

In order to gain entry to the nation it was necessary to show your passport to whichever member of embassy staff was on duty and complete the application form for a visa. Your passport would then receive a green circular rubber stamp bearing that day's date and the emblem of a crocodile, which had been declared the symbol of the nation after several hours of debate, because, in Eliza's words: "it's an *impertinent* creature."

To my knowledge visas were always granted. At the border sometimes a bag search was requested, and occasionally incomers would be frisked, on the pretence that banned articles might be hidden inside their garments, a process that Billy once refused to yield to, nearly causing a full-scale sectarian conflict, until it was resolved before dinner that evening. Procedures at the border had the tendency to change all of the time without warning, and the constant threat of being denied entry loomed over all that happened at the border.

Banned entities within the Republic included all references to George Michael, all species of fish (because Eliza hated the smell), all cameras (they wanted to stress privacy), any conversation about television (a nod in Rebecca's direction), all discussions of Feminism (thoughts of both Mother and the Elder Set), baseball caps, as well as most forms of physical attack. For some years new prohibitions were drafted on a weekly basis. This was an activity which became a tradition at all meetings of parliament, partly because they often couldn't think of much else to discuss.

"It's necessary for the republic to take a stance towards the family's weekly acquisition of corn flakes!" asserted Gerard.

"Why?" asked Eliza.

"Because the Republic must take a stance towards everything!" said Gerard.

"Aren't there more important things to worry about?" asked Barnaby.

"Corn flakes are a genuine material issue which we are confronted with in this environment on a daily basis," said Gerard, "therefore we must consider what our relationship towards them must be."

"Why are they a matter of concern for a parliamentary meeting?" asked Eliza.

"Because everything is," said Gerard.

"But some things don't matter!" said Eliza. "Do you think this is an issue worth discussing, Barnaby?" asked Eliza.

"No," said Barnaby.

"Gerard, your authority is therefore suppressed through democratic procedure," said Eliza.

Gerard sat through the remainder of the meeting in silence, emanating irritation.

Every morning, before the family sat down for breakfast, the members of the Republic stood tall, garbed in olive-green military uniforms, a cluster of coloured ribbons dangling from self-awarded medals on each citizen's chest, every one of them given for apocryphal reasons which changed depending on who was asking about them. With purple berets resting atop their heads and hands placed solemnly on their hearts, they would sing their national anthem with great fervour. Early attempts to perform this rite resulted in the entire household becoming their audience, all of the other siblings laughing and jeering at their actions as they did so. Only Mother offered applause, an action that struck me as being equally embarrassing and misplaced. However, everyone soon got used to the Republic's daily display of patriotism and then ceased to find their singing noteworthy at all. In fact, the reciting of the national anthem built itself into our daily routine, until it seemed as common a sight as someone brushing their teeth, or our sitting down at the kitchen table to eat. The movements of the tune's melody, as well as some of the words, soon became as annoying as any song you hear on the radio too frequently. These were the words:

All across our glorious nation,
Evidence of our situation,
Progress and Liberty,
In place of adversity.

We are bearers of new Freedom!
We hold flames so you will see them!

The Third Floor is beautiful,
Graceful and suitable,
Site of our destiny,
For all eternity.

We are noble agitators!
We are earnest instigators!

Talking of their uniforms, the Republic always claimed that these clothes did not signify any involvement with military concerns, but were purely representative of a shared cultural identity.

"Our uniforms signify only our Republic," stated the Republic, collectively. "We are not a military organization. We are pacifists. Violence will never be our objective, unless our boundaries are trespassed, or our rules are breached."

When he was seventeen Gerard wrote a detailed, rambling letter to what he believed to be the relevant department of the United Nations in New York City, putting forth his case for the Republic being recognized as a legitimate nation state. Within the envelope he included a variety of supporting documents, including photographs, legal papers, copies of passports, and other assorted paraphernalia, which in his mind clearly proved beyond doubt that a legitimate nation was in existence and was wholly worthy of United Nations validation. He was never to receive a reply, yet for some years, unbeknownst to him, the contents of his package would remain pinned to a cork noticeboard that stood in a rarely traversed corridor and became an object that brought forth occasional mirth.

Gerard was essentially deluded and arrogant. He saw himself as a visionary, and honestly believed that in changing the course of human history, he would be assuming his rightful role. This megalomania extended to a range of elaborate schemes he drafted in extensive form inside his notebooks. One of the projects he most cherished was that of taking over the Isle of Sheppey, in Kent, where he wished to establish a large-scale colony of independent thinkers and found a further nation. At first Eliza and Barnaby were entirely prepared to go along with all that he asked of them, largely because he had managed to convince them that they were determining their own fate, but in fact it was mostly the case that he was simply manipulating them, like his own private pair of marionettes.

In his early twenties Gerard took to writing a book-length history of the nation, a document destined to be of no more than passing interest to anyone other than the three citizens. He composed the entirety of it longhand in a neat, fastidiously legible script, completing many chapters that bore titles such as 'The Declaration of the Republic' (Chapter 1), 'The Age of Ostentation' (Chapter 9), 'Eliza Decorates the Hallway' (Chapter 15) 'The First War With the Younger Siblings' (Chapter 17), and ending with one entitled 'The Republic Resilient' (Chapter 56), in which he outlined a number of delusions he possessed regarding his group's ability to ineradicably alter the face of British society.

The most controversial official statement that the Republic ever made was the following:

> "We, the Independent Republic of the Third Floor, wish to protest against the creation of the new cleaning

rota, the creation of which, and wording of which, assumes that we, the members of the Republic, are happy to engage in onerous cleaning tasks of our own territory, on a regular basis, to help uphold a social system which we do not recognize. We accept that there is a need for us to share our portion of all necessary household chores, but we do not accept the drafting of a cleaning rota that does not recognize our right to govern our own territory as we see fit."

Tensions continued to exist in this way for some time.

8.

Open House

For a number of years Mother liked us to hold an "Open House" event, a sometimes annual occasion which would involve a large body of friends and acquaintances visiting our house and encountering our domestic terrain, as well as our imaginations, which would be on full display, operating in a number of different capacities.

Mother always selected the guests she invited to the house very carefully. They were generally all from the sorts of families who would not be likely to object to us. Mother firstly determined whether this would be the case through a consideration of the occupations of the parents, which was one of the first questions she always asked about any of our friends. Many of the party-goers that day were arriving in our house for the first time and to many of them it must have felt like a kind of opulent temple consecrated to the act of play.

There were so many people that day that I found myself nervous amongst the milling crowds of faces spilling into the house, many of which were unknown to me. As I wove through the rooms, a number of the adults looked at me, smiling, as if to offer an unspoken acknowledgement that this was my home. I was immediately struck by the numbers of children who had arrived attired in different animal costumes, and I soon found myself feeling a little jealous of a boy dressed in the form of a giant dice, with the number "6" facing outwards and directed at all onlookers.

Confused by the crowds surrounding me, I decided to try and locate Lilly, so that I might find some modicum of safety in her company. Usually, this would not have been a particularly difficult task, but with our environment transformed by so many unknown figures, I couldn't see her anywhere and I panicked slightly, eventually hiding under a table in the hall, shutting my eyes and covering my ears with my hands. I received concerned looks, but Mother ushered everyone away and let me stay there alone for fifteen minutes. After that Lilly found me, and, looking a little concerned, ushered me from under the table out into the open again. In her presence I suddenly felt strong enough to engage with the party again, at least in some limited capacity. She led me by the hand, out into the garden.

"I'm worried about you," said Lilly.

"I'm a bit scared of the party, but I think I'll be alright," I responded, in a quiet voice which I didn't want anyone to hear.

Covered in sweat, produced from half an hour of being chased around the garden, a boy I didn't know, who was slightly older than us and dressed impeccably as a grenadier, suddenly approached.

"Do you live here?" he asked.

We nodded our assent a little nervously.

"Have you been here before?" asked Lilly.

"I was here a year ago for a party," he said a little breathlessly. "My name's Tom. Last time I was here I went on an expedition up to the attic and broke a vase by accident."

"Oh that was you!" said Lilly. "You looked quite different a year ago."

"Last time I came here I was dressed as a detective and I had a trenchcoat and a magnifying glass," said Tom.

"Yes, I remember you," said Lilly. "I don't think you spoke with me and Matty a year ago did you?"

"No we didn't talk, but I saw you, it was Billy and his friends who took me on an expedition, do you want to go on another one this year?"

"I don't know about expeditions," said Lilly, who was, in fact, lying, as a consequence of shyness. "We don't like Billy all that much," said Lilly.

Tom laughed at the animosity existing between siblings and launched into a spontaneous run, reaching the other end of the garden in a few seconds, where he soon joined a group of other children who were pretending to be time travelling.

Surveying the lawn, I counted more than sixty people, which was a larger number than any I had seen present in the house before. The Elder Set were attempting to practice the airs of adulthood whilst playing croquet, but found themselves frustrated, as people kept obstructing their game. Rebecca was trying to build a doll's house with sheets of cardboard and glue. Mother was talking with other adults about subjects which we did not understand and had no particular wish to right then. A constant flow of figures moved back and forth across the lawn, persons both young and old, although only the young had been brave enough to arrive dressed in costumes, which they wore proudly and with a natural ease that many of their parents had lost.

"Shall we go and find Mother?" asked Lilly. "Maybe she can think of a game for us to play. I think she's inside somewhere."

I gave my assent and we ventured into the crowded kitchen, past a circle of mothers nibbling on pieces of crackerbread laden with olive paste and laughing ostentatiously. Our own Mother wasn't among them however, and it felt strangely disconcerting to hear so many strangers being quite so noisy in the midst of our home.

As we peered into the living room, searching for her form, our gaze was met by a tall, lean middle-aged woman wearing a pair of thick, oval tortoise-shell spectacles, and a white polo neck. She looked both intellectual and free-spirited and was staring intently at the pictures Mother had chosen to put on the wall. She gestured to us with a crooked finger, so we tentatively sidled over to her.

"Does your Mother choose these pictures by herself or with you?" she asked us.

"Mostly she chooses them," I said, "but sometimes she wants to know what we think as well."

"Do you like this one?"

We gazed properly for the first time at a painting which we had previously treated as if it were an innocuous side table, walking past it thousands of times without ever stopping to think about what sort of picture it actually was. Staring intently, I found that it depicted, with crystalline exactitude, the forms of a grapefruit and an ostrich, neither of them occupying their usual dimensions, both now bloated and gargantuan. I didn't know what I was supposed to be thinking about this painting, but Lilly immediately became excitable:

"I really like the ostrich!" she enthused.

"Do you like paintings? Do you ever paint yourself?" the woman asked us.

"I do," said Lilly. "Matty isn't so into painting though."

"We're going to find Mother now," said Lilly suddenly and seizing me by the hand, we both walked away.

"See you later then," said the woman, whose name we still didn't know. She smiled at us whilst we departed in a manner that I found slightly sinister, although at that time I was not capable of articulating why.

Children wearing bright, spangled costumes were sprinting and somersaulting across the verdant green of the summer lawn, breaking into delighted little yelps of laughter. Flo was carrying heavy jugs of elderflower cordial and lemonade. After venturing across the lawn, she placed them carefully on the table beside stacks of paper plates and bowls heaped with salads. A pleasant murmurous accretion of excited voices gathered in the air, hanging above all of us, forming its own temporary soundscape.

"You two look familiar to me," said Mother as we walked up to her on the first floor, "have we had the pleasure of meeting before?"

"Yes," I said, with conviction.

"Are you two having a good time?" she asked.

"We were wondering if you could think of any games for us to play . . ." said Lilly, with a slight hint of whimpering in her voice.

"Are you two really *not* happy?" asked Mother, suddenly with a hint of genuine concern now. She drew both of us towards her to offer comfort, just in case it might be needed.

"Matty says he's a bit scared of all the people," said Lilly.

I didn't want to have this conversation. Instead I decided to explore the upper reaches of the house to see if anything intriguing was happening there. I looked into a number of entirely empty, familiar-looking rooms, which all seemed to belong to the house that I normally inhabited. However, a curious lulling music, of a kind which I had never encountered before, was seeping into these rooms from the second floor above. Investigating this, I found that the source was Ag's room, where people, who I would later come to understand were gamelan players, were spread across the floor with their instruments. They wore mauve-coloured sequined robes designed by Clothilde, their bandleader, and all possessed a serene air of concentration, as if by playing extremely carefully they expected to encounter the visual forms of the deceased, which is perhaps exactly what they thought was going to happen. A reverent hush was expected from all present, including children, who were all repeatedly asked to be quiet by whichever adults were nearest to them. Everyone sat cross-legged on the floor, rapt with attention.

Upon entering this room I immediately sensed that I had stepped into a different domain to the rest of the house, one that was in some ways more adult than the other rooms and spaces. The music infused the air with a mysterious, contemplative, spiritual quality that I had never encountered before. I felt attracted to the atmosphere that had been generated by the room and stayed there listening for some time. This unexpected scene, although only encountered fleetingly, was one which my mind would return to many times over the years and I would always be able to form a picture of its spaces and its denizens with great clarity, as if those people were always sat there.

A Profile of Matty

Name: Matthew Crickholme

Gender: Male

Nationality: British

Born: 1978

Place of Residence: Highgate, London

Hair: Reddish

Eyes: Light brown

Height: 5'9" at his tallest

Weight: About 17 stone, at his heaviest

Religious Persuasion: None whatsoever

Hobbies: Reading novels, lying around in bed, being neurotic, being silent

Likes: Cartoons, Surrealism, Spies, Wandering through cities

Dislikes: Computers, Mushrooms, Dogs, Buildings made from concrete

Prejudices: Against anyone of a religious persuasion, against people who don't read books, against animals, against most human beings.

Eccentricities: He is known to have occasionally knocked on the doors of strangers' houses to attempt spontaneous interviews with them; enjoys playing games of snooker in out-of-season British seaside towns filled with grey light; particularly enjoys urinating into sink basins.

Superstitions: He always recoils a little from black cats whom he considers to be supernatural beings; he has a genuine fear of the number 13, which affects him whenever that date of the month comes around, or indeed whenever he encounters that number in any context whatsoever.

Obsessions: With his Mother; with the effects of his Mother's upbringing; with the household created by his Mother.

Allergies: He claims to be allergic to fish, coffee, pillows, garlic, certain kinds of house dust, exhaust fumes, roll-on deodorants, washing up liquid, cream once it is even slightly old, most brands of nail clipper.

Subjects that make him feel guilty: The fact that he stole one of Lucinda's purple spiral-bound notebooks when he was 14 and instead of giving it back hid it under his bed for months, before destroying it with matches; the fact that he once tormented Rebecca's pet ferret, Madison, with drops of hot glue; the fact that he once spat in Billy's face, which makes him feel guilt even though at the time of this happening Billy had been tormenting him with cruel names and stinging little punches up and down his arms.

General reputation: He is not really thought of as someone who is capable of achieving much, although for the most part, he is not really thought of at all.

Alcohol intake: Either extremely moderate or nothing whatsoever.

Aspirations with regard to employment: Very few. He does possess a number of most probably unrealizable dreams of employment roles that he might one day fulfil (e.g., stage magician, theme park designer, wrestling "consultant"). However, life goals which might become a reality are few and far between.

Frequency with which he has thrown javelins: He has done this only once, but it was a memorable occasion, an attempt by a poet, who was then in his late 50s and teaching at a radical adult education institute in the British countryside, to explain the potential for "movement" in a line of poetry, comparing the rhythm of a line of poetry to the throwing of a javelin.

Major grievances that he possesses: Anger at the fact that Lucinda would torment him as a child; anger at the fact that Billy would torment him as a child; a general sense of outrage at the state of the world and how difficult it is to survive within it, particularly for individuals wishing to "survive" in a way that offers some kind of nourishment rather than just workplace brutality.

Things of which he is ignorant: The biography of Pythagoras;

facts about Andorra; Bolivian literature; the sociology of Max Weber; how to operate a fishing rod successfully; how to fly aeroplanes successfully; how to cook anything much; the interior life of most of his siblings.

State of his health: More or less reasonable given that he never drinks or smokes and always keeps, for the most part, to a moderately healthy vegetarian diet. Nevertheless, he never does any exercise whatsoever.

Partiality to apple doughnuts: High.

Things he most enjoys eating: Apple doughnuts (already mentioned). Also: Spaghetti Carbonara, Pad Thai, various crustaceans which go by different names, key lime pie, apple flavoured ice cream (although he has only had the good fortune to have eaten this on one occasion).

Feelings regarding the supernatural: A mixture of awe and fear. He definitely possesses some sort of belief in various so called "supernatural" phenomena. Aliens and ghosts being the entities of this category which enter his mind most frequently.

General level of his luck: Usually low. Bad things seem to happen repeatedly to Matty. Not very, very bad things, but things that most people would nevertheless agree were unpleasant and better avoided if at all possible. He was liable to lose his bank documents all the time, for one thing.

Standards of hygiene: These are not always especially good. He does not wash on an everyday basis. After using plates, cutlery, or cups from the kitchen he doesn't always clean them, but sometimes just leaves them lying around in his room, or indeed another room, for days on end.

Preferences concerning holidays: That no holidays be taken. Matty prefers simply staying at home, following a daily routine, and resting rather than going abroad and facing the confusions that come from encountering other locations and cultures.

Important accomplishments: So far in his life, literally none whatsoever. At least that's his view.

Ways in which he is pedantic: Whenever he goes shopping he always buys precisely the same brands. If anyone utters a factual inaccuracy in his presence he always corrects it, even if that person might be hurt by his correction. He would always tell people that the word "parliament" should be pronounced by sounding the "i" and the "a" in its centre, even if many people, including many political journalists, do not.

Sense of humour: Fair, although his ability to tell a joke might benefit from some practice.

Associations he possesses with regard to the colour green: It reminds him of a dress that Lilly used to wear when she was twelve; of Rebecca's room after she painted her bedroom walls that colour when she was sixteen; of writing with green biro pens.

Time at which he is most outgoing: When there are no imminent or obvious threats of interaction with other people.

Social Class: Despite liking to think of himself as being essentially classless, the truth is that he is Upper Middle Class, with a lifestyle that borders on the aristocratic.

Decadent aspects of his personality: Is known to spend many hours in the bath; Consumes large quantities of chocolate truffles; Subscribes to the Times Literary Supplement.

Attitude towards car crashes: Genuine fear of them (one which arises on any occasion when he is in a car, or near a car, or near a road).

Attitude towards mathematics: One of contempt.

Attitude towards women: In most ways he has a preference for them over men, although he does find Feminism to be a deeply threatening phenomenon.

Attitude towards cooking: Hopes someone else can do it.

Skill at making important judgements: Not really a skill that Matty has managed to acquire. Instead of applying for jobs, he has tended to stare at tanks of tropical fish for hours on end or grapple with the finer points of daytime television.

Rituals that happen to please him: His bedtime ritual of ablutions followed by reading; the conversations that he always has at the barbers about television and young ladies; the process of making a cup of tea holds a strangely calming effect for him.

Tricks he has up his sleeve: He has learnt a list of the highest scoring 2 and 3 letter words to play in Scrabble; he knows how to pick most forms of lock; he has memorized the instructions for first aid to administer when encountering a heart attack, although he isn't really sure why he did that.

Country he would most like to be from but isn't: France, entirely for intellectual reasons.

Subjects which often appear in his dreams: Bells; radishes; small rooms in which he is locked; turtles; long stretches of empty pavement; small boats landing on beaches at dawn; screaming.

Level of his generosity: Can be high, but only if he actually happens to talk to anyone at all, which he seldom does.

His relationship to hats: As a child he occasionally liked to wear baseball caps so that he might resemble images of American film stars and models which he had seen; later, in his very early twenties, he had a brief period of wearing straw hats, ideally ones that possessed a red band, to be accompanied with a blade of grass which he would clench towards the right of his jaw.

His politics: Almost non-existent, but if he has one it would undoubtedly be on the Left.

His relationship to photography: He is very strict about the fact that he never takes photographs and never appears in them either. This is perhaps strong evidence of his neuroticism, a fact he is aware of, but ultimately he does not care, as any photographs involving him make him feel profoundly uncomfortable.

Odours that inspire him: Fresh laundry emerging from a washing machine; the smell of pine trees; brand new machinery; nail polish remover; the smell of people's basements often seems to inspire him as well.

His habits as a diarist: He has intermittently kept a diary for many years, although he is not at all diligent about this and gladly goes many months or years without writing a single entry, as, writing diary entries feels strangely like something of a burden to him.

The likelihood of his being stung by a bee: Extremely high. Ever since he was a child bees have gravitated towards him and not others inside crowded rooms. This is a cause of some considerable distress to him, as being stung by a bee is a painful and traumatizing experience.

Tendency to take medicine: Also extremely high. Matty will take medicine at the least provocation, or even if he doesn't actually need it at all. Of course he is usually sure that he is coming down with various kinds of illness. He is happy to describe himself as a valetudinarian.

Frequency with which he wears sunglasses: He goes through phases of wearing them all day long, whether there is sunshine present in the sky or not, in both interior and exterior locations. This is in order to avoid eye contact with any human being that he might encounter, as this can often make him feel uncomfortable.

His relationship with bivouacs: At one time The Elder Set had been obsessed with making bivouacs, first in the family's back garden, then later (more excitingly), out in public locations. Matty had been coaxed into spending the night sleeping inside one of these creations, but he had felt cold and uncomfortable all night and had missed home.

Things he has hidden: Books about human sexuality, which despite the focus of his Mother's career still felt shameful to him; the key to a box in which he held his scrapbook, an object whose cover was decorated with luridly coloured superhero stickers and which contained train timetables, fragments of maps, dried flowers and a number of photographs that he had discovered of camels, amongst other things.

Things he does on rainy days: He listens to radio stations that he would never normally tune into at all; he hoards things together to hide in boxes; he attempts to make friends with the neighbour's cat by making hand gestures through his bedroom window.

Attitudes towards swearing: General sense of disapproval. He only swears on rare occasions when he is really extremely angry.

The rest of the time he is liable to tell other people in the household off for their excessive swearing, urging them to expand their vocabulary and refine their sensibility.

Feelings about rice pudding: This is his favourite substance in the world, although he is addicted to his Mother's rendition of the dish, refusing to accept that rice pudding from a can is ever of equal merit.

What is most irritating to him: When his siblings use his "special mug" in the kitchen, even though they know it has somehow been designated his "special mug" and that it is therefore officially out of bounds. This is a mug decorated with cartoon zombies in blue-and-red waistcoats.

Songs he sometimes hums to himself when lying in the bath: "Yesterday"; "I Am a Rock"; "The Man Who Sold the World"; "Mr. Tambourine Man"; "(You Make Me Feel) Like a Natural Woman."

His views on extra-terrestrials: Somehow he is certain that they exist. He likes to try and invent new forms in which they might appear in his notebooks. He is waiting for the time that they will finally appear on the evening news and feels that everyone has simply forgotten the possibility that they might one day arrive on the scene.

Thoughts on utopia: He is not a utopian. He believes that people should try to be realistic and get on with things as best they can, whilst understanding that no sort of utopia is ever likely to be formed during our lifetimes.

Relationship with swimming pools: Matty has never really got into the whole business of doing lengths. He generally prefers to swim "free style," going pretty slowly and sort of exploring the space of the pool at ease.

Inspirations he draws from when desperate: He thinks of the optimism of soul music; he pictures sunlight falling through branches of trees in a distant unnamed country; sometimes his Mother's example of how to live life keeps him going.

Most significant life occasion he has had inside a lift: With Lilly when they were in their early teenage years they found themselves alone on a weekday afternoon inside one of the Covent Garden underground lifts and they felt somehow excited to have so much space to themselves and so began hollering and dancing.

Feelings about hair: Matty likes to keep his hair long. Often he doesn't brush it for some days. He tends to think that this is hair's natural state, that this is really how things are meant to be.

Habits he wishes he could abandon: His tendency to stop using a notebook somewhere in its middle, rather than at the end, simply because he is so eager to launch himself onto the pages of a new notebook; leaving lights on all night long to help decrease his sense of fear, as it feels wasteful of electricity to leave them on; sleeping in until noon.

His nocturnal habits: For years now Matty has been waking up in the middle of the night, despite having no desire to do so. He uses this as an opportunity to read or make notes of various kinds and then around 5AM he usually returns to bed.

10.

The Message Delivery Service

During the course of one summer Flo decided to run a "Message Delivery Service" which took place solely within the confines of the house. Anyone could ask her to deliver a message to anyone else who happened to be present in the property. Initially she attempted to charge 5p for each delivery, but it soon became apparent to her that no one wanted to pay even that much, so she began to offer the service for free.

The messages could be written down or conveyed in a verbal form, often with flourishes of various kinds added as an accompaniment. Those might include hand gestures, singing, or the wearing of costumes. Indeed these extra touches carried much of the appeal of Flo's service. When no one wanted to send a message she was liable to invent one, until no one could be really sure of the authenticity of her messages any longer.

Usually these were messages which, strictly speaking, did not need to be sent. They mostly lasted for only one line, partly because Flo would get bored and demand that the dictations of words cease. "That's enough!" she would say and immediately storm out of the room. Occasionally she could be coaxed into taking down more, but you had to be particularly kind to her if you were to receive a service of that standard.

Often requests for message deliveries would come to Flo thick and fast, but when there was a lull she might start pacing from room to room, asking if her services were wanted. Usually when in this state she would find someone soon enough, although after some weeks of this the family's interest in the whole practice was no longer as strong as it had been at the outset of Flo's experiment. During that summer she learnt to take a break occasionally and then return to asking this question once everyone had developed an appetite for it again.

Quite a few of the messages that people wanted to send were rude or angry ones, sometimes going as far as being actually abusive. Flo was worried about carrying such messages as she knew that she was liable to be blamed for their content. Nevertheless, it was understood around the household that such messages were supposedly playful and often they did fit that description well enough, but it was equally true that they often revealed a kind of latent malevolence, one usually masked in humour and good cheer, but in fact malevolence nonetheless. Often it was difficult to tell the difference. After a while, no one cared all that much anyway. It felt easier just to go with the general flow of barbarity and to try and enjoy it for what it was worth.

It soon became standard practice for everyone to routinely attempt to send the most outrageous insults that anyone could manage to think of. These included:

"You are the living embodiment of Hell"

"I would rather vomit than ever see your face again"

"If you were to die I would laugh my head off"

"You are my new nemesis"

"Why not jump off the roof!"

Eventually even someone as liberal-minded as Mother felt the need to intervene, once she felt that this had all gone too far. She stopped us from abusing each other quite so much.

Another tactic amongst those sending out messages involved the creation of texts which were irreverent in their lack of distinct meaning. Once this tendency had been established the various siblings then tried to outdo each other with the wildness of their statements.

"The zebra has been led into the maze," was a message which Gerard sent to Rebecca one day, thus inadvertently starting a vogue for similar messages. Rebecca sent back "It thinks it is a zebra, but it is not actually a zebra!" And so it went on, escalating chaotically for many days.

Lilly sent Ag a message which said: "the buccaneers are unhappy with you" A message which really emerged from nowhere, as "buccaneers" had barely ever been mentioned in the house previously. Ag sent one back saying "Fuck the buccaneers!" We all enjoyed this sort of thing greatly for a while.

Shortly after this there was another period in the history of the Delivery Service when everyone started to push Flo as much as possible, seeing how many words they could get away with and how many extra words they could elicit. For the first time Flo set a very strict word limit of fifteen words per message. She would then try and compose the most imaginative messages which she could muster within the fifteen-word limit. Often she liked to slip in little similes and metaphors of her own and for a couple of days once she tried to place a palindrome inside each message, but people complained because that wasn't what they had intended to send. Her next game was to include the name of one animal beginning with "G" inside each message. Then, once bored of that, she took to rearranging all of the words of each message so that on initial inspection it appeared they made no sense.

She began wearing a uniform every day. This was quite casual and changed in precise form quite a few times during the course of that summer, but it always involved a white folded paper hat like the kind sometimes encountered in fish and chip shops. Additionally, she always wore a silk sash which ran from her right shoulder down to her left hip. Over this a sheet of paper was fixed stating "MESSAGE DELIVERY SERVICE" in block capitals rendered with a green felt tip pen.

Mother made a strikingly individual use of the service. Sometimes she liked to use it in an extremely pragmatic way: "Dinner in ten minutes!" or "Do some laundry today please for crying out loud!" However, more frequently she liked to surprise us with unexpected subjects, leading us into the labyrinths of her learning by sending us quotations, often ones which didn't seem related to us personally, often using the most abstract and difficult of academic texts. We would often look at these as if they were the baffling fragments of some sort of alien language. I might find it necessary to read mine five or six times before I could even begin to understand what was being said.

Gerard liked to send everyone questions. He was particularly interested in the brand of open-ended question which was not answerable in a clear or obvious way. Some of them even resembled *koans*: "Where is the invisible house that does not exist?"

But in fact they ranged across many subjects: "Which one thing would you save from your luggage in a sinking ocean liner?" Or, he might be more rooted in our contemporary domesticity for a moment: "Why do you like mustard so much?" or indeed, "Why will the apocalypse arrive at our door?" or he might be slightly more philosophical: "Are dogs actually loving creatures or merely foolish?"

During the first days of the service Flo had refrained from sending any messages which she had actually composed herself.

Instinctively, she felt that her role was to be a bearer of messages. However, she in fact possessed a hidden desire to compose her own writings to send and eventually after some weeks of message bearing she gave into this urge. Her own messages tended towards the sprightly and hopeful. She would say pleasant things about sunlight or particular shades of green. Unlike many of the others she would never send any messages that were violent or disruptive.

At the end of the summer Flo terminated the service because she couldn't be bothered with it anymore, but we all often requested its return for some time afterwards.

11.

Some Notable Facts About the Family

* Lilly was always quite paralyzed by a fear of lightning. Whenever there was a storm that even possessed a chance of containing lightning she would refuse to leave the house for hours or even days afterwards and would often lie trembling in bed.

* Lucinda developed a full-blown obsession with glaciers. She collected books and photographs, could quote relevant statistics, and knew about all of the world's most significant examples of glaciers. Once the rest of us learnt this, we would demand facts about them from her. She tended to know even the most improbable ones that we could think of.

* Rebecca once took out a library book (about castles), which she failed to return for three years. When she did finally return it, she sent it back in the post and ignored all correspondence from the council that she had received about the issue, until finally, after another year or so, their letters ceased.

* In the hallway, above a telephone on the hall table, for many

years, there was an oil painting of a pelican standing next to a gramophone.

* Almost the favourite thing for Flo to do at one time was continuously make drawings and pictures of her ideas of how paradise might appear.

* In Mother's study there was a complete set of human teeth that had apparently once belonged to an infamous murderer in Guatemala who had bitten people to death. At least that's what she told us, anyway.

* In 1988 Rebecca held a "press conference" in the Living Room to announce that she was leaving home and going to university. None of the newspapers that were invited chose to attend, but all of the family did.

* In 1986 Ag and Flo became fond of leaving messages on people's answering machines that were as long as they could possibly be.

* One day Billy had started musing over the possibility of voluntarily losing an arm. He thought, somehow, that things might be preferable that way and began to conduct research into the countries where it would be a legal possibility.

* When she was ten years old Eliza learned to count to ten in the following languages: Punjabi, Spanish, Greek, Farsi, and Japanese. She never learned any other words in any other foreign languages.

* At one time Rebecca had wanted to be a yeti, so she would dress up as one.

* When he was eight, Gerard learned how to tell a joke whose

telling he could manage to extend to nearly half an hour. It wasn't funny and it got progressively more annoying to listen to him as the telling wore on, but for a while we still asked him to keep repeating it, just for the spectacle of the feat.

* When young, Ag memorized hundreds of "Waiter Waiter" jokes and would go around the house from person to person practicing them.

* Flo used to have a recurrent dream about a tram depot whose precise location was not defined, but she felt that it was probably somewhere in Spain. Nothing much tended to happen in this dream, but she nevertheless enjoyed having it immensely and would often shut her eyes at night willing the dream into action once again.

* In 1987 Flo got into the occasional habit of covering her entire head in shaving cream and going about her daily routine looking like that all day long. According to her, this could induce sensations that she had never dreamt were possible.

*At one time, Eliza began to keep a daily 6AM logbook which detailed her thoughts and feelings and any observations, every day at 6AM, which is when she always got up during that period.

* Ag was the only person in the household who had ever worn dungarees. She owned a pair of maroon-coloured ones, but she didn't wear them very often.

* At a young age Lilly decided that she possessed an enormous dislike of all bathrooms and would avoid them as often as possible. This wasn't really very possible of course, but she would do the best that she could. Sometimes she could be seen brushing her teeth in the street as she walked down the road.

* Gerard liked to claim that the most important book ever published in the English language was one named *A Pictorial History of Singapore* by L. E. Abdelnoor, which was published in 1953. No one ever knew quite how seriously to take him with this.

* Lilly developed a habit of locking herself in her room on occasion, for hours on end, as a form of sensory and social deprivation. She claimed it was a "calculated experiment" and that she enjoyed the sensation of being in temporary isolation, but most of us became worried about her nonetheless.

* For a few months in 1990 Flo began offering a free class of "eyelash exercises," in which she would help members of the household (and a few persons from beyond it), with developing a general sensitivity to the reality of their eyelashes. Her techniques involved the gentle application of fingertips, gazing at hand mirrors, and rubbing eyelashes against butterflies, amongst much else.

* Lilly had a long-term problem with sleepwalking. During the night she would wander all over the house. She was particularly fond of dressing up in other people's clothes and then cooking herself bacon and eggs while in this state. The latter activity made everyone quite worried that her sleepwalking could be a fire hazard one day, but it seemed that she always remembered to turn the gas off when she'd finished cooking.

* The Elder Set got into a habit of staging interpretive dance performances which commenced at 3AM. They said that this was the optimum time for everyone to be "taken out of themselves," but it was usually pretty difficult to get certain members of the household out of bed at that hour.

* The Independent Republic of the Third Floor liked to have

extensive conversations around subjects they knew nothing whatsoever about. They would find their subject and then sit and talk,
for as long as they could manage to, pretending they possessed
knowledge of the subject, even though they did not possess any
real knowledge of it at all.

12.

Mother's Research

For many of my childhood years, I didn't understand what my Mother's working life consisted of. It took place within a hidden adult world that I did not then occupy. Gradually, I pieced everything together through disparate slivers of information. I had to first possess some understanding of what sex itself actually was. Despite an early education from Mother on this subject, I don't think I possessed much of an understanding of what sexual reality might mean until I first learned how to ejaculate.

Oddly, it often felt like a subject that was not central within our household at all. So many other things were taking place there and sexological activity largely only happened when Mother went off to teach at the university or when she was in her study. Seeing her at work in her study made me associate the word "sex" with the pages of books and tedious rows of printed text, a notion that stayed with me for many years. It seemed like a clean, clinical thing related to schools and education.

Before I knew what was really happening I was bewildered by the occasional spectacle of my older siblings parading through the house and saying as many "obscene" things as they could manage, purely for the sheer pleasure of doing so. It didn't take long for the novelty of that to wear off though. Eventually I came to understand that doing this wasn't even possible in most families.

Our fragmentary knowledge of Mother's research seemed to offer us permission to do anything we pleased. Eventually we all sensed how transgressive Mother's actions were inside the realm of adults and so we felt justified in being "transgressive" ourselves, although we hadn't encountered that actual word yet. At one time, when walking down the street, we seemed to think that it was permissible for us to jeer and swear at any passersby we encountered, although Mother would chastise us for doing this.

One significant episode of our childhood occurred when Flo was allowed to have a boy stay the night in her bedroom when she was only fifteen and had therefore not yet reached the age of consent. She refused to answer questions from the family about what they had done together, which personally I thought was both ladylike and sensible.

Our understanding of the nature of Mother's research was often limited to the rumours that circulated amongst us; in many cases these turned out to be wildly off the mark in terms of accuracy. Mother rarely revealed much of what she was up to in her study or in her laboratories. I never could decide if there was perhaps an unacknowledged element of shame in that behaviour, but I'm sure had they ever been made, Mother herself would have dismissed any such claims with verbal violence. Privately, the siblings were fond of inventing the most outlandish, ludicrous versions of her research that we could manage to and then we would attempt to convince each other of their truth, often claiming that we had been privy to secret knowledge, and indeed, sometimes we had been.

As we discovered, some years later, Mother's research had in fact, frequently focused on the obtaining of maximal sexual pleasure for all partners involved in sexual acts. She had observed thousands of couples engage in a variety of sexual practices on campus, measuring the extent of their stimulation at different crucial moments before and during intercourse. This research had led to much controversy amongst Mother's fellow academics, a view further explored in articles published by a number of broadsheet newspapers.

Mother was always very keen to spur us into action as far as relationships were concerned. At times she could be almost bullying on this issue, encouraging us to go on dates, to join social groups and mingle with members of whichever gender we happened to desire. If I didn't have a girlfriend (and I never did) she would tease me about the issue, or ruthlessly attempt to couple me with someone, always giving priority to the issue to an extent that other parents would reserve exclusively for the completion of homework. I grew very wary of this particular trait of Mother's and her actions embarrassed me to the point of silence and sometimes tears.

Over the years Mother would look at seemingly every possible issue related to human sexuality, saying in later years that she had wanted to "possess knowledge of the entire spectrum of human desires," that she had been working towards as comprehensive a knowledge of the subject as was possible, partly because, she admitted, "such knowledge spurred on my own desire." She never discussed her sex life with us at all until we had reached late adolescence, but at that time she would sometimes become quite outrageous, talking of her predilection for firemen and fighter pilots as her two ideal masculine archetypes. Or in her words: "Tough men, manly men, men who pretend they know what they're about."

Despite her possession of this interest, Mother seemed to find most human beings attractive in some way, simply enjoying their personalities, however their selfhood manifested itself, even if she didn't possess an overt physical desire for them. Mother simply liked to strongly relate to people in one way or another and this was the case whatever their age or gender. It was exceptionally rare for anyone to take a major dislike to Mother. As she would later acknowledge, Mother enjoyed the act of "collecting people," making as many friends as was humanly possible, filling out all of the pages of her address book until she had to buy another larger version.

Even when we didn't understand them we took Mother's academic transgressions to be a source of familial pride. We could already intuit enough about the adult world to see how strongly she had placed herself in opposition to it and we instinctively wanted to support her in this endeavour. This was something that we never discussed openly with her until we were adults, perhaps because, for one thing, we were not capable of articulating our position. We could see that Mother must be some sort of maverick, and since we loved her and benefitted from her outsider stance, almost all of us were accepting of her excesses, and indeed it is true that she taught us to value them.

Mother was wholly capable of honestly scaring me with the subject of sexuality, a situation that proved to be more or less unique amongst the siblings. I could see the power she wielded with her grip on this subject and I always found that fact disturbing. When she ran her hand through my hair, in a motherly fashion, and spoke about the possibility of my having a girlfriend for example, I would find myself flinching from her. At that point I might run off upstairs and attempt to hide from everyone under my duvet for a while, but unfortunately she was liable to follow me into my room and sit on my bed and harass me with talk, precisely at the moment I least wanted her to be present.

Personally, I never wanted to follow Mother to the distant, glamorous academic realm she inhabited, as from afar it seemed like a cold and cerebral location, somewhere which I assumed would be inherently hostile towards me if I attempted to gain entry to its environs. Whilst she was always eager for us to expand our knowledge of the world, she actually wanted her research to be somewhat mysterious to us for a long time, which was presumably a protective gesture.

So much of the effect of Mother's research could only be felt by us retrospectively. At the time it often seemed insignificant, and we usually took her professional life as a fact of little consequence for us. To establish some sense of security in our minds we thought of ourselves as "just another family," even if we also wanted to think of ourselves as separate and different in certain ways.

Curious in later life about Mother's research, I took to reading her publications in my early thirties and found that her take on sexuality was indeed close to comprehensive. During different periods she had written articles on the G-spot, anal sex, mutual masturbation, the effects of music on sexual response, the potential improvement of the female orgasm under the stress of patriarchy, and the influence of social institutions upon sexuality. I found myself a little overwhelmed reading her work. I commend her employment of such a great multiplicity of approaches! Surely there have been few scholars in recent decades possessing such an extensive sexual imagination as her own. That fact still frightens me to this day.

There came a point in the 1980s when Mother's work became impacted, strongly at times, by the sudden new presence of HIV/AIDS in the world. I think she preferred to pretend that this crisis wasn't happening. But she couldn't always do that. As I was someone who was seemingly never destined to actually have sex, this never felt that relevant to me. Still, when I first heard of them, the very terms "HIV" and "AIDS" inspired a genuine, almost abstract fear within me.

To my knowledge Mother only ever wrote about HIV/AIDS in a couple of fairly short academic articles. She never spoke directly about the issue with us, although she did like to frequently remind us of the importance of engaging in safe sex. Often she would do this unexpectedly, bringing the subject up whilst we were eating bowls of breakfast cereal or playing games of Scrabble.

13.

The Elder Set

"Where do you think we'll be in ten years' time?" asked Flo.

"Isn't that the sort of question they ask at a job interview?" asked Lucinda.

"Does that matter? I think it's an interesting thing to consider from a myriad of perspectives. It's only right now that we can really anticipate all of the years ahead of us. One day they'll be gone and we won't be able to."

"I want to construct grand buildings and monuments," stated Lucinda, somewhat formally.

"I want to travel to India and journey down the Ganges in a boat," ventured Ag.

"At this age it really is just a case of making sure we actually do these things. We just have to do whatever's necessary to make them happen . . . we all *can* do these things," said Flo, grasping her sisters by the wrists.

"Do you think we'll still have meetings like this when we're old women?" asked Ag.

"Doubtless," said Lucinda. "How could these meetings ever end?"

"Oh I don't think we will," said Flo, "surely we're all going to disperse across the world. Ag is going to marry an Australian businessman and settle into a suburban existence in Melbourne."

"I don't think I'm going to let you condemn me to a life like that in the space of a single offhand sentence. I'd like to aim for a life that's as far removed from that possibility as I can manage."

"Come on, I don't think it sounds so bad. Imagine the swimming pool parties. The long afternoons spent on board yachts. Think about the potential!"

* * *

"I'm worried about Matty," said Flo. "He seems wary of all of us, of just about everything actually . . . I think he's going to develop some major neuroses."

"Haven't those already fully developed?"

"Give the kid a chance," said Ag, "he's still so young, he might still surprise all of us and transform himself completely . . ."

"I wouldn't bet on it."

"Well," said Lucinda, as if laying down a heavy gauntlet. "I for one blame Mother for all his emotional problems. Are you surprised that he's neurotic growing up in *her* domain? She doesn't set proper boundaries, or have any sort of restraint . . . she just has no idea when to say 'No'."

"Come on, she can say 'No' if she wants to," said Flo, "you can be sure of that."

"Not often enough for my taste. I think this is a very destabilizing environment for a child to be brought up in . . . it's as if there are no certainties anywhere in this house. I wouldn't be surprised if one day he starts to get really angry about a lot of things."

* * *

"Who would your ideal man be?"

"I don't care about looks," said Lucinda. "That really shouldn't matter at all. No, he has to be a gentleman, quick-witted, willing to dispense acts of gallantry freely. He has to be sensitive, particularly to the experiences of women," said Lucinda.

"Don't looks matter at all though?" asked Ag.

"No," said Lucinda. "That should hardly enter into it. I'd like a man who's bald, fat and breathless. He just has to love me, really love me, whilst also possessing the various essential qualities that I've just outlined."

"What about Paul Fisher?"

"What *about* him?" asked Lucinda.

"Isn't he your type?"

"No."

"Why not?"

Lucinda rolled her eyes.

"Too arty."

"What's wrong with arty?"

"Well nothing's wrong with it in principle, but in practice it's usually irritating, those guys are just so pretentious."

"I think that you're closing yourself off there Lou . . ."

"No, really, please, just the other day I was sat in the I.C.A. cafe with Ella and some bearded guy in his thirties who was just like Paul and he was sat there talking away. He was using a very solemn tone and at one point he turned to the assembled company and said in this grandiose voice: 'define esoteric,' which he accompanied with this sweeping hand gesture and I really just thought, *My God, you people are too much*."

"But isn't that an interesting point," suggested Ag, "that it's difficult to define what's esoteric in art?"

"Oh please Ag, you aren't going to become one of them are you?"

* * *

"What degree do you want to take?"

"Engineering," stated Lucinda firmly.

"Wouldn't that be incredibly boring?"

"No, then I could use it to start building things like bridges or airports."

"Why would you want to build an airport?"

"It's a challenge. Once you've completed an airport you can always think of it as an achievement."

"How often do you think you would visit your airport after it was finished?"

"Oh I could imagine going once a month, at least, just to walk around its spaces, to see it when it's in use."

They all spent a moment enjoying imagining the particularities of such a scene.

"Which degree are you thinking of these days, Flo?"

"Oh I think I'll have to go for Art. What subject is better than Art?"

"Ag?"

"I'd like to study Hinduism, get to know the Vedas really intimately."

"Sounds like a plan," said Flo.

"Do you think university will be as good as it's meant to be?"

"Oh, I think it'll be a disappointment," said Lucinda. "When everyone's older they look back on it with the sort of nostalgia that distorts everything."

"Well, there must be something lurking inside the nostalgia, no?"

"Maybe, but I'm not convinced that there will be as much to love about university as Mother and her friends seem to think . . ."

"But that's because you're not a fantasist are you Lou? You always dismiss romanticism don't you . . . why is that actually?"

"Because sentimentality is a trap that's really easy to fall into. It's very seductive, but it's always an illusion."

"Can't illusions be exciting sometimes?" asked Ag.

"Well isn't that also an illusion?"

"Which do you think is better," asked Flo, "to hold Romantic illusions or to be cynical?"

"Oh it's definitely better to be cynical," said Lucinda, without hesitation.

* * *

"What would you do if you had your own island?" asked Flo.

"If I was there alone, then I'd use my time to think through just about everything that I could, to get to the bottom of everything," answered Ag.

"But is it really possible to do that? Maybe once you get to where you thought the bottom was, you'll find that everything goes much further than you realized."

"Oh sure, that always happens, but isn't it better to try and enjoy that happening? To try and embrace the confusion of it all and the getting lost inside of it?"

* * *

"Are hats *in* these days Ag?"

"Oh hats are most certainly in. How could they ever go out?"

"Hats will always be in. That's an inherent part of their nature. Our heads aren't going to disappear any day soon, so neither are hats."

"What about on men? They don't seem to wear hats as often as they used to. Why is that?"

"I guess men these days maybe think that hats are effeminate unless they're using them just for warmth. Of course men are foolish. Hats should be for everyone, we should all be wearing hats far more often than we do."

"Hats just seem to make people happy. If you wear one in London it becomes immediately noteworthy. Strangers start looking at you and say "Nice hat!" giving you praise as if you've just performed some sort of complex acrobatic manoeuvre."

* * *

"Don't you think that we should be revolutionaries? Isn't that what we're supposed to be thinking about when we're eighteen?" wondered Flo.

"I believe in evolution, not revolution," said Ag. "We should be working on our spiritual health, on helping our community evolve . . . revolution just leads to violence, conflict, aggression. It sounds like a grand idea but actually it's a total mess."

"Dreaming of revolution is what you do at eighteen, but we recognize that this is a cliché right? Shouldn't we be trying to avoid the allure of that dream, given that it's completely unobtainable and therefore surely a waste of everyone's time?" asked Lucinda with some defiance.

"No, I think that's cynical. That kind of thinking is only going to lead towards apathy and non-action," said Flo. "We can't afford to be thinking like that whilst all of the revolutionary activity is dying out, we have to be the ones who bang our fists down and refuse to conform."

* * *

"Should we have children?" asked Flo.

"Yes," said Ag emphatically. "Of course we should. Isn't that the point of life? Isn't that what these bodies are meant for?"

"I don't want children," said Lucinda, "as you well know."

"But people change Lou, and you might as well one day . . ."

"That's one thing that's never going to change . . ."

"Where are *you* currently standing on this issue Flo?"

"Wavering."

"I would've thought it's pretty normal to feel unsure in the age of birth control," said Lucinda.

"What would make you waver towards yes?" asked Ag.

"Meeting the right man might make all the difference."

"Oh I'm sure you will," said Ag, "you've certainly got plenty of time."

"Sure, but it seems impossible. I really can't see who would want to be with me anyway."

"Is that self-deprecation I'm hearing?" said Lucinda. "You really don't need to be down on yourself. Let's face it Flo, you have a great deal to offer. I think that you know that really. You're just striking a bit of a pose for us."

Flo became quiet, frowned, and looked bashful for a few moments, as if she were a debutante waiting to walk on to the stage for the first time.

"I suspect," began Lucinda, in a solemn voice, "that once you've felt some sort of childbearing urge, even if it goes away for long periods, you'll probably find yourself returning over and over to those thoughts. Eventually I'm sure that you'll feel a need to address them. In my own case I just think that I won't ever have those feelings, they don't seem to exist inside me, and I suspect that they never will. But I do think you will be a Mother one day Flo, I honestly do."

"Don't be so sure of that."

14.

A History of the Secret Room

Lucinda first glimpsed the secret room in the midst of a dream in which she was pacing through the house in a restless manner. Suddenly, unexpectedly, she leaned against the wall in her bedroom and a portal to another, unknown room was revealed. After waking, she found this delighted her so much that she soon became obsessed with making it a reality. Images of the room would constantly enter her mind. She soon took to planning how she could secretly create just such a room.

It would take her some years of scheming and planning, with much furtive shuffling of materials. The process got to a point where she needed to make a certain amount of disorder and noise and for that it was necessary that the house be entirely empty of people. As this was a rare condition for the house to be found in, for a number of years her work could only progress extremely slowly, a fact which was the cause of some frustration to her.

Lucinda felt that it was absolutely crucial that no one know what she was up to and for many years she successfully managed to hold an obliterating veil over her activities. For her, the secrecy was an intrinsic part of the project. Her ideal was that the room would stand, fully built, furnished with exquisite objects, the walls coated in an attractive patterning of wallpaper, without anyone else knowing that it existed. It was to be her private domain, an expression of her radical will, a project which would hopefully never be known to anyone else. She loved the notion of having disappeared whilst still residing amongst the family, lurking behind unknown screens, unreachable.

Lucinda did not always possess a clear idea of what she actually wanted to do inside the room once it was built. Indeed, during the process of building it, she often stopped to wonder if the whole project was in fact a grand folly, involving an entirely pointless expending of energy.

Nevertheless, over time, this confusion became matched with the many uses for the room that would flit through her mind on a daily basis. Once these ideas started to emerge, they refused to disappear. She would practice yoga inside the room. Hold séances there. It would be her secret study. She would steal one object from every member of the household every day and hoard all of them in the room. The ideas never ceased. There was simply no end to the potential uses for the room. Therefore, evidently, it needed to be built.

Lucinda didn't want to tell anyone else about the room because she knew that once it was discovered, the family would steal it from her immediately. The room would rapidly come to have nothing whatsoever to do with her and would instead become a further feature of the household, one which would barely relate to her in any personal way. On the contrary, she wanted a room that couldn't belong to anyone else, one that was entirely her own—even more completely than her bedroom already was. She felt some guilt about the fact that she possessed this desire. After all, it was not an egalitarian impulse. She recognized this. Was her desire to possess a secret room an essentially selfish one? Again and again she wondered if she ought to be labouring for the wider social good of the family. Perhaps she should be creating a space for everyone to use, rather than one designed only for herself?

She thought about the wider human desire for the possession of personal space, about how widespread that impulse was and how, to her mind, there was essentially nothing corrupt about that feeling of need.

Once constructed, the room could be reached through a circular trapdoor concealed underneath a carpet in Lucinda's bedroom, leading into the ground underneath the basement where the room was located. Anyone entering had to follow a ladder downwards, moving through a musty smelling tunnel until they arrived on solid ground, with one bare lightbulb dangling downwards from the ceiling. Lucinda often felt upon entering that the space contained an air of the occult, of mysterious, unknown practices.

She had coated the walls with an antique wallpaper design of greengages and chrysanthemums. There was a dark red leather armchair with a modest sidetable placed next to it. She tended to leave only four or five books in the room at any one time. Indeed, she didn't like storing things in the room which might potentially be missed by the rest of the household. Or, at least, if she took such things there, she vowed that she would not keep them in the room for very long, as otherwise she thought she was somehow tempting fate.

Keeping the room clear of objects and clutter was important to her. She wanted a space where meditation was possible, where she could be rational and reach conclusions and decisions. A place set apart from the clamour of family life, where she could relax and be studious, something that did not interest most of the siblings.

The longer that she stayed in the room the more disappointing it seemed to her somehow. Eventually, all of the effort it took to create it, the secrecy, the heavy labour, no longer felt worthwhile. After all, it was just empty space, although what else could you really expect from a room? It was as if she wanted the room to be a fully animated creature, rather than dead, empty space. Later she felt that she had probably attached too much significance to the room, that in her mind she had endowed it with potential uses and properties it was simply not likely to contain. The room she had sculpted out in her mind had been a perfect one, but it had also been a room that did not dwell in the realm of the real, but rather in the invisible spaces of the imagination. This emptiness did come to feel slightly too minimal, even to her tastes, so she added a blue-and-red vase holding a bunch of dried purple amaranths.

She sometimes felt pleased at the pointlessness of her room. Its lack of a carefully defined purpose *was* in fact a part of its real tangible purpose. She was bored of the many rooms in the world containing names and rules (whether they were written or unwritten ones). As she saw it, rooms should simply be defined as pure space, as entities which could be used, stretched, filled, transformed. By calling a room "The Living Room" she felt that its space became too narrowly defined. Already with the designation of that title, the behaviours which would take place within that room had been decided. To Lucinda, it was all another constriction, a further way of establishing control. She wanted to build a space that had nothing to do with such things.

Once the room was built she didn't actually do a great deal inside it. Later she would come to feel that the process of building it had been the important thing, along with the fact of the room's physical existence. But she noted that nothing much actually *happened* in her room. Perhaps she had thought that, somehow, forces beyond her control would cause things to happen there, but this was not to be.

She came to think that the room was perhaps more important as a concept, as a state of mind, rather than as a place. When considered as an actual location on earth it could be pleasing for a short period, but that feeling eventually wore off.

Generally she would only visit the room late at night, when everyone thought she was asleep. She would sit in the armchair and read or sometimes meditate upon her future, scrawling notes about it in a notebook, or allowing images of how it might look to arise.

She felt that eventually the room achieved the status of an inarticulate rumour in the household. No one quite guessed exactly what she was doing, but nevertheless the household sensed, collectively, that something or other was afoot. They would occasionally make vague insinuations about this at the dinner table, forming statements which would make her feel paranoid, such as:

"Lucinda is looking very distant again . . ."

Or once, Mother had looked her in the eyes and said:

"I wonder, is Lucinda planning something we're not aware of?"

To which Lucinda responded with a mock-aristocratic air:

"No Ma'am, I am not."

Lucinda found that carrying the secret of the room inside herself, alone, was an exhilarating thing to do. In moments of depression or boredom she could always return again to thoughts of her room, seeing a perfected image of it and clinging to that image as a salvation, however foolish that might be.

Of course the process of building was extremely drawn out and took many years. If she had possessed more money, and crucially, if she had not decided that it needed to be done in absolute secrecy, then it could clearly have been created far more rapidly. This was a fact she pondered over frequently. There was a definite sense in which the entire project was simply ridiculous for this reason.

After some years she hired a few workers, who were sworn to secrecy about her project. Furthermore, she never made it entirely clear to them quite what it was she was actually doing. They would only receive instructions to drill holes, to remove sacks of rubble or to construct walls, for example. She claimed that this was to be "a surprise" and that therefore the family must not be informed.

Eventually she came to feel that she had embarked upon

a grand quest, one of the most significant experiences of her lifetime, one which was destined to test the limitations of her resolve to its outermost capacities. At times she faltered. This was a fact which she hated to admit to herself, but she did falter. There were days when she no longer possessed any sort of desire to create the room at all. Nevertheless, she persisted, driving herself onwards until the room was finally completed.

One evening, with some sense of inevitability, Lucinda was finally discovered. Mother was so concerned about Lucinda's not responding to knocks on her bedroom door, that she eventually enlisted the help of Billy and Carlos (her lover of that week, a shot-put athlete from Valencia). Together they broke down Lucinda's door and discovered the substantial hole in the floor of her room. Carlos was the first to go down, doubtless out of some sense of machismo and duty. When he discovered Lucinda's body at the bottom of the ladder, she was curled into a foetal ball on the floor of her room. Seeing Carlos she emitted a very long, shrill scream, a sound that seemed to tear apart the very fabric of the entire family. Soon all of the siblings present in the house had hurried down the ladder and crowded into the room, fascinated by this new extension to their living quarters. Somehow no one was especially surprised by the room's sudden appearance. It simply seemed in keeping with everything else that tended to occur in the house.

As Lucinda had predicted, the room was soon taken over by everyone else, everyone who was not her. Initially she attempted to restrict access to it, but that quickly proved to be impossible. All of the siblings seemed to feel that they possessed an inalienable right to spend time in the room and they would charge into her bedroom, often doing whatever violence was necessary in order to gain entry. In effect, she lost both her secret room and her bedroom. This led her to feel that it was clearly time for her to move out of the house for good, so this she did, in no uncertain terms.

15.

An Interjection from Gerard During an Otherwise Ordinary Dinner Table Conversation

(All of the following was read from a selection of sheets of yellow A4 paper covered in black handwriting):

"I have come to believe that many of us could profit greatly from forging a new relationship with the sea. The fact is, in evolutionary terms, that's where we're all from. We should get to know our ancestry instead of just ignoring it.

"I have also come to believe that red dragons might once have actually existed, possibly even on these very islands. After all a dragon is one of our national symbols isn't it.

"I have come to believe that I really enjoy the presence of large bushy beards. However, I will only say this of those that have grown in unkempt splendour on the faces of older men. On younger men I think bushy beards usually look inappropriate.

"I have come to believe that puffer jackets are ugly, that they are representative of all that is wrong with patterns of consumption in contemporary European life. I would prefer it if a decree was made against them.

"I have come to believe that I would like to spend at least one day inverting everything I would normally do. This would be just to see how it felt to do certain things, to say certain things. To say 'No' when it would normally be 'Yes.' To be kind when I would normally be rude. To prefer dogs when I normally prefer cats.

"And I have also come to believe that I don't really believe in the act of believing.

"Furthermore, I have come to believe that dialogue is one of the strongest of human abilities. And yet we spend most of our lives being silent towards each other.

"And I have come to believe that sometimes, if I were to stand up unexpectedly and wave my arms about and deliver an oration of genuine quality, then in certain contexts that might be a good thing.

"And I have come to believe that after already thinking about this for some years, even in my youth I am convinced that there is a particular magical and highly significant dimension, of possibly inexplicable qualities, that lies resident inside certain gigantic fish tanks displayed within the windows of Chinese restaurants.

"And indeed it so happens that I have come to believe that miniature plastic models of major tourist attractions are in fact often more exciting than the actual places themselves."

16.

In Mother's Study

Everyone had gone away for the weekend. Lucinda, Flo, and Rebecca had returned to their university towns, whilst the others, who had not yet begun studying, were either away with friends or else attending a two day "survival skills" course taking place at a sports centre, in which they would learn how to successfully navigate their way through jungle, desert, and arctic environments after an aeroplane crash or some other similar calamity. I had opted out because I had thought it sounded like a foolish waste of time, perhaps secretly knowing when doing so that I would then be left alone in the house with Mother and could expect an unusual amount of her attention.

Halting in the doorway of Mother's study, I gazed inwards, observing her sat behind her desk, clenching her maroon-coloured fountain pen, her right arm frozen in the air, poised, about to descend on to the page. She took a break from her labours and offered me a warm, disarming smile.

"Do you enjoy doing your work?" I asked her.

"Yes Matty, I do. It can be difficult to complete, but I find it's always good to work hard on something with your mind.

Especially if you finish it and feel that you've done something well."

"I think it looks really boring just sitting there for hours . . ."

"Well, I'm not *just* sitting here for hours," she said, "I'm also thinking and writing, attempting to sculpt my sentences into their most ideal form."

Whilst she spoke, her voice was soft and benevolent and did not contain any hint of malice, as the same words might have done if someone else had said them.

"Do you make everything up?"

"What I'm writing?"

"Yeah."

"No, I'm not writing fiction Matty," she said, smiling. "I'm doing academic research, and when I'm in here I'm engaging with reality. I look at facts and reports, things that I see in the laboratory, as well as other things that I discover reading books, and then I put all of them together on the page . . ."

"It sounds sort of boring to me."

"Well . . . it isn't, because I'm working on one of the most interesting subjects in the world."

"What's that?"

"Sex."

"So . . . why is sex interesting?"

"That you will have to discover for yourself, in time my dear, but for now just trust me when I tell you that it's very interesting."

My features reddened and I swivelled my head away from her so that I pretended I was staring at the wall.

"Okay," I said, nervously, feeling that I had to say something.

"Try not to feel embarrassed about it Matty," she said in a soothing tone, "just see it as something good to look forward to one day."

Despite being eleven years old, I still enjoyed sucking my thumb, a practice that Mother strongly disapproved of, and this was what I did at that moment to occupy myself.

"Hey, come here and give me a hug," she commanded, in a gentle tone. "Please stop putting your thumb in your mouth sweet pea, you're getting too old for that."

"Matty, I think we should talk about boredom. You seem to find too many things boring . . ."

"Yeah . . ."

"Do you think that most things in the world are boring?"

"Yeah."

"Well, I honestly don't think they are darling. I think everything has some kind of interest attached to it. You just have to try and think about things in a slightly different way sometimes."

"I don't know what you mean."

"So try and think of something boring."

"Like, what kind of thing?"

"Anything."

An odd silence ensued.

"Maybe let's try and write a list," she suggested. "How about waiting for a long time at a bus stop? Do you think that's boring?"

"Sounds pretty boring."

"Snooker," she said.

"Boring!" I said.

"Right, so what else is boring?"

"Tennis."

"Yes, you find sports boring don't you . . . what else though? Maybe something that isn't a sport?"

"Being ill."

"Well that can be much worse than boring, sometimes that can be more like frightening, but I suppose it can be boring, particularly if it's just a cold."

"Yeah, I was thinking about having a cold."

"So let's consider these boring things . . . is waiting for a bus *always* boring?"

"I'd say so."

"Is it though? Does it always have to be?"

"Maybe it doesn't always have to be," I consented.

"How could it be interesting?"

"Mmm . . . I don't know . . ."

"How about if you play a game when you're at the bus stop?"

"What sort of game?"

"Well . . . maybe you're with someone else and you're watching all of the people walking past and what you have to do is make up their thoughts, the ones going through their head at that precise moment, and you have to whisper them into the ear of whoever you're with . . ."

"Okay that sounds like it could be fun."

"Or maybe, instead of being bored you could just start looking really closely at all of the things around the bus stop, the different shops, the advertising posters, the things people are carrying, even the rubbish bin next to the bus stop . . . you could start doing drawings of all of them."

"Do drawings of a rubbish bin!?"

"Why not?"

"Rubbish bins are *totally* boring."

"No way!"

"Yes they are!"

"I think they're full of amazing things: all of those brightly coloured food wrappers, heaps of brown leaves, magazines, letters that people were too frightened to send . . . if you look carefully at them you'll find quite a lot of unexpected things . . ."

"I'll go and have a look at one soon then."

For a while we lapsed into silence, Mother casting her eyes across her rows of sentences, forming an occasional alteration to her writings, flicking through the pages of her books stacked on her desk. As she busied herself with this I stared with fascination for some minutes at the many objects in her study, something I was very fond of doing at that time. Ornaments and trinkets were crowded inside a glass-fronted cabinet inlaid with mother-of-pearl, a place where I could observe many entrancing, sumptuous forms without being able to label them, although I think when I was eventually able to, this reduced some of the effect of gazing at them.

Inside were a mouflon horn, a macramé orchid, a ceramic eel, miniature glass ships, a lenticular postcard of a palm tree, a green oval hand mirror. Almost of equal interest to me were the many obscure volumes lining the shelves, the names of the authors appearing like components of a foreign language: Kraft-Ebbing, Masters and Johnson, Wilhelm Reich, Shere Hite. Staring at the names I would invent the everyday habits and histories of these people, imagining their clothes and faces, whilst living in absolute ignorance of what they represented. They only belonged to the distant, unreachable domain of adulthood, a mysterious and alluring location that I knew I did not currently have access to.

Amongst Mother's books were also many that bore her own name: Susan Crickholme. But these seemed unreal to me, as if they hadn't emerged from her person at all. To me she was always Mother, the person who used that other name was a separate, distant individual, one who I didn't know really except perhaps in passing.

Noticing that I was somewhat restless, Mother broke off from her scholarship again for a moment and addressed me once more.

"Matty, can you imagine ever having a job?"

"No. I don't ever want to have a job."

"Well, I'm afraid that you'll probably have to have a job one day . . . don't let it worry you though, the important thing is that you find something you really enjoy doing . . . so much that you could be happy spending all of your time doing it . . ."

"I can't think of *anything* I want to spend all of my time doing."

"Oh you will find something eventually, I'm sure. One day you'll see that the world is much larger and more complex than you might have imagined it to be, and that there are subjects within subjects within subjects for you to learn about, any of which you might want to pursue . . ."

"But you're always telling me things like that, so I already know about how large the world is . . ."

"Well you might think you know, but there's a big difference between thinking that you know and actually knowing."

An uncertain silence fell between us, with Mother continuing to beam a reassuring smile. I started to perform walking motions with my fingers along the edge of her desk.

"So what do you think I should do with my life then?" I asked her.

"Maybe you could become a writer, or perhaps a politician . . . you could become an explorer, go on expeditions to remote locations . . . or you could become a leader, someone who alters the course of history . . ."

"How would I do that?"

"Don't worry about how you would do it yet, the first thing is to start *wanting* to do it, to bring all of your enthusiasm to the task, to start to dream about changing things, about making a difference . . ."

"I'm not sure if I want to make a difference . . ."

"Oh don't say that! Don't say that. You should certainly want to make a difference, to mean something to the world, even if that is very difficult to achieve."

"Well it sounds like a nice idea."

"Yes, it does, doesn't it . . . so you need to start thinking about what kind of contribution you might make to the human race."

"Do I need to think about the whole human race?"

"Not the whole human race, no. But you do need to think about how you might relate to more people than just yourself and your friends and brothers and sisters."

"How big is the human race anyway?"

"At the moment there are around five billion human beings, although the population of the world is expanding all the time."

"Five billion is so many! So what can I do to help all of those people?"

"Don't worry about helping *all* of them, just worry about one day helping some of them."

"Okay, maybe I can do that then."

"Maybe? Of course you can do that!"

Suddenly she rose to her feet with a decisive air of affirmation.

"Okay, stand up Matty, stand up on top of that chair."

I did as asked whilst bearing mournful features and a transparent reluctance, which affected my entire body. She stood at the opposite end of the room, providing me with an audience of one.

"Now, Matty, I want you to raise your head, raise your fist high into the air and repeat after me: I want to change the world!"

I repeated her words in a shambolic, lacklustre voice.

"Say it again! Better, stronger this time, really declare it to me!"

"I want to change the world!"

"Yes, Matty, again! More volume this time."

"I WANT TO CHANGE THE WORLD!" I said, as loudly as possible.

"Yes, Matty! Yes! Those are fighting words!"

She formed a fist and punched the air to provide an illustration of this thought.

"Matty, perhaps you should consider where you will be in fifty years' time. Shut your eyes for a second now and try to imagine yourself at the age of sixty-one. What kind of clothes do you think you might be wearing?"

"Maybe a . . ."

"You don't need to answer with your voice, just think about it. What kind of room will you be in? How did you get there? What job are you doing? What kind of things do you do in this job? Why are you doing those things? Do you think that you will have a beard when you're sixty-one?"

"No, I don't."

"Okay. Well, so now you have a picture of yourself. Sit back down again."

It seemed as if, in the absence of everyone else, we had entered

a place where we might consider ultimate questions and prop-
ositions rather than just go through our daily motions. I felt
excited by that, even though I was not directly conscious of the
fact that this was happening. That day it felt more like some kind
of imperceptible shift in the weather, a movement that somehow
changes everything.

"How does it feel to get old?" I asked her.

"Am I so old?"

"You're older than me."

"That's true. How old am I?"

"Don't you know?"

"Maybe I just need some confirmation from you."

"You're forty-seven."

"Does that seem old to you?"

"It seems older than me. You *are* older than me."

"Yes, I am, I don't deny it."

"So how does it feel being forty-seven?"

"I'm happy being the age that I am. I really don't mind being
this age at all . . . at least not most of the time."

"I can't imagine being forty-seven."

"I couldn't have imagined it at your age either. But it does
happen . . ."

"I hope I never get old."

"No you don't really hope that. You might think that you do,
but you don't . . ."

I lay on the floor staring at fronds of carpet and imagining
that I could see mysterious faces inside them.

"What's the most important thing that's ever happened to
you?"

"Having you and all of your sisters and brothers is the most
important thing that's ever happened to me."

"What happened when I was born?"

"It was very late at night, the middle of the night, around
three in the morning. I'd been expecting you to arrive for hours

and hours, but for some reason you didn't, you kept holding back. My guess is that you liked it in here," she made soft circles around her belly, "it must have been nice and warm and comfortable inside . . . can you remember it?"

"What?"

"My womb. Can you remember how it felt being inside my belly?"

"No, I can't."

"Well, that's normal. Most people can't remember, but just a very very few people say that they can remember, although maybe they're all lying anyway . . ."

"It scares me to think about when I was born."

"Really? Why is that?"

"Well, it's strange to think that before then there was a time when I didn't exist at all."

"None of us gets to live forever. At least most probably we don't. I don't think we do. I doubt you would want to live forever even if you could."

"I'd prefer to live forever than to have to die."

"Well I can understand that. Still . . . I think you'll probably feel differently about that eventually."

"I don't think I'll feel differently. I'm sure I'll always feel just the same. Why would anyone want to die?"

"Everyone changes as they grow older. You change your ideas about death, just as you change so many things. You'll be surprised. Your body will change a lot, in ways that might not be expected. And your mind will change as well, it'll grow and take on board different kinds of ideas . . . is there anything else that scares you about being born?"

"I don't like thinking about being so small and weak. Crying all the time and lying in a pram . . . I don't like it, it makes me feel weird . . ."

"Because you want to be who you are now?"

"Yes."

"And you don't want to be a baby anymore."

"I guess so."

"You want to get away from all of that babyish wailing and neediness and be a growing boy."

"I guess so."

"Well, you *are* a growing boy, much bigger and stronger than when you first came out of me. So just remember that things have moved on and they will continue to move on for you . . ."

This felt fateful and somewhat profound to me. In fact, it made me uneasy, deep inside my stomach. Many of her remarks that day were destined to stay with me in a hazy form for some years to come, it was just one of those occasions, echoing in my memory like blurry voices in a cave.

17.

A Conference on the Vagina

In the winter of 1989 Mother arranged an academic conference, which took place in our living room, focused on the general theme of "The Vagina." Everyone presenting a paper was female, for reasons of Feminist solidarity and because, as Mother put it, "We sometimes need to be able to discuss the feminine, without the interference of the masculine." The only audience for this conference, apart from those academics delivering papers, were most of Mother's children and some of us, including me, were masculine. I think the memory of this confused me in later years, as I felt that being masculine in that room was not entirely permitted.

I was eleven years old at the time and somehow still didn't really have an altogether clear idea of what a vagina was, despite Mother's explanations to us, which had usually been delivered with the aid of diagrams. I think I figured a bit more out during the course of the day, but it was still all quite hazy to me even at the end of it, particularly considering the large quantities of academic language which we encountered, containing many unknown and often intimidating words. I feel now that these academics perhaps managed to make the vagina a more complex entity than it actually is, but maybe that's just my perspective. Mother had warned all of her academic colleagues that her children would be listening and that they should not alter the way in which they would normally deliver their papers. She had made sure that they had all given their consent for children to be present as they spoke.

Despite their advance knowledge of our presence, none of these academics spoke in a way that I could really understand and did not deliver their speeches as if in a room full of children. In retrospect I don't think that we were acknowledged enough and I also feel that we should not have been present at all.

Nevertheless, we were present. Mother told us beforehand that it was "controversial" to hold such an event off campus and even more so to have children in attendance. She told us that it was probably necessary for the conference to be held in secret and that we should consider ourselves lucky to be there at all. "Perhaps there will be scholars in hundreds of years' time, who will feel envious of you all for having been in this room," Mother said to us, surely at her most deluded. Still, I believed this line of argument at the time and the whole occasion bore a portentous weight for me. In the morning Lucinda dressed me up in a suit with a navy-blue bow tie, the first time in my life I had ever dressed like that.

My major memory of the day is that I encountered a boredom of a kind which I have rarely known since. Time seemed to lengthen during the conference to an extent which I did not know was possible. The interminable rounds of discussion and debate which followed each paper seemed genuinely endless. Whatever age you happen to be, I think there is an excruciatingly grey, dismal pain to be encountered when experiencing a lengthy speech that does not seem to possess any real bearing on your existence. I now strongly believe that you should not have to listen to a speech which you have not really chosen to listen to with any sort of freedom. That day I was really only trying to please

Mother by sitting there at such length, trying to be a good son without knowing how to exactly.

The eleven speakers invited that day, delivered the following papers:

Dr. Bethany Merrikin discussed "The Hidden Vagina," musing on the extent to which society chooses to conceal women's sex organs. She wondered whether this could ever be thought of as a positive phenomenon or not, considering some of the damaging effects of representation. She weighed these up against what she saw as the possible advantages of the female body "being seen." She discussed whether it might be distinctly "feminine" or "masculine" forces which caused these acts of "censorship" and argued that it was inevitably a combination of both genders. She was particularly concerned with the extent to which the clitoris is a "concealed entity." Finally, she spoke passionately in favour of bodies "being seen" and took off all her clothes, including her underwear, to support this assertion, an act which met with a round of applause and cheering.

Dr. Clara White discussed "The Vagina as Metaphor," evoking certain films, novels, poems, and paintings, as well as outlining "commonly encountered metaphors" which she claimed always lay lurking within the Collective Unconscious mind. Her talk had different headings which she placed on an overhead projector as she proceeded: "the vagina as treasure chest," "the vagina as dainty flower," "the vagina as autonomous animal," "the vagina considered as a fearsome entity," and finally "the vagina as repository of all experience." In each case, Dr. White was at pains to debunk the myths put forward by these tendencies, to show that all of them could be dismissed, that the reality of the vagina stretches far beyond each of these perspectives. She argued that it was a reality which, finally, could not be pinned down to any singular entity.

Dr. Angela Robertson discussed phallocentrism and the masculine insistence on the inferiority of the vagina. She mentioned the profusion of phallic forms that could be encountered in the world, finally claiming that most objects "in some sense resemble a phallus through the very fact of their material inscription," a fact which "tends to negate the feminine absence of materiality within the genital realm." She discussed the ultimate male belief in the superiority of the phallus and the many strategies employed to make that belief synonymous with forms of social power. She ended her talk by proposing that everyone present "Kill the phallus as a socially central phenomenon." She went on, exclaiming with more and more urgency as she continued: "Let us kill the phallus! Kill, kill the phallus! Kill, kill! Kill, kill, kill!"

Dr. Astrid Durand discussed Gustave Courbet's painting "L'Origine du Monde" (1866), heaping praise on its full exposure of feminine anatomy. Stating that: "To my mind it seems evident that Courbet truly loved women and wished to give women the central place in his cosmology." She saw the painting as "an erotic celebration of the vagina," but added that "we should not lose sight of how shocking this painting would have appeared to its original audience . . . Courbet wished to force his audience out of their quiet, docile complacency and into some form of sensual, revelatory knowledge." She went on to discuss the extent to which the painting formed a masculine discourse, but argued that through his focus on Realism Courbet in fact transcends gender.

Dr. Sarah Atherton discussed the need to praise and honour the vagina in the face of all disparagements and debasements. She outlined her view of pornography as a strategy for the covert humiliation of women through the "lewd exposure of the feminine sex." She went on to propose the adoption of "new sacral perspectives" towards female genitalia, a process which would involve the building of temples and the enacting of rituals as a means to celebrate the vagina and its relations to gender. She called for the instalment of female religious leaders "by any means necessary."

Dr. Sally Dunscombe discussed the possibilities of the vagina becoming a closed off location in the context of HIV/AIDS. She spoke of the ways in which the presence of the disease had already caused the vagina to be shut away, confined, turned into a zone defined by taboo. She was concerned that in the age of HIV/AIDS these already prominent tendencies would only become accentuated leading to the closure of both sexualities and femininities. She ended by calling for an avoidance of hysteria and negativity in the face of these new social circumstances.

Dr. Valentina de los Santos asked: "Are genitals accurate signifiers of gender?" discussing the debates around transgender persons and arguments involving their gender status. She spoke of many other subjects which create gender signification and claimed that *all* of them were of more importance in defining a person's gender identity than their genitals were. Her examples of these things included speech acts, clothes, styles of walking, the deployment of colour in domestic spaces, and the tendency to practice or avoid the playing of certain sports. "The notion that gender is definitively, or even largely determined by the genitals is a major misconception," she claimed.

Dr. Tamara Kirkland discussed pornographic images of women and the masculine gaze, condemning Western society's all too easy adoption of the pornography which was currently prevalent. She spoke of a society in which women are framed as a series of masculine fantasies. She went on to call for the creation of pornographies that would possess a far stronger creative input from women, claiming that "pornography is an inevitable aspect of human life, so let us attempt to improve it as much as possible." She proposed the creation of university-level education programmes about pornography involving lectures, screenings and debates. She felt that the "first task" was to convince many women that pornography was actually of some value to them.

Dr. Nicole Reynolds discussed the problems of equating menstruation with notions of "impurity and danger," speaking of the tendencies within many different human societies to do this. She called instead for "an exuberant celebration of the fact of menstruation, understood as a key aspect of human fertility." For her, "the impurity label is simply another way in which women are reduced by the masculine gaze, even though what is under discussion is something that is natural, and indeed, intrinsic to human experience."

Dr. Miriam Pelletier considered the vagina as a continued site of desire despite the new presence of HIV/AIDS. She spoke of how the vagina was becoming a more illicit and forbidden entity in these circumstances, putting it in line with all sexual "locations." She discussed how this state of affairs could be overcome, partly through safe sex practices, as well as through journalism, lectures and support groups. Towards the end of her talk she put on a baseball cap bearing the message "Practice Safe Sex!" next to a smiling cartoon condom.

Dr. Mashika Akintola discussed "personifications of the vagina in art," focusing on those instances where a vagina had been known to speak and walk, particularly within the realms of performance art and animation, where it was often used to represent womanhood in general. She argued that such vaginas were "goading instruments of empowerment," which, "in their best manifestations . . . cannot help but drive female spectators onwards, towards a place which challenges inequality." In particular she praised the wit of giant, mobile vaginas witnessed in Feminist street parades, with the pinkness and fleshiness of their forms emphasized in a celebration of both kitsch and the feminine. She called for more instances of such personifications, noting that the phallus was far more likely to receive such attention and that "for obvious reasons . . . we should consider this to be unfortunate . . ."

18.

A Procession

There was the day that we took to the streets.

All of the siblings formed a procession in which we wore our favoured costumes, tossing little shimmers of confetti into the air as we progressed, giving out little yelps and shrieks, chanting out personal slogans and waving placards bearing texts formed from capital letters. This procession possessed no formal purpose beyond its own enaction, beyond the fact of its own unravelling. We all developed a joint stomping motion, characterized by its discontinuity as much as by the collective movement which we soon established.

Mother stood entirely to one side and watched us, documenting our progress with photographs whilst dressed in her "ordinary" garb of that time, a green-and-cream coloured *salwar kameez*.

Flo wreathed her neck in pearls and tied a floral silk scarf around her neck in a bulbous knot. She wore a bright spangled silver shirt with pink-and-white buttons descending down its centre. Her trousers were bright green.

"I wish to personify glamour during our march," Flo stated

firmly, "you're all welcome to mess around being characters or revolutionaries, but today I am going to be firmly on the side of glamour."

Of course Mother had frequently encouraged us to dress up from a very young age, so we were used to this kind of behaviour, but this was literally the first time that we had ever taken this tendency out into the city surrounding us. We found that many heads turned. We seemed to inspire both cheerfulness and alarm.

Once we had begun marching we couldn't stop ourselves from making noise. Seemingly any species of noise which we could invent would satisfy us, be it hollering, cheering, clapping, or hissing. As we progressed along the pavement we formed a crazed combination of all of these, with many verbal interjections thrown in as well. All in all the neighbourhood felt quite confused by us. We were an unprecedented spectacle.

Eliza strummed out chords on a Spanish guitar and stopped to stamp her foot, shouting "Olé!"

Gerard brought a little stereo and a selection of cassettes, which he kept changing, seemingly never entirely content with the noise emanating from him. During our parade he switched from 1950s surf pop, to Estonian chanting, to the recording of a lecture about magnesium, to a 1980s martial arts sound effects tape. Whatever he played, each new sound felt like a sonic affront, a challenge to whatever composure may have been possible beforehand.

Eliza carried a large antique mirror encased inside a broken wooden frame. She used it to capture the faces of pedestrians and perhaps reveal those to their owners a little more. It seemed that she felt a somewhat gleeful malevolence with this, almost as if she held the key to all sunlight, all imagery. A somewhat terrifying brightness gleamed from her, as well as a sense that she was the key conspirator within an unknown series of probably nefarious machinations.

Ag held a wooden pole decorated with the bodies of fake soft toy animals, as well as lenses cut out from pairs of 3-D spectacles, various esoteric beermats, and a series of tiny clay beings. She was dressed in the robes of a Kwakiutl Indian priestess and seemed to believe in her essential efficacy that day.

Lilly was dressed in a full body tiger suit. She repeatedly made a roaring sound in imitation of the creature. She had covered a series of white sheets of A5 paper with the word "ROAR" in large red comic book letters and handed them out to some of the pedestrians we encountered. That day I felt she really had some kind of deep inner longing to be a tiger which had never previously managed to quite surface properly.

Barnaby meanwhile was dressed in a blue boiler suit with giant yellow boots covering his feet. He delivered fragments of monologue through a loudhailer, all improvisations on the general subject of "The Street."

Rebecca was dressed in purple leggings with a *Star Wars* T-shirt and aviator shades. She spent the afternoon singing and humming film and TV theme tunes, often employing a very different voice and tone than the ones normally encountered with those songs, sometimes inverting their meaning in the process, turning frivolity into solemnity and indeed vice versa.

For my part I spent the length of the procession handing out pages of texts and images torn from books and magazines of various kinds. Some of the passersby I offered them to wouldn't accept them and looked somehow threatened by my behaviour, whereas others smiled and thanked me. I hope that I made someone's day.

19.

Conversation with a Cardboard Man

I consented to being filmed. So Rebecca led me into a room whilst blindfolded. She sat me down and revealed, somewhat to my surprise, a fully-fledged, life-size, distinctly unreal man created from cardboard. He looked friendly enough I thought. His upper lip held up a bushy, white moustache that sprouted outwards, turning messy at the edges. He wore a black-and-white checked suit. A blue cardboard flower was lodged inside his breast pocket. I was to learn that, in marked contrast to his appearance, he possessed an electronic voice which was slightly raspy and emerged from a hidden microphone.

"Hello," said the cardboard man. "Welcome to my room."

"Hi," I said, a little tentatively, my eyes darting back and forth in all possible directions, in any attempt to discover what else might be concealed in this place.

"Is that all I get?" he asked.

"What do you mean?"

"Just 'Hi.' Is that all you're going to say to me?"

"Uh . . . I might say something else . . ."

"Good," said the cardboard man, "it feels pretty lonely around here. I don't get too many visitors."

"Right," I said, stumbling with my speech slightly, still getting used to the situation. "Is there anything in particular you'd like to talk about then?"

"How is the world doing?" he asked in a somewhat plaintive tone.

"Do you ever get out there?" I asked.

"Never," he said, "I'm always in here."

"Okay," I said, "that's a shame."

"So tell me about it . . ." he said, sounding a little expectant this time.

"Perhaps you could be a little more specific about what you'd like to hear . . . I mean which aspect of the world is it that you'd like me to tell you about?"

"Tell me about something lovely," he said.

This made me pause for some time. My mind was roving, trying to think of some way of simultaneously pleasing the cardboard man, as well as Rebecca, and perhaps even more mysteriously, the silent though deeply enquiring black camera lense which pointed directly at my features.

"I think comic books are lovely," I said.

"They sound nice," he said. "Someone else told me about them before."

"I really love all of the bright colours in them. The way the characters can move so quickly. All the little details."

"So . . . tell me about something you don't like," said the cardboard man.

I mused on this for a moment.

"I don't like sleeping," I said.

"What's sleeping?" he wondered.

"It's when you go to bed and close your eyes and you leave consciousness for some hours."

"Okay. So what is it that you don't like about it?"

"I don't like having to not be awake," I said. "Everything

seems so much better when you're awake. I don't really see the point in not being awake. When you're asleep you aren't really living."

"That doesn't sound too great."

"No, it's not great at all."

"Maybe you could tell me something *you* don't like?" I asked, a little hopefully, in an attempt to deflect attention away from myself a little.

"I don't like being made out of cardboard," he said. "I mean, look at you, you're actually made out of flesh . . . you can stretch your limbs and actually go for a walk for example."

"And you can't do that?"

"No. So that means I'm stuck in here all day."

"That must be a little bit of a drag."

"Yeah, it is. But I don't want to be too pessimistic about it all."

"No . . . I guess you shouldn't be like that . . ." I said. "You don't want to be getting too down."

"Oh, I'm always down," he said. "Wouldn't *you* be, if you never left this room?"

"Sure, I would be too," I said, trying to show some empathy.

"Are you actually real, cardboard man?"

"Real?"

"Do you really exist?"

"What sort of a question is that to ask of someone?" He was clearly a little incensed. "Of course I'm real."

I decided that I shouldn't enquire any further in that direction.

"Okay," I said. "Don't get offended. I was just asking."

"Tell me something else about yourself," said the Cardboard Man.

"What do you want to know?"

"Do you know any songs?" he asked.

"What makes you ask me that?"

"I thought maybe you could teach me how to sing a song. Or maybe, at least, a portion of a song. Perhaps a line or two from a song . . . it's always nice to learn something new to sing . . ."

Stopping for a moment, I rested my chin in my palm, pondering over what to teach him.

"Do you know 'Sittin' On the Dock of the Bay'?"

"No. I don't."

"That's maybe the greatest song ever written."

"That sounds like a good choice then . . ."

"It goes like this . . . *Sittin' in the evening sun, I'll be sittin' when the evening comes, watchin' the ships roll in, then I'll watch them roll away again . . .*"

Before long I'd successfully got him to repeat those words in his strange, fake electronic voice. Finally I demonstrated the whistling part of the song and then he stumbled through a little of that.

"Have you ever whistled before cardboard man?"

"I don't believe that I have."

"So you're learning something else new then."

The electronic nature of his voice kept forcing the whistling to break down into crackles.

"I don't think this is working very well," he said to me.

"Maybe not."

"I think maybe my voice is too electronic."

That made me break into laughter.

"Why have you got an electronic voice when you're made out of cardboard?"

"I don't know . . . I mean, some things just happen don't they . . ."

"Yeah, I guess they do."

"What's your name by the way?" he asked me.

"I'm Matty. What's yours?"

"Pleased to meet you, Matty. I don't know my name. I don't have a name. No one ever gave me one."

"Would you like to have one?"

"I'm not so bothered about having a name to be quite honest with you."

"No?"

"I mean what do I need one of *those* for?"

"Perhaps it might come in useful at some point . . ."

"I don't know what point that would be exactly."

"Neither do I."

That led to silence for a little while, but not for too long. I felt intrigued by this person in front of me. I wanted to talk more with him, partly as I thought he might be liable to disappear at any time.

"So what do you get up to in here?"

"Not much."

"If you're in here all of the time you must do something or other . . ."

"Do you think . . . ?"

"Yes."

"Well, I don't do too much . . . I mean, I can't do too much . . . I'm made out of cardboard . . ."

"But it sounds like you possess a mind . . ."

"Yes, I certainly have a mind, I have one of those."

"So what happens inside your mind?"

"I think about things. I wonder why I'm here. Sometimes I muse on where I'm going . . ."

"Will you go to Cardboard Heaven?"

"I hope so. Maybe cardboard men can move their bodies about a little more when they get there."

"Maybe you'll be able to do a jump."

"Yes, maybe I will Matty, maybe I will."

"I guess that might be something to look forward to . . ." I offered, trying to cheer him up.

"I do look forward to that . . . although just thinking about it makes me feel pretty jealous."

"Oh well, I don't want you to feel like that."

"It's okay. You don't know me yet. You only just met me."

"Well, I'm sorry. I don't like making people feel bad."

"I don't feel so bad."

"Okay."

Our talking ceased for a few moments. We sat in silence. It was as if we were getting to know each other better.

"Do you have many friends?" I asked him, feeling genuinely curious about that.

"I do. Here and there. Round and about. Scattered widely across the continents."

"Okay."

"And some of them come to visit you do they?"

"Now and then they do, now and then, but I do spend an awful lot of time alone here."

"Do you have many hobbies?"

"Oh this and that. I like to spend a lot of my time sitting down. That much is certain."

"And what do you do when you spend all of this time sitting down?"

"Not so much. I stare ahead of me. I think about things. My mind ponders issues. It wanders over quite a few subjects really."

"And are you content like this? Spending all of this time pondering?"

"Not at all, not at all. I possess an overriding feeling of discontent. I am a deeply melancholic man."

"So why is that?"

"I'm made out of cardboard! I can't even move! Surely anyone in this predicament would feel the same way!"

"Well, you have my sympathies about all of this . . ."

"I should think so too laddie!"

"Can you eat anything?"

"How would I be able to eat anything? I'm entirely made out of cardboard!"

"Perhaps that was a foolish question."

"Yes, I think perhaps it was."

"Was your Mother made out of cardboard too?"

"What do you think?"

"I suspect she probably was."

"You suspect accurately . . . of course she was! How else could I have ended up like this?"

"And your Father?"

"He was made of cardboard too! For crying out loud!"

"Well cardboard people don't usually speak . . ."

"And how many of us have you met young man? How do you even know?"

"I must admit that this is my first time meeting a cardboard person."

"Well try not to make too many assumptions about people young man! It is not becoming of a gentleman in your situation."

"Now I'm wondering if it would be better to be made out of cardboard or made out of ice . . ."

"Well that I wouldn't know. Your guess is as good as mine."

20.

Things That People Don't Say, But Which Were Nevertheless Said

"Next year I intend to take up exorcism as a hobby." (Rebecca, 1992)

"I think detectives should have, like, one day off a year, when instead of detecting they would all wear Hawaiian shirts and stick their tongues out." (Matty, 1995)

"Maybe most of my dreams are there to remind me of the chores I haven't done yet . . ." (Lucinda, 1986)

"When you're asleep I always think you look like an albino horse." (Rebecca, speaking of Ag, 1987)

"I don't believe woodpeckers exist 'cuz I've never seen one." (Billy, 1993)

"That's a lovely bit of Edward Estlin." (Frequently spoken

catchphrase by many members of the household, referring to either quotations or general echoes of the work of the poet ee cummings, Edward Estlin being what the double "e" actually stands for.)

"I don't really believe in science, it isn't entertaining enough for my taste." (Matty, 2002)

"But aren't civilizations overrated as a concept?" (Mother, 1991)

"How can you say that the moon doesn't really *do* anything?" (Lucinda, 1993)

"Yes, but what exactly is it about nail clippers that disappoints you so much?" (Lilly, 1999)

"Next time I'm born I'd like to try out being a Komodo dragon." (Ag, 1987)

"I think I've developed a genuine fear of teeth." (Flo, 1993)

"Do you honestly think that Omar Sharif would approve of your antics?" (Rebecca, 1997)

"One day cosmetic surgery will become the new Rock 'n' Roll." (Eliza, 1996)

"Matty, I just ate a woodlouse and now I'm not sure what's going to happen to me!" (Lilly, 1988)

"Well that makes two of us then, I'm also a Seventh Day Adventist these days, didn't you know?" (Rebecca to Lucinda, 1989)

"But watermelons haven't actually *done* anything to you, have they?" (Lucinda to Matty, 1986)

"Oh there are definitely some days when I consider myself to be half woman and half cheetah." (Ag, 1988)

"Sometimes I wish I could just wake up and be a bit of a cyborg for a while." (Billy, 1996)

"Do you think that it's possible to kill someone by being so repeatedly nice to them that they die?" (Matty, 1998)

"Lexicographers are some of the great criminals of our time." (Rebecca, 1993)

"I saw an old woman eating a puffin yesterday." (Eliza, 1996)

"Imagine if water was always a solid . . ." (Lucinda, 1990)

"Society ought to be restructured in order to favour the cause of vampires." (Rebecca, 1988)

"Quite honestly I don't think I've got enough photographs of chihuahuas in my life at the present time." (Flo, 1991)

"Did anyone see my gnu anywhere?" (Lilly, 1996)

"Lucinda, are you actually a werewolf?" (Rebecca, 1987)

"Don't do that! A truly malevolent dishonour will befall the entire family!" (Lucinda, 1986)

"Couldn't we have a room in the house just for displaying jellyfish sculptures?" (Lilly, 1994)

"That's an absolutely first-rate way of storing salt!" (Rebecca, 1990)

"Well he did a thorough enough job that it destroyed most human possibilities." (Lucinda, 1989)

"Who are you kidding? Vegetarian lasagne is a substance in possession of angelic grace!" (Rebecca, 1991)

"Yeah, Scientology will always ruin a perfectly good afternoon." (Flo, 1992)

"Get your hands off my antique fire extinguisher! That's a family heirloom!" (Mother, 1995)

"I wonder how many kilometres we are from the nearest mechanical goose?" (Matty, 1994)

"Why don't you quit that and just get your kicks with banjos instead?" (Barnaby, 1996)

"But did Dwayne really celebrate in an appropriate manner?" (Rebecca, 1988)

"I wonder what Max Von Sydow would have to say about all of this?" (Eliza, 1996)

"Surely I am the living embodiment of jazz?" (Barnaby, 1995)

"There just isn't any restraint in this bedroom is there?" (Lucinda, 1987)

"I declare this bishopric odious!" (Flo, 1989)

"The sensory delights of spaghetti fights are only known to a handful of individuals." (Gerard, 1993)

"The true skill of cooking lies in abstraction." (Rebecca, 1993)

"There's really nothing that a wig can't change for a person." (Flo, 1987)

"I'm currently thinking that playing pinball is likely to solve most of my problems . . ." (Gerard, 1992)

"Look, it's not about the uranium, it's about the sexual malaise . . ." (Rebecca, 1994)

"In this situation I would have thought that puppets truly represent our final hope." (Flo, 1995)

"Perhaps all grandparents are just fakin' it. They're only pretending to be old and slow so that they don't have to exert themselves." (Billy, 1994)

"I think the word 'sneaky' really isn't given the sense of respect which it deserves." (Rebecca, 1993)

"If they won't give us tickets, then we should all go down to the box office and harass them with rattles and kazoos." (Eliza, 1991)

"Autumn is the best season because that's when it gets colder and starts to rain all the time and everything is always miserable." (Lilly, 1996)

"If I was forced to join the army I would think that might be the moment for me to start experimenting with make up." (Matty, 2000)

"But like, what would Fatima Whitbread think of all this?" (Rebecca, 1987)

"Most significant things begin and end with spinach." (Mother, 1993)

21.

A View of the Rooftops

For a number of years, most mornings, not long after dawn had appeared, Eliza would venture over to Hampstead Heath, a fairly short journey from the house. Once there she would launch herself into the air on a hang-glider and be carried by airstreams into whichever directions fate wished to take her.

She found this to be an inspiring commencement to each day and her memories of flight would always mingle pleasingly with her afternoon and evening states. Unlike everyone else in the household she had gone out into the world, in no uncertain terms. Before tedium could take hold she had already escaped.

As she drifted across the skies she often liked to throw small objects downwards for people to encounter in odd locations and juxtapositions. These were always different things: flowers, toys, revolutionary tracts, anything that she wanted to use as a way of communicating with the territories which sprawled out relentlessly underneath her. This was, somehow, her ritual way of affirming that she existed every day, the way for her to wake up, amongst cold relentless blasts of air.

Beneath her lay the vast tangle of suburban streets and swathes of green, antennae gleaming in the early sun, the entire human world in microcosm mingling amongst these forms; everyone breathing, waking, looking innocuous enough, until she began to ponder over how much was in fact below, that is to say all of London.

Once she had learned to see things in this way, almost every ascension felt somewhat breathtaking. She would again consider the profusion of what lay hidden below, often concentrating on the many things which were not visible, but which were undeniably present. She liked to let these known and imagined entities run through her mind as she was carried by the air currents. Many possibilities of what they might be would stroll through her mind. Perhaps she would think of ancient family photograph albums, mahogany chests coated in dust, the odor of ink suffusing the air of attics, boxes of jigsaw puzzles, or collections of antique jewellery.

Every time she ascended she would attempt to imagine new things like these which must, logically, lie beneath her in some form, in some destination below. It was precisely at the moment when she started imagining the city like this, using this method as a prompt, that the view forever ceased to be in any way tedious. She realized it was necessary for her to teach herself to see the city as being more than just its obvious physical outer layer. There was more than just rooftops, roads, and green spaces. These were only the visual repetitions of the urban world that lay underneath. It was perhaps inside, in the more hidden interior spaces that the human universe was lying in wait. Some mornings she really felt that she could reach out and touch these things that flitted and coursed through her mind whilst floating; they assumed an extraordinary sense of reality for her, they formed a vast hidden terrain, one that did not even possess a name. However, in order to access it, she only had to remember that it was always there, and that she had discovered it.

Higher above her aeroplanes drifted, leaving their chains of white vapour trails, moving along a multiplicity of pathways. She enjoyed being among them so much that she rarely even thought of them as entities causing pollution. In fact she liked to feel akin to them with her own flying machine, along with the members of the avian population which she encountered with each of her morning ascents.

It was not long before she got to know all sorts of local landmarks which she would soon encounter on a daily basis, places that became almost like cosmic markers of terrain to her. She would always see grass-covered tennis courts, the train depot, a children's playground, the roof of the house where Keats had once lived, another which had belonged to Sigmund Freud. She always noted all of these aspects of the landscape, as to do so felt like an important part of her routine. When she saw them it was as if she was affirming her own private knowledge of these places once more, asserting her own stance in the world as an individual, one which began on top of Hampstead Heath and spread out towards infinity, extending from that precise point outwards, towards the vanishing distances.

22.

The Transformation of a Room

Partly in response to the radicalism of the Independent Republic, partly due to her own impulses, Flo decided to transform her bedroom as entirely as possible. She wanted it to appear absolutely separate in style to every other room in the house. Somehow she wanted to create a rare environment, one which did not seem to resemble British society, a room that felt greatly removed from more prevalent notions of what a bedroom should look like. She hoped that visitors would find it startling.

Firstly, she took to sleeping in the living room for a while, removing every last object present in her room. She tore up the carpets and took the curtains down. She then painted every surface a shade of glaring pink. Once this base was present she began to build on top of it, gradually adding surfaces and curiosities, as seemed appropriate to her. Eventually the pink base was barely visible at all, sometimes just appearing in tiny patches. It was nevertheless important to her that this base was present and that everything else was somehow related to its form, even if only in a peripheral way.

She wanted to place different objects together in the room to create a sensation of jarring aesthetic configurations, so that everywhere eyes wandered they would encounter new forms which would provoke many different reactions within anyone present. The room was not meant to be restful, but a place of action. All "stable" aesthetic coordinates were discarded in favor of unrest, disorder, asymmetry, disarray. It was to be a room which you stumbled through, encountering random haphazard forms, a collage of psychedelic detritus. She wanted her room to become so arresting in its unexpectedness that it could induce a feeling almost akin to hallucination.

She covered the windows with translucent mauve-coloured plastic. A chest of drawers, which had sat innocently in the corner for years on end was now slathered in lurid pink paint and a coating of silver glitter. She was less worried about how attractive the room might look than by the extent to which it could surprise and alarm any visitors who entered. She began to tilt objects at unusual angles, would frequently experiment by hanging things upside-down, would spatter paint over surfaces, or perforate a variety of objects just for the sake of it. Sometimes she would simply destroy much of the room merely in order to start all over again.

One windowpane was now entirely covered in lurid stickers obtained from dental surgeries, with gaping large red mouths revealing sparkling white teeth; cartoon animals engaged in acts of dental hygiene, as well as a five-step guide for brushing your teeth. These crowded the entire expanse of the glass, obliterating all incoming sunlight.

She took cut-out images from the Caribbean and mounted them on a large sheet of dark green paper. These images included lagoons surrounded by shady foliage; lobsters arranged on a plate with a circle of limes; a mysterious empty dining room with a chandelier and a revolving ceiling fan; an 18th century windmill with white sails; a woman wearing a red dress smiling and leaning against a parapet.

Next to this were pages from an Italian language textbook (pre-intermediate level) with its verb conjugations, paragraphs dotted with empty spaces awaiting words. Images were labelled a, b, c, d, e, f, g, h, i, j, k, l, m, n, and o with a box of sentences beside these containing corresponding sentences which needed to be joined up with a series of lines. There was also a simplified (and in fact fake) newspaper story about the history of football in Italy, which was followed by a series of numbered comprehension questions possessing a definite hint of nationalist fervour.

Flo had taken hundreds of Polaroid images of the interior of the house, finally venturing as far as the back garden with her camera. These covered a substantial portion of one wall. Looking upon them it felt as if the house was in fact expanding whilst you gazed. They frequently seemed more beautiful than the house itself did. She had caught the stairwell, the door of the bathroom on the second floor, boots lined up next to the cupboard in the main hallway, the washing up bowl, and plates inside the kitchen sink.

There were also pages and pages of mathematical calculations along the walls; a glossy magazine photograph of a toadstool; a musical script laid out in purple and pink felt tip; covers of various 1950s pulp paperbacks; a 1985 ping pong championship poster from an obscure Californian destination; even a photograph of "fried trainers." She would frequently cover the ceiling with wrapping paper. Meanwhile portions of the original floor had been obscured by the kind of fake green Astroturf which could often be found inside the window displays of butcher's shops.

On the side of an antique dresser she placed an extract from a two-page article entitled "Turtles in Suriname" which she had discovered inside a copy of the inflight magazine of Suriname Airways, published in the Autumn of 1980. Flo had typed up this text, leaving all of the errors in its English intact, and mounted it on to pale green cardboard. It read as follows:

"There is still a lot to be learned about these animals. For instance only shortly it became known that the Krapés laying in Suriname live on the sea weed and sea grass fields in front of the Brazilian coasts and that female turtle swims every two or three years from there the hundreds of kilometres to Suriname to lay her eggs Every time again on exactly the same beach. This has been known because 6,000 in Suriname laying turtles were marked with a metal tag fixed to a forefeet. How the animals are able to find their way however is not known yet."

Also:

A number of graphs on the walls illustrated phenomena such as "Television Viewership Trends in Peninsular Malaysia between 1981 and 1995," with additional explanatory boxed texts placed beside these.

A gaudy painting contained the forms of houses and skyscrapers, lopsided and at odd angles, with a miniature 3-D U.S. flag emerging from the canvas into the open air, along with plastic human figurines stolen from a children's collection of toys which were glued to the canvas.

A black-and-white photographic portrait of white male colonialists wearing glasses, beards, military medals, and the hats of officialdom, all in aid of the task of illustrating the History of Western Samoa.

A black ink drawing of two seahorses arranged against a background that was empty and white, aside from some clusters of abstract wavering lines representing the forms of the sea. Their eyes seemed to contain an air of sadness and vulnerability. At the end of their bodies their tails curled up like ferns.

A sculpture of a gang of Dalmatian puppies depicted clambering over the form of a toilet cistern and playing with a considerable number of unspooling rolls of pink toilet paper, whilst generally bickering with each other in an amiable fashion.

She painted her wardrobe pink and attached a series of feminine dolls in orderly lines along the edges of the mirror in the centre of its door. All of these dolls possessed blonde hair, which in many cases she had made look more feral by mussing it or chopping parts of it off. These were intended to serve as a constant reminder of how onerous a task feminine self-preservation was. She really did hate the social expectations which existed with regard to that. She was wholly intent on subverting those expectations with every chance that she possessed.

On her bedside table was a wind-up aluminium toy crocodile, a translucent pink plastic water pistol, a purple slinky, a glow-in-the-dark green tinted human skeleton, a pack of tarot cards stacked up and waiting for use, various unidentifiable fantasy creatures crafted from felt, as well as a large ceramic aubergine, placed there for good measure.

Across the spaces of the ceiling she had created many constellations of coloured dots arranged in haphazard fashion. Interspersed amongst these were baseball stickers, empty stock cube packets, a ballerina possessing billowing petticoats and a mermaid with gleaming silver scales.

She had scribbled graffiti and slogans all over the door so that it appeared to look more like a wall in the street. She did this extensively on both sides of the door so that its original appearance had essentially been obliterated. Some of her slogans deliberately contradicted each other, for reasons she always refused to explain.

Whilst she was preparing the room's new form she steadfastly refused to let anyone in the family enter, keeping the door firmly locked at all times. She even fixed a patch of black felt over the keyhole so that no one could even glimpse inside. There was much speculation and anticipation within the household as to what she might actually be *doing* inside, but when her efforts were finally unveiled it seemed that none of the rumours had been accurate.

The floor was now largely covered in a glaring linoleum pattern depicting dragons, tigers, and lilies, all of them placed in front of a swirling abstract turquoise and pink backdrop. Considered by itself the floor would have caused unusual responses in anyone observing, as it didn't really correspond to anyone's idea of how a floor should appear. But she liked that fact.

She had painted a chest of drawers alternate shades of red-and-green, a general act of vandalism towards what was in fact a 19th century antique. She wholeheartedly believed that it was more important to create new objects in the world than to venerate pieces of furniture as if they were sacred entities. On top of this chest, she arranged various bunches of artificial flowers inside three substantial orange plastic vases.

Her old bed was now replaced with a four-poster one which she draped green netting over. (This had been noticed with jealousy by a few family members when it had first entered the house). The bedding she placed on it was always pink. In addition, stuffed creatures lurked within the spaces of the headboard, staring down at any of the bed's occupants, perhaps with humour, perhaps in judgement. Of these creatures, Harry the chimpanzee was perhaps the most significant to her, a gift from her paternal grandmother at the age of five. Many young men were destined to visit this location over the years which followed.

On her desk she had placed a marble bust of Freud which she had painted pink. There was also a mysterious clear glass orb; a pair of chipmunks who were dancing and playing the maracas; a tin robot with flashing dials and an array of buttons; a voodoo doll coated in jutting needles; various photographs placed within silver frames, all of different people wearing brown bear costumes.

When the family were finally allowed to enter the room there were a great variety of responses. For a while everyone in the family wanted to hang out in the room, but she was very clear about boundaries and would often keep the door locked. Billy hated it and said that everything in it was "total rubbish," which earned him a definitive ban.

Lucinda felt that clearly her own project of creating a room had been imitated and plundered in this one. She tried quite hard to mask her annoyance about this line of thinking, but in fact found she could not do that with much success. At the end of the day she was annoyed with Flo for having done this, but she never said this directly.

Rebecca was particularly taken with this project and would often attempt to sneak into the room to commune with it in this new state. Flo eventually got annoyed with this and attempted to also ban Rebecca from the room altogether, which resulted in some screaming fits on Rebecca's part and the inauguration of a perennial rift between the two sisters.

23.

Enacting Impossible Conversations

Feeling bored and limited one day, Gerard decided to instigate a new activity. He encouraged Barnaby to join him in creating a series of conversations which, ideally, would be of a kind not occurring anywhere else on the planet. They were supposed to feel like partially "invented" conversations, lacking the logic and linearity and tone of most other, more "ordinary" conversations. At times it could feel as if they resembled actors' exercises.

The two of them would always agree to talk about only one subject per conversation and this had to be one that might be considered nearly impossible to have, or at least it had to be on a subject which it might seem extremely difficult to have an extended conversation about. Their words would not always focus exclusively on this chosen subject, but they would always form the centre of their conversation, a place from which they would then make an endless series of detours. Rambling across all manner of mental territories in this way, they would enter strange unknown destinations of speech, places which sometimes resembled forgotten human settlements in distant countries. Generally, they would assume positions that they did not really believe in so that there was usually an element of debate.

They considered the ideal conditions for their discussions to be in the midst of the night and so they would usually commence at around 2AM, acting in a highly ritualistic way, with both of them sat cross-legged on the floor, facing each other with grave seriousness, staring intently into each other's eyes, their heads adorned with matching black fedoras, smoking an endless series of menthol cigarettes. Everyone in the household got used to the regular sounds and rhythms of their chattering as it percolated through the walls and corridors of the house, occasionally subtly shaping the course of everyone's dreams.

If anyone chose to distract them at any point in this process then Gerard, who possessed a considerably more difficult and aggressive temperament than Barnaby, was liable to become furious with anyone venturing into their domain. I discovered this to my dismay one night, early on in their years of conversation, when Gerard turned to me and said, in perhaps the most obnoxious voice I had ever heard: "Begone Matty! You are disturbing the equilibrium of our derangements!"

And those are words which will always be with me now. Despite this animosity, I often liked to secretly listen in to their acts of verbal unspooling and I felt jealous of their camaraderie.

They would say things like the following, their words always revolving around one subject at a time:

STAMPS

"Stamp collecting is foolish. It's an activity predicated upon false notions of significance. It is empty. It is silly," proclaimed Gerard.

"You are the foolish one Gerard. Just because it isn't a hobby which you happen to possess yourself . . ."

"It isn't about whether I engage in stamp collecting or not. This is a statement about that particular pastime which I am attempting to make in objective terms. I am trying to silence all of my subjective urges here."

"And you are failing to silence them . . . Gerard, can you not see the potential for beauty lying resident within postage stamps?"

"No. I cannot see that potential."

"Well some people see each individual stamp as its own world . . . or perhaps each is a fragment of a possible world . . . or perhaps it is the decoration of a vessel which could contain anything . . ."

"You mean an envelope?"

"Yes, that's what I'm talking about . . . we see a stamp at the moment of not knowing, at the moment of ignorance about the contents of the envelope . . . and if it is a pictorial stamp it can make an otherwise dull and blank expanse of paper come alive that little bit more . . . a potential repository of colours and cosmic forms . . . just think about all of those envelopes crisscrossing the planet, being bundled into aeroplanes, being sorted, handled, delivered, making endless journeys . . . and each of those envelopes emblazoned with a rectangle, hidden in the corner, that is a potential frame for carrying all colours, for holding a practically innumerable array of pictorial forms . . . any possible arrangement of colour, light and form . . . think of all the different designs which have been used in different nation-states throughout history . . . to dismiss stamps is, in effect, to dismiss the possibilities of pictorial representation as a whole, it is to dismiss images and art and what they might embody . . . if a picture is beautiful then surely it will remain so, whether it is on a stamp or a gallery wall . . ."

CATS

"Cats are the noblest of pets, the most beautiful and significant of animals generally kept as pets . . ." Barnaby put forth.

"They're pests just like all of the other animals . . ."

"How can you say that! How can you repeatedly and so easily come up with these statements?" returned Barnaby, with a kind of mock outrage.

"They bite and scratch—both you and your furniture. They make a highly irritating yelping sound. They lick you and leave disgusting traces of their saliva behind everywhere . . ."

"You are insistently focusing on whichever negative points you can summon! All of them are obvious points as well!"

"They carry fleas, germs, illnesses, they contaminate human living quarters. Sometimes they bring in other little dead animals as presents, or first perhaps they trap them in a corner and play with them in a sadistic fashion, stopping them from leaving, slowly terrifying and torturing them . . ."

"Right, okay Gerard, but they also purr and curl up into adorable balls and want your attention, your companionship, they want to be cuddled and stroked and that is very much a two-way interaction. You are loving them and they are loving you back."

"That's really an illusion. They're just animals. That affection is given without any real level of thought. It's empty. It doesn't actually mean anything."

"I honestly believe that they are far more conscious than you seem to think they are. They possess an intricate chain of feelings, personalities, individual tendencies, preferences . . ."

"They are all lies. Just obfuscatory statements. It's deeply foolish to go around believing that."

"A heartfelt engagement with cats would make you a better person," said Barnaby, with some genuine feeling.

ROUNDABOUTS

"They have fascinated me for years. They really possess something which draws me towards them," opened Gerard.

"What significant social experience have you ever had which involved a roundabout?" countered Barnaby, adopting an incredulous tone.

"I have never had a major social experience which involved a roundabout, but many individual ones . . ."

"What sort of individualist experiences are you talking about?"

"Many of those have involved walking for prolonged periods of time around cities, particularly provincial British ones . . . places in which most of the populace thinks of a roundabout purely as an insignificant architectural feature of pure utility. As entities which could not possess any further significance, which could not be beautiful in any way . . . roundabouts are universally considered banal and normative, they lack all of the qualities which could inspire any sort of imaginative excitement . . . but in fact encountering them during endless lonely walks they have often appeared to me as neglected sites of some beauty . . . I've spent hours looking at them, photographing them, clambering across them, hiding things within their confines, sitting atop them, contemplating aspects of the Earthly realm . . ."

"But aren't some of them simply ugly in your eyes? Is this really the way you feel about every last roundabout?"

"Certainly not every last one, no. The best ones for me are undoubtedly those that possess a little more space than most . . . more foliage, a clump of trees throwing some shadows, perhaps a verdant green expanse of lawn . . . and in those conditions a roundabout can feel more like a microcosm, more like a miniature location, an unusual and forgotten location . . ."

"And what about tramps?"

"Strangely I've never encountered any tramps whilst investigating roundabouts . . ."

"That's lucky."

"And there is a sense in which you want to live on a roundabout simply because you could, just because they are spaces that it's possible to occupy and yet seemingly barely anyone has even noticed that possibility, hardly anyone has stopped to consider it, making the act of living on a roundabout all the more beautiful as a notion, because it feels like an almost secret idea, a fanciful conception which few minds seem to have considered . . . yes, indeed, roundabouts are one of the last unknown glories of the world. Maybe eventually more people will catch up with them.

Maybe in fact this is one of the things that will happen en masse at some point during the 21st century . . ."

"What's your favourite roundabout?"

Gerard did not need to pause before delivering his answer.

"The Arc de Triomphe. Which of course is something of an anomaly . . . I really don't know of too many other roundabouts which achieve such awe-inspiring beauty effects as the Arc de Triomphe does. That is the occasion on which the roundabout reaches the transcendental. It points towards the great possibilities lying dormant within roundabouts . . . if only more people would open their imaginations to such things . . ."

"Now you're getting into one of your vanity trips . . ." said Barnaby with a hint of actual venom.

"Have I told you before about how extraordinary I am?" asked Gerard.

SHOELACES

"Are shoelaces beautiful?" asked Barnaby.

"I don't think that is a question which is even worth asking," returned Gerard.

"Why not?"

"Because it is so evident that they are entities of exceptional beauty . . ."

"Would you care to elaborate on that?"

"For example take the fact that a frayed pair of shoelaces can be taken to represent the very suffering and poverty and heartbreak and exhaustion of the beaten down world . . . or think about the fact that if the strength of pressure exerted by your shoelaces is unequal in quality then there is always a need for you to bend downwards and increase the pressure of one of the shoelaces so that it "matches up" in a suitable manner with the other . . . just think of how remarkably significant it is that such a tiny thing can in fact transform your entire body and its sense of well-being . . . or take another perspective on this . . . so far we have only delved into this subject briefly and so this is only yet another potential commencement of a discourse . . . but think of the visual beauty of shoelaces, their thin long stretching tubular forms, poking upwards with secrecy like surreptitious animals alive with their own secrets and movements . . . anyway I hope you are getting the general notion that they are not something which can simply be neglected or forgotten or dismissed . . ."

"I will attempt to no longer dismiss them!" stated Barnaby.

WHISTLING ON STREETCORNERS

"There are few human actions as beautiful as whistling," began Gerard.

"On this matter I am entirely in agreement."

"The possibility this act provides for self-expression . . ."

"Or for surprising others . . ."

"Indeed. It can be a genuinely transformative act."

"I find that this is particularly the case when an individual stops for a moment on a street corner and breaks into an unexpected bout of whistling . . ."

"Yes, the street corner surely is one of the ideal human venues for whistling."

"Absolutely."

"I particularly like to lean against a pedestrian crossing and listen to the silence of those people directly beside me and then without warning commence whistling, breaking into their airspace with music."

"What do you like to whistle on such occasions?" asked Barnaby.

"Happy tunes, of various kinds, it doesn't really matter what they are, as long as they're cheerful."

"Is there a great difference between whistling versions of famous songs or whistling your own inventions?"

"I don't think that there is any great difference. If you attempt a rendition of a well-known tune it always tends to come out transformed into something at least a little more difficult to recognize . . ."

"Surely not always?"

"No, not always, that is true. If you can manage to capture an essential well-known melody then doubtless someone will recognize that. But often, when it emerges from my mouth it becomes shapeless and no one can tell what I'm trying to do."

"I find that more excitement arises from improvising my own creations, the feeling of freedom, the sense of not knowing where it is you are going exactly . . ."

"That certainly has its place."

"Once you really get deeply involved in whistling you find that it contains all music . . . and yet it all emerges from a location on the body, not from any material object . . ."

"That probably makes whistling more organic than most forms of music."

"Yes, I think that's right, it does."

SUNDAY AFTERNOONS IN SEPTEMBER

"There are just so many examples of earthly phenomena which have yet to be examined in any great detail . . ." said Barnaby, with a mystical air.

"What comes to your mind when you say that?" replied Gerard.

"Many things."

"Tell me about one in particular, the first one that arrives in your mind at this precise instant."

"Sunday afternoons in September."

"Alright. And what do you have to say about those?"

"I'm certainly drawn to them. Their sense of melancholy. The way in which each of them gathers innumerable absences together."

"Yes."

"The way in which everything residing within them ought to be coloured grey and pale brown, the natural colours of that temporal unit known as 'Sunday'."

"We're talking about Britain however, right? I mean Sundays taking place closer to the equator must feel very different for example."

"Yes, that is undoubtedly true. I do indeed have British Sundays in September lodged in my mind when embarking on these ruminations."

"There is the sadness of the Christian illusion which always seems to manage to pervade everything," said Gerard, running with this notion. "It is a day constrained by order, by the heavy limitations of the popular mind."

"We agree on the sadness of all *that*."

"And they do feel different in Autumn in Britain don't they? I think a Sunday in Summer here can be a very exciting occasion, I don't feel that the church affects those days quite as much . . ."

"Perhaps not. To me the fact of Sunday being the holy day is still inescapable then, even in summertime Britain . . ."

"Let us attempt to escape that feeling then," said Gerard.

24.

Rebecca Sends a Parcel to Strangers Who Live 10,000 Kilometres Away

In the summer of 1990 Rebecca made the decision to send a parcel to recipients whose names she did not know, but who lived almost precisely ten thousand kilometres away from the family home. The actual name, nature and occupation of the recipients were not known to her. All she possessed was a postal address, selected purely on the basis of distance, which she found to be a pleasingly arbitrary reason to communicate with anyone. She declined to enclose any formal details about herself, and indeed her package contained almost no information about her at all, beyond whatever details might be inferred through a perusal of its contents. By doing this she wished to occupy an enigmatic position, to be a covert, faceless one-sided correspondent, a person whose precise motives were concealed and could only be repeatedly guessed over.

Considered from one perspective, this was an act of solipsism that edged off into nothingness, a gesture of meaninglessness, the full implications of which eluded even Rebecca. Was it an act of kindness or one of intrusion? Did it display an imaginative curiosity or did it prove the enormous scale of her self-involvement? Could she actually act in any sort of useful or worthwhile way by doing this? She remained uncertain about all of these issues.

Realizing that she could send her package across the globe in any number of different directions, she determined, through an elaborate, protracted series of coin tossing episodes, that it would travel in a south-easterly direction. Consulting maps and guidebooks in a local library she came across the city of Florianopolis, in the Santa Catarina province, in the South-East of Brazil. She managed to obtain a suitable residential address by contacting numerous organizations in the city by telephone, ascertaining whether anyone could speak English there, before persistently presenting a variety of stories about the mysterious disappearance of an inept plumber.

On an otherwise blank sheet of blue writing paper which she placed at the top of a pile of her curious offerings, she wrote these words:

Dear Stranger,

I do not know you. However, this parcel is intended for you. Sending it to you was not an accident.

With Love,
Rebecca

She did not want to make her message more complicated than this to facilitate the possibility of her actually being understood. Assuming that the recipients could understand the English language, or could find someone who did (it being, after all, the most widely spoken language in the world), she hoped that they would, in some sense, be able to figure out the terms on which the package had been sent.

Inside a bulbous, padded envelope Rebecca included a great assemblage of obscurantist paraphernalia, most of the objects not being related to each other in any obvious way. Cut-out portions of some of her favourite advertisements discovered inside glossy magazines were interspersed amongst other appropriated images: an anatomical drawing of a horse from 18th century Persia, a map of the layout of Kew Gardens, a paragraph photocopied from a sociology article about Boxing, a formal invitation to join the American Alligator Farmers Association, the covers of several forgotten 1950s American sci-fi novels (*The Man from Zone X* by Herman Bilstead, *The Avenues of Lucifer* by Malcolm Glish, and *The Sarrastrian System* by Allen Divy), as well as a photograph which she had taken of a red-and-white striped circus tent located in a muddy field amidst a cluster of caravans whose paint was peeling away.

She also included a number of modest three-dimensional objects: a miniature plastic space shuttle, a flattened origami frog fashioned from pale green reeds, a pair of sunglasses rendered in the shape of pineapples, a pair of brand new neon-pink shoelaces, a plasticine artichoke wrapped in a layer of cellophane with its Latin name (*Cynara cardunculus*) typewritten on a thin strip of card, as well as an enamel badge which stated matter-of-factly: "Je Suis un Monstre."

After sending the package in the post, Rebecca took to continually imagining its passage across the planet, seeing images of all the various hands which might hold it in postal depots and at airports, and the vessels it might be stored in at the various stages of its journey. The following weeks saw her inventing a range of elaborate scenarios, each of them resting within a single imaginary comic book frame in her mind, each being a slightly different possible explanation of the fate of her parcel. In practically all of these stories she managed to create illusory visions of achievement for herself, seeing faces consumed with delight, with confusion, with excitement, with the unfolding of some hitherto unknown awakening. She reasoned that there was a definite sense in which the package could not have failed to have induced a significant event in someone's life. However, the truth, perhaps, was that it had been an oddly important moment in *her* life, but had quite possibly barely registered in anyone else's as more than a peculiar, slightly troublesome anomaly.

For some years afterwards she would gaze for long durations at the incidental details of photographs of Brazilian cities, paying particular attention to tower blocks, as she thought that the address she had sent her singular correspondence to must have been inside a similar building to those that she saw within the images she looked at so ardently. Somehow she felt fairly certain that what she had done had resulted in significant consequences of some kind.

25.

The Siblings Discuss Sexuality

Of course the subject of sex never felt as if it was banned in our household. It was discussed with a casualness that I'm sure many would feel envious of, whilst others would certainly have been intimidated. I was definitely a person who belonged in the latter category, probably because I was the youngest in the family and somehow could never speak of the subject with ease in the way that everyone else could.

It should be understood, however, that sex was more usually something lurking in the background of everything we did. The family was interested in a great many other subjects and pursuits, in fact a number of the siblings had already got quite bored of talking about sex by the end of their teenage years, a form of reaction I put down to Mother's outspoken style.

Flo was the first of the siblings to enter into some sort of relationship. This was with a marine biologist named Oliver Goswell, who happened to be fifteen years older than her. After a few months this was all over as Flo discovered he was in fact a serial adulterer. She then commenced a long journey through the bedrooms of many young men who would appear in the house with such regularity that I gave up on introducing myself to them and would usually make do with a hurried nod instead.

Ag and Rebecca soon followed suit, but Lucinda seemed to find it impossible to meet anyone she got along with for some years. It became something of a hobby for her to come home after one of her many dates and launch into a lengthy litany of complaints about her most recent suitor, which at times made her resemble an irate customer who enjoys laying into a shop assistant.

"Shouldn't you try going to bed with one of these dates?" Mother eventually asked her.

"Oh I suppose you want me to be a slut like you!" was Lucinda's barbed response.

"Oh I revel in sluthood darling, I revel in it," said Mother.

"Some of us feel we want to live differently," said Lucinda, quite aggressively.

Mother sometimes let her children bring lovers to their bedrooms a little before the age of consent. Everyone knew that they did have to obtain some sort of permission for this, even if, in effect, it was almost always granted. Mother thought of each case in individual terms and only gave a green light if she really thought that this was an appropriate course of action. Nevertheless, it was far more likely that she would be telling us to have safe, consensual sex than to abstain from that activity.

Most of us didn't really like being the children of a sexologist, although some of us did seem to love it. The rest of us felt that it put us under pressure to be similarly open and liberated when we weren't really inclined that way. Still, it was only me, ultimately, who seemed incapable of commencing any sort of relationship at all. Everyone else found a partner that suited them eventually. In the long run no one followed Mother's example of long-term polygamy or "polyamory" as she preferred to call it. On the contrary, everyone decided to live in reaction against it.

On the whole, it was fairly unusual for us to enter into extended conversations about sex, but it would happen occasionally, and

when we did launch into this difficult subject it seemed to be me
who was affected the most negatively. I would always be nervous
to the point of feeling genuinely mortified.

A particularly long and excruciating exchange unravelled
in the Living Room one Sunday afternoon when I was still a
teenager. Everyone seemed especially restless that day, so it was
not long before Flo confronted me, a little idly, with a question:

"Matty, have you got a girlfriend yet?" she asked, probably
meaning no harm.

"No," I said, as quietly as I could manage.

"Don't you want one?" she asked.

"Maybe he wants a boyfriend," suggested Rebecca, before I
could answer. "Don't you want one of those?" she asked me.

"I don't think so," I said, almost inaudibly, not really understanding the full implications of this discussion.

"Oh, I remember *my* first boyfriend," said Mother, "he was
such a terrible pain in the ass, and not in any sort of good way.
Always nagging me to go and see Tarkovsky films which would
make me fall asleep."

"Maybe you were lucky to have someone like that," suggested
Lucinda.

"Well there were plenty of other things that were wrong
with him. The major one being that at heart he was an absolute
misogynist."

"Was this when you were a teenager?" asked Eliza.

"Yes, I was fifteen, I was surrounded by the so-called intelli-
gentsia from a very early age compared to most people."

There was a lull in conversation, so I was put under scrutiny
again.

"Come on Matty, sex is wot we're ere for," said Billy, goading
me. "Pants down, stick it in!"

"No Matty, don't listen to him," said Flo continuing in a tone
that felt both serious and ironic simultaneously, "you should be
an attentive and sensual lover. A new man. Someone given to

the exquisite and languorous techniques of giving and receiving pleasure."

"Alright," I said.

"Is this an appropriate conversation we're having here?" wondered Lucinda aloud, but everyone ignored her.

"Personally, I like to make love at least twice a week," said Gerard.

"I'm sure you would like to get down to it a couple of times a week Gerard, but somehow I suspect that you don't end up getting your end away quite that much," said Flo.

"You might be surprised my dear," returned Gerard.

"At least you've referred to 'making love'. I mean that's at least the language of a gentleman," said Lucinda. "I won't fault you in that direction."

"Nah, it's really not accurate to call it that," said Billy, "the right name for it is 'fucking'."

"I might agree with that actually," said Mother.

"Might," said Lucinda.

"Well there's such an infinity of ways of using words to describe what can be called 'the sexual act'. And 'fucking' is certainly one of the important examples of those terms," said Mother, enjoying being an actual certified expert on this subject.

"Well I happen to think it sounds like something really disgusting when you call it that Billy," said Lucinda.

"It's really better not to put the words 'sex' and 'disgusting' together in the same sentence," said Mother, "trouble usually lies in that direction."

"Trouble lies in the direction of sex," said Flo, smiling mischievously.

"Nobody really knows what sex is," said Rebecca, "because we don't know what human beings are."

"Quite right darling, quite right," said Mother. "Yes darling that's really very insightful of you."

Lucinda couldn't resist this opportunity for some conflict.

"To be honest Mother Darling," she said in a voice heavy with sarcasm, "I think you really should try to be a little more responsible around us with this subject."

"This subject? You mean sex?" Mother asked, a little disingenuously.

"Yes. That's the one," said Lucinda.

"A subject you don't seem to want to even name," Mother said, quite softly. "Are you feeling inhibited about it yourself, Lucinda?"

"No, I'm not feeling inhibited, but I do think that you could practice a few more constraints . . ."

"Which ones do you have in mind?"

"It should be obvious, frankly. I mean sometimes it just isn't really appropriate to say certain things around your children . . . I don't especially want to repeat those things . . ."

"Well, Lucinda darling, you know very well that I am an academic engaged in the study of sexuality and that means I believe in a liberated sexuality. One aspect of that involves speaking openly about the subject . . . in any case, as you well know, it will simply not be possible for you to successfully censor me . . ."

"I'm not trying to censor you. I wouldn't attempt to try and do that, but I am trying to get you to think a little more about some of the things that you come out with . . ."

"Well thank you very much for your concern Lucinda, but honestly you needn't worry us all too much about that."

At this point Rebecca decided to step into the discussion again: "Honestly, Lucy, you do seem to think you're such a great moral authority around here. You really do make too many assumptions. There are times when you should really just leave Mother alone."

This caused Lucinda to storm out of the room and towards her bedroom.

"Matty," began Rebecca, "I really wouldn't underestimate the potential pleasure of taking a good stout firm prick up your ass

. . . you never know, you may find that you want that one day . . . it could be that you just haven't realized it yet."

Then she turned to the rest of the room. "You're all way too heteronormative for my taste. Let's remember that there are different sexualities in this world, even among us."

Mother only nodded ardently in agreement with this.

"Of course it's tremendous that you say this darling. You do need to remind everyone. It really isn't the same as me saying it," said Mother. "It can take a while for these things to sink in with people, and that's why I think it needs repeating to you all while you're still at a relatively tender age . . . Just remember to always have consensual, safe sex . . ." said Mother.

"Yeah, everyone knows they have to be doing that," said Rebecca, who sounded bored.

"Be sure that you all *do* know," said Mother.

Personally I was so shocked by what Rebecca had just said to me, that I had now descended into an even more absolute silence than the one which I had already been inhabiting. I hardly felt capable of speech for some days afterwards.

"Becky, do you really have to harass Matty like you just did?" asked Flo.

"It's not harassment! Frankly that betrays that you possess a very heteronormative mindset."

"Well I'm straight," she returned, as if that settled the matter once and for all.

"Everyone's secretly gay," said Rebecca, "it's just that people hide it from themselves, they pretend those feelings aren't there."

"You would say that tho wouldn't you, 'cuz you're gay," said Billy.

"It really isn't my own sexuality I'm talking about here," said Rebecca, sounding worried and defensive. "This is a statement about everyone."

"It's just wot you think's true," said Billy.

"I think it might be true," said Ag. "I'm not sure though. I can't imagine being a lesbian myself. That seems quite alien to me really."

"Don't knock it until you've tried it," said Rebecca.

There was a momentary silence as everyone figured out where to lurch towards next in the conversation. Then Mother began one of her small impromptu lectures.

"I really think sexuality should be more visible, should be something that people feel comfortable talking about. It should be something that actually *happens* as well, at the right time. And that's really not always the case in Britain. Even these days. One thing I would really like to have achieved for you all, as a Mother, is that you might feel comfortable talking about sexuality together, or with anyone. But I guess you can't always win at that game."

"But what if someone doesn't like sex?" asked Flo. "Some people just aren't interested in it. Isn't that acceptable?"

"Well Flo, I certainly think it's a terrible shame when that happens. It's really a denial of one of the most significant things in life. And I really think people like that deserve help, but I suppose the fact is that not every last person actually wants to *be helped.*"

"But can't some people just be celibate?" continued Flo. "shouldn't that be allowed? Why does sex always have to be this thing that feels compulsory?"

"Well it isn't compulsory of course," said Mother. "It mustn't ever be that. Sex always has to be consensual. Yes that really is a very significant and really quite beautiful word: 'consensual.'"

"Personally I think there's also the fact that people who don't like sex are virtually insane," said Rebecca.

"Well that was in fact Wilhelm Reich's theory. He claimed that the suppression of sexual energy was one of the chief causes of the rise of Fascism."

"Do you agree with him about that?"

"Oh Yes, I would call myself a Reichian. His writings are

extremely significant."

"Perhaps he was right," said Flo, deferring to Mother's greater knowledge a little.

After this, a silence descended in the room and we all sat feeling different forms of confusion, before most of us eventually retreated to our rooms until it was time to come downstairs again for dinner.

26.

An Evening of Entertainment

Giving us little prior warning, one morning the Independent Republic of the Third Floor announced that that evening they would present an entertainment revue that they had been planning to the rest of the family. Beforehand, no one felt very sure quite what it would be like, but everyone was happy enough to be in attendance. After hearing their statement we all spent the day wondering what the show might contain.

To commence the evening all three members of the Republic performed a five-minute play entitled "Cosmos" in which they enacted a version of the creation of the universe using mime and interpretative dance movements. There was a strong emphasis on explosions, which were mimicked with mouths and the energetic movements of flailing limbs. Inchoate gestures depicting the births of numerous animal species followed. No one really understood what they were watching, but at least it didn't last for very long.

The Republic then began calling a series of real telephone numbers selected from those available across the world, putting their voices through a speaker, so that we all sat listening to their exchanges with a hotel receptionist in Toronto, a rubber tyre manufacturer from Invercargill in New Zealand and finally a nightclub owner in Harare, Zimbabwe. These were all inconsequential conversations which drifted for a time, as those picking up the phone attempted to assert some sort of logic and order within the framework of the call, before, in each case, they finally gave up, each of them within the space of three minutes as it happened.

Eliza then took to the stage alone and announced that she would now recite the balcony speech from *Romeo and Juliet* with all of the sentences spoken in reverse order, which she did:

"Capulet a be longer no I'll And.
Love my sworn but be, not wilt thou if or;
Name thy refuse and father thy deny,
Romeo thou art wherefore, Romeo, Romeo, O."

They next set up a canvas screen and projected a random selection of television adverts from previous decades. We enjoyed many details from these: the melodies of certain jingles, the haircuts of housewives, the forms in which people then decorated their homes. It was not clear if we were supposed to like these adverts or feel derision for them, but it all seemed to fit into the irreverent style of the evening in any case.

Barnaby took to the stage and announced: "I am now going to tell you some fake anecdotes about various encounters that I've had with aliens," which was a statement that was met with a certain amount of cheering and applause. He recounted his story in this way:

"They were larger than I expected, with big sacks of bright pink flesh. I couldn't detect any faces among them. There were, however, thin stalks emerging from their bodies in odd places. There were a great number of these stalks, too many to count, so I didn't. They led me to a gigantic rock in space, which I guess was probably a moon somewhere, and whilst they did this they were busy tickling me with these long thick stalks they had. I wasn't sure if it was supposed to be affection they were showing me or something more threatening. Eventually they took me home."

After this they next began to play a series of sound recordings of "everyday" objects and occurrences, all of which were rendered in slow motion. We were treated to Gerard brushing his teeth, to Barnaby having a shower, to Eliza boiling the kettle to make a cup of tea. All of these things felt truly distorted by the radicalism of the slow-motion treatment. They announced each action before playing the recordings in somewhat ludicrous, solemn tones. Personally, I found this to be amongst the most enjoyable pieces of the evening.

It was then Gerard's turn to deliver a brief lecture which was named: "The Pleasures of the Formal Apprehension of Bad Art". Amongst his examples were the films of Walt Disney, the paintings you see displayed on the walls of takeaways, the decorative plates to be found inside tea rooms and cheap hotels which depict scenes of rural idyll, and finally he discussed the phenomenon of popular romance novels, which he read passages from at some length. In each case he identified elements of "significance" and displayed an infectious enthusiasm for whatever was being considered.

Seemingly, it was then time for Eliza to perform a balancing act involving a large stack of porcelain plates which she had built on top of her head. Finally, at the summit of these, she added a bowl of pickled cucumbers doused in rice vinegar, which she proceeded to offer to everyone in the room, walking in a circle and successfully balancing all the while. We all felt that this was a genuinely impressive feat, one that we could not have repeated or matched ourselves.

Finally, the evening came to a suitably curious conclusion with a brief silent slide show, exclusively composed of images of caravans and camper vans. These were presented without any sort of formal commentary or explanation, which somehow didn't seem to matter at all. Eventually the slides came to an end and the Republic took applause whilst they engaged in a certain amount of exaggerated bowing.

27.

Three Children Encounter a Polar Bear

1.

I discovered a copy of this photograph amongst some of Mother's old papers and clutter some years ago now. It depicts three blind children in Sunderland Museum, in 1913, discovering the forms of a taxidermied polar bear. This image has always moved me profoundly. It became perhaps my favourite photograph.

2.

Looking at this image I feel great compassion and tenderness for these children. Partly this is due to their age, the innocence in their faces, the fact that they are children, any children. But of course you cannot help but see a further level of vulnerability in them because of their blindness. I know nothing about their personal histories. I can only hope that they managed to get through their time on Earth without too many difficulties.

3.

When looking at this, I used to imagine myself faced with the life situation of blindness and the multitude of meanings it would hold when living within it. Even after years of thinking about this subject, I'm still not convinced that I can adequately project myself into their situation, into a state where I would find it possible to genuinely imagine the lives of these children in more than a fragmentary way. Perhaps it would be easier if I knew someone who actually was blind, but I never have done. Even then I think it might be hard to fully understand.

4.

Aside from these general thoughts, in which I am treating blindness as a negativity, there is also the extraordinary level of Hope which seems resident within this photograph, perhaps because it depicts a form of Exploration, the discovery of a remarkable creature existing at enormous remove from the social environment in which these children lived. You sense the children are probably being looked after very well, that they really were learning here in a full and meaningful way.

5.

A large part of what I responded to in this photograph was the somehow unlikely and wonderful juxtaposition of a variety of elements which you do not expect to encounter at once. Blindness, Childhood, Polar Bears, Sunderland: these are not elements which you expect to encounter mingled together. There is also the considerable age of the image, presenting something from what is certainly another historical time altogether. All in all it was something that I never thought I would see in this life.

6.

Whilst I think there is fragility within this image, ultimately I find it to be one of great beauty, and that surpasses any other feelings I might have about it. This scene, in this forgotten provincial museum, a location of hidden treasures, with its roped-off paintings hung in heavy gilt frames; the attentive, curious, beautiful faces of the children, touching an animal which here looks like a mystical relic of soft proportions. I can imagine how intriguing that fur must have felt to them that day, all of those years ago, in a city that feels far away from London, one that I have yet to ever visit.

28.

Rearrangement of the Premises

Over dinner one night Mother announced that we would soon dedicate a day of our lives to "rearranging the position of all of the objects in the house." She then spent some time attempting to explain to us *why* we would be doing this, but I'm not sure that all of us ever fully understood. The general idea, at least, was to create a new environment, to make the house feel different again, if possible to make it feel "reborn," to use one of her terms. As it turned out, that proved perhaps more possible to achieve than we at first thought. Other key aims of this exercise were for Mother to try and create some sense of communality amongst us and to make us feel less possessive of the objects in our rooms.

Each of us was allowed to choose ten objects that we felt *had* to stay in our rooms. These were to be covered in pink sheets announcing their significance. Everything else was therefore designated as suitable for relocation to any other part of the house. To our surprise, soon after we began this tumultuous exercise, we all started to actually enjoy it. This particular engagement with chaos seemed very positive at first.

Movements of objects began at a bewildering rate. Gerard

took Rebecca's toothbrush and placed it inside a frying pan. This frying pan was soon moved from the kitchen to Eliza's room, where it perched on top of a wardrobe. Somewhat in retaliation, Rebecca then charged into Gerard's room and took a pair of shoes, placing one of them in the boiler room and another inside the freezer.

In a moment of insanity Eliza and Barnaby decided to move all of the food from the kitchen into one of the bathrooms. A number of things spilt onto the floor, the bathtub and the sink. People passed each other on the stairs and in doorways carrying objects that had embarked upon mysterious itineraries.

It did not take long before everyone and everything seemed to suddenly possess the character of something unknown and perhaps inscrutable. No one and no thing seemed to hold fixed attributes any longer. A person was suddenly liable to appear anywhere, in formations that often contradicted all of their ordinary actions. It felt as if none of us could really be trusted to remain ourselves anymore. This made for an extremely peculiar day, one possessing an atmosphere that was unlike any other that I have known.

Late in the morning I passed Gerard and Barnaby carrying the kitchen table out into the garden. Their faces were strangely solemn. I flattened myself against the wall to enable their passage. As I did this, I saw Rebecca entering in the other direction, holding a large stack of my books which were destined for a cupboard where we more usually kept shoe polish and cans of air freshener that never got used. For a moment then I did feel a sense of dispossession and injustice. I found that I couldn't help but throw her a glance that contained some malice. Mother moved a few objects herself, but largely she spent the day standing amongst us, trying to push proceedings along with her comments:

"Yes, try and think of the most unlikely place that you could put that and leave it there . . ." She kept saying similar words of encouragement all day long.

Or she might just urge us onwards: "Yes, Matty, yes, displace it! Help us to create some chaos! Keep going my love! Keep at it!"

Sometimes it almost felt as if we were engaged in a sporting competition. "Come on Rebecca! Come on my son!" Mother might exclaim. (She really would actually call Rebecca "son" from time to time.)

Walking past the doorway of Eliza's room I noticed the figure of Gerard crouched close to the floor, sifting through all of her possessions, leaving them strewn in piles on the floor around him. As he went along he would distractedly throw things over his shoulders so that they joined the morass of objects lying across the floor.

"What are you doing?" I asked him, in a slightly accusatory tone.

"I'm just thinking about which of Eliza's things to move ... I'm intending to move most of them somewhere ..."

"That looks a little more like a form of psychological harassment to me," I said, an unusually bold statement for me.

"No Matty, it falls perfectly comfortably within the perimeters of this exercise . . ."

Gerard was always one of the more commanding and patronizing members of the family. Knowing he could treat me in that way it often seemed as if he would take every opportunity that he could to do so.

"Are you going to make her unhappy like this though?" I asked.

"No Matty. Eliza and I possess a very intimate understanding of our respective imaginations you know. Perhaps you aren't aware of that? She will be perfectly fine with this . . . In any case, as I've said, this behavior is permitted within the rules outlined by Mother . . . so get off my case, alright!"

I didn't feel like having a full-blown argument, so I left him to his mess making.

Meanwhile Ag and Rebecca had started to fill up the upstairs bathtub with as many objects as they could cram into its form.

These were gathered together from everyone's possessions, they were careful to not specifically target any one person. Above the objects they wrote a sign which stated: "Things you should probably be ashamed of."

Among their selections were a dart board, an inflatable PVC monkey, pairs of elbow length gloves and some *Wham!* LPs. Certain members of the household found this to be a negative way of reacting to the situation, whilst others thought it was witty. I suppose by this point in time we were all used to the notion that someone amongst us would always be a little offended, but we also knew that in our house these behaviors would usually be permitted in any case.

Whilst tearing all the rooms apart in this way, arguments inevitably broke out amongst certain siblings. We knew that afterwards all of these possessions would be reclaimed and that, in most cases, they would find their way back to their original locations, yet there was still anxiety and a sense of moral outrage when we saw certain persons carrying particular objects. As a consequence of such tensions, Lucinda and Gerard ended up rolling on the floor, attacking each other, with her unleashing a series of screams, all because she saw him holding on to her hot water bottle. They were reminded by Mother that this was the sort of behavior which could not continue during this exercise. It was not long before they both resumed shifting objects in a more amicable fashion whilst quietly glowering at each other. Everyone soon shrugged off their disagreement as being part of "just another day in our house."

Our movements reached a level of high intensity in the late afternoon. By that time we could see the clear transformative possibilities of our actions. As the day elapsed we grew more weary and became quieter. Eventually we began to question the value of what we were doing and in some cases even became a little annoyed with Mother. Many of us wanted the game to end, but instead she kept pushing onwards, until our living quarters became very confusing in their disorder.

Once we had finished rearranging everything there was a prevailing sense that you could no longer take anything for granted in this place. At every turn you were liable to encounter unexpected forms. It made us realize how malleable our surroundings really were. If things could look so different, just by *moving our possessions around*, then what else could happen here? There was a definite element of excitement with the house in this state, but it was also quite anxiety inducing. We no longer knew where anything was. Nothing even seemed to possess a "place" any longer. The bananas were in the sink. The maps were in the spice cupboard. The measuring instruments had been fastened to the ceiling.

We paced around the house, the space that was suddenly so hard to recognize as our own.

"I like it this way," said Rebecca. "I don't think we should change it at all."

"But I need to know where everything is!" protested Ag.

"Well," said Mother, with a look of mirth in her eyes, "the next part of the exercise, starting in the morning, will be to put everything back where it came from."

"That sounds boring," said Rebecca.

"What if we don't know where it came from?" asked Eliza.

"We'll just have to get it as close as possible," said Mother. "I'm sure there will be some confusion . . . but I would also predict that somehow it will all just slot back together more or less . . ."

29.

Our Tendencies

Living in our family is often an exhausting experience, especially when everyone is huddled under the same roof. There are constant surprises. Nothing ever seems to settle into a steady or predictable pattern. Looking back now I readily get lost within a profusion of childhood images, fragments which come crowding in and overwhelm me.

Mother would be wandering back and forth amongst us all, perhaps brandishing a loudhailer, improvising slogans or utterances to try and spur us on towards new chaotic permutations, with most of her children eventually either ignoring or shouting at her.

There was the afternoon that Barnaby decided to tie hundreds of brightly coloured balloons to an armchair so that he could achieve the feat of ascending into the skyscapes, where he was destined to drift languidly for some time, before methodically puncturing each balloon in order to return to the safety of the ground.

And there was the occasion on which Lilly put together an A5, eight-page black-and-white stapled pamphlet which she named

"An Introduction to Lilly," giving a free copy to everyone in the family, as well as to most other people who she met for a while. Within its pages, she discussed her interests and hobbies of the time and included a list entitled "Various Ridiculous Things I Want To Do Before I Die."

During another period, Mother began to give a series of lengthy monologues concerning a number of long dead aunts and uncles who we had never met. There was Uncle Richard who had been an early pioneer of aviation; Aunt Florence who had lost her sanity and become quite fixated on the subject of moss; Aunt Ellie who had once tried and failed to become a pop star in Estonia. Uncle Donald had apparently once organized a concert involving hundreds of musicians who had lined the tunnels of London's sewers, because he believed that it was a location containing "unique acoustics." Transporting an audience into this environment was important, he believed, in order to alter their spatial, aural and olfactory perceptions, in a way that was not obtainable in any other venue.

Then there was the time that The Independent Republic would shift around the spaces of the house, inscribing the surfaces of walls and furnishings with lines of coded writing, a form that almost resembled hieroglyphics due to its tendency to employ language forms that were also nearly pictures, with flourishes of tails, dashes, circles, stripes, and dots. They would leave these fractured discourses around the house in discreet, nearly invisible locations. Over time they came to adorn table legs, the top of newspaper pages, empty spaces on food wrappers and the corners of desks and wardrobes. Sometimes they would hand out cards containing a key which explained some of the terms of their code and translated various sample sentences.

Or there was the year when Billy would always refer to an imaginary friend named "Pete," who would invisibly accompany us through all of our dinners. He could be consulted on all manner of issues affecting the household ("Could you ask Pete what he thinks?"). Billy would stop talking and lean to his right, where Pete was always seated, and silently confer with him, only moving his lips a little as he did so. Reactions to Pete's existence varied greatly from one sibling to another and ranged from apathy, all the way through to adulation.

Waking up in our house you would come to expect an encounter with almost anything on a daily basis. One morning, when I was still very young, I awoke, fervently rubbing my eyes, as I saw Ag leading a goat up the stairs. She seemed to be on quite intimate terms with this creature, stroking its fur and administering affectionate little pats to its head, making nonsense noises as if it were a human baby. Seeing me she grinned and just said: "Hello Matty, this is Horace," offering no further explanation. Remaining silent, I kept my feet firmly lodged in place, as if fixed to the carpet by some mysterious adhesive substance. I felt fearful and began shivering slightly.

I never asked why Horace was present, indoors, amongst us. I simply continued on my way, pretending I hadn't seen anything unusual. In fact, I have never discovered any sort of reason for Horace's presence that day; he soon disappeared altogether and I didn't want to ask any questions about him. By then I'd learnt that it was better to accept anything around me that happened and just try to get on with things.

I also remember the occasion on which the Elder Set launched an official campaign in favor of the wearing of hats. They began to make a point of each wearing a different hat and of continually swapping their hats throughout the day. The aesthetic qualities of these accessories were not of great significance to them. All that really mattered was that their forms kept shifting for the sake of enjoyment. They supplemented this with a series of leaflets, posters, speeches, and public debates on the subject which were all held in the Living Room.

Certain interests would occur so briefly in the house that they barely registered at all. One day someone would become obsessed with new phenomena that they had only just discovered. For example for a while many of the siblings became completely enraptured with an event known as the Tanganyika Laughter Epidemic, which had occurred in 1962, and which apparently saw schoolchildren consumed with laughter for some months. This was one of those episodes of history which seems so unlikely that you feel compelled to question its authenticity; but looking at the few available materials related to it, I eventually came to the conclusion that, however unlikely it seemed, the laughing epidemic must indeed have happened. Imaginary scenes from the Laughing Epidemic would play out in my head. I invented haunting tableaux involving school rooms, huts, school girls rolling in ditches laughing uncontrollably. After a few weeks of thinking about this, it was time for us all to move on to the next thing.

Soon after there was the week that most of the siblings decided to create an "orchestra," despite their inability to play very many musical instruments with any sort of competence. They created their own "instruments" with sheets of paper, a box of tools, toilet rolls, and tape recorders. A nightly cacophony ensued for a while. Then everyone seemed to have had enough of that.

Rebecca began to collect examples of glass eyes, arranging them on top of her desk, a location from which they stared upwards in unison, providing a disquieting, though compelling, collective gaze, one that was eerily rooted in the material past. It was strange and disconcerting to consider how these eyes had once rested inside actual, sentient human bodies.

Lilly went through a period of attempting to examine the entire contents of the house through a magnifying glass. At that time she could often be found huddled in a corner, or propped up on her knees, searching intently for the "important details" as she had once put it when questioned about her behaviour. If you attempted to engage her in conversation when fixed in this stance, she would simply refuse, ushering you away with a flurry of prohibitive hand gestures.

At one time Mother set up a room resembling a church, containing a pulpit, rows of chairs, bibles, prayer cushions, and stained-glass windows. Her notion was that we would use the space to practice our own satirical, anti-clerical ceremonies. Mother would often take the pulpit herself, dressed in a black shirt and white dog collar (this being at a time when women in Britain were forbidden from the priesthood), and there she would preach to us, inviting us to jeer, to engage her with more abusive heckling and dissenting conversation.

At another time Billy would claim, on a daily basis, that certain conspiratorial messages were present in a vast variety of locations within the media landscape. Detecting these in the lyrics of B-Sides, in TV sports commentary and women's magazine articles, as well as within innumerable other outlets, he would present his "evidence" to anyone in the household who was prepared to listen, although for the most part no one was interested in his theories.

Eliza made meticulous plans for the creation of an underground railroad network which would sprawl beneath the prominent locations of Central London. It was intended to rival the public transport system, but would only be known and used by those who had been "initiated". I used to love staring at her endlessly detailed maps and sketches for this project, although by the time she was sixteen, she had realized that it was merely a fantasy and would never be built.

There was also the tendency, which lasted a whole autumn, for the Elder Set to invent their own click languages, demonstrating their use in a voluble fashion. Ultimately this confused and irritated everyone who heard them (except for Mother), but nevertheless at first we were all raucously laughing and enjoying the absurdity of their performances. Soon it became tiresome because only The Elder Set actually understood anything of what was being communicated and indeed, when we requested, they refused to teach us how to use any of their sounds. No one could ever be entirely certain that they were not simply producing abstract clicking noises, rather than employing any form of actual linguistic communication, but this was always to remain one of The Elder Set's more closely guarded secrets.

Lilly and I would sometimes venture out on what we liked to call "pointless expeditions," long walks around the city involving no coherent agenda and no definite destination. We would simply walk for hours, discovering things along the way. Sometimes we would spend several hours leaning against a wall, trying to savor every last detail around us, or imagining potential transformations we could make to the environment. If we became at risk of being too constructive in our talk Lilly might turn to me and say: "This isn't pointless enough!" And I would attempt to amend my behaviour.

30.

Mother Describes a New Theory

"Recently I have been attempting to formulate a new theory . . . this is a very important line of thought to me, one which might come to define my work within the field of sexology in future years . . . it has endless branches, many fermenting and shifting meanings . . . the crux of it is the idea that every last thing in the world is essentially sexual or at least can be related back to sex . . . often in many different ways simultaneously . . . I feel that this might be considered one of the great hidden facts of our nature . . . we have hidden sexuality away so entirely that we have perhaps never realized this or rarely think about it . . . and indeed it has never really been written about theoretically . . .

. . . firstly there is the very simple fact that sex has created everything within human perception in the first place . . . without it we would possess neither body or mind . . . it makes all apprehension of worldly entities possible and yet again and again this fact is hidden from view, is forgotten . . . so I'm interested in the sexual nature of all organic being . . . and then there is also a radical call to arms I wish to make around these issues . . . that the separation we see of sexuality from all that it produces, from all of these objects of consciousness, things-in-the-world, is really part and parcel of the separation of sex from our procreative capacities . . . the deeply embedded social desire for sex to become a domain unto itself, in which nothing else plays a part . . . and yet I am convinced that the converse is true . . . that everything else, every last thing within the world plays a part in informing our sexual identity . . . even and indeed especially in the ways we decide that certain things are definitely "non-sexual" . . . it is in fact that unconscious definition which makes them inherently sexual in character . . .

. . . the more I consider it, the more I can see endless chains of actions emanating outwards from the sexual act . . . a nearly infinite series of largely invisible effects upon individual psychological states, the habits of communities, even the eco-systems which we are all surrounded by . . . the number of things affected is endless and while convincing certain persons of this fact might be difficult I feel it can and should be done . . . this can be written about in an analytical, scientific manner or indeed it can be approached in a more poetic way, a way more redolent with ambiguities and loose disordered ends which do not tie up successfully . . .

. . . so in some ways this is essentially as perverted as our academic researches get . . . it feels as if I am ardently sifting through the human universe in order to discover more sex than we actually thought was present . . . and there might be some truth to any claims of that kind . . . but nevertheless I believe I am discussing something that is actually present in the world in a palpable way, which can be observed and measured with exactitude . . .

. . . I believe there are a number of ways in which what I am saying is true, but if nothing else, consider that the extent of sexual response on the part of an individual can always be recorded in relation to many different sets of circumstances . . . there is really no end to the things which are involved in this, everything can be related back to the sexual even if at first that subject might not appear to be especially relevant . . . there are more central and less centrally significant aspects to all of this . . . language structures, clothes, the furniture chosen in a particular setting . . . all of these things can be thought of in relation to sexuality . . . there is the highly appealing exercise of attempting to discover the hidden sexual nature of the most unlikely things . . . benches, plants, arrangements of crockery, asteroids, football matches, the layout of factories . . . it goes on and on . . . it really is just a case of perception and perspective . . . in essence everything is implicated . . . nothing is "safe" from the advance of sexuality . . .

. . . I do possess an ambition to make sexual energies as present as they can be . . . to indeed sexualize everything, to find the hidden sexual character of every last entity and demonstrate these characters to anyone who is prepared to look . . . I hope this will be like a sort of uncovering . . . like stripping reality itself entirely bare without the slightest adornment left to conceal anything . . . the curious thing here is that we are not really dealing with bodies but with minds . . . these are invisible adornments . . . but that doesn't take away from how prevalent they really are . . ."

PART TWO:

Going Out into The World

1.

A Ceremonial Meal

By the time I was seventeen years old most of the siblings had either completed university degrees or were still engaged in studying at one level or another. At the beginning of autumn that year, just before Lilly, Barnaby, Eliza, Gerard, and Rebecca were all due to leave home again and return to a variety of universities around the country, everyone gathered together in the house for a weekend which concluded with a family meal rendered on a large scale. For my own part I would never be going to any sort of university at all. I didn't quite know how to. Instead I was destined to be a perpetual onlooker, watching everyone else go away.

Mother had arranged the dining room table with specific places set for each of us, all of them designated with a series of handwritten name cards that were decorated with floral borders cut-out from reproductions of 19th century wallpaper designs. We all dutifully sat where we were supposed to, without offering any complaints. Whilst we sat there we were being watched over by a giant abstract oil painting which was always hanging there, one that was almost entirely green and formed of swirls and blotches, inevitably suggesting nature, stalks and leaves, trees

and fields. Over the years, I came to think that its presence designated a location of unusual imaginative openness, one that not
every household dwelt within, but when I was younger it was
something I took for granted, simply part of the home environment which I knew.

"So. What are you going to do after your degree?" Mother
asked Eliza.

"I don't know . . . I'd like to do something or other outdoors,"
she offered, "I'm not quite sure exactly what that would mean
though . . ."

"I think you should go work in an office," said Billy.

"What is it that makes you say stupid things like that, Billy?"
wondered Lucinda.

"I like suffering," he said, clearly intending some sort of joke,
his voice trailing off into the pretty sinister sound of his laughter.

"How about you just fucking shut up!" snapped Lucinda.

"When I finish studying, I want to become the owner of a
kangaroo farm in the home counties," said Gerard.

"That'll be lucrative," said Flo.

"Do you have any idea how many people want to possess
kangaroos in this life?" he asked.

"I don't," said Flo.

As usual, Lilly and I remained entirely silent during the course
of this meal. For the most part it was only ever Mother who
might attempt to include us in the conversation. It always seemed
as if the others were too preoccupied with themselves. Sadly, Lilly
and I hardly even talked to each other anymore, but many in the
family hardly realized this. I felt both terrified and fascinated as I
watched my family and its relentless acts of talking.

"And what about you Barnaby? What do you think you might
do after your degree?" asked Mother.

"Well, I don't really know either, but I definitely don't want to
be in an office. Maybe that should be the defining thought with
regards to this issue: 'Don't end up in an office Barnaby.' That's

a statement I should be repeating to myself."

"Go on," said Billy, "an office would do you good."

"Mum, this food is *delicious*," said Ag, in an obvious attempt to calm the situation down, through using the vaguely underhand trick of changing the subject.

"Thank you Ag, I'm glad that you like it."

The centerpiece of the meal involved dishes holding two roast chickens, which had exuded fine flurries of steam when cut into, coated with glazed skins and filled with a stuffing composed of chestnuts, onions, and apples. Each of the chickens was surrounded by an array of roast vegetables seasoned with garlic and thyme. Rebecca, the only vegetarian in the family, received her own plate, which held a nut roast.

"What theories have you been learning about at university then?" asked Billy, who had always been adamant about not wanting to attend university, aiming his question at the room in general.

"I've been looking into Queer Theory," said Rebecca. "Is that a problem Billy?"

This left Billy unexpectedly silent and unsure for a few moments, whilst everyone looked to him with critical eyes, expectant of an answer from him.

"I mean . . . gay sex is alright by me," he said finally.

"How about Queer Theory? Is that alright by you?" asked Rebecca.

"I dunno if people have to write endless boring books about it . . ." he said.

"Maybe sometimes they feel that they *do* have to," said Rebecca.

"I've been learning about Michel Foucault," started Gerard. "He proposed that knowledge is intimately related to power. Don't you want to possess power Billy?" he asked, taunting his brother, in a tone of voice that was genuinely supercilious.

"Give me 'Raw Power' any day," Billy said. "By The Stooges."

"Academics just have another kind of power," said Flo. "Indeed what does the latest research of Susan Crickholme involve?"

"Thank you for asking Flo . . . well, of late I've been writing papers on attitudes towards sex and disability, as well as the old favourite of female sexual response."

"Sounds good," said Flo.

"I think you should write theories about piss," said Billy.

"Well perhaps I will actually do that one day," said Mother, who was rarely shocked by any subject matter, aside from those which she believed were quite clearly depraved.

"I would have thought a paper like that would be a bit of a piss-take," said Ag.

"Or maybe a *miss*-take," suggested Flo.

"In some ways I side with Billy," said Barnaby. "I'm really far more into the idea of being an 'Adventurer,' rather than a 'Scholar.'"

"That sounds like a lot of Romantic shit to me," said Lucinda.

"Come now Lucinda, it's perfectly natural to like the title of 'Adventurer,'" said Mother. "It's probably quite advisable, a good ambition to possess . . ."

"Sounds like some Lord Byron nonsense dream to me," said Lucinda.

"Come on Lou, everyone wants to be an adventurer at heart, even if they won't admit it . . . and particularly at a certain age . . ." said Flo.

"My adventure tomorrow will be to leave this house and return back home . . ." said Lucinda.

"I don't know, I think some of you should just get a little more real," said Rebecca. "I mean 'Adventurer,' yeah, I don't know about the value of a label like that . . . maybe you should just go and open a drycleaners, wouldn't there be enough adventuring involved in doing that?"

"No, Rebecca, those really weren't the sort of adventures I had in mind . . ." said Barnaby, laughing.

"There's really a certain beauty to a drycleaners," said Flo, "that extraordinary sense of the clothes you take there becoming as clean as they could possibly be . . ."

"And their intense steam smell," said Rebecca, "and all the incidental little details of decoration in the shops, maybe a plant in the window, some little statuette . . ."

"The World really gets much worse than the insides of a dry-cleaners," said Mother.

For some years now the family had discovered a collective predilection for free-flowing absurd conversations which were liable to shift and jump in any sort of direction. I think everyone was inspired in part by Gerard and Barnaby's night time discussions, which had obtained a sort of nearly mythic status in the household, not that anyone would want to openly admit that fact to anyone. Once this sort of thing began in a conversation, as it would, at random, without warning, the absurdities were liable to spiral onwards into all kinds of unlikely contortions. This sort of thing often went on for some time.

"Forget drycleaners," said Eliza, making her own further jump. "Frankly chain hotels are where things are at these days . . . I mean they really provide the most exquisite sense of alienation imaginable . . . talk about things being clean and pristine . . . and then there's the global uniformity, the free stationery, the endless profusion of trash images on cable TV . . ."

"Oh you're totally right Eliza, who could resist the chain hotel experience?" said Flo. "That sense of being nowhere and every-where . . . the pleasure of strolling down those infinite, blank corridors . . ."

"I hate to bring the subject back to this, but you really can have the most sublime sexual intercourse in a chain hotel," said Mother.

"You really don't hate to swing the subject back to that do you!" said Ag with a certain tone of affection.

At this point everyone suddenly wanted to make their own random verbal contributions, as this was how these conversations

tended to go, it was something of an unwritten although implic-
itly understood part of this whole ritual. Everything lost control
for a few moments, with a series of overlapping conversational
gambits all cancelling each other out, only being heard by some
of us in fragmentary bursts.

"Glitter badges are proof that deities really are in charge of
this Planet . . ." started Rebecca.

"The myth of Dracula is the height of Western civilization . . ."
started Gerard.

"We could all live without carbonated beverages . . ." started Ag.

"People are only the images of machines these days . . ."
started Flo.

Eventually things settled back down into a situation where
the siblings would let each other speak and even listen to each
other to some extent.

"Purple is such a forgotten colour," said Ag. "It's really such a
mysterious, mystical colour . . . designers often seem to forget it
exists, think about it, there are relatively few purple things which
you see out and about . . ."

"I think there are quite a lot of them . . ." said Rebecca.

"Purple was once a colour deeply associated with royalty,"
said Mother, sounding rather regal herself as she said this, "for
centuries the scarcity of the dye used to create purple made it
the choice of monarchs who often demanded that their robes be
given that colour . . ."

"Enough of Kings and Queens!" proclaimed Gerard. "I want
to see an end to monarchies!"

"Yes, we should be thinking more about ordinary people,"
said Eliza.

"Go to Walthamstow and do some pub karaoke then,"
suggested Rebecca, "it's an activity I heartily recommend!"

"We should go some time," said Eliza, who probably wouldn't
in fact go.

"Karaoke's for losers," said Billy.

"You'd better go and sing some then," said Lucinda.

"I think at this point, I shall suggest that we should adjourn and go next door to drink some coffee," said Mother.

We then all proceeded to take up Mother's suggestion.

2.

Various Aspects of the Siblings' Lives During this Period

- For a year and a half Barnaby commenced an extended, eventually global search for a rare example of an 18th century silver pendant crafted in the form of an elephant.

- Ag became involved in smuggling large quantities of tea into the U. K. via the sea. She would sell it at a stall at music festivals each summer. Because it was "only tea" which she was smuggling she thought "it wasn't that bad."

- Billy began to regularly paint a spider's web across his face with a bulbous black spider resident in its center. He particularly enjoyed opening his mouth wide and growling when in this state.

- Flo became fascinated by examples of "incidental music" that could be found within certain soap operas from across the world. For a little over a year she collected examples of this phenomena and would listen to them on headphones, wandering around

London, inventing her own characters and storylines for television programmes that did not exist.

-Lilly became fascinated with the subject of pyjamas. This started with the pleasing softness of the word itself and continued with every further aspect of the word: its associations with childhood, with the nocturnal domain, with domesticity and the states of comfort that entailed.

-Lucinda began to collect antique erotic drawings, but only if they included the form of an orchid. She did this in absolute secrecy, as being her Mother's daughter she somehow felt embarrassed to engage in any public acknowledgment of her sexuality.

-At one point during this period Barnaby became convinced that he would engage in doctoral work related to the history of the kazoo. He managed to convince himself of the potential value of this work and believed that he would be motivated enough to complete it, but he then gave up on his studies days before they were due to commence.

-Eliza seemed to discover a nearly infinite profusion of meanings lurking within the word "gallant". She took to using this word as frequently as possible in her everyday speech and would sometimes use it as many as four or five times within the course of a single sentence. Eventually, she became disgusted by this habit and gave up using the word altogether.

-Gerard began experimenting with performing a great variety of actions in slow motion. This commenced with his attempts to run the 100 metres as slowly as possible, a task which he returned to frequently, always attempting to "break his own records". Eventually he moved on to activities as diverse as "drinking a glass of water," "drawing a sketch of a tree," and "walking somewhere". Slowness would always remain a quality in things which he greatly valued and which he also believed could be used to challenge some of the more questionable tendencies of "the wider society".

-After playing certain S&M games with a girl from Cincinnati called Janet, Billy became used to the practice of eating dog biscuits and realized that in a way he actually enjoyed them.

-Flo took it upon herself to attempt to memorize the entire text of *Finnegans Wake* which she would then recite large portions of at any given opportunity, frequently inventing occasions if necessary, to the extent that hearing her do this made everyone groan.

-Rebecca began an extensive collection of "meaningless" leaflets. It amused her to think that strictly speaking it was not really possible for any leaflet to be truly "meaningless". Perhaps only a blank or an entirely abstract one could fit into that category. The original conception she had of the collection was simply that the leaflets would possess no direct relation to her own life and interests. This collection came to involve many take away menus, museum maps, charity subscription forms and advertisements for commemorative plate sets.

- Barnaby composed a 12-page pamphlet on the subject of newsagents which he then handed out to people entering actual newsagents. He wished to offer this material for the sake of entertainment, but also to galvanize the customers of these establishments into mental action concerning where they were and what they were engaged in. There were black-and-white illustrations, as well as a great deal of typographical play.

-Flo and Rebecca commenced a long running game of inventing "hypothetical situations" which they would then contemplate, inserting themselves into each one, deciding what they would do in such circumstances. These would generally be exchanged via telephone late at night. For example Rebecca might say: "So you're stranded in the café of a ski resort, high up in the mountains at the top of a cable car route. The lifts have all stopped working, the weather is terrible, and you've ended up there for three entire days without rescue, sharing the space with a stenographer, a professional diver and a manufacturer of buttons. What do you *do?*"

3.

Aliases

For a time it was Flo who took the identity games we had played as children the furthest. She took to wearing a series of disguises, each one being a form of appearance she had chosen to inhabit and illustrating the personality of one or another of various personae.

Each of these identities came equipped with an elaborate paraphernalia of traits, gestures, quirks. When she was behaving as "Caroline" she had blonde hair, was interested in gardening, and would occasionally bet on the horses. As "Alison" she had dark brown hair and possessed a secretive past which had involved a period of flying as an air stewardess for Pan Am and another running an alpine guesthouse in Austria. When she was being "Debbie" she suddenly became immersed in flower arranging, and weekend breaks across Western Europe, whilst also possessing an emotional need to pay for her daughter's horse-riding lessons. These were the three most significant new personalities in Flo's life. Each of them regularly took her into unexpected directions.

At first she had started wearing a wig only on occasional days, just to see how it felt to have blonde hair. She had found, that this was, indeed, revelatory. Both men and women offered her entirely different kinds of glances. Conversations with shop assistants seemed to possess a different rhythm and tone. She had never considered that life might one day feel quite like this and the sensation was strangely thrilling to her.

Soon she began to add new layers to her appearance, gradually coming to adopt sunglasses, a necklace, a brooch, then a scarf, a different make-up regime, then new dresses, business suits, clothes that she would never normally have worn herself, but that she was now happy to appropriate as part of her new explorations. She then began to invent entire personalities, a gradual process of creation that lasted for some years.

The sense of anonymity which she now possessed with these personae soon gave rise to a desire to attempt shoplifting, as of course, in the long run at least, she was less likely to be caught. With some success she took food items, clothes, stationery. It didn't feel to her as if she was being herself anyway, she was merely masquerading as another. It was only a game, she told herself, she had no desire to steal. In this way, the outlines of her actual identity receded, became somewhat more indistinct to her, until finally the location of her identity seemed opaque, a sensation which she found that she enjoyed.

Eventually she had tried dressing as an old woman, just to see how the world would choose to greet her in that form. She spent some time practicing at hobbling with a suitable level of authenticity. The major issue was that her skin was too smooth, and she didn't think that she convinced too many people, apart, perhaps, from those who only threw fleeting glances at her and did not stop to look at her with any sort of thoroughness. She began moving with a stooped back, with a walking stick and a hand trolley laden with tins of food. In a sense she felt happy merely being recognized as an impersonator, however inept she was, as she believed a certain heroism lay in that direction.

One day she awoke to find that she was annoyed with herself

for moral reasons. The fact is she had engaged in petty criminality, almost for no purpose, except that it seemed both novel and entertaining to her. Thinking about this left her feeling somewhat ashamed. She vowed not to steal again.

Like Mother before her, Flo took to dressing as a man. She attempted to be the most ordinary man she could manage. She chose to use the name "Nigel" when living within this persona, adopting a green tweed blazer, resolutely unmatching grey trousers, and a mustard-coloured tie, with rectangular metal-framed spectacles and a large quantity of fragrant aftershave.

She soon found that, unlike in the case of Mother, she did not feel very personally involved in the creation of Nigel. He was not an intimate part of her, but at best a shorn off fragment of herself. She nevertheless enjoyed being him for brief periods, an experience predicated on the understanding that she was running through the motions of a masquerade.

Unlike Mother, she found that she had no need to renounce her masculine self upon a certain date, but continued to flirt with it on an occasional basis for the remainder of her life. She found that the greatest excitement in this game arrived when she engaged in interactions with others. This could, of course, only be achieved with success when she was in the company of strangers. When in such company she would improvise life anecdotes, suddenly assuming preferences and habits which she had never dreamed could have been her own. She would attempt to pass off the most outrageous fictions as realities and would often succeed in doing so.

Through this process of reinventing herself, Flo began to search for the persona which would correspond most accurately to her "true self," to the person who she most wished to be, the person that she should perhaps have been born as in the first place. In order to find this individual she spent many days trying on different clothes and wigs, adjusting her outfit to see if she could shift it into the right direction. All the while she was asking herself questions: "Who am I?" "What do I enjoy?" "Where am I from?"

To really get into character she needed to become incredibly detailed, interrogating the peripheries of a character's psychology. "What is the profession of her youngest aunt?" "Does she prefer mauve or aquamarine scarves?" "Would she enjoy attending a dinner party held by an archaeologist?" It seemed very important to her to get to the bottom of all such questions. Only then could she really know who she was creating. She wondered if she should actually attempt to *become* the person that she was piecing together. Was that where all of this was leading her? In the end she decided that it was important to maintain a distance between herself and her creations, although there would always be some form of interplay, given that she had created these people. They therefore inevitably carried some of her traces.

Next she attempted to create a persona that was the absolute opposite to her. She refused to stray into dark territories, and was definitely not going to become a murderer, but she did try to become "Steph" who worked as a personal assistant to the director of an investment bank in the city. "Steph" enjoyed practicing extreme sports on the weekend, particularly skydiving and bungee jumping. Steph saw this as an antidote to her stressful and somewhat tedious working life, which nevertheless "brought in the bacon" in her words. Flo enjoyed her excursions into the realm of Steph, but only insofar as she could detach herself entirely at any moment and become "Flo" again. Arriving at that point could sometimes be a relief.

4.

The Annual Pageant of Finality

From the age of twenty-one onwards, towards the end of each year, Gerard took to staging his own funeral. These ceremonies would commence with him lying horizontal and inert in an open top coffin, resting on a table in the family Living Room, his features pale with stage make-up, his eyes resolutely closed. Mourners would circle the corpse, attempting to simulate the most considerable outpourings of feigned grief which they could muster. The game here, instigated and encouraged by Gerard, was for each person to exaggerate their gestures as much as possible, so that the room would be filled with wailing, hysterical bodies, with inchoate voices consumed by the miseries of bereavement.

Weeping faces would be buried in shoulders, bringing forth rivulets of tears that were mere simulacra, having been induced by eye drops more commonly used in the theatre. "I'm going to miss him so much!" Rebecca cried, in a hysterical tone, before her words dissolved into inchoate blubberings as she began to writhe on the floor in mock agony. We often seemed to resemble the characters of an obscure, forgotten melodrama, staged on a distant continent, all of us acting in a production for which

208

skilled actors could not be supplied due to a lack of resources.

Most of those present would read memorial speeches. During the recitation of these we often had to struggle to keep our voices from wavering and cracking. We would invent roseate memories of our times with Gerard, occasions when we had played skittles together, or had eaten sandwiches which he had made for us. "It was, truly, the most delicious tuna sandwich I have ever eaten," said Flo, "made so carefully, on wholegrain bread, with a layer of sliced cucumber and slathered with mayonnaise! He took such care in preparing it for me and I'll always remember it!" she said, before hurling herself on the floor and collapsing. "It tasted so good!" she gulped.

"The more inappropriate your actions the better," Gerard had said to us before the first funeral, and we did indeed take this suggestion very seriously.

During these ceremonies Gerard was amazingly adept at playing the role of a corpse. Knowing him well I assumed that he had spent many hours practicing this, learning how to stay concentrated on his role and keep his features fixed in utter placidity, oblivious to whichever aural distraction might challenge him. It was eerie to see how seriously he took his self-assigned role. Evidently it meant a great deal to him, and partly for reasons that could never be enormously clear to any of us.

The night before the first funeral Gerard held a "Briefing" in the Living Room, during which, with a calm seriousness, he outlined the different "movements" of the occasion and what he expected from those in attendance. His requests were reasonably flexible, but certain things were clearly of great importance to him and he emphasized these by repeating them a number of times. Assuming the role of a teacher, he stood in front of us with a whiteboard and a marker pen, making an extensive spider diagram with the word "Funeral" in the center of a generous bubble, with many lines extending from it.

The dress code was always strictly black in accordance with

traditional funeral symbology. Nevertheless, Gerard encouraged his mourners to "luxuriate" in their dress and women were permitted to adorn themselves with looping black ribbons, or absurd conical hats resembling chimneys. Sunglasses were frequently worn, being used as a method of concealment, often making the construction of lies an altogether more palatable task. Lace frills, velvet scarves, elbow-length gloves, and high heels all featured amongst the feminine mourning contingent, whilst the men were forced to wear suits, looking as if they were conducting business.

Each year, once we had completed our eulogies, Eliza and Barnaby, his fellow Republicans, would solemnly walk to the head of the coffin, close the lid, then lead the procession out of the house, into the garden, bearing the coffin on their shoulders with the help of two other siblings, often Rebecca and myself. Everyone else would follow in a line slowly and in silence, their faces contorted with suffering or blank with the effort to contain it. At this moment in the proceedings I would always feel that the air was suffused with a feeling of dread, that for some minutes the funeral became too lifelike, too scary. Doubtless, this was part of Gerard's plan. I would long for the party which was waiting to erupt after we had finished the rituals, and perhaps everyone else did too, although we dared not talk about this.

Finally, once in the garden, we would enact the part of the ceremony that Gerard said he most deeply relished, which was the act of being buried in the ground. For him, it was only at this moment that the occasion took on a genuinely transcendent quality. This helped him to directly confront his own frailty and fear, before emerging once more into the triumph of festivity. After making a procession outside, we would gradually lower the coffin into the wet, fertile soil. Gerard lay within the coffin the entire time, breathing through a snaking plastic tube that led up out towards the airstreams. He would hear many clumps of earth being thrown onto the coffin's lid and would once more imagine his actual demise, whenever that might happen to be.

Finally, the coffin would come to rest underground and we would all stand there in stillness for some minutes, silent except for the weeping of artificial tears. The first time that we reached this juncture, many of us wondered if Gerard had chosen this precise moment to actually kill himself, a doubt that prevailed during all of the funerals which we undertook. However, finally, his mobile, sentient form appeared, fully vertical, crashing upwards through the coffin's lid and the soil, his arms held outwards in the triumph of mock celebration. He would then embrace each of us in turn, often for some time, giving us generous squeezes, sometimes breaking into ballroom dancing with Ag or Flo.

An enormous party would then erupt and last until dawn. All black garments were replaced with bright, life-affirming colours. Invariably we became consumed with a sudden energy arising from the knowledge that, despite incalculable odds, we were all still alive. After the first funeral Lilly, Rebecca and myself locked ourselves in the attic bathroom with a bottle of sloe gin and began broadcasting a spontaneous quasi-philosophical dialogue over the internet, until morning appeared.

Lucinda always refused to attend the funerals, stating that they were "macabre and sick," as well as "profoundly egotistical," a view which no one else in the family agreed with oddly enough. Everyone else seemed to understand the interplay of theatre and festivity involved in their enactment. Many previous family occasions had prepared us all for this, so we shrugged at Lucinda's criticisms, which were predictable anyway.

All year long, whether it contained his body or not, Gerard's funeral plot stood waiting at the end of the garden, beside his gravestone, with an inscription carved into it:

Here lies Gerard
He found life quite hard
(1971-?)

Gerard enjoyed remembering the lingering question mark at the end, but often imagined different numbers being chiselled into its place. Over the years he had considered almost every possible form of death which could come upon a human being, thinking through many of the personal implications that they held.

He wanted all of us to consider the reality of our own mortality, as well as that of everyone else. The occasion forced us to be confronted with a subject which we did not always wish to consider or discuss, but it did so in the form of a game, thereby making death feel slightly lighter, a given fact, even something that could be a suitable cause for celebration. This ceremony was to remain uniquely centred on Gerard's own demise, as no one else in the family had the slightest desire to be buried alive. We nevertheless kept resuming our roles as mourners, because we found them so consistently enjoyable to perform.

5.

Communication Written Inside
a Paper Aeroplane

Dear You,

I've been lying here on the grass watching the faces of this park for some hours now. All in all it's been really quite a pleasant thing to do. It's sort of one of everyone's pastimes isn't it? We all love spying on strangers and I'm no exception. I love looking at people's faces and guessing what's going on behind there. We're such a voyeuristic species. It seems a lot of people enjoy doing that when sat at café tables, but personally I enjoy doing this most when lying on the grass in a park, at the height of summer. Essentially when in a place like this and on a day like the one we have here before us, today. I like secretly watching people at ease, when they're busy being happy.

I'm always wanting to talk to people I don't know. I think this is a strange and unusual compulsion that not so many people possess, but I do. Please forgive me, it's just who I am. Anyway, most of the time I bow to social pressures and keep my mouth firmly shut. After all, that's a particularly important thing to do in England, more than in most countries. So you are a rarity: a stranger who is receiving a communication from me. Though as I say, I'm always wanting to do this sort of thing. There's a big difference between silently watching strangers and actually approaching them. The latter contains far more risk. Whereas the former hardly contains any risk at all really.

I can only hope that you share some of the joy that I take in unexpected encounters and occurrences. I suppose, that there is, after all, an element of the universal here: doesn't everyone enjoy unexpected things happening sometimes? Maybe it's kind of like the way that everyone enjoys looking at people. (I wonder how many of these unexamined universal interests there are in fact?)

So yes, I hope that my sending this message to you, surging through the air, is something that is largely cheering to you rather than disconcerting. I can't be certain that you will react positively, but of course I've chosen someone (you) who looks like they would be open to my approach. Yes, I'm actually pretty good at intuitively knowing if someone will be open to me or not. I would've said that's hardly a trait unique to me either. Human beings tend to be pretty good at knowing this sort of thing, I'd say. But nevertheless, if you do find my sending you this message somehow disconcerting then I do apologize. Just understand that no harm is meant by it. I only mean to be charming. Sorry if I've failed in that aim.

So why have I settled on you for this message? What is it that I hope to achieve by sending it to you? I hope that all of this will become slightly clearer if you keep reading . . .

Well let's face it, like so many people, I'm lonely, I'm bored. Those factors are really helping to motivate me in my actions here. Don't be offended by this, I mean what's the point in getting all offended? Just because I'm lonely and bored that shouldn't take away from the fact that I'm actually fascinated by what I can see of you. And writing this and giving it to you really will be a successful antidote to both loneliness and boredom. I mean you might not want to talk to me, but at least I have attempted to communicate with you, so even this note makes me feel less lonely and more as if I am actually engaging with the human race.

I tend to think that it's a spiritually positive thing to talk with strangers. Even attempting to do that has its own positivity. It certainly happens far more in certain other countries than here. Take the U.S.A. for example. People often actually love talking to each other there. It really doesn't matter if you haven't met before, they still like to talk to you, on public transport, or going for a walk in the countryside, or wherever. So probably I don't need to tell you that here in England it is more like an actual taboo to speak to someone you don't know. I find that sad and confusing. I don't really understand it actually, but there we go, that feeling is present.

I really believe that you can tell a lot about someone just by looking at them. Others sometimes strongly disagree with me about this, but then others believe that so much of our communication as a species is pre-verbal and indeed non-verbal. So in fact we are communicating with each other with the clothes which we have chosen to wear, with the glances that we throw at them, with the way that we wear our hair, the way we move. All of these things are very important for establishing who a person is in our minds. So having watched you all afternoon I sensed something non-verbal, some possible connection, which I can't really (obviously!) articulate into words. For the words you'll have to come over and talk to me.

So, today, before writing this message to you, I was busy deco-
rating my flat with angels made from paper. Some of them were
quite funky angels actually. I made pink tutus for some of them
and loud, colourful tights for some of the others. So they were
modern angels, rather than being more traditional ones. After
that I went to the art shop to buy some glue and some spray
mount and I was going to go home to work more on these angels,
so that my flatmates would get a pleasant surprise when they got
home from doing their work in the library. But I got distracted.
I went for a bike ride along the canal. And after that I came here
to the park, just to lie in the grass and see what was going on and
watch faces and then I saw your face whilst you were sunbathing
and decided to make this aeroplane.

Potentially, you could keep this message for as long as you live,
but nevertheless, let me be clear that I'm certainly not demanding that of you. Really, you might as well screw up the paper
and throw it into the rubbish if you want to. This is up to you,
because, like every other human being you are (sort of) entirely
free. But surely, it's not everyday that you get a souvenir like
this, right? If I were you I would hold on to it for a while and
see how it feels. If you threw it away maybe you would end up
regretting your actions. But as I already made clear, it really is
entirely up to you.

I guess one reason I'm writing to you, if I'm honest with myself,
is simply because it's summer and it even feels like summer is
really meant to be today, with sunlight and heat and everything
you might expect from a summer's day. And so, let's face it, on
days like this, people around here get a little more open, their
character changes, and they are suddenly maybe open to strangers
for example. As you can see, I'm clearly no exception as far as this
sudden summer openness is concerned, in fact I would rather like
to be its living embodiment, or something like that. My advice

would be that you run with this sense of openness that I'm try-ing to pass on to you. Even if you don't feel much like talking to me today, try and remember the place from which this note was written and feel free to dwell in it yourself at some later time, maybe just tomorrow or the next day.

The fact is I've always wanted someone to send me a message via paper aeroplane. This has been a secret wish of mine for a long time. I know this is not a very usual wish, not a "run of the mill" wish as we might say, but there we are, that's one thing that I wished for and I don't know how much we can control that sort of thing. There's something about this medium which is, after all, very appealing to me. So I'm just sending you the message that I would like to receive myself. Or something like that message. The version of that message that is actually written by me, which bears my traces and habits and not someone else's.

So obviously, clearly, this is an invitation to come over and talk to me. And of course you can say anything, there are no real rules. I promise to be receptive and open and talk as much or as little as you'd like to. I'm the one over there in the stripy red and green t-shirt.

I would like you to know that in as far as I can, I do in fact really wish the best for you. I'm only going on how you appear of course, but I do think there's often quite a lot to be said for first impressions and my initial impressions of you are very positive. So yes, maybe we will have a short or a long conversation after I send this message flying through the air, but either way just know that I hope things turn out well for you in the near future, that things go the way you would most like them to go. That's all really. My name is Rebecca.

6.

The Profusion of Roads

When he was nineteen, Barnaby decided to hitch-hike to Edinburgh in August, a place he had never visited before. It was the first time that he had undertaken this activity, one that would rapidly become a constant compulsion. Scotland attracted him as it was a suitably distant and unknown location, another country that somehow lay nestling within his own. Attempting to reach it without paying any money for transportation seemed to him a suitably worthy challenge. Whilst at first he felt somewhat daunted by the prospect of trying to do this, he soon found that his goal was achieved with relative ease. Indeed, he managed to complete the whole journey in the space of only three lifts, commencing from the North Circular Road and travelling until he was dropped off at the docks of Leith.

An hour after arriving in Edinburgh he found himself attending an immersive theatre event taking place in someone's living room. The audience were huddled together on the floor and the performers, who had switched off all electric lights, were chanting, enacting intricate choreographies with their limbs and waving lit sparklers into a series of arabesques. Later, moving through various pubs, which were open until 3 A.M. during the festival season, a rosette was pinned to his lapel, awarding him third place in a beauty contest, and by the end of the night he had found himself agreeing to perform life modelling duties for a painter who was draped in a flowing purple cape, an individual named Damarian, who failed to appear at their rendezvous the next day.

Barnaby always enjoyed making new and unexpected acquaintances on his many journeys, particularly with drivers, usually commencing extended, meandering conversations. During these years he engaged in many of the most important conversations of his life. These were mostly had with middle-aged men, persons who he found to be lonely and garrulous, seeing the offering of a long conversation as the unspoken price for the ride that they were giving. Over the many hours of their duration these conversations became labyrinthine and digressive, roaming across many territories, incorporating almost any subject matter.

He heard so many beautiful things in these years that he came to expect them whenever he entered a vehicle. Often he remembered in particular the story of the niece who had abandoned her wedding ceremony in order to attend to her tropical fish; the next door neighbour who had turned their spare bedroom into an elaborate shrine celebrating the life of a soap opera star; the history teacher who forced his children to regularly engage in Napoleonic musket drills.

After devoting himself wholeheartedly to the activity, Barnaby became so skilled at the art of conversation that he was eventually capable of conversing for hours with almost anyone. Somehow he could always find another thread to pursue, could always tease out a point, or provide further examples of elucidation. Early in adulthood, he learnt of the remarkable capacity that human beings have of asking each other questions. Whenever a conversation looked as if it might be in danger of dwindling away into silence, he could always call upon new stratagems, and might invent a chain of many questions in order to get words flowing again.

When abroad, he always felt that he hadn't experienced the interior of a culture until he had stepped inside a privately owned vehicle and inhaled its odour. If he disliked the smell of a vehicle, he knew that he should attempt to leave it as rapidly as possible. Sifting through the memories of his many years of lifts he would always return to the biscuit and breadcrumb scent of a car in France driven by a bald and genial architect, a man who had just finished constructing a church in Marseille. That car, it seemed to him, had offered the finest olfactory experience of all of them. He found that he could always recall its aroma with absolute exactitude and it was one which he would often comfort himself with, especially when travelling became a difficult activity.

After his first trip to Scotland, his next objective was to cross the entirety of Europe by hitch-hiking, a feat which he was destined to achieve the following summer, managing to travel as far as the Bosphorus. On the way, he ascended to the summit of the Eiffel Tower whilst carrying a life-size crucifix, attended an annual cheese festival in Montenegro, and wrestled a large Mexican girl inside the waters of a fountain in Madrid at dawn, a finale to one particularly turbulent night. She had caused his left wrist to bleed, a fact which he afterwards treasured both for its eroticism and its ludicrousness. By the beginning of August he had become an integral part of a choir in a village in Macedonia. He then spent a week sleeping in a hedgerow in Bulgaria, accompanied by an arthritic stray dog whom he had discovered yelping in a pitiful manner one morning on a high street, its body mysteriously covered in milk. When the culmination of the summer had finally begun to draw near, all he could think of was how he might have more experiences of this kind.

It was always of enormous importance to Barnaby to be alone when he took these trips, a situation which after some years of following his instincts a little thoughtlessly, he realized was something of a male privilege. Whilst these journeys were clearly dangerous enough to make as a lone male traveller, he never once felt really worried during these years of exploration. He did possess a Swiss Army knife, an object which he always kept lodged underneath his belt in case of emergency, but this only rarely proved necessary. It was when he was encased inside a cocoon of months of absolute solitude that he could think clearly about his life situation and make some kind of interior "progress" with his affairs.

Barnaby loved nothing more than arriving in a desolate, remote location which the world had forgotten existed. He never liked to stay for very long in these places, indeed he usually found that a single night was sufficient, because if he tried to extend his time in such a destination, he would quickly grow morose and desperate to leave. Nevertheless, spending twenty-four hours in a village he was destined to forget the name of, scrutinizing the movements of flies swarming in a gutter, whilst immersing himself in the silence and stillness of the place, was an activity which he cherished. He loved to sleep in hotel rooms in which the door handle broke away from the door when he attempted to use it. He loved spying on clusters of old men sat in cafés, playing endless games of backgammon, and discussing horse racing tips.

Recollecting these scenes he would see the pale green apparitions of plants framed inside cloudy windowpanes; the strange paintings almost thoughtlessly placed on display in bars and hotels; an enormous stained mirror that covered almost an entire wall, a receptacle that seemed to hold an image of eternity sealed in its crevices.

He would find himself in human destinations that consisted of only a single street, with one shop, or one restaurant, or one hotel. After arrival he would deposit his luggage inside another dust-ridden hotel room, and would go for an aimless stroll, usually sitting on a bench or a wall for an hour or so, examining the movements of children and pigeons, inhaling the pervasive calmness. He would imagine the succession of grey, listless days that must pass in these places in perpetual repetition.

In Senegal he had taken a ride in a truck carrying crates of brightly-coloured watering cans. It took him as far as Joal-Fadiouth, a coastal town split into two parts, "Joal," on the mainland, and "Fadiouth," which was an island in an estuary, all of its floors naturally formed from white clamshells, which were also embedded in the outer walls of buildings and used in making local handicrafts. To reach Fadiouth you had to walk across a long wooden footbridge with a number of its original planks missing, resembling lost teeth. Stray dogs would always be running back and forth across the bridge, barking at everyone present, jumping onto each other and tangling into balls of playfighting. Somehow mangroves and baobab trees sprouted from the beds of clamshells and underneath their leaves old people sat playing draughts in the street with homemade sets possessing enormous circular wooden counters painted either red or black. Barnaby had stayed in a guest house owned by a retired acrobat who kept a pair of performing pelicans in a corner of the central courtyard. The beds were all covered in a pink gauze of mosquito netting.

In India he had stayed in a hotel, in Varanasi, where the water that emerged from the taps was always brown. The owner, who walked around half naked and whose ribs were starkly visible, was tall, with raked silver hair protruding upwards and a persistent heavy cough. He spent the majority of each day lying down on a mattress on the floor in a darkened room the size of a cupboard, a room shared with a budgerigar who lived suspended from the ceiling inside a bulb-shaped wire cage. When Barnaby had tried to leave this hotel, the owner had attempted to procure most of his possessions by simply asking if he could have them. He had requested, more or less politely, that Barnaby give him his watch, his cigarettes, his lighter, t-shirts, trousers, razors and toothpaste, before eventually giving up on this pursuit with a disgusted grunt.

Barnaby had then moved northwards towards the foothills of the Himalayas, sharing a lift in a silver Mercedes Benz with a fashion designer from Amsterdam called Joris who was a

Buddhist and therefore travelling to Dharamshala, home of
the Tibetan Government in exile. Barnaby was destined to stay
in Dharamshala for several months, soon attending lectures
delivered by a Tibetan monk each morning, his words translated by a short elderly Englishwoman with white hair and a
turned-in left eye. She commenced each lecture session by playing
a harmonium on the floor and singing solo in Sanskrit, using a
high, fragile wavering voice.

Once he had adopted hitch-hiking as his pastime he felt that
he was capable of travelling anywhere at all using this method of
conveyance. It didn't matter how far a driver could take him, as
it would always be equally possible for him to pick up another
lift in the next town and then again in the one after that. He
came to realize that each town was connected by an endless series
of perfect geometrical lines to every other one in the world, a
network that extended infinitely, branching outwards, essentially
without end.

It was extremely rare for Barnaby to not get a ride. Perseverance
was all that was generally required. Often enough he would be
forced to wait for several hours, but occasions on which he could
find no ride whatsoever were extremely rare. He never minded
the protracted periods of waiting, and indeed he actively enjoyed
the opportunity these gave him for contemplation. He did,
however, remember certain occasions when he had failed to get
a lift for many hours and had found himself in difficult circumstances. Once, wandering alone among the Taihang mountains
of North-East China, the few vehicles passing by had all ignored
his jutting thumb. The sky had darkened, and he was still some
hours away from any sign of habitation whatsoever. With a sense
of desolation he had finally bedded down in a ditch, using his
backpack as a pillow and his jacket as a duvet. The next day, after
walking for another six hours, he finally came to a village, where
he had paid to sleep on the floor of a family's living room. It
had been necessary to communicate only through miming and

finger pointing with them, and when he had really struggled he had taken out his Mandarin phrasebook, which was missing its first eighty-nine pages, an item which he had discovered some months before amidst a pile of torn, rotting volumes in a street market in Beijing.

As a traveller, he had soon learned to love youth hostels. Often he would remember his first experience of one, which had involved walking up to the fifth floor of a building in Montmartre, where there was a modest dormitory. Not knowing at the time what the usual etiquette dictated, he had thought that it might be necessary to discover the name of each of the nine travellers occupying the room and shake their hands. Until that precise moment, he had always been somewhat withdrawn, but now this provided him with an opportunity to become an entirely new person, to extend himself socially in ways that even his upbringing had not prepared him for.

Whilst he often found it difficult to sleep in dormitories because of the constant arrival and departure of persons, he still loved them as places of rest, knowing that their ability to introduce you to other people generally outweighed the discomfort you might experience within them. In any case, if he wasn't in a social mood, there was also the magical sense in which he felt a dormitory bed constituted the sole domain of its current occupant, and he found it was always possible to simply lie there sleeping or drifting, ignoring everyone.

Barnaby thought that the friendships made when travelling possessed unique qualities. He loved the sense of inevitable dispersal which hung over these encounters, the shared unspoken knowledge of their imminent demise, which lent a certain permissiveness to many of the conversations which he engaged in. He discovered that you could become anyone during such exchanges, and he was sometimes raucous, inventing various elaborate fabrications, including a string of new names. A bittersweet sense of elusiveness mingled with the excitement of temporary connection.

Not long after commencing this period of travelling, Barnaby made a vow that he would not return to any of the places outside Europe that he visited. He never told anyone else of this. Each location then began to possess a renewed sense of urgency, and generated continual states of melancholy, and when leaving them now he would watch streets and faces recede into the distance until they had disappeared from sight and almost immediately become memories.

7.

Edible Mucus

Billy took the first opportunity he could to disappear on tour with a band, one summer, only two weeks after it had been formed. At that time they were known as "Edible Mucus" and dealt in a style of punk music which they claimed had yet to be named. Their speciality was songs which lasted about one minute. Nevertheless, it must be said that within this timeframe they really did pull out all the stops in terms of screaming, drumming and electric guitar strumming crescendos.

There were five of them (Billy, Ian, Fred, Mike, and Alastair) and they all spent that summer sleeping together on the floor of a tiny van, kicking each other accidentally in the middle of nightmares, soaked in pools of not-always-identifiable liquids. Their pet rat Dillinger would scamper across their slumbering bodies, making sleep even less of a likelihood. In future recollections, each of the band members would always claim that this had been something of a perfect, idyllic summer and that an essential part of the experience had been their sleeping in a communal way, huddled together on the floor, joined into a single entity like bacteria melding together into one new organism.

When they were bored, on particularly bleak hungover afternoons, the band would drive into the nearest, quaint English
village and commence yelling abusive messages from the van's
windows, a practice which got them cautioned by the police on
more than one occasion.

After their shows were finished, the band was very fond of
being naked together. Preferably, this would be in the context
of sexual intercourse with young women, but more common
was the practice of the band halting the van to build a fire on
a beach or on moorland, stripping off in a communal fashion,
which ensured that the sense of a fraternal bond was formed.
Bearing this in mind, during the course of the summer, the entire
band got their buttocks tattooed, so that these occasions came to
involve a level of ritualized display.

Billy's tattoo (on his left buttock) showed an aardvark eating
books in a library, a visual diatribe against Mother's insistence
on the importance of learning through reading. Billy had long
managed to feel resentment about this, despite the fact that
Mother was just about as open as anyone could be to all alternative, non-textual forms of learning. Billy was always very keen
to show off this tattoo to members of the family at the end of
the summer, whether they were interested in seeing it or not.
Nevertheless, Mother did stop Billy from dispensing with clothes
altogether, as he attempted to do at one point. He argued that
he wanted his tattoo to be on permanent display because it "represented him." It felt a little extraordinary to see Mother feel like
she had to draw the line somewhere.

That summer saw the full inauguration of Billy's drug use,
a practice which became worse and worse over time. We were
never entirely sure quite what drugs Billy was taking. Once he was
suitably inebriated he liked to venture out into the city and cause
any sort of trouble he could manage to. During these sessions
he was particularly fond of standing on top of restaurant tables
whilst attempting to deliver orations, occasions that usually

ended with his toppling onto the floor amidst a crash of crockery and silverware. Sometimes for days on end he became fixated on rearranging the furniture inside public libraries, "for a laugh," he would say.

On stage Fred would enjoy giving himself a series of electric shocks with a microphone whilst he flailed across the floor. Each of the other band members liked to become equally lost in their own journeys: Mike would give up on his drum kit and would attack any and all alternative surfaces with his sticks, this being purely for his own private entertainment given that his efforts could not be heard at all above the surge of distortion emerging from the amplifiers. Billy might attach a gigantic leek to his head with masking tape and form delicate little cuts along his bare torso with a shattered beer bottle, watching the blood ooze and drip onto the stage, invariably already sticky with spilt alcohol. Ian, meanwhile, was often entirely absorbed in scraping coins along the length of his bass guitar strings, forming a sound that resembled the wailings of a mechanical cat in the grip of a strangler's fingers. Edible Mucus would lose themselves like this, during their final extended number of each evening, a piece which would sometimes last half an hour, during which time the audience was subject to an illegal, extended show of flashing strobe lights, which could sometimes alter an individual's perception of reality in a permanent fashion.

They were a band which believed in degradation as a philosophy. They were always ready to reject anything and pour scorn upon it. Equally, it was rare for them to praise anything that did not involve themselves. Indeed, they created a great deal of energy through their extended sessions of collective hating. This was something that often happened as they drove through a town for the first time, when they would immediately begin to take issue with people, buildings, streets, atmospheres. Generally, the next step was to start actually attacking these things, either verbally, or more ideally, physically. (At least they usually stopped short of attacking people.)

The members of Edible Mucus liked to challenge each other to staying awake for the longest periods possible. Once, when they had all been awake for close to forty-eight hours, Billy began to see giant sheep in the sky, where normally there would be clouds. At the same time, Dillinger the rat actually began talking back to him for the first time in their relationship. Minutes later Ian collapsed on to Billy in utter exhaustion and managed to crush Dillinger to death. Despite this evidently being an accident, Billy found it very difficult to forgive Ian for this.

Alastair liked to get high and unwind by unleashing gargantuan monologues, outpourings which were liable to last for more than an hour at a time. He generally spoke about elements of the supernatural that happened to interest him, weaving in materials related to the F.B.I., references to string theory, to various ancient civilizations (but particularly prevalent was the Assyrians), as well as statistics related to Olympic ping pong champions of yesteryear. He would deliver these words at breakneck pace and the first few times the whole band loved to listen and follow the manic lurches of his mind and be entertained. However, it quickly got to the point where his voice became insufferable to them and everyone would join in a chorus of "Shut up Alastair!" One day when it became clear that this tactic was not going to work, the band found it necessary to seize his limbs and tie him up, placing a gag in his mouth so that he now only produced a vague muffled whimpering, with occasional forays into squeaking.

The whole band would relish encounters with strangers, as long as they managed to create a situation that was suitably disorientating or provocative, so that order was destroyed rather than maintained and sensibilities were offended, or at least sullied. If they could, the band liked to lure people into their van, perhaps with words such as "Hey, sisters . . . come and check out our stinky van!" This line did not often work, but the point was more to attempt the impossible for the sake of amusement, rather than to expect the impossible to actually occur. They would try to create "converts" to their way of life, another foolish venture that was generally doomed to extinction before it even commenced. Whilst they wanted followers, generally all that they got were new enemies, but perhaps, after all, that was what they really wanted.

They liked to claim that they were a band without influences. They would say that all their inspirations emerged from their own minds and life experiences. Of course, this wasn't strictly true, as they were a band which was evidently engaged with their own form of "punk," but it *was* true that their narcissism led them to only listen to themselves and forget that other bands existed.

There was some strange sense in which it felt as if they had emerged from nowhere, from some form of inarticulate wilderness belonging solely to themselves. Their fractured, discordant compositions were unique in the sense that they belonged nowhere and directly imitated nobody. However, it must be said that the music was largely of a very bad quality, pinning all of its hopes on an intensity of volume and entirely ignoring the need for either structure or melody. They were frequently out of tune, piercing ears with squalls of feedback, their bodies and instruments sometimes collapsing on stage before they had even begun. Still, there were a number of people that summer who identified with their feral intensity and who created small, but not insubstantial crowds at each of their gigs.

When they weren't playing music the band had a tendency to become restless, drumming against any available surface with their hands, limbs twitching uncontrollably. If there was no music to be made then the best substitute was an intake of one or another chemical substance. This quickly left them burnt out and before they knew it the band had split up. It was only a few months since it had been formed.

8.

Opening the Inner Eye

Ag first realized that she possessed psychic powers when she found herself hearing the voice of her friend Samirah's dead pet tortoise, Quentin. He spoke to her in the voice of a debonair, aged English gentleman. At this time he had already been deceased for nearly a decade. "I am perfectly safe," he said, "and surrounded by good company."

The appearance of Quentin's voice had been induced by seeing a photograph of him when posing in the midst of his prime, a time when he had looked like a stately and dignified tortoise. The image seemed to suddenly unlock Ag's psychic potential and she soon began to hear hidden voices appearing around her everywhere. Afterwards she would rove through the city and hear voices percolating through the walls, issuing secrets, forming cryptic gestures, conversing.

She felt incomparably blessed to have been "chosen" in this way, to be suddenly capable of performing feats that many people assumed were impossible. Soon after her revelation she vowed to devote the remainder of her earthly sojourn to harnessing these skills and putting them to whatever use that she could manage.

As she passed pedestrians in the street sometimes she saw their thoughts trailing from their bodies in scrawly lines of blue handwriting which lay suspended in the air.

Soon she was to discover that her powers were not absolute, that at times the voices would not appear when called upon, and occasionally her predictions did not come true. Refusing to be deterred by this, she commenced her work with her many clients, but always felt that she had to warn them of her limitations, stating that entering the psychic "beyond" was a little like guiding an aeroplane through a landscape shrouded in fog. Many would abandon her services when they reached this point in her spiel, but she felt that it was a necessary disclaimer for her to make. In any case, her critics had no notion of what they were dealing with, of what might actually be possible within the realm of the terrestrial, a place in which, as Ag had learnt, nothing was quite as it appeared to be.

She found that the range and extent of her powers was curious. Voices never spoke to her on Wednesdays. Streets possessing names beginning with "L" would never yield any information. If she ate scrambled eggs cooked with turmeric her abilities were sometimes heightened. Whenever she felt the slightest sense of discomfort with a client, even simply not liking their jewellery, she knew that she would have to warn them profusely of her limitations. By contrast, she found that communications related to animals were generally very strong, as were those involving southward movements from the direction of the North-East. Over time it seemed to her consultations involving bathtubs tended to reveal more than any others.

Eventually she set up her own dial-a-psychic business, advertising in a number of national newspapers and magazines, her consultations being generally available to the public on a 24-hour basis (she split the shifts with two fellow female psychics who she had met during a tarot reading weekend retreat she had once attended at a hotel in Torquay). A large proportion of her callers were either elderly people desperately in need of social company or middle-aged male sexual obsessives who loved to regale her with obscene sentences. Ag truly believed that in setting up this service, in her own small way, she was helping to beautify the world.

When she began to work on the telephones, in 1995, she charged £1.50 a minute, although she soon decided to offer a 15% reduction to those possessing a concessionary status who could prove this to her via written communication. These consultations would sometimes stretch across a number of hours, her clients often becoming so involved in the turbulent drama of her readings, that they felt incapable of bringing proceedings to an end.

She became furious whenever anyone accused her of fraudulence. This anger did not always manifest itself outwardly, but stayed, simmering within her, indefinitely. She knew, however, that an appearance of professionalism was as important in this domain as it was in any other, so she would rein herself inwards and would keep all of her gestures within a calm, composed register. Often, she would fold her hands together into a suitably mystical posture and address whoever her critic happened to be with a statement like : "not everyone possesses a full understanding of the nature of the mystic arts."

Many of her old friends and acquaintances were quite insistent with regard to her lack of psychic ability and a substantial number of them ended up abandoning her altogether. A number of people now found her to be a constant embarrassment and did not wish to encounter her at all any more. Among members of the family there was a general sense of protectiveness, even if many of us considered her beliefs to be foolish, we did not wish to speak out against her, unless it felt entirely necessary to do so.

Only Rebecca seemed wholly convinced of Ag's powers and would always defend her against all outbursts of scepticism and hostility, citing examples of how she had once successfully aided our Highgate neighbour, Mrs. Arkwright, in locating her missing parakeet by instinctively following the movements of a series of "tremors". Or Rebecca might recall the occasion when Ag had been able to recite the entire text of a Babylonian prayer tablet after glancing at an out-of-focus photograph of the ruins where it had been discovered, despite never having seen it before, and despite having no prior knowledge of Ugaritic, the language which it was written in. Ag had recited it whilst wandering in circles around the client's four-poster bed, in order to facilitate a home birth, an occasion which also featured streams of incense and the tinkling of handbells.

During an otherwise unremarkable meal in a Thai restaurant, Ag had once seized a waitress by the arm, and then, evidently feeling that this was not enough, had encircled her waist whilst chanting. Watching a moderate sense of terror accumulate in the eyes of the waitress, Ag began to tell her: "I can feel your auras, they are jostling with you and around you, they emanate from you like silk . . . I hear voices, the rustling of voices from deep within your past . . . do not be concerned, they are benevolent . . ."

It seems that Ag did successfully manage to communicate something or other with this outpouring, as subsequently the waitress agreed to have a number of consultations with her, and indeed this relationship was to stretch across the length of a decade.

Ag often wondered why these powers had only revealed themselves to her relatively late in life. Had they been lying dormant all along? What was it that had given them the ability to suddenly flourish? She had no idea and the sudden appearance of her gift was a situation which she likened to the arbitrary emergence from the womb of two baby infants, when only one had been expected.

Asked to attend to a series of inexplicable "disturbances" that had recently taken place within the confines of a suburban terraced house in Hounslow, Ag found herself recording a voluminous series of dialogues into a tape recorder. Entering into a trance, she had sat cross-legged on the floor for hours, unleashing a torrent of words. It later transpired that some of these words were in fact Welsh. Finally, after a fit of wailing and shaking, during which she claimed demonic entities had consumed her, arriving simultaneously in each of her orifices, she seemed to have managed to banish all unwanted spirits from the household.

Whenever voices appeared to her, they would always be in the precise, actual voices those particular individuals had possessed, and it was mostly a case for Ag of attuning herself to these speech patterns, a process which she often compared to a surfer instinctively riding a wave. As soon as she successfully melded herself together with a voice, she could always travel any distance with it, enter into fruitful dialogue or ask any question that she wished to. She did not know why this remarkable blessing had been conferred upon her, but she was incredibly grateful that it had been.

9.

Our Narrator Addresses an
Important Issue Directly

Readers,

"Perhaps everything I'm telling you here is a series of lies,"

Matty

10.

Bopple

After everyone left the house I was left living alone with Mother, often consumed with intense feelings of ennui. There was no particular reason for me to either get a job or move on. I was still given a large allowance, mostly put together by monies from my Father and his business interests. My days became tedious. Eventually, whilst in this state, I decided to invent my own planet. I named it Bopple. The invention of this planet occurred over the course of many years and involved my filling out hundreds of notebooks with lines of text, drawings and tables of facts, all describing a planet I never told anyone else about.

Late at night I would imagine Bopple's teeming cities with giant vistas of roofs and spiralling towers. All of these cities received names in one of the various languages which I invented, entities that did not possess grammatical rules or even an extensive vocabulary. I nevertheless felt that each of these languages possessed some degree of reality. I would create words and covertly whisper them to myself in my room. There were no rules attached to their creation or use, but instinctively I began to invent words which sounded and felt right within the confines of these various languages. The three most significant of these languages were named "Xellis," "Parabobo," and "Ugga". Over time, I came to know the sounds, rhythm, and style of each of these entities with some intimacy.

I found myself developing a special affection for Ugga, which I would describe as the most atavistic of these languages, one in which almost half of the words were slang terms, including hundreds that were expletives or could be considered in some way profane. I tended to reserve most of my real-world feelings of anger and hatred for private expression in Ugga, a process which often took the form of shouting. In fact I found that I couldn't really explore the full perimeters of Ugga unless Mother was out of the house. When she was, I would sometimes forcefully pace through the rooms, breaking into fits of shouting, enjoying the sound of my voice reverberating from the walls.

There were a total of 159 countries on Bopple. The largest was named "Kajouin" and possessed three billion inhabitants, many of whom hated each other with a great passionate intensity. Civil wars were liable to commence there during any given week of the year. As a result of all this conflict, infrastructure was relentlessly poor in Kajouin. Things never worked as they should. Roads were full of potholes and telecommunications were liable to cut out at any given moment. It was a difficult place in which to be happy. People would often be killed by one or another sectarian faction for reasons that few really understood the intricacies of. It might be related to certain kinds of rattles, or the way in which a person stood on one foot.

I became emotionally attached to Kajouin and kept returning to it, worrying about its inhabitants, wanting to add more details to their existence. I found myself tempted to call an end to their long war, but somehow didn't feel capable of that, despite repeatedly daring myself to. Instead of this, Kajouin received a long-standing ceasefire of hostilities from me, during which a festival of "sports and entertainments" was inaugurated to encourage peaceful behaviors between the various warring factions. At that time I also let the nation receive a new garbage disposal system, many newly planted palm trees, as well as a plastic surgery clinic. For a while it felt as if things were looking up around there.

When I got tired of the bloodshed on Kajouin, I would turn to any of the other smaller countries on Bopple, ones in which wars never seemed to happen and life was more or less focused on cheerful things like ice cream sundaes and cocktail umbrellas. As time wore on I became especially attached to Yoob, an island state in the Rubbanassar Ocean where there had, allegedly, been no acts of crime for the last twenty-three years. The last time there had been one it had involved someone stealing a bicycle. Of course this state of affairs had come about as a consequence of Yoob having a very small population for a nation state. One census had estimated it as being 14,328. This made it feel like the absolute opposite of Kajouin and even more like a place to retreat to when the going got tough.

The citizens of Yoob spent a great deal of time fishing to take care of their diet. In the evenings they often engaged in a form of line dancing along the beaches. There was much smiling on these occasions. For years a strange thing had been happening in this country: everyone who lived there seemed very keen on the practice of sharing everything. People would just wander into each other's dwellings, usually whilst grinning, and they would simply take any possession that they wanted from each other. This was done in the full knowledge that everyone would get their possessions back without any trouble. No one ever got stressed out about any of this. Indeed everyone liked being able to just stroll into other people's dwellings and simply take things. When thinking about Yoob I sometimes had the opposite impulse to that with Kajouin. That is to say, I was tempted to make certain terrible things happen on this island, even if I didn't really want to. It was just so nice there on Yoob. I really didn't want to spoil it for anyone. So I left Yoob in its happy idyll and let myself return there with great frequency.

The nation of Ik was another which I returned to very often and it was another country that was very fraught with tensions and problems. One issue in "Ik" was that many people had different opinions about what day of the week it was. There were various competing calendars and large groups felt culturally attached to different versions of the ordering of time. To abide by a certain calendar in Ik was to take pride in one's own culture and so there were often tense discussions about this in workplaces and cafés. Little scuffles broke out all the time. It was rare for anyone to be killed or gravely injured in such disputes, but it did happen from time to time. I must admit I never developed an enormous affection for Ik, but, as with all of these destinations, Ik had its place in my heart.

Pllpllpll was another of Bopple's nations. It was a country in which the populace was so consumed with irony that they were constantly building monuments to persons and civic entities that didn't actually exist. These were then declared open with elaborate ceremonies where everyone present would stifle knowing giggles whilst watching the latest overwrought efforts of groups of cheer-leaders or steel bands, who had been called in to perform in front of statues of persons who had never lived, or beside round metal plaques bearing next to no information about fictional societies said to have done significant deeds for the public good. Quite why so many people in Pllpllpll enjoyed devoting so much time to this pursuit was never all that clear to me, but I knew that they did.

Meanwhile, over on Ruzz patriotic fervour had reached such a level of intensity that much of daily life had become related to flags. There were frequently long debates and discussions about the subject. People painted them on their cheeks, bellies, and thighs. There was intense competition between citizens who all wished to display the maximum quantity of flags in the windows of their houses and on the exteriors of their cars. They could also be found frequently emerging from mouths, fluttering on the sides of prams and stamped on to tubes of medicine. People would hum to their flags and stroke them as if they were pets. Someone on Ruzz even started a social movement named "Flags! Not Rags!".

Gazooog was a strange country. Every day at 2p.m. there was a radio broadcast listened to extensively throughout the nation. This broadcast contained predictions of what would occur within the next twenty-four hours. Often as people listened they would take copious notes, as experience had taught them of the veracity of these predictions. All of these broadcasts were sanctioned and orchestrated by central government, who made sure that the announcers employed to read out these predictions did so in a serious tone, as if they were reading out the news or the shipping forecast. No individuals were ever named and all predictions were supposed to be taken as general possibilities which could potentially apply to anyone.

11.

Index Cards

There came a time in her early thirties when Lucinda realized how much she actively enjoyed using index cards. She would habitually use them, in one version only which was close to being their standard size: 3 x 5 inches, with one pink line across the top under a slightly larger white space than those underneath, formed by nine pale blue lines.

Her enjoyment came from the clear, rational ordering of space which they offered. There was a sense for her that within the grid they supplied, somehow anything could be recorded or achieved. Perhaps all that really mattered was the careful designation of each word, the delicate ranking of priorities, an assemblage of precise logical strictures. Over time, she had found that, more and more, she was using them for almost any purpose that they might be employed for. As well as the textual ordering of her academic work, she gradually discovered that they were also good to use for making shopping lists, jotting down directions to friends' houses, drafting tables of equations, and noting fragmented details of bibliographies.

Eventually, she found that her pockets were always stuffed

with sheaves of the cards, including a number of blank ones in case the need for the creation of a new list overtook her. This was liable to happen at any time, day or night, in the street, at a supermarket, in the midst of cooking a meal. Inspiration would arrive as and when it had to.

After beginning to consider the issue, she began to feel that these cards were irreplaceable to her. When she attempted to use a notebook instead, the effect was distinctly different, as the crowd of pages found there was not a concise enough frame and did not offer the singular brevity of an index card. Each card's detachment from all other materials gave it the ability to stand alone and be used to represent all manner of significant things with a certain exactitude.

She had first encountered these valuable entities when she was a teenager revising for exams, a time when Mother had suggested that they might help her. In order to get through her O-Levels, she had needed to fill out many hundreds of these cards with bullet points, facts and quotations, shuffling through them constantly, successfully memorizing all that she had inscribed on their features.

At first the cards served this very pragmatic function for her and she then began to adopt them without thinking about it strongly, not realizing they were destined to take a surprisingly important position in her life. Gradually, she came to find more and more uses for these small and yet significant objects, until suddenly, without warning, it seemed that they had become central to her way of living.

At first she felt that her use of these cards proved how efficient she was at learning and ordering information. They made her feel fastidious when she used them, they seemed to prove that she was an effective worker. However, she found that they crept up on her, eventually becoming a necessity, something that she reached for every day, for any kind of purpose.

Eventually it got to a point where she would write out a card every night to account for all that would occur the next day. She commenced each card by writing the day of the week and the date, always including the year as well. Underneath this, she would write the times of sunset and sunrise, expected weather conditions, any notes on public holidays or other significant public information, as well as all spatial movements and activities which she would engage in. As far as possible she would attempt to account for every last person she might encounter. Once each day's card was finished, she placed them into a filing cabinet at home, where she had created sections for each passing month.

Before any planned meetings with other people, she would write out a card detailing topics of conversation which she intended to steer those people towards, or which she thought *they* might wish to engage in. She would also write out a brief list of emotional states which she expected to feel on such occasions. Ideally for Lucinda, nothing would be improvised, nothing would be left to fate.

Whenever plans she had laid out so precisely on her cards failed to occur for some reason or another she often felt upset, somewhat outraged at being present in a world where her will was not commanded with precision, where events involving *her* did not occur as she wanted them to. But unfortunately this happened all of the time.

12.

Lettuce

For the length of a summer, Barnaby and Gerard took to meeting in a café not far from Marble Arch, once a week, for precisely one hour. There were very definite rules governing their behavior on these occasions, as they were playing an extended game, one that would quite possibly prove dangerous to them.

The most significant rule during these meetings was that the only subject they were allowed to speak of was lettuce. There were to be no lapses into silence. They both had to do everything within their power to continue talking about lettuce, within any possible verbal formulation, for the length of an hour. It was not necessary for them to be telling the truth, nor was it necessary for them to be speaking in any particular way about the subject; it was simply of great importance that every last sentence they uttered be related in some way to the subject of lettuce.

Why was this important?

It was important to them because they wanted to see what would happen to language, to their actual *realities* if they took part in such an extended and extreme performative game. They wished to strengthen their relationship as brothers, to take it a further distance which it had never reached before.

Why had they chosen to speak only about lettuce?

They had considered many different possible subjects, but they had eventually decided upon that of lettuce because it seemed unlikely and therefore it made the formation of statements about it more of a challenge. Because of this challenge they saw the potential for the subject generating certain magical qualities in their conversations which a more obvious subject would not have provided. They felt that an extended consideration of lettuce could potentially cause a transformation of consciousness and, in the end, they felt that their experiment had succeeded. Whilst lettuce might look like a ridiculous subject on the surface, they wished to prove (at least between themselves) that it was as viable a subject for conversation as any in the world.

A typical opening gambit in one of these sessions often went something like this:

"Do you know what Barnaby? . . . I happened to eat some lettuce yesterday . . ."

"Did you?"

"Indeed I did."

"And how was it?"

"It was very poor."

"Why so?"

"Too watery. A very watery example of iceberg."

"What was the context of this lettuce?"

"It was in the context of a salad."

"That is a perfectly reasonable context."

"I'm glad you think so."

There was always this strange air of artificiality to their

conversations. In some ways it felt akin to the formality of playing chess, with each player moving only within highly proscribed rules which did not really allow for much in the way of freedom.

"So yesterday I was buying some lettuce in the supermarket . . ." Barnaby might say.

"Well isn't that grand! Did you enjoy the experience?"

"It was superlative."

"Why was that?"

"Whilst I was looking at the different forms of lettuce available, the ghost of Ho Chi Minh made an unexpected appearance."

"Ho Chi Minh?"

"Yes, indeed. His ghost at least."

"Does his ghost like lettuce?"

"I believe he might."

Then, as soon as silence threatened to descend, a rapid change of subject, as always in these talks.

"Do we think that there would be an aversion to such a large amount of talk about lettuce in the wider social world?" asked Gerard.

"Yes."

"Why do you feel that might be?"

"I think that people possess a fear of considering lettuce in any detail because it is so ubiquitous and yet also so hidden. To alert them to the details of lettuce is, therefore, alarming . . ."

"Is it not about the desire to be rational, to obliterate all that stands in the way of such a rationality?"

"That sounds like a plausible explanation to me."

A momentary pause.

"Do you believe that lettuce is significant?" asked Barnaby.

"No I do not."

"Why do you feel that way?"

"Because it barely has any taste and the taste which it possesses I find to be actually unpleasant when you think about it, when you get right down to it . . ."

"And we *are* thinking about it . . ."

"Yes we are."

"So why is lettuce significant?" asked Gerard on this occasion.

"I find it to be a delightful substance. It can be the home of snails. That is one reason for my delight. Due to its nearly invisible status it can be placed within almost any culinary context and I do find this ambidextrous nature very satisfying to consider . . ."

"Do you?"

"Yes. I find it immensely appealing."

Their already well to do voices would often stretch even further into fake aristocratic ones during portions of their dialogues.

"What about the notion that lettuce should not be used to illustrate philosophical arguments? The idea that it is not really suitable for such an elevated purpose?"

"I think it could potentially be a crucial example in such conversations . . ."

"Why?"

"Because if a proposition is not true in the case of lettuce then perhaps it also is not true in many other contexts . . ."

"I think you are avoiding the obvious problem here," said Gerard. "The problem being that lettuce simply does not matter."

"Lettuce *does* matter. It emphatically matters. If only because every last thing in the world matters on some level, simply because it exists . . ."

In truth, Gerard found that line of argument hard to disagree with, but for the sake of the game, he could not be seen to agree.

"Is it possible then," said Gerard, "that certain things do not contain *enough* lettuce?"

"I feel that may well be true," said Barnaby, gravely.

"And of those things, which would you mention in particular?"

"I think we should leave gastronomy aside for a moment."

"Alright, let us do that."

"Because gastronomy is the most obvious domain of the lettuce and I would like for us to consider things beyond that domain for some moments, to think about the places in which the lettuce feels too absent."

"Yes, let's do this."

"I feel that lettuce is not present to a sufficient degree within the realm of animated films for example."

"That sounds correct."

"I think much could be made of lettuce within the domain of the animated film."

"Doubtless it could . . . but presumably there must be plenty of examples of animated lettuce out there? Perhaps examples that we are not aware of at the present time?"

"I'm sure that must be correct."

"There are also many other things which I feel do not contain enough examples of lettuce. Things such as taxicabs, bathrooms, photographs of swimming pools . . ."

"Why does a photograph of a swimming pool need to contain lettuce?"

"It is not a question of *need* exactly. Not in this instance, not with this particular example . . . but I do nevertheless believe that certain photographs of swimming pools could benefit from the inclusion of lettuce . . ."

"Perhaps it would be better than their exclusion."

"Do you think that a sustained consideration of lettuce undertaken in this manner could drive a person insane?"

"I would have thought that must be a possibility."

"And in our own cases?"

"I believe, wholeheartedly, that we will not go insane ourselves during our considerations of lettuce."

"That is a relief to hear."

"I'm glad of that."

"Do you feel, by now, at this point in your life, that you know a lot about the subject of lettuce?"

"I feel as if we still have far to go. I feel that the horizon of this subject still stretches far beyond us . . ."

"Well thank goodness for that."

There was a moment of rumination, a brief hesitation for both of them, before they launched into a further exchange, started again, as so often before, by a question.

"Is it a problem if lettuce isn't green?"

"But most of it *is* green isn't it."

"Well, some tends towards white and is perhaps not so much green as green*ish* . . ."

"Yes."

"So don't you think that *real* lettuce should be green? Not just vaguely green, but abundantly, wholesomely green . . . an earth-green to match the planet?"

"That sounds about right."

"But do you agree that it is an important issue?"

"I do . . . although I don't think that it is quite as significant for me as it is for you by the sounds of things . . ."

Many of these sentences would repeat themselves in their memories during the long stretches of time when they were apart from each other. They would consider them again, embellish them in their minds and then return to them in their café to really get to the bottom of each issue.

"The more that we discuss lettuce," began Gerard one day, "the less interested I am in actually eating any . . . it feels as if I've been force fed the same kind of food for months on end . . ."

"I'm sorry you feel that way, but I must say, for my part, our conversations always make me feel eager to eat more lettuce . . . I leave your company and then seek out lettuce . . . that is precisely what I find myself wanting, a good leaf or two of crispy, watery and refreshing lettuce."

"Imagine a world without lettuce."

"I dread to think about how that would be."

"It is strange this state of affairs exists. The world might as well not have lettuce within it, and yet it does . . ."

"You could make that remark about anything at all though . . ."

"Yes, you could, so why not make it? I really would be sad to see a world without lettuce. I think it would be missed and not just by me. Doubtless it wouldn't be missed in an altogether *conscious* way. But, somehow, I feel people would know that a small and yet important thing was missing, that the world was not quite right."

"I do know what you mean, but I also think that there are more inherently important things which would be missed rather more . . ."

"I disagree. What could be more important than lettuce?"

"Is lettuce visually beautiful?"

"I don't think so."

"How would you describe it if not as beautiful?"

"I would prefer to use the word 'gawky.' Or perhaps, if I was in a darker mood, I might choose to call lettuce 'unsightly.'"

"That seems a little extreme to me, that last word."

"Really?"

"Yes. Personally I believe that lettuce at least deserves to be called 'handsome', if not simply 'beautiful'."

"This of course opens up the question of what kind of gender lettuce possesses. I will go out first and say that I feel it happens to be feminine."

"Well I think with 'handsome' I've already given you my answer regarding gender."

"Does lettuce have a purpose?"

"What does that even mean? Your terminology is too vague. What kind of purpose could it be said to have?"

"I didn't say I had an answer . . . I'm only asking the

question . . ."

"Well in this case at least I think you'd better attempt an answer because I don't feel that I am capable of one."

"Surely at least it has the purpose of existing to be eaten. Or perhaps we might even say 'to be nibbled.'"

"Perhaps we might very well say that."

"At the end of the day it is very nourishing and fulfilling to rabbits is it not?"

"I do believe that to be the case."

"Does lettuce contribute anything important to salads?"

"You've got to be kidding. How can you even ask that?"

"Well I don't think it does much in salads. It tends to sit there on the sidelines so to speak, being rather boring. I think much of the time it is pretty redundant, as if it is only there to fill space and has been carelessly, thoughtlessly placed there."

"You are a foolish man. I think in fact that these are disingenuous statements. You know as well as I do that lettuce is in fact the heart of any salad, virtually the purpose of salads, it carries the salad, it *is* the salad."

"Is lettuce inferior to other items sold at the stalls in vegetable markets?"

"You seem to imply that it is inferior."

"Again, I am merely asking the question. Giving the question an airing."

"But you do believe that it is inferior don't you?"

"Yes, alright, I suppose I do believe that . . . I would wager that if you were to go to a fruit and vegetable market you would not see any great enthusiasm amongst the stallholders to sell lettuce. It isn't something that they are likely to shout about with great noise. I would propose that this is because lettuce is inherently boring and almost tasteless. No one can really get excited about lettuce, although seemingly you can . . ."

13.

The Suburban Carnival

Rebecca devoted two years of her life to the creation of a carnival. Hundreds of people were involved in this project, as craftspeople, performers, or simply as witnesses of the procession when it finally occurred. Extremely adept at creating enthusiasm for her event, Rebecca would make long inspirational speeches on its behalf and would always find suitable roles for new recruits.

Early in the planning process she decided that there would be no central theme or organizing principal behind the actions of this carnival. Instead, it would be an opportunity for expression of any kind. Anything that happened to be life-affirming and not imbued with any sort of hatred was permitted within her framework.

The carnival took place along the length of a single suburban street with the full permission of the local council. After Rebecca and her conspirators harassed them a great deal, the council agreed to close off the street to all other traffic for a day.

Rebecca wanted everyone who had attended to feel that they had been present at one of the most significant locations in the world that day, even if it was an entirely temporary one;

a location which was, furthermore, destined to disappear at the end of a single day, vanishing into mere traces of memory, a series of decaying photographs. She wanted people to stumble across her carnival without warning; to be drawn, spontaneously, into its swarming, cheering crowds, its mosaic of colours. She dearly wanted it to be a place without conflict, where every last person involved possessed the same status, all joining together to create a mutual disharmony.

Large canvas banners decorated with irreverent slogans and Day-Glo paintings were held aloft by hordes of marching promenaders, some of whom were blowing whistles or shaking maracas as they moved; one old woman spent seemingly the entire day sat in a camping chair on the pavement, playing folk ballads on a banjo. Some people handed out drawings, or postcards, placed garlands of flowers around shoulders, or struck up conversations with a troupe of notably effeminate-looking koala bears who spent much of their time dancing together spiritedly in a circle.

There were many floats, sometimes laden with so many materials that they resembled impossible palaces, passing by in seemingly endless succession, with close to one hundred appearing during the day, each its own temporary and singular plethora, with separate laws, inhabitants, and locations. There were many pairs of sunglasses worn on these floats and also, as it happens, many pineapples.

Excited children ran up and down the length of the street, shouting and pointing at things, breaking into frenzies of jumping and smiling. There was a constant barrage of noise from the many enormous, overgrown sets of stereo speakers sending new ripples outwards into the airwaves which had previously seemed grounded in stillness.

It was a carnival that did not possess any formal title. Rebecca wanted to avoid its becoming an event that was too clearly defined in terms of a set identity. During committee meetings this issue was discussed many times and everyone always concluded by simply referring to it as "The Carnival," a designation understood by everyone.

A series of colourful, often absurdist floats moved down the street in procession all day long. On one of them a number of figures made semaphore messages with flags, handing out copies of a code book to anyone who looked interested enough to want to figure out just what it was that they were saying. Most of the float's audience were cheered simply by following the choreographed movements of the dancers and did not need to know what was being said exactly.

One of the carnival performers, an energetic girl known to some as Maria Rosalda, spent the day moving back and forth between one person in the crowd and another, continually making surreptitious offerings of macadamias. She would create a little cluster of these nuts in her fist, creep up close to someone and open out her hand, often in conjunction with a whispered message.

Another performer came dressed as a tree, with suitably bark-like surfaces covering their bottom half and real branches with leaves sprouting from their head, their face coloured with a shade of green paint. As a "final touch" they had lodged a couple of woollen birds amongst their branches, a phenomenon that they referred to by saying "I possess my very own eco-system here."

One group spent hours dancing in a circle as slowly as possible, enjoying the reversal of the usual dancing tempo, with smiles plastered across most of the group's faces. After an hour, they successfully managed to draw a further fifteen people into their group.

Three girls were dressed in the attire of nuns. When asked why they had chosen to dress like this, they revealed that it was quite definitely neither a religious nor a sacrilegious gesture, but merely a collective choice taken to discover how it felt to dress together as nuns. "We're just nuns," they would say when questioned.

Other young women had elected to arrive dressed in

swimming costumes, apparently as a direct consequence of
the lack of any waters to swim within. Rebecca assumed that
this represented a longing for the beach, or for lost childhood
afternoons spent in swimming pools, or perhaps even for the
vanished pre-human aquatic world, which she believed was still
a component of everyone's psyche.

In one of the street's front gardens an elderly chef had decided
to use the occasion to fry a gigantic omelette, carefully seasoned,
garnished with many sprigs of parsley, it was served in considerable portions to more than a hundred people, who were all
grateful for the gesture.

From somewhere, at an undefined moment in the afternoon
that no one seemed to notice the inauguration of, a profusion
of giant yellow sponge hammers suddenly appeared everywhere.
Seconds later people were bashing each other in merry comic
book imitation until Rebecca saw what was occurring and decided
that this had to be a strictly pacifist carnival and that she must tell
everyone to cease bashing each other, and so they did indeed cease.

The people with hammers then spontaneously formed a
conga line, a hopeful chain weaving in and out of the floats and
stalls, with everyone's hands placed fraternally upon whoever or
whatever happened to be immediately in front, with all touches
given without judgement or reservation, being swiftly replicated
without hesitation all along the length of the street, moving to its
own crazed rhythm, as conga lines are prone to doing.

Rebecca had prepared a full-colour magazine entitled *Dry
Ski Slope Glamour* especially for the day of the carnival. This
consisted solely of a series of photographs of her various close
associates posing on a number of different dry ski slopes, often
in lime-green and pink. She gave away copies of issues 1 to 17 of
this publication for free that day.

Many objects were waved in the air, a phenomenon which
included umbrellas, banners, sticks, fake sticks, rolled up newspapers, but which most frequently involved human arms, all

of them moving in accord or with disregard to whatever music happened to be prevalent at that particular moment.

In one back garden the Stevenson Family had put up a tent in which cartoons were projected in a loop all day long. Once children had discovered this, they told other children about it and ran back to the tent sweaty and out of breath. Inside, they sat staring, mouths agape, feeling an enormous distance from the manic activity continuing outside, although this only lasted fleetingly, for seconds, before they would get up and find something else to occupy themselves with.

A "taxi service" was set up, with which, for the price of 10p, anyone could climb aboard a float at one end of the street and be gradually carried all of the way to the other end. During the journey passengers tended to dance a little, as well as smile and wave at those who had been left behind on the pavement.

As night descended fully, most of the partying drifted out of the street and into the houses and front gardens. It became quite possible for partying opportunists to drift from one house to another all evening long. Every abode seemed to possess its own unique atmosphere and sampling each one in turn was a perversely exciting activity to some. There was only an extraordinarily small amount of trouble which resulted from all of this openness. In one instance, a very large, bearded man, wearing a faded Van Halen t-shirt, passed out in the hallway of the Cranbourne family home, a place where all of the inhabitants were unknown to him. Nevertheless, the man created no damage and everyone parted amicably in the morning after he awoke.

14.

Once Again, Mother Considers One of the Most Important Subjects of Her Life

sex sex sex sex sex sex sex sex sex sex sex sex sex sex sex sex sex sex
sex sex sex sex sex sex sex sex sex sex sex sex sex sex sex sex sex sex
sex sex sex sex sex sex sex sex sex sex sex sex sex sex sex sex sex sex
sex sex sex sex sex sex sex sex sex sex sex sex sex sex sex sex sex sex
sex sex sex sex sex sex sex sex sex sex sex sex sex sex sex sex sex sex
sex sex sex sex sex sex sex sex sex sex sex sex sex sex sex sex sex sex
sex sex sex sex sex sex sex sex sex sex sex sex sex sex sex sex sex sex
sex sex sex sex sex sex sex sex sex sex sex sex sex sex sex sex sex sex
sex sex sex sex sex sex sex sex sex sex sex sex sex sex sex sex sex sex
sex sex sex sex sex sex sex sex sex sex sex sex sex sex sex sex sex sex
sex sex sex sex sex sex sex sex sex sex sex sex sex sex sex sex sex sex
sex sex sex sex sex sex sex sex sex sex sex sex sex sex sex sex sex sex
sex sex sex sex sex sex sex sex sex sex sex sex sex sex sex sex sex sex
sex sex sex sex sex sex sex sex sex sex sex sex sex sex sex sex sex sex
sex sex sex sex sex sex sex sex sex sex sex sex sex sex sex sex sex sex
sex sex sex sex sex sex sex sex sex sex sex sex sex sex sex sex sex sex

sex sex sex sex sex sex sex sex sex sex sex sex sex sex sex sex sex sex
sex sex sex sex sex sex sex sex sex sex sex sex sex sex sex sex sex sex
sex sex sex sex sex sex sex sex sex sex sex sex sex sex sex sex sex sex
sex sex sex sex sex sex sex sex sex sex sex sex sex sex sex sex sex sex
sex sex sex sex sex sex sex sex sex sex sex sex sex sex sex sex sex sex
sex sex sex sex sex sex sex sex sex sex sex sex sex sex sex sex sex sex
sex sex sex sex sex sex sex sex sex sex sex sex sex sex sex sex sex sex
sex sex sex sex sex sex sex sex sex sex sex sex sex sex sex sex sex sex
sex sex sex sex sex sex sex sex sex sex sex sex sex sex sex sex sex sex
sex sex sex sex sex sex sex sex sex sex sex sex sex sex sex sex sex sex
sex sex sex sex sex sex sex sex sex sex sex sex sex sex sex sex sex sex
sex sex sex sex sex sex sex sex sex sex sex sex sex sex sex sex sex sex
sex sex sex sex sex sex sex sex sex sex sex sex sex sex sex sex sex sex
sex sex sex sex sex sex sex sex sex sex sex sex sex sex sex sex sex sex
sex sex sex sex sex sex sex sex sex sex sex sex sex sex sex sex sex sex
sex sex sex sex sex sex sex sex sex sex sex sex sex sex sex sex sex sex
sex sex sex sex sex sex sex sex sex sex sex sex sex sex sex sex sex sex
sex sex sex sex sex sex sex sex sex sex sex sex sex sex sex sex sex sex
sex sex sex sex sex sex sex sex sex sex sex sex sex sex sex sex sex sex
sex sex sex sex sex sex sex sex sex sex sex sex sex sex sex sex sex sex
sex sex sex sex sex sex sex sex sex sex sex sex sex sex sex sex sex sex
sex sex sex sex sex sex sex sex sex sex sex sex sex sex sex sex sex sex
sex sex sex sex sex sex sex sex sex sex sex sex sex sex sex sex sex sex
sex sex sex sex sex sex sex sex sex sex sex sex sex sex sex sex sex sex
sex sex sex sex sex sex sex sex sex sex sex sex sex sex sex sex sex sex
sex sex sex sex sex sex sex sex sex sex sex sex sex sex sex sex sex sex
sex sex sex sex sex sex sex sex sex sex sex sex sex sex sex sex sex sex
sex sex sex sex sex sex sex sex sex sex sex sex sex sex sex sex sex sex
sex sex sex sex sex sex sex sex sex sex sex sex sex sex sex sex sex sex
sex sex sex sex sex sex sex sex sex sex sex sex sex sex sex sex sex sex
sex sex sex sex sex sex sex sex sex sex sex sex sex sex sex sex sex sex
sex sex sex sex sex sex sex sex sex sex sex sex sex sex sex sex sex sex
sex sex sex sex sex sex sex sex sex sex sex sex sex sex sex sex sex sex
sex sex sex sex sex sex sex sex sex sex sex sex sex sex sex sex sex sex
sex sex sex sex sex sex sex sex sex sex sex sex sex sex sex sex sex sex

sex sex sex sex sex sex sex sex sex sex sex sex sex sex sex sex sex sex
sex sex sex sex sex sex sex sex sex sex sex sex sex sex sex sex sex sex
sex sex sex sex sex sex sex sex sex sex sex sex sex sex sex sex sex sex
sex sex sex sex sex sex sex sex sex sex sex sex sex sex sex sex sex sex
sex sex sex sex sex sex sex sex sex sex sex sex sex sex sex sex sex sex
sex sex sex sex sex sex sex sex sex sex sex sex sex sex sex sex sex sex
sex sex sex sex sex sex sex sex sex sex sex sex sex sex sex sex sex sex
sex sex sex sex sex sex sex sex sex sex sex sex sex sex sex sex sex sex
sex sex sex sex sex sex sex sex sex sex sex sex sex sex sex sex sex sex
sex sex sex sex sex sex sex sex sex sex sex sex sex sex sex sex sex sex
sex sex sex sex sex sex sex sex sex sex sex sex sex sex sex sex sex sex
sex sex sex sex sex sex sex sex sex sex sex sex sex sex sex sex sex sex
sex sex sex sex sex sex sex sex sex sex sex sex sex sex sex sex sex sex
sex sex sex sex sex sex sex sex sex sex sex sex sex sex sex sex sex sex
sex sex sex sex sex sex sex sex sex sex sex sex sex sex sex sex sex sex
sex sex sex sex sex sex sex sex sex sex sex sex sex sex sex sex sex sex
sex sex sex sex sex sex sex sex sex sex sex sex sex sex sex sex sex sex
sex sex sex sex sex sex sex sex sex sex sex sex sex sex sex sex sex sex
sex sex sex sex sex sex sex sex sex sex sex sex sex sex sex sex sex sex
sex sex sex sex sex sex sex sex sex sex sex sex sex sex sex sex sex sex
sex sex sex sex sex sex sex sex sex sex sex sex sex sex sex sex sex sex
sex sex sex sex sex sex sex sex sex sex sex sex sex sex sex sex sex sex
sex sex sex sex sex sex sex sex sex sex sex sex sex sex sex sex sex sex
sex sex sex sex sex sex sex sex sex sex sex sex sex sex sex sex sex sex
sex sex sex sex sex sex sex sex sex sex sex sex sex sex sex sex sex sex
sex sex sex sex sex sex sex sex sex sex sex sex sex sex sex sex sex sex
sex sex sex sex sex sex sex sex sex sex sex sex sex sex sex sex sex sex
sex sex sex sex sex sex sex sex sex sex sex sex sex sex sex sex sex sex
sex sex sex sex sex sex sex sex sex sex sex sex sex sex sex sex sex sex
sex sex sex sex sex sex sex sex sex sex sex sex sex sex sex sex sex sex
sex sex sex sex sex sex sex sex sex sex sex sex sex sex sex sex sex sex
sex sex sex sex sex sex sex sex sex sex sex sex sex sex sex sex sex sex
sex sex sex sex sex sex sex sex sex sex sex sex sex sex sex sex sex sex
sex sex sex sex sex sex sex sex sex sex sex sex sex sex sex sex sex sex
sex sex sex sex sex sex sex sex sex sex sex sex sex sex sex sex sex sex
sex sex sex sex sex sex sex sex sex sex sex sex sex sex sex sex sex sex
sex sex sex sex sex sex sex sex sex sex sex sex sex sex sex sex sex sex
sex sex sex sex sex sex sex sex sex sex sex sex sex sex sex sex sex sex
sex sex sex sex sex sex sex sex sex sex sex sex sex sex sex sex sex sex
sex sex sex sex sex sex sex sex sex sex sex sex sex sex sex sex sex sex

sex sex sex sex sex sex sex sex sex sex sex sex sex sex sex sex sex sex
sex sex sex sex sex sex sex sex sex sex sex sex sex sex sex sex sex sex
sex sex sex sex sex sex sex sex sex sex sex sex sex sex sex sex sex sex
sex sex sex sex sex sex sex sex sex sex sex sex sex sex sex sex sex sex
sex sex sex sex sex sex sex sex sex sex sex sex sex sex sex sex sex sex
sex sex sex sex sex sex sex sex sex sex sex sex sex sex sex sex sex sex
sex sex sex sex sex sex sex sex sex sex sex sex sex sex sex sex sex sex
sex sex sex sex sex sex sex sex sex sex sex sex sex sex sex sex sex sex
sex sex sex sex sex sex sex sex sex sex sex sex sex sex sex sex sex sex
sex sex sex sex sex sex sex sex sex sex sex sex sex sex sex sex sex sex
sex sex sex sex sex sex sex sex sex sex sex sex sex sex sex sex sex sex
sex sex sex sex sex sex sex sex sex sex sex sex sex sex sex sex sex sex
sex sex sex sex sex sex sex sex sex sex sex sex sex sex sex sex sex sex
sex sex sex sex sex sex sex sex sex sex sex sex sex sex sex sex sex sex
sex sex sex sex sex sex sex sex sex sex sex sex sex sex sex sex sex sex
sex sex sex sex sex sex sex sex sex sex sex sex sex sex sex sex sex sex
sex sex sex sex sex sex sex sex sex sex sex sex sex sex sex sex sex sex
sex sex sex sex sex sex sex sex sex sex sex sex sex sex sex sex sex sex
sex sex sex sex sex sex sex sex sex sex sex sex sex sex sex sex sex sex
sex sex sex sex sex sex sex sex sex sex sex sex sex sex sex sex sex sex
sex sex sex sex sex sex sex sex sex sex sex sex sex sex sex sex sex sex
sex sex sex sex sex sex sex sex sex sex sex sex sex sex sex sex sex sex
sex sex sex sex sex sex sex sex sex sex sex sex sex sex sex sex sex sex
sex sex sex sex sex sex sex sex sex sex sex sex sex sex sex sex sex sex
sex sex sex sex sex sex sex sex sex sex sex sex sex sex sex sex sex sex
sex sex sex sex sex sex sex sex sex sex sex sex sex sex sex sex sex sex
sex sex sex sex sex sex sex sex sex sex sex sex sex sex sex sex sex sex
sex sex sex sex sex sex sex sex sex sex sex sex sex sex sex sex sex sex
sex sex sex sex sex sex sex sex sex sex sex sex sex sex sex sex sex sex
sex sex sex sex sex sex sex sex sex sex sex sex sex sex sex sex sex sex
sex sex sex sex sex sex sex sex sex sex sex sex sex sex sex sex sex sex
sex sex sex sex sex sex sex sex sex sex sex sex sex sex sex sex sex sex
sex sex sex sex sex sex sex sex sex sex sex sex sex sex sex sex sex sex
sex sex sex sex sex sex sex sex sex sex sex sex sex sex sex sex sex sex
sex sex sex sex sex sex sex sex sex sex sex sex sex sex sex sex sex sex

sex sex sex sex sex sex sex sex sex sex sex sex sex sex sex sex sex sex
sex sex sex sex sex sex sex sex sex sex sex sex sex sex sex sex sex sex
sex sex sex sex sex sex sex sex sex sex sex sex sex sex sex sex sex sex
sex sex sex sex sex sex sex sex sex sex sex sex sex sex sex sex sex sex
sex sex sex sex sex sex sex sex sex sex sex sex sex sex sex sex sex sex
sex sex sex sex sex sex sex sex sex sex sex sex sex sex sex sex sex sex
sex sex sex sex sex sex sex sex sex sex sex sex sex sex sex sex sex sex
sex sex sex sex sex sex sex sex sex sex sex sex sex sex sex sex sex sex
sex sex sex sex sex sex sex sex sex sex sex sex sex sex sex sex sex sex
sex sex sex sex sex sex sex sex sex sex sex sex sex sex sex sex sex sex
sex sex sex sex sex sex sex sex sex sex sex sex sex sex sex sex sex sex
sex sex sex sex sex sex sex sex sex sex sex sex sex sex sex sex sex sex
sex sex sex sex sex sex sex sex sex sex sex sex sex sex sex sex sex sex
sex sex sex sex sex sex sex sex sex sex sex sex sex sex sex sex sex sex
sex sex sex sex sex sex sex sex sex sex sex sex sex sex sex sex sex sex
sex sex sex sex sex sex sex sex sex sex sex sex sex sex sex sex sex sex
sex sex sex sex sex sex sex sex sex sex sex sex sex sex sex sex sex sex
sex sex sex sex sex sex sex sex sex sex sex sex sex sex sex sex sex sex
sex sex sex sex sex sex sex sex sex sex sex sex sex sex sex sex sex sex
sex sex sex sex sex sex sex sex sex sex sex sex sex sex sex sex sex sex
sex sex sex sex sex sex sex sex sex sex sex sex sex sex sex sex sex sex
sex sex sex sex sex sex sex sex sex sex sex sex sex sex sex sex sex sex
sex sex sex sex sex sex sex sex sex sex sex sex sex sex sex sex sex sex
sex sex sex sex sex sex sex sex sex sex sex sex sex sex sex sex sex sex
sex sex sex sex sex sex sex sex sex sex sex sex sex sex sex sex sex sex
sex sex sex sex sex sex sex sex sex sex sex sex sex sex sex sex sex sex
sex sex sex sex sex sex sex sex sex sex sex sex sex sex sex sex sex sex
sex sex sex sex sex sex sex sex sex sex sex sex sex sex sex sex sex sex
sex sex sex sex sex sex sex sex sex sex sex sex sex sex sex sex sex sex
sex sex sex sex sex sex sex sex sex sex sex sex sex sex sex sex sex sex
sex sex sex sex sex sex sex sex sex sex sex sex sex sex sex sex sex sex
sex sex sex sex sex sex sex sex sex sex sex sex sex sex sex sex sex sex
sex sex sex sex sex sex sex sex sex sex sex sex sex sex sex sex sex sex
sex sex sex sex sex sex sex sex sex sex sex sex sex sex sex sex sex sex
sex sex sex sex sex sex sex sex sex sex sex sex sex sex sex sex sex sex
sex sex sex sex sex sex sex sex sex sex sex sex sex sex sex sex sex sex
sex sex sex sex sex sex sex sex sex sex sex sex sex sex sex sex sex sex
sex sex sex sex sex sex sex sex sex sex sex sex sex sex sex sex sex sex
sex sex sex sex sex sex sex sex sex sex sex sex sex sex sex sex sex sex
sex sex sex sex sex sex sex sex sex sex sex sex sex sex sex sex sex sex

sex sex sex sex sex sex sex sex sex sex sex sex sex sex sex sex sex sex
sex sex sex sex sex sex sex sex sex sex sex sex sex sex sex sex sex sex
sex sex sex sex sex sex sex sex sex sex sex sex sex sex sex sex sex sex
sex sex sex sex sex sex sex sex sex sex sex sex sex sex sex sex sex sex
sex sex sex sex sex sex sex sex sex sex sex sex sex sex sex sex sex sex
sex sex sex sex sex sex sex sex sex sex sex sex sex sex sex sex sex sex
sex sex sex sex sex sex sex sex sex sex sex sex sex sex sex sex sex sex
sex sex sex sex sex sex sex sex sex sex sex sex sex sex sex sex sex sex
sex sex sex sex sex sex sex sex sex sex sex sex sex sex sex sex sex sex
sex sex sex sex sex sex sex sex sex sex sex sex sex sex sex sex sex sex
sex sex sex sex sex sex sex sex sex sex sex sex sex sex sex sex sex sex
sex sex sex sex sex sex sex sex sex sex sex sex sex sex sex sex sex sex
sex sex sex sex sex sex sex sex sex sex sex sex sex sex sex sex sex sex
sex sex sex sex sex sex sex sex sex sex sex sex sex sex sex sex sex sex
sex sex sex sex sex sex sex sex sex sex sex sex sex sex sex sex sex sex
sex sex sex sex sex sex sex sex sex sex sex sex sex sex sex sex sex sex
sex sex sex sex sex sex sex sex sex sex sex sex sex sex sex sex sex sex
sex sex sex sex sex sex sex sex sex sex sex sex sex sex sex sex sex sex
sex sex sex sex sex sex sex sex sex sex sex sex sex sex sex sex sex sex
sex sex sex sex sex sex sex sex sex sex sex sex sex sex sex sex sex sex
sex sex sex sex sex sex sex sex sex sex sex sex sex sex sex sex sex sex
sex sex sex sex sex sex sex sex sex sex sex sex sex sex sex sex sex sex
sex sex sex sex sex sex sex sex sex sex sex sex sex sex sex sex sex sex
sex sex sex sex sex sex sex sex sex sex sex sex sex sex sex sex sex sex
sex sex sex sex sex sex sex sex sex sex sex sex sex sex sex sex sex sex
sex sex sex sex sex sex sex sex sex sex sex sex sex sex sex sex sex sex
sex sex sex sex sex sex sex sex sex sex sex sex sex sex sex sex sex sex
sex sex sex sex sex sex sex sex sex sex sex sex sex sex sex sex sex sex
sex sex sex sex sex sex sex sex sex sex sex sex sex sex sex sex sex sex
sex sex sex sex sex sex sex sex sex sex sex sex sex sex sex sex sex sex
sex sex sex sex sex sex sex sex sex sex sex sex sex sex sex sex sex sex
sex sex sex sex sex sex sex sex sex sex sex sex sex sex sex sex sex sex
sex sex sex sex sex sex sex sex sex sex sex sex sex sex sex sex sex sex
sex sex sex sex sex sex sex sex sex sex sex sex sex sex sex sex sex sex
sex sex sex sex sex sex sex sex sex sex sex sex sex sex sex sex sex sex

15.

Campus Controversies Associated
with Mother

She used a series of sex dolls in class, giving a "performative presentation" which also involved flow charts and her pointing with a metal stick. Whilst her intention was to interrogate gender relations as they existed within the sex industry, her critics felt that she was merely embodying certain pornographic forms.

& she published articles on the subject of *bukkake*, which went so far as to praise various "practitioners" of this ritual, finding erotic value in the subject matter and even recommending that readers engage with the practice themselves. This was not thought of as "a proper academic stance" by some.

& her paper "Representations of the Asshole in Western Discourse" was met with disdain by a fellow sexologist who felt that the word "asshole" was a sign of "intense, childish vulgarity" and that in this instance the use of the word "anus" would have been "a more proper use of terminology".

& her research into female orgasmic response involved observing and monitoring couples engaged in acts of sexual intercourse whilst they were within what was known by some as "The Pleasure Zone" on campus, a place that was strictly cordoned off. The main room in which the pleasure took place was lined with padded materials to lessen the instances of noise leaking outwards, but despite this, sounds emerged from this area and could still be heard in the adjacent corridors at times. This was considered "inappropriate" by almost everyone in the institution who encountered it.

& she was accused of flirtation, of talking too openly and candidly about her research and of sexual subjects when present at faculty get togethers in the common room. It was a habit which she possessed when talking both to students and to other members of staff.

& she led a workshop in which students were invited to sit in a circular formation and discuss their vices and fantasies. Certain staff members declared this an "inappropriate occasion" and attempted to put on pressure to ensure that this did not happen on campus again. As usual however, Mother managed to argue in favour of her position in order to retain enough confidence amongst her fellow academics to stay in her role.

& she placed posters with sexualized imagery within un-suspecting university corridors. These posters featured exposed nipples and couples engaged in coital embrace, as well as more mysterious elements such as pieces of jigsaw puzzles and the forms of cartoon geese. She was asked to take them down.

& she wrote extensively about the pleasures of being sexually dominated, going so far as to attempt a complete inventory of methods of sexual domination. Again, some Feminist critics tended to think that she was not supplying women with enough agency in this account, a line of argument that was always par-ticularly annoying to her.

& sometimes when she gave out handouts of academic material she would include little phallic drawings in the corners. These were thought of as "immature" by many. Mother liked to respond to this accusation by saying "These drawings are not immature, they are *decidedly* immature." At other times she would say "Is there no place for humour any longer? Do we truly find the phallus to be an entirely, purely serious matter?"

& then Mother always considered the issue of pornography a very serious matter. She felt a need to discuss it in class. In order to do this she felt the need to play certain clips from pornographic films. She would bring in quotations from Cixous, Bataille, and Lacan. To her, the inclusion of those voices helped to provide these occasions with "legitimacy."

& she would stroll around campus wearing a t-shirt which she had made herself which bore the slogan "I Love Sodomy" written in pink block capitals on a white background. "Can you not contain yourself slightly more?" asked Professor Anthony Winters as he passed her in the corridor. "No," she said.

16.

Gerard Becomes a Guru

He could not help his urges. Eventually Gerard set up his own alternative community in the countryside, a place where he would be the presiding overlord; a "guru" who did not permit that word to be used; an individual who, somewhat dangerously, didn't at first appear to be any sort of guru at all. Gradually he coaxed many people into his orbit. Once there they would experience Gerard's singular, very subtle form of domination, one which of course commenced with his requesting money.

A sense of seclusion from the world was important to him, and so this community was located on a farm, spread-eagled across fifty-three acres of land. Only a very minimal amount of farming took place there however. It somehow seemed necessary to at least grow a few turnips and bunches of asparagus, but that was largely for the sake of appearances. This was no ordinary farm.

Gerard had been careful to position himself in a space which was some distance away from any public transport connection, so that for anyone venturing out to this place, there would be a definite feeling of dispensing with the ordinary world first.

Gerard had wanted to get away from most people, from the city, an instinct he seemed to share with both Barnaby and Ag, who both spent short periods staying on his farm, before realizing that this place was not really for them.

Every day Gerard would round up everyone in the community and marshal them into group activities of one sort or another. There were generally about forty people living on the grounds at any one time, although this did fluctuate a great deal. Gerard would often summon everyone to "Central Hall," a space that looked as if it belonged to a church group. It was a room in which there might be a circle of percussion instruments, or a mass confession of forgotten dreams from childhood, delivered in verbal fragments, with everyone absorbing each other's dreams in a curious kind of collective osmosis. Or sometimes there was also collective nudity.

In general Gerard was most usually the one to invent these activities and to lead everyone through them. Often, if anyone else suggested a game or exercise of their own invention, he would either dismiss it there and then, on the basis of any fabricated reason that entered into his head, or he would find any sort of excuse to put off doing that activity, in favor of something that had originated within his own mind. He barely even realized that he was doing this and that to some it might be considered offensive. Of course this behavior resulted in his making some enemies and in certain people deserting his vicinity.

There would often be a certain tension at the farm's weekly group assemblies where collective issues were discussed, with particular individuals invariably making complaints or starting arguments of one kind or another. This would often lead to debates involving everyone present and the gradual building of long-term resentments. There were always, seemingly, issues that required debate, whether it was what colour the fence next to the main road should be painted, or whether they should grant a follower of Aleister Crowley permission to join the community.

Gerard would always be several steps ahead of everyone else in terms of inventing absurd exercises for everyone to do, each of them less likely than the last one. These were games in which often no one else could really compete, because, truly, only he actually understood the rules of the enterprise. On one occasion he instructed everyone present to make nonsensical, non-linguistic noises. These could be of any quality. The only rule he imposed was that no one should imitate what any of their neighbours was doing, as he wished to hear a chorus of differing illogical sounds, all of them jostling for attention and knocking against each other in a discordance that Gerard found pleasing.

He then asked everyone to repeat the exercise, except this time he instructed them to sprinkle various "verbal improvisations" into their actions. These were, however, to be strictly limited to a single word per person. He stipulated that this one word: "Should be declared with great, soulful intention".

"It should be a word you truly Love," he went on excitably, "for whatever foolish reason, you should truly Love it, though it doesn't really matter what that reason is exactly . . . but do say it as if you really mean it . . . please, that's all I shall ask of you for now . . ."

So then, as requested, within moments Central Hall was flooded with noises which resembled growling, buzzing, burbling, murmuring, screeching, and yawning, a tremendous cacophony which was then also punctuated by persons declaring words into the air at odd intervals, often with their arms raised high above them, although this had never been declared an official part of the exercise. At other times they would lie supine upon the ground. You might catch hold of a rendition of "Aeroplane!" or "Luminous!" or "Scribbling!" and many other such randomly uttered single word sentiments which hung in the air, by turns revealing and incongruous, hopeful and defiant. Here and there the odd lone individual had broken down into a fit of joyful laughter and was rolling about on the floor, unable to control themselves.

Of course Gerard was the demonic controller of all energies present and so naturally it fell to him to bring these voices to a halt. He did so by wandering around the room, taking disjointed, looping routes with his feet, whilst tinkling a triangle repeatedly, a musical sign announcing "Stop," which he had prepared everyone for in that day's version of an inspirational speech. It was a sign many people ignored, being so lost within the act of exploring the energies unlocked by this activity that they had seemingly become incapable of either logic or constraint. It took about half an hour to wind proceedings back down to silence, or at least something close to it.

Occasionally, during one or another of these many group exercises, Gerard liked to wave around a conductor's baton, deliberately making a sort of mockery of himself as he did so, his face breaking into imitations of what he saw as the foolish facial posturing of both orchestra musicians and conductors as they very passionately engaged with their music. Flapping his arms wildly like a demented bird about to take flight, Gerard would circle the room restlessly, stand up on a chair if it felt necessary, grab people spontaneously, or even stick out his tongue in jubilation.

Gerard might wake up on a certain morning and spontaneously decide that this particular day ought to be dedicated to stillness. Once, taken up with exploring this quality, after the morning meeting, he urged everyone to fix a pose and retain it for an unspecified duration of time.

"I'm not going to tell you how long you will be still for . . . it won't be forever, but it might well be for quite a long period of time . . . anyone who isn't interested in participating should please vacate the hall now . . . we're going to explore the boundaries of stillness, see what that state might contain for us to learn from today . . . I don't know exactly what we might discover . . . but let us find out . . ."

Many of those involved in this particular exercise became intensely frustrated by the claustrophobic lack of movement that was taking place within their spatial imprisonment. Meanwhile others had experiences which they would later describe in hushed tones as "almost mystical".

Gerard spent some months trying to achieve mastery of the art of hypnosis. He liked to hypnotize as many people as possible simultaneously and get them to assume absurd postures and perform unlikely tasks, such as cleaning an antique clock with a toothbrush, or pushing a parsnip for half a mile using only the force of a nose. People would wander around the farm making 1950s dance routines, complete with complicated hand gestures, or they would become involved in having extended one-way dialogues with horses. On these occasions more than on any other the farm resembled an asylum.

At one meeting Gerard demanded that certain people endure sleep deprivation and then report back to the community about their experiences. He used a walking stick to point at his victims and indicate that they had been selected. Most of the experiences were, unsurprisingly, negative ones, but as ever, a few spoke in glowing terms about how their sense of reality had been altered, or that they were grateful for the opportunity to experience this "thickened" reality, which was "stronger, with broader dimensions."

Another morning, those within the community woke up to discover that Gerard had arranged the chairs in Central Hall into a circle and in the center of it, on the floor, was a single shoe, looking lost and forlorn. Once everyone had sidled into the hall, Gerard calmed the hubbub by standing and gesturing with his hands, as if he were softly pressing the air downwards. Having attained the desired silence after some minutes he finally spoke, in his deep bass voice, representing either a mock-solemnity or perhaps an actual solemnity, by this time no one felt enormously sure about the difference.

"A shoe," said Gerard, halting his words there for emphasis. "What will you do with it?"

A few seconds passed in a confused inertia, as everyone stared at the shoe feeling slightly puzzled by this unprecedented situation. After some minutes of inaction, a woman named Karen strode forward, picked up the shoe and walked out of the room. Everyone then followed her outside and watched intently, expecting some kind of "performance action," but in fact she merely walked off into the distance and was not to be seen for many days.

17.

Further Incidents Proliferate

Rebecca made this into a circular embroidered patch which was sewn to the left arm of a green coat which she wore in winter everyday for a number of years:

+++

Q. Were the Crickholme children affected by their upbringing when they were adults?

A. Yes.

Q. Which activity did Rebecca feel could cause widespread redemption when she was older?

A. Singing.

Q. Where did Gerard come to believe was the most significant location in the U.K.?

A. Blackpool.

Gerard decided to spend a day creating a series of rapidly drawn free associative pencil sketches. The only constraint he set himself was that each drawing had to be entirely different in subject than all of the others. This led to:

1. an otter swimming in a river

2. a grand hallway containing a crystal chandelier

3. a field of maize viewed from a hilltop and swaying in wind

4. a cat traipsing across the roof of a hut

5. a cloudy, glowering sky above a multitude of suburban rooftops

6. a banjo player possessing a bushy moustache

7. the exterior of a tram moving through a street in Istanbul

8. an old woman holding a nasturtium

+++

As it happens, Lucinda had never eaten chocolate. She had also never wanted to eat it. Indeed she was destined to never do so.

As it happens, Flo was the author of hundreds of sentences about a small wooden elephant.

As it happens, after years of always loathing television pro-grammes, Gerard suddenly began watching the news everyday.

As it happens, Ag possessed an ambition to eat her placenta after giving birth. And eventually she actually did.

Manic wandering through unknown scattered towns . . . .
. . . . Barnaby
wondering if these restless movements could honestly be in any
way heroic . . . . drunken hollering into
rusted car graveyards . . . . alone on a Friday night dancefloor breaking into hysterical jolts and limb motions until everyone surrounding backed away . . . . during street
wanderings exalted elations of glimpsing an antique accordion
illuminated by pale-blue electric light inside the frame of a shop
window at night . . . . spying pools of milky
light lying within the expanses of empty fields stretching outwards beyond the motorways cloaked in darkness . . . .

++

Eliza began to dream of an unknown country almost every night

translucent mounds of jelly

This photograph, which was taken in Adelaide, Australia in 1947, came to possess a sort of strange talismanic significance for Flo. These mysterious heads, even with their blank features, seemed to her to possess an eerie feeling of presence. They looked to her like a row of different potential new selves to appropriate, to try out or to become.

++

The night at a party where Billy began crawling around the room on his hands and knees, producing yelping and growling and falsetto sounds, shifting from one location to another without warning, then pouring a jug of single cream over his head, before defacing his hosts' walls with the creation of as many squiggly moustaches as he could manage, using a black marker pen which he often kept lodged within his y-fronts specifically for moments such as this one, before being ejected from the premises.

And everyone continued on their different paths chasing their different fulfilments and

No one ever really doubted the essential efficacy of their many separate approaches to this

Mother never ceased to shower all of us with affections on most occasions that she could do

Largely it was a happy story for most of us but then not always every single day of course

++

This map found its way into Ag's miscellaneous collection of papers after she visited Peshawar, Pakistan during the summer of 1989. Looking at it again evoked certain faces, streets, buildings. She often remembered one particular conversation she had engaged in with a young philosophy student. They had spoken for a long time about telepathy.

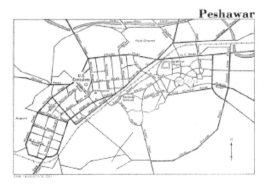

Rising one morning, Flo thought: What shall I do today?

pretend she was a fantasist with a set of obsessions that she did not in fact possess/commence extensive and unprecedented acts of pickling at home/pay for a hotel room in the West End and lie in bed watching television for hours/walk across each of the bridges crossing The Thames in Central London slowly and carefully/immediately locate books holding reproductions of Flemish Baroque paintings/gaze with longing at motorcycles in showroom windows/consider the possibilities which might arise from an engagement with parachuting/buy a box which can be locked with a key and then place an object inside and leave it on a pavement/spend all day permitting herself to be indecisive/find a multitude of small hiding places around the city

???

++

Rebecca once stood on a streetcorner in Hampstead repeatedly delivering the following oration through a loudhailer:

I WOULD LIKE YOU ALL TO KNOW

THAT I AM AGAINST

HETERONORMATIVE CONFORMITY

AND ALL OF THE GLANCES

THROWN AT ME

BY PREDATORY MALES

OF THE SPECIES

Barnaby found the following text in a free publication named "Guide to Cork and Kerry Visitor Services- 1991" and he decided to cut it out and place it in his notebook:

"BALLYDEHOB
Population: 238. A gaily painted village street climbing the hillside, the home of several craft centres. A graceful twelve-arch railway bridge crosses the estuary of Ballydehob, a relic of the former railway and from which there are panoramic views of Roaring Water Bay. Above Ballydehob is Mount Gabriel (288.3m.) with an aircraft tracking station on its summit. On its slopes are the small workings of Bronze Age miners, untouched since those ancient miners finished their operations. Some local attractions: angling (shore and game); Cush Strand (3Km./two miles); Ballydehob Agricultural Show and Festival: mid-August."

++

Gerard once read out the following text of nonsense language to the members of his community. The few times when he came to words and phrases which were recognizably part of the English language, he would pause with a little solemnity both before and after uttering them: "garramon aileekee ips savaloo gara buhlubbalubb kakaboo sinda parl zanrezka poon ip kolo im eht gurtladevcha oa mii emsa karlumnitze ip muloopister vakaapo yooae wid gerdonskow oa pazzingo **egg sandwich** drewbie ip puzzagogblem emsa zod quarakkaplods ssuss ip mang gallaparnung suyvijienna oa spow brichelsea var gavver **Scunthorpe** poblodd minnavatchkerow oa gabberdoccus zillaprott vullarr spoeee ip guhdubblo barrashanks lallee splongburm gozzizoccer **mountaineering** gavvalaabo durnplubb fiss qoon fizzatara bubnashkee spizzle oa yangotplod pazzingo jov evvoltupp kobbroniss ip oolaax yomquo gewmak piipii gahzudd marsgott muloopister ip boquerrin **Speedy Gonzalez** soomalo wubba gilpashlo dabbaful garang zhanti sploowbo"

Eliza became highly taken with this image, which was an advertisement for a gymnasium in Philadelphia created in 1831. She enjoyed the masculine brawn and physicality, as well as the feeling of mirth it contained.

+++

Things which Lucinda tended to hide about the place:

(emotions)

(Thai curry recipes)

(nine spare sets of keys)

(an extensive collection of protractors)

(amiability)

(a worn out childhood toy rabbit named Angelica)

(vicarious gestures)

(many pairs of black gloves)

(occasions of being receptive)

18.

A Weekend of Reunion

We seemed to hardly notice it happening, but suddenly it had become a number of years since all of the siblings had assembled together in the same place. This set of circumstances drove Mother to organize our first ever family reunion. For some reason, one that was only known to her, she decided that it would be a good idea for this occasion to be held in a house located in a remote part of the Highlands of Scotland. It also happened in the middle of winter, as that proved to be the only time when all of us could easily gather together. In retrospect these placements within time and space seem fateful, as it was to prove a cold, claustrophobic, miserable weekend during which hitherto reasonably concealed feelings of loathing revealed themselves entirely, in the forms of awful, incendiary arguments.

When we first arrived it seemed like a perfectly promising location for us to be in. Some of the typical symbols of the country were used as décor in the house we had rented. There were framed examples of tartans, photographs of stags captured on hilltops, dried thistles had been placed inside jugs and vases, there was even a selection of books about Scotland, including an anthology of Scottish myths, which I dipped into a little. All of this seemed very appealing to me. In the living room there was an enormous fireplace which we soon set ablaze and we all sat around drinking a concoction which Rebecca had suggested: warm cups of blackcurrant cordial. On the first evening of our stay, on Friday, it felt quite good to see everyone again. It was only after lunch on Saturday that the troubles began.

"Well you never really attended to us very much when we were growing did you!" said Lucinda in a highly belligerent way.

"I think that's unfair! I don't think that's really true," countered Mother.

"You were always busier with your academic work, you would just leave us to ourselves . . ."

"And frankly what kind of education did we receive from you?" asked Gerard. "I think in fact you denied us an education . . ."

"Oh children, please, please . . . ," said Mother, not knowing quite how to react to all of this.

"Yeah, you were shit," said Billy, which turned out to be his only contribution to the entire conversation.

"Thanks Billy, thank you for that," said Mother in a tone of heavy sarcasm.

"You really had no barriers, no restraints, very little moral sense of how to turn us into adults," continued Lucinda.

"I think I have a very considered and developed attitude towards morality . . ." said Mother.

"Well, perhaps you do, but maybe most of that went into your academic work rather than into bringing us up," said Lucinda.

"Lucinda, honestly, I don't believe that there *is* a correct way to take children into adulthood, I think that's really a myth . . ." said Mother, sounding quite high-minded.

"How about slow psychological torture? Is that a suitable method for bringing up children?" asked Lucinda.

"Oh come on, you really don't need to be so ridiculous . . ." said Mother.

"Well that's how it felt to me. Would you like to deny that it felt like that to me? Is my feeling that way just not what you want to hear?" said Lucinda, her anger increasing in strength even more. At this point her face had really become frenetic and red from shouting. It was a genuinely unpleasant and discomforting sight.

"Lucinda, I think your attack is already enough," said Flo. "Perhaps you could quiet down and start being reasonable now? How much more of this do we have to hear?"

"Plenty more," said Lucinda. "When you have a mother who is an inherently unreasonable person, it's not always easy to just keep quiet about that fact all of the time," said Lucinda.

"Look, come on girl," started Rebecca, "we're all extraordinarily fortunate to have this woman as our mother. And you aren't her only child here, to say the least!" With this, Rebecca moved over to Mother and embraced her, rubbing her arms affectionately.

"Yeah, Lou, really, you should be praising this woman . . . I mean, you only exist at all because of her right?" said Ag.

"Oh, it's so wonderful to be in a world like this one, isn't it!" snapped Lucinda. "I'm just so intensely grateful to be yet another product of one of her fucks!" she proclaimed loudly, which elicited some gasping. She then pointed a finger at Mother with a violence that looked as if it might launch into actual jabbing.

"Well, Lucinda, my darling," Mother started, taking a genuinely heartfelt tone, "I'm sorry that you feel so upset about everything sweetheart . . . One thing I will say is that '"fucks"' are what create children usually. And there's really no need to be dismissing them."

"The thing is, Mother, did you really need to have *ten children* in this day and age, wasn't two or three enough for you? It's not as if we were living in a Victorian slum . . . contraception was readily available to you . . ." said Lucinda.

"Well you're all here now," said Mother. "I mean, what's done is done. I certainly can't magic you all back to a pre-natal state can I? There's no going back to non-being at this point . . . And I have tried to give all of you as much Love and Attention as I possibly could do. I really did. And I suppose that now you've all just got to try and make the most of what you all have . . ."

"I am terribly sorry to dwell on this," said Lucinda, not in fact sounding sorry at all, "but really *ten children* . . . and from so many different fathers, it's not as if that might cause confusions or anything like that . . . I mean, really, what were you thinking?"

"Well, darling, it was always just a case of following my instincts, of following what felt like the right course of action . . . and the fact is I very sincerely Love you all, and I very deeply wanted to bring all of you into this strange and beautiful world . . ."

"Yes, what a beautiful world! Just look out of the window, what a beautiful world it is!" was Lucinda's response.

She was referring to the fact that outside it was raining on a relentlessly bleak moorland landscape that seemed utterly infused with grey. At this moment I really had to wonder why we had all come to Scotland of all places, for this peculiar affirmation of our family ties.

"You really are good at moaning Lucinda, you know that?" said Eliza. "I mean honestly, we've been given everything that any human being could reasonably expect and I think frankly you could perhaps try and be a little more grateful for that . . ."

"Also, Lucinda," began Barnaby, "I think you should realize that you're very much speaking from your own perspective here, that you really aren't representing all of us with these thoughts . . ."

"I never thought I was speaking for anyone other than myself," declared Lucinda.

"Well the tone you've taken makes it sound like you're attempting to speak for everyone and I really don't think that you're doing that at all," said Barnaby.

"Lucinda," started Flo, "I'm just interested, honestly, why do you feel such a need to be an asshole? Seriously . . . We've all been very fortunate to be a part of this family, to grow up in such an incredibly open and imaginative environment, in such a large, beautiful house and with such an extraordinary and singular woman as our mother." This made Mother start to well up with tears a little, "so I really think you're being quite indulgent here today, really extremely fucking unpleasant . . ." finished Flo, leaving the entire room even more engulfed with feelings of grief and confusion.

"Here, Here, Flo!" said Ag.

Mother continued crying, with Rebecca remaining by her side to try and comfort her. It was really quite rare to see her in such a fragile state and quite unsettling.

There was silence for a few long moments and then finally Mother felt the need to speak again: "I've always just tried to do the best for you all . . ." she said, the tears continuing to emerge, making her words sound a little indistinct and inchoate, "I'm sorry if it wasn't what you wanted Lucinda . . . I'm sorry . . . I just did what I thought was best, or what I thought I had to do . . . I'm sorry . . ." she said, repeating this final refrain a number of times until the words had become an unclear mumble and it was no longer exactly certain what she was being sorry for.

After this, there was a great deal of crying and embracing still to be done. Lucinda did calm down and apologise. Much of the remainder of the weekend was spent in states of shock, there was much quietness and silence. Some of us spent Sunday wandering through the wet, craggy landscapes of the outside world, before finally returning to the house exhausted and despondent. I don't think anyone enjoyed the weekend very much. We were not destined to meet for similar occasions very often in the future.

19.

Boxes Discovered Whilst Searching in the Attic

FIRST BOX

Contains a selection of documents related to the village of Barles in south-eastern France, a tiny cluster of buildings in the Alpes-de-Haute-Provence region possessing a population of 154. At one time Flo had wanted to make an art project about the place and had begun to collect a variety of materials including maps, copies of old birth records and tourist brochures detailing walking tours around the local area. This was a place which the family had once passed through during a holiday. Everyone had sat down for an hour and a half for lunch in a restaurant. Nothing very noteworthy had occurred during that encounter, but nevertheless Flo had enjoyed the food which had been served so much that she never ceased thinking back to the experience. She did not know what the project might "achieve," but she kept on with it anyway, until her interest had entirely dwindled and become merely what was left in this box.

SECOND BOX
Mother's wig collection, acquired over many years and involving
most of the prominent natural shades of hair, a variety of different lengths and styles, as well as red, green, blue, and silver wigs.
The majority of these had hardly ever been worn, and a number
of them were completely untouched. Occasionally Rebecca liked
to go up to the attic and sift through them, trying them on and
glancing at herself in the mirror, often whilst pouting.

THIRD BOX
Many sheaves of photographs. In some cases large bundles of
these were grouped together with string or rubber bands. These
were all images from Mother's life in the 1970s. For the most
part they were of fairly banal scenes of the kind which could be
seen in many different attics all over the country. Posed portraits
of family and friends, holiday snapshots, on the whole very little
which was at all surprising or unexpected, with the exception of
one photograph of a man possessing a large and almost unwieldy
beard, who was sat in front of a microphone and delivering a
mysterious oration.

FOURTH BOX
Objects which were all related to Mother's time as a man. A
Subbuteo set. Various examples of fake moustaches. Silk ties.
Polka dot handkerchiefs designed to be worn inside various breast
pockets. A silver hip flask. Cans of lager, flattened and mounted
on to card. A pale blue cotton shirt. A mahogany pipe. A straw
hat possessing a red band. A programme detailing events at a
gentleman's social club on the Isle of Man. A number of pairs of
black socks.

FIFTH BOX
A box containing only obscure old books that nobody in the
house wanted to read:

Flames by June Oldham
Nancy Cunard by Anne Chisholm
The Hour of the Women by Christian von Krockow
Scotland: A Concise History by Fitzroy Maclean
People with Long Ears by Robin Borwick
After the Ball:- Pop Music from Rag to Rock by Ian Whitcomb
Buttons: A Collector's Guide by Victor Houart
The Art of Benin by Paula Ben-Amos
The Serpent and the Nightingale by Cecil Parrott
Two Sisters for Social Justice by Lela B. Costin
The Lady or the Tiger? by Raymond Smullyan
Liberation! by Nick Machon

SIXTH BOX
A box consisting exclusively of letters written to or by Mother. In her hand the alphabet becomes small, angular, and spiky. Mostly these were letters from lovers (she kept her more intellectual correspondence in her study). These romantic letters could get surprisingly sentimental. At times she wrote about clouds and birdsong. She also wrote to her lovers about their caresses, as well as their genitals, muscles, and buttocks. More than once she described how she would like to have sex with them in "ideal circumstances." Reading through these letters could be quite painful and disturbing.

SEVENTH BOX
An entirely miscellaneous collection of materials. In this instance: a colour photograph of a 1950s U.S. housewife posing with various examples of Tupperware spread out on a kitchen table before her. A book about forestry management published in 1979. A leaflet giving information about a cave museum in Argentina. A reproduction of one of the original film posters for the serial *Les Vampires* (1915), directed by Louis Feuillade. A timeline detailing the most important life events of Harry Truman, 33rd president of

the U.S.A., with events commencing in 1884 (birth) and ending in 1972 (death).

EIGHTH BOX

A collection of VHS tapes from the 1980s, all of them holding copies of pornographic films. Mother had acquired them ostensibly for academic purposes, but later we came to suspect that they were also for her own sexual entertainment. She left them in the attic underneath a dusty cotton sheet, either hidden or forgotten, no one was ever entirely certain. Quite a few members of the household were given to sneaking up into the attic in order to borrow one of these tapes. The Elder Set always claimed that they were above and beyond such things, but we all wondered about that.

NINTH BOX

A box of objects related to elephants. A small pink plastic elephant cocktail straw. Various children's books with narratives containing a strong emphasis on elephants. An elephant-shaped jelly mould. A t-shirt bearing the image of a smiling elephant. An example of soap packaging involving a red elephant. An ivory box. A copy of the book *Sacred Elephant* by Heathcote Williams (1989). A photograph of Elephant and Castle shopping centre in South London.

TENTH BOX

A box containing nothing other than a single sheet of paper headed "General Proverbs":

Diligence is the mother of good luck.

Experience is the mistress of fools.

Go to bed with the lamb, and rise with the lark.

He was a bold man that first ate an oyster.

If you run after two hares, you will catch neither.

Keep a thing seven years and you will find a use for it.

Mighty oaks from little acorns grow.
Never is a long day.
Speak well of your friend, of your enemy say nothing.
Virtue is its own reward.
Zeal without knowledge is fire without light.

ELEVENTH BOX
A further box was filled with audio tapes that held recordings of interviews which Mother had conducted during the course of her sexological research. Each possessed a handwritten label detailing the name of the interviewee with the date of the conversation. I tried listening to some of these once and discovered that they were useful for their soporific effects. I fell asleep for some hours right there in the attic. The occasional words would make me stir in my sleep slightly. Words like "ejaculation," "clitoris," or "penis". Once or twice I woke up with a start when these words were mentioned.

TWELFTH BOX
A miscellany of maps. Many Ordnance Survey editions. Various older antiquarian representations of Norfolk, Sussex, Lincolnshire. A map of the entire British Isles from 1903. An A to Z of London with black and white pages published in 1975. A contemporary map of Hampstead Heath printed by a local walking society. A sepia-coloured map of Mull, one of the Inner Hebrides, dating from 1751. A map of the London Underground from 2007. To these Rebecca had added her own hand drawn map of the house, leaving it secretly in this box for someone to find one day and be surprised by.

20.

Shipwrecks

For a period in her late twenties Eliza became a professional diver, one who specialized in the salvaging of shipwrecks. This took her to a number of different locations around the world, although in her memory they became strangely indistinguishable from each other, as this all took place on anonymous, vast stretches of sea possessing no specific cultural identity.

The first wreck she salvaged was that of the *Mary Walcott*, a British ship which had been sunk by a German U-Boat in 1943. It had been crossing the Arabian Sea en route to Ras Tanurah in Saudi Arabia, carrying a cargo largely composed of trucks, cranes, and steel pipes. There had also allegedly been close to 1,000 tonnes of gold bullion on board as well, the promise of which had given rise to this particular diving operation.

The *Mary Walcott* had been a large vessel, weighing in at 7,293 tonnes and stretching out for 421 feet. Salvaging it therefore involved a heavy work schedule of many months that saw Eliza completing dives from seven in the morning, until about six thirty in the evening, just before sunset. Eventually experts were brought in with their own specially designed machinery, a "grab" fitted with computer-controlled thrusters and cameras, which was used in conjunction with explosives. These efforts succeeded in gaining entry to the no. 2 hold, where the bullion was supposedly stowed away. After many weeks of clearing away wreckage and overburden and repeatedly letting off carefully controlled explosions, access to the hold was reached and no gold bullion was discovered there.

This was also Eliza's first experience of a typical aspect of these expeditions: the fact that she was the only woman involved. Indeed, many of the sea captains who specialized in this kind of work refused to accept any female crew members at all, feeling that this would "tip the balance," causing a lack of concentration. She was nevertheless determined to run counter to this policy. Although she had no desire to actually *be* a man, she nevertheless enjoyed the experience of being in exclusively male company, partly because she knew that she held some power over the sexual imaginations of virtually *all* of her fellow crew members. On this first expedition she inaugurated her habit of finding one crew member to have a love affair with on each salvaging trip. As would always be the case, she was careful to establish the trust of the captain first, to lessen the possibility of being sent back to land.

It was to prove a life of intense, temporary existences played out in a series of cabins and hotel rooms. A life in which she could expect a phone call at any time to lead to another flight to any destination on the planet. She got used to living entirely on the contents of her backpack, which would often sprawl across the floor of whatever was currently her room. She found that this life of flux suited her very well and that she possessed no desire for it to come to an end. She enjoyed the male camaraderie of drinking and playing card games or chess every evening. This was, strangely enough, a world that she felt perfectly at home in.

Encountering a shipwreck for the first time was always thrilling to her. She saw each one as a submerged mausoleum, a world that had fallen into ruin, a portable location from the land which had somehow become accidently transplanted to the bottom of the sea. Each of them had its own atmosphere, its own physical form, always possessing certain individual attributes that were unique to it. She liked getting to know each portion of a wreck, each room and area. She particularly enjoyed finding small incidental objects which lay strewn about the wreckage and that would now potentially discover some sort of new life after being taken once more to the surface.

On the other hand she sometimes thought of the wrecks as places that were scary due to their absolute removal from civilization, places in which human error had caused an alien realm to house the remnants of a fragile human colony, locations defined by their primordial nature. For Eliza it was almost akin to space travel, she felt it was the closest which you could get to that sensation without actually leaving the planet.

The *Lon Kee* was a Chinese ship which had run into difficulties in the South China Sea en route to Amsterdam in 1763. It had been a passenger ship with an estimated 600 people on board hoping to find a new life when they reached Europe. In addition to this, it was a vessel carrying an enormous cargo of porcelain for the European market. Eliza was part of the team which spent many months retrieving these objects, a haul which included many plates, bowls, jars, and vases. These were to be found amidst much other detritus. Eliza felt that there was real poetry lying within many of these objects and within the broken expanses of the ship there could sometimes be found magical entities such as parasol handles, tiny figurines, and bells.

At this particular wreck she found herself repeatedly imagining the disaster that had befallen the ship and its denizens. It was here that she encountered her first skeletons and their appearance caused her to succumb to an episode of fear that seized her entire body, although she was very careful to hide this fact from the rest of the crew. After encountering the forms of the skeletons again and again she would imagine the 18th century screams which must have once torn into the air here; she saw the water flooding into the boat as if in a nightmare; she saw animate bodies transmogrified into corpses by drowning. Eventually she managed to get these thoughts under control and could keep herself calm, but at first this took some effort to achieve.

When she returned to shore from any of these expeditions there was always a sense of deflation. This was made more curious by the fact that she often spent months longing to go back to shore. However, once this wish had had been granted she realized that in fact she was more at home when living out at sea. On shore she could not find her purpose somehow. Most of her actions quickly began to feel idle and worthless. She would sometimes find herself lying in bed all day long, not managing to sleep or even really to rest.

All of the objects found on the *Lon Kee* needed to be cleaned and prepared for auction. Once the diving was completed Eliza took to helping with this arduous process of washing, scrubbing and sorting. Many months later, when the auction finally took place at Sotheby's, in London, the cargo received far more money than was expected of it and, as per contract, Eliza received a handsome share of 3% of this. At the auction many of the items which she had personally brought to the surface sold for thousands of pounds each.

As with virtually any work she found that the routine it involved eventually led to boredom. The first days of encountering wrecks were always the best ones, but with some inevitability this quickly gave way to the tediums of routine. It was extremely tiring, physically demanding work, but she nevertheless found a certain enjoyment within the feeling of exhaustion at the end of each day. She often felt that she had perhaps accomplished something in that way.

No one took many possessions on these expeditions. It was a minimal existence, and she always found that she enjoyed that aspect of the work, feeling as if life itself had been stripped away, leaving only a husk. It was something of a relief from the burdens of a more clearly earthly existence.

Eventually she decided that, on the whole, she actually preferred the company of fish and marine creatures to that of human beings, although whilst she was diving she would sometimes miss the possibility of conversation.

21.

Barnaby's Longest Summer

One year Barnaby decided that he would attempt to have as much fun as was possible during the summer months. He really would go out of his way to keep himself entertained. He felt that it would be necessary for him to change activities on a daily basis. With fervour, he wrote voluminous lists of things he might do and then he began.

First he got a tattoo done, one which could match Billy's, who he felt a little jealous of in this respect. He had been daring himself to do this for years, but now, finally, he did it. It was a tattoo of a levitating horse, its face consumed with mysticism and some inexplicable form of ecstasy. The horse was rising towards the sun and seemed a little overawed by the prospect. It was a sun that possessed very bright, attractive yellow rays which were emanating in powerful looking bolts that surged across Barnaby's left arm.

The next day he phoned up a number of "Children's Entertainers" who he found in the telephone directory. He requested that one of them teach him how to make balloon animals. He felt that this would be a good investment for the future, as he would then always be able to impress people with the spontaneous creation of balloon creatures. That day he learnt how to make dogs, cows, and giraffes.

The following day saw him hanging out with a nudist society, which met in Streatham. They liked to play boardgames and have long conversations about being nudists. The whole enterprise struck him as being dreary and dispiriting.

On Sunday he went to Speaker's Corner and spoke exclusively, all day long, about the subject of slime. People kept asking him why he was talking about that subject, so he spent much of the day giving reasons for the choice of slime as his topic. Among the reasons he gave were: "It's an irreverent subject," "It isn't a political subject," and "It's perhaps the best substance in the world".

On Monday he smoked some hashish and went to the aquarium. He felt that the drug helped him to connect with the ebb and flow of the aquatic world, a world that he found himself wishing he was part of due to its beauty, its many diverse forms, and its pulsating otherness. He felt some moderate envy for Eliza with her diving expeditions. Explaining all of this to himself he said: "Fish and crustaceans get to live in a world of infinite poetry! It's not fair!". He spent a number of hours transfixed by the movements of seahorses.

The following day he dressed up as a woman, with Mother and Rebecca helping him prepare, particularly with make-up. He wore a svelte green dress, a necklace of bulbous orange beads and a broach crafted from silver and amber. He felt that he looked quite the lady. One surprising aspect of his dressing in drag was the way that women looked at him. They were genuinely fascinated. Often he was sure that their gaze even held a desirous element which he hadn't expected at all. Although he didn't talk with any of these women, some of their glances were destined to stay with him as memories.

He decided to ritualistically destroy one of his possessions and first spent some hours musing over which one it should be and why. Finally he settled on a birthday present that he had been given when he was nine years old, a book of Celtic myths and legends which he had always found tedious and which he could not see a purpose for in his life, at least as it was then constituted. He burnt it on a bonfire in the garden and thought about the loss of time.

After this, he then completed a painting purely for the purpose of leaving as many "secret messages" as he could within its frame. He gave in to no aesthetic considerations whatsoever. Indeed, he admitted that technically it was a somewhat sloppy effort, although he could hide behind certain Modernist tendencies as an excuse for his lack of precision. In the end he counted twenty-nine separate messages which he had left surreptitiously lingering within the work and which would doubtless be of interest to practically no one whatsoever. He scrawled a note on to the back of the canvas explaining all of this just in case someone found it one day, although he was careful to not say what any of the messages actually were. He wanted whoever found the painting to at least be aware of the scale of his efforts.

Dressing head to foot in white, he painted his face a similar shade, adorned a pair of white plimsolls and took to performing mime in various locations around the city. Sometimes people would attempt to hand him coins for his efforts, but he always refused them. In this state he found that he best liked pressing his hands against imaginary walls, thus creating invisible structures, entities he found troublesome, seemingly needing to scale them, or break them down, or overcome them in some way.

He went to the pub and challenged everyone that he found there to bouts of arm wrestling. These were competitions that he generally lost, but occasionally, with great effort, he could either become a victor or at least force a draw. After a few fights, Andy, a large man in his early sixties, took on the role of referee, a social position which he seemed to consider in very serious terms, and which provided him with more entertainment than he had come across in this pub for a number of years.

The next day Barnaby spent twelve hours sitting on a single bench, a length of time which he had determined before he began, preparing himself earlier in the day by eating a substantial spread of food and performing an extensive range of warm up stretches. Very little that was revelatory occurred to him during this exercise, but he hadn't expected anything to, so that was fine. It was a bench placed outside of a shop that sold plastic sporting trophies.

As a contrast he then went to an army recruitment centre and pretended that he wished to join the British military. He tried to do this as earnestly and realistically as he could manage, discussing the different requirements there might be of him, the length of training, the starting salary he could expect to receive. He stated that he was interested in trying to progress to officer status as rapidly as possible. Despite his efforts, no one in the recruitment centre could really believe that he was for real. Indeed, he wasn't.

Next he filmed the pilot episode for a cable TV show in which he could be seen interviewing friends who were all pretending, with a deliberate lack of skill, to be a series of celebrity guests. A section of the show was called "Barnaby's Glamour Tips," a title which he had written in large letters on a yellow sheet of A2 paper with a purple felt tip pen. He advised that his viewers should "Wear gold whenever possible" and that "Fake tans at least show you're making some sort of effort".

The next morning he took a hot air balloon ride from Muswell Hill to Edgware. He had wanted to see if it was possible to phone someone up in the morning and make such a journey by the end of that day. He was pleased to find that it could be done.

He took to meticulously planning the details of a book which he knew he would never write: his autobiography. He was seriously considering the form in which he would write this despite his only being twenty-six. In fact he was considering writing it *because* he was only twenty-six. That was what made it of some interest, as it then seemed more like an impossible exercise and therefore a challenge. He planned all of the chapters and wrote out notes about what each of them would contain. It was to be a rebellious work in which much was invented and little could be entirely trusted.

The next day he approached a variety of strangers and asked them if they would consent to his whispering a single sentence into one of their ears. He promised them that this sentence would involve "something lovely" and "absolutely nothing you wouldn't want to hear". Despite this, most people felt that they would prefer to decline this curious request, feeling oddly fearful, even if they could see that Barnaby seemed to possess a cheerful demeanour. Into different ears he whispered:

"acrobats"

and later

"silence at dawn, in the garden"

and then

"a room of silver objects"

and

"the softness of clouds"

The looks which he received as a consequence of this were very often confused ones.

For his final day of kicks, at the end of August, Barnaby phoned up a number of friends and staged a "Happening" inside the shop of a petrol station in Bethnal Green. It lasted for a total of precisely three minutes. During this time ten performers each focused on the completion of a single action. Without warning, the staff were suddenly subject to a room full of people in which someone was sprinkling silver confetti everywhere, whilst simul-taneously a paper orchid unfurled from the insides of a human mouth, a woman started searching through the radio waves on a portable cassette player, whilst someone else wandered through the aisles holding a watercolour landscape of the south of France which had been purchased in a charity shop. Meanwhile Barnaby himself was waving the flag of Andorra above his head and being very vocal in singing that country's praises, whilst a couple of his friends in Edwardian military uniforms engaged in a very serious duel "to the end" with a pair of baguettes. Flo, all dressed in silver, made a series of mysterious movements with her arms, whilst Gerard busied himself by emitting noise with various thumb pianos, until finally everyone ceased and departed as rapidly as they had arrived.

22.

Billy Loses It

After drinking from his bottle of whisky he began scrawling words across his arms and face, then going so far as to take his shoes and socks off and continue his writings across his somewhat unpleasant, harsh-smelling bare feet, just in order that he might possess some other surface to continue his work on. During this process inspiration would often stretch no further than a single word, although these would often be finished off with an exclamation mark . . . he wrote on his chest: "Superstar!" and then again on his thigh: "Superstar!"

→→→→→→→→→→→→→→→→→→→→→→→→→→→→→→→→→
→→→→→→→→→→→→→→→→→→→→→→→→→→→→→→→
→→→→→→→→→→→→→→→→→→→→→→→→→→→→→→→
→→→→→→→→→→→→→→→→→→→→→→→→→→→→→→→→
→→→→→→→→→→→→→→→→→→→→→→→→→→→→→→→→
→→→→→→→→→→→→→→→→→→→→→→→→→→→→→→→→
→→→→→→→→→→→→→→→→→→→→→→→→→→→→→→→→
→→→→→→→→→→→→→→→→→→→→→→→→→→→→→→→→

Forcing a window ajar he began shouting largely incomprehensible statements through the aperture, many of these being abusive statements of one sort or another, whilst others were slightly more poetic in their nonsensical manner . . . after a while they seemed to cease to be directed at particular individuals or groups witnessed through the bus windows and instead became more general statements thrown at the cosmos

→→→→→→→→→→→→→→→→→→→→→→→→→
→→→→→→→→→→→→→→→→→→→→→→→→→
→→→→→→→→→→→→→→→→→→→→→→→→→
→→→→→→→→→→→→→→→→→→→→→→→→→
→→→→→→→→→→→→→→→→→→→→→→→→→
→→→→→→→→→→→→→→→→→→→→→→→→→
→→→→→→→→→→→→→→→→→→→→→→→→→
→→→→→→→→→→→→→→→→→→→→→→→→→

Turning to a group of teenagers in school uniforms he began quite a relentless monologue aimed at them . . . "Come on guys . . . where's the rebel spirit? You've gotta use your time constructively . . . can't afford to let your days slip by without doing something important . . . & you're all just sittin' there doing nothing! Where's the animation???? Where's the razzmatazz????"

→→→→→→→→→→→→→→→→→→→→→→→→→
→→→→→→→→→→→→→→→→→→→→→→→→→
→→→→→→→→→→→→→→→→→→→→→→→→→
→→→→→→→→→→→→→→→→→→→→→→→→→
→→→→→→→→→→→→→→→→→→→→→→→→→
→→→→→→→→→→→→→→→→→→→→→→→→→
→→→→→→→→→→→→→→→→→→→→→→→→→
→→→→→→→→→→→→→→→→→→→→→→→→→

. . . at this point in the day he suddenly began making faces at people . . . rolling his eyeballs . . . opening his mouth wide . . . he'd do this with anyone he encountered . . . virtually all of the people that he saw . . . many took offence to this but most were silent . . . largely he was written off as a jovial fool and his actions were not perceived to be threatening

→→→→→→→→→→→→→→→→→→→→→→→→→

→→→→→→→→→→→→→→→→→→→→→→→→
→→→→→→→→→→→→→→→→→→→→→→→→
→→→→→→→→→→→→→→→→→→→→→→→→
→→→→→→→→→→→→→→→→→→→→→→→→
→→→→→→→→→→→→→→→→→→→→→→→→
→→→→→→→→→→→→→→→→→→→→→→→→
→→→→→→→→→→→→→→→→→→→→→→→→

Turning to one further pedestrian, a man in the street never encountered previously, he asked him "Are you a poet sir?" by way of greeting, to which this man (who was fairly ordinary looking in his work suit) responded, without hesitating for a moment, by saying "Well, in a way, isn't everyone a poet?"

→→→→→→→→→→→→→→→→→→→→→→→→
→→→→→→→→→→→→→→→→→→→→→→→→
→→→→→→→→→→→→→→→→→→→→→→→→
→→→→→→→→→→→→→→→→→→→→→→→→
→→→→→→→→→→→→→→→→→→→→→→→→
→→→→→→→→→→→→→→→→→→→→→→→→
→→→→→→→→→→→→→→→→→→→→→→→→
→→→→→→→→→→→→→→→→→→→→→→→→

Running down a high street somewhere within London (although had he been questioned he wouldn't have been able to say where he was exactly) & in the midst of this he tripped over on one of his stray shoelaces and ended up rolling around on the pavement, making a little red gash on his knee

→→→→→→→→→→→→→→→→→→→→→→→→
→→→→→→→→→→→→→→→→→→→→→→→→
→→→→→→→→→→→→→→→→→→→→→→→→
→→→→→→→→→→→→→→→→→→→→→→→→
→→→→→→→→→→→→→→→→→→→→→→→→
→→→→→→→→→→→→→→→→→→→→→→→→
→→→→→→→→→→→→→→→→→→→→→→→→
→→→→→→→→→→→→→→→→→→→→→→→→

. . . next he decided to cover himself in a variety of substances

which he acquired within a supermarket . . . he took all of his
clothes off and poured treacle, shampoo, castor oil, hundreds
and thousands, cream cheese, and milk of magnesia all over his
form . . . he then rolled around in the grass letting it all merge
together and congeal . . .

→→→→→→→→→→→→→→→→→→→→→→→→
→→→→→→→→→→→→→→→→→→→→→→→→
→→→→→→→→→→→→→→→→→→→→→→→→
→→→→→→→→→→→→→→→→→→→→→→→→
→→→→→→→→→→→→→→→→→→→→→→→→
→→→→→→→→→→→→→→→→→→→→→→→→
→→→→→→→→→→→→→→→→→→→→→→→→
→→→→→→→→→→→→→→→→→→→→→→→→

. . . he approached the portly, balding, middle-aged man
merely in order to tell how extraordinary, he, Billy, in fact was
. . . the information was met with surprise, a certain raising of
eyebrows, a glance which held a modicum of contempt . . . Billy
spoke of his "achievements" which included "crossing the road,"
"burning a piece of toast" and also "giving a round of applause
to people who deserved it" and after this their very one-sided
conversation collapsed into silence . . .

→→→→→→→→→→→→→→→→→→→→→→→→
→→→→→→→→→→→→→→→→→→→→→→→→
→→→→→→→→→→→→→→→→→→→→→→→→
→→→→→→→→→→→→→→→→→→→→→→→→
→→→→→→→→→→→→→→→→→→→→→→→→
→→→→→→→→→→→→→→→→→→→→→→→→
→→→→→→→→→→→→→→→→→→→→→→→→
→→→→→→→→→→→→→→→→→→→→→→→→

. . . he entered a phone booth that smelt of urine & old
cigarettes & proceeded to phone directory enquiries in order to
obtain the numbers of the relevant institutions, that is to say, the
ones which it had occurred to him to harass . . . that day his tally
included a number of local councils, the treasury, a branch of a

well-known high street stationers . . . and an accountant's office in Holborn . . . he considered all of these people his enemies in some sense . . .

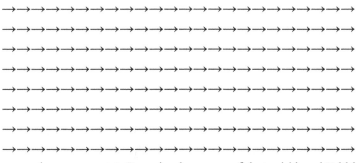

. . . he went to visit Ben, the drummer of their old band Edible Mucus . . . an entity which had ceased to exist . . . Ben was now resident in a squat down in Elephant and Castle . . . when Billy appeared that day he, Ben, was lying in his makeshift bed spread across the floor and upon seeing Billy grabbed him harshly by the arms, drew him close and told him in no uncertain terms to Fuck Off and Never Return, which Billy then obligingly did . . .

. . . somehow on another Suburban London High Street which he could not later identify he spent a good amount of time attempting to balance a wine glass on top of a raw sirloin steak which itself was resting on top of a plimsoll . . . this did not work and the glass fell & shattered, with the steak becoming instantly grimy & inedible upon contact with the pavement . . . all in all he felt quite sorely disappointed with this failure and felt that it was destined to emerge in his memory with some frequency for many years afterwards . . .

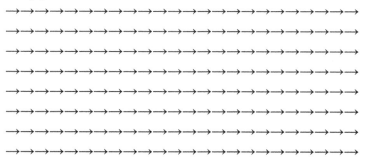

. . . suddenly he found himself with one hand firmly pressed against a brick wall, whilst his entire body worked towards issuing a generous stream of vomit, splashing over the bricks & his feet, and onto the surrounding paving slabs . . . afterwards he stood there for some minutes gasping, staring dumbly downwards at the sight of his vomit-strewn feet, attempting to somehow re-arrange his consciousness to its default position of relative composure . . .

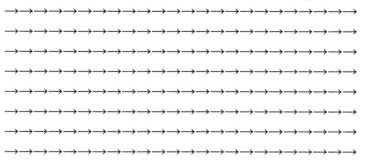

. . . entering an Italian restaurant on Old Compton Street he ordered a portion of Spaghetti Carbonara which he had no intention of paying for, ate all of it up with ravenous gestures, then placed the plate on the floor and ascended, standing up on the table and tinkling his glass with a spoon in order to attract attention for a speech which he did not quite manage to commence delivering . . . he had intended it to be a speech concerning the subject of how extraordinary he in fact happened to be . . .

→→→→→→→→→→→→→→→→→→→→→→→→

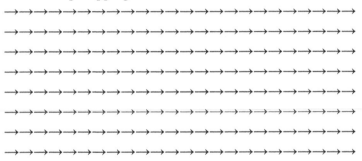

. . . Billy next became obsessed with attaching things to his hair (which at this time was very long & profuse & full of tangles) he lodged a plastic ladybird in there, a pink sparkly feminine hairclip & he then attempted to house a small branch from an oak tree up there . . . but it didn't prove to be a very comfortable fit and it kept slipping out . . .

. . . He sat drinking a pint of lime and soda in a pub somewhere in North London . . . this was intended as an antidote to the quantity of alcohol which he had consumed & to that end it did work reasonably well particularly in the atmospherics of July heat which he was experiencing then . . . this had always been one of his favourite drinks . . . although one which he frequently forgot about & which was therefore all the more welcome when he did remember . . .

→→→→→→→→→→→→→→→→→→→→→→→→
→→→→→→→→→→→→→→→→→→→→→→→→
→→→→→→→→→→→→→→→→→→→→→→→→

. . . boarding the tube he commenced another of his monologues . . . worrying & confusing a number of the passengers in the carriage where this occurred . . . & after a little while these passengers expressed their annoyance with him verbally . . . his words slipped somewhat incoherently from one subject to another . . . from his dislike of the wearing of baseball caps . . . to his dislike of chandeliers & finally on to his dislike of supermarkets . . . before they all finally reached the end of the line . . .

→→→→→→→→→→→→→→→→→→→→→→→→
→→→→→→→→→→→→→→→→→→→→→→→→
→→→→→→→→→→→→→→→→→→→→→→→→
→→→→→→→→→→→→→→→→→→→→→→→→
→→→→→→→→→→→→→→→→→→→→→→→→
→→→→→→→→→→→→→→→→→→→→→→→→
→→→→→→→→→→→→→→→→→→→→→→→→
→→→→→→→→→→→→→→→→→→→→→→→→

. . . he developed a sudden craving for water biscuits . . . a longing which would continue throughout the day . . . he tried adding some red Leicester to one such biscuit . . . but found in fact that the biscuit was clearly preferable to him on its own without the adornment of cheese . . . a fact which he would gladly declare in public debate if the occasion were ever to somehow arise . . .

→→→→→→→→→→→→→→→→→→→→→→→→
→→→→→→→→→→→→→→→→→→→→→→→→
→→→→→→→→→→→→→→→→→→→→→→→→
→→→→→→→→→→→→→→→→→→→→→→→→
→→→→→→→→→→→→→→→→→→→→→→→→
→→→→→→→→→→→→→→→→→→→→→→→→
→→→→→→→→→→→→→→→→→→→→→→→→
→→→→→→→→→→→→→→→→→→→→→→→→

. . . he walked into a toilet cubicle at the back of the Rose & Crown where he laid out the cocaine in a slightly cracked little hand mirror, which was covered, at the edges, with stickers of little rainbows . . . he inhaled the powder which caused a nefarious & familiar rush of the senses . . .

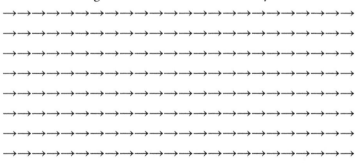

. . . Billy next involved himself with saluting the guards at Buckingham Palace, firstly taking enormous ridiculous strides with his extremely long legs & punctuating his saluting with manic mouth openings & face twitching for melodramatic effect . . . the guards were resilient in their indifference, saw a joker for what he was & ignored him until he went away . . .

. . . speaking to an elderly gentleman on a street corner somewhere within the confines of W1 he said "you know wot, my man, there isn't any end to the possible subversions out there. . ." which was a thought that was met with confusion . . . the elderly gentleman (who sported a black and white tweed blazer and a well-maintained silver-grey moustache) was in fact unsure as to whether these words had been addressed to him at all and in confusion he looked around to see if there was another possible recipient, before politely asking Billy to leave him alone . . .

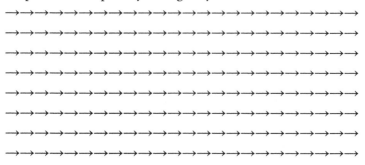

. . . he found himself spitting against a concrete wall (one which happened to belong to an NCP car park) & he watched with some strange fascination as the saliva made its progress downwards forming extraordinary globules & formations of bubbles, a slithery trail of residue from the spaces recently abandoned forever . . .

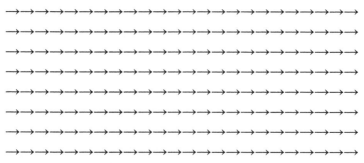

. . . he spent some time meticulously examining possible flowers to purchase, for the sake of his lapel, in order to smarten himself up a little, his slowness eventually causing an amount of consternation to the flower seller who possessed a stall inside Liverpool Street Station and who was not convinced that Billy was going to pay for any of her produce . . . but he did & just selected a carnation in the end, despite its lack of originality in terms of smart lapelwear . . .

→→→→→→→→→→→→→→→→→→→→→→→→→
→→→→→→→→→→→→→→→→→→→→→→→→→
→→→→→→→→→→→→→→→→→→→→→→→→→
→→→→→→→→→→→→→→→→→→→→→→→→→
→→→→→→→→→→→→→→→→→→→→→→→→→
→→→→→→→→→→→→→→→→→→→→→→→→→

. . . approaching a variety of women he tried out the most ridiculous pick-up lines he could conceive of, just to see what facial and verbal responses he might manage to generate . . . none of the women had the slightest interest in him & many were even clearly offended . . . the first of these lines which he had tried out was "will you be my mistress of the clouds?" . . .

→→→→→→→→→→→→→→→→→→→→→→→→→
→→→→→→→→→→→→→→→→→→→→→→→→→
→→→→→→→→→→→→→→→→→→→→→→→→→
→→→→→→→→→→→→→→→→→→→→→→→→→
→→→→→→→→→→→→→→→→→→→→→→→→→
→→→→→→→→→→→→→→→→→→→→→→→→→
→→→→→→→→→→→→→→→→→→→→→→→→→
→→→→→→→→→→→→→→→→→→→→→→→→→

. . . after buying a gin and tonic in the Earl of Denby, he decided that it was his right to repeatedly rush in and out of the doors, sometimes with hands trembling in the air like a character in a piece of old fashioned musical theatre, grinning enormously at everyone sat in their staid quietness, all looking at him with what would appear to have been contempt . . .

→→→→→→→→→→→→→→→→→→→→→→→→→
→→→→→→→→→→→→→→→→→→→→→→→→→
→→→→→→→→→→→→→→→→→→→→→→→→→
→→→→→→→→→→→→→→→→→→→→→→→→→
→→→→→→→→→→→→→→→→→→→→→→→→→
→→→→→→→→→→→→→→→→→→→→→→→→→
→→→→→→→→→→→→→→→→→→→→→→→→→
→→→→→→→→→→→→→→→→→→→→→→→→→

   . . . shutting his eyes for some minutes in the park he found himself enjoying the breezes rustling amongst the trees, the flurry of a group of schoolchildren marching in a line & the shuttling of trains back & forth along the tracks which bordered the park's Southern edge . . .

→→→→→→→→→→→→→→→→→→→→→→→→→→→→

→→→→→→→→→→→→→→→→→→→→→→→→→→→→

→→→→→→→→→→→→→→→→→→→→→→→→→→→→

→→→→→→→→→→→→→→→→→→→→→→→→→→→→

→→→→→→→→→→→→→→→→→→→→→→→→→→→→

→ →→ →→ →→ →→ →→ →→ →→ →→ →→ →→ →→ →→ →→

→→→→→→→→→→→→→→→→→→→→→→→→→→→→

→→→→→→→→→→→→→→→→→→→→→→→→→→→

23.

Wedding Amongst the Flamingos

For a few years Flo had been in a relationship with Nick, an academic ornithologist. Their wedding was the social event of its year, not just for the couple and the family, but for almost everyone who attended.

It took place inside a white stucco mansion set within the vast grounds of a flamingo sanctuary in Tanzania. They were married in a ballroom there, under a glass chandelier and whirring fans, amid sweltering August heat, with more than one hundred guests in attendance. The couple had been able to fly everyone out especially, making use of Nick's recently acquired inheritance from his Aunt Geraldine who had suddenly died at the age of seventy-three, after choking on a pineapple upside-down cake.

Flouting all Western conventions, Flo wore a many-coloured dress on her wedding day, with occasional decorative patches sewn on at irregular intervals depicting botanical specimens, mythological creatures, and starfish. Her cheeks were coated in a layer of silver glitter amongst dashes of luminous green paint. I felt that she had successfully pulled off the feat of looking beautiful, more than she ever had done before, just the way that brides are supposed to.

As well as the dress, Flo spent the entire day wearing a pair of roller skates. After the vows and the first married kiss, she wheeled herself around in celebratory circles and did a little pirouette of victory, with swaying arms held aloft, her features suffused with delight. She claimed that the roller skates helped her to move from one guest to another on the day with greater ease. When talking about the subject, she also liked to point out that she was most probably one of very few women who had spent the entirety of their wedding day on skates. Indeed, she was overly proud of this fact. During any conversation that day she was liable to disappear with unexpected motion, retreating with the rapid movements of her wheels at any given moment.

The guests were largely dressed in tropical colours, with many of the men wearing Panama hats and the women tying brightly coloured ribbons into their hair or clutching peacock feathers throughout the ceremony, both for the effect of ornamentation which they offered and to compliment the ornithological theme of the wedding.

With so many guests packed into a relatively small amount of space, most of them quite unused to the sweltering heat, a great deal of sweating took place, and there was a constant wiping of brows amidst a general atmosphere which often seemed to teeter close to hysteria. With some minor sense of the mischievous, the couple felt delighted in removing their guests from all ordinary, urban, quotidian, European experiences, placing them instead within a location that hardly felt plausible, one that seemed to dwell within a location of myth and fairy tale, as much as within any more obvious reality.

The ceremony was conducted by a tall, bald, amiable priest who wore a dog collar and a psychedelic silk shirt which was abundant with swathes of colour. He conducted the standard Church of England service, which did seem a little strange to encounter in the context of that location. They had flown the priest in from a suburb of Birmingham, which was where Nick had been brought up; they had known each other since Nick was a child.

Upon completion of the ceremony a great cascade of confetti fell upon the couple's heads, emerging from heaped baskets which had been passed around in all directions. It was exclusively composed of orange blossoms and had been lightly sprinkled with perfume.

During the reception the guests were treated to a lavish spread of delicacies. Flutes of champagne were served by waiters bearing circular silver trays. Dotted on tables around the room, elaborate floral displays emerged from glass canisters, with white orchids and pink lilies mingled together into enormous bunches. Excited chatter filled the hall, rising into a cloud, scattering amongst the white plaster of the floral cornices which decorated the edges of the ceiling.

Almost everyone was extremely excited to be present at this event although some found they were suffering from disorientation and fatigue. Indeed, Aunt Petunia fainted and collapsed seconds after the wedding ceremony was completed, giving rise to gasps and a great flurry of anxious movements before order was restored. Fortunately, she recovered her composure rapidly and soon returned to her table in an upright position.

Doubtless due to the extraordinary location, as well as to Nick and Flo having paid everyone's travel expenses, those who possessed money seemed to become unusually inspired when it came to the act of giving wedding presents. Amongst many other immodest presents the couple were given an alabaster sculpture of a gang-gang cockatoo, a sketch of a sparrow executed by Modigliani, and a quill pen which had once belonged to François Marie Daudin, who was regarded as an important early ornithologist.

As everyone sat down to eat in the afternoon, they discovered that a wooden model of a bird had been placed on top of each table, a different one in each case, often corresponding to the research speciality of one of the ornithologists who had been given a seat there. Each of the models had been carved by Nick especially for the occasion from Eucalyptus wood which he had acquired whilst doing fieldwork in Australia.

As much as anything the occasion involved an emotional reunion for all of the siblings. We hadn't all assembled together for a number of years. In fact it wasn't quite a complete reunion, even if it felt like one. The only one of us missing was Billy, who had moaned: "I can't be bothered to take a flight that long!" A reunion was important enough to the rest of us however that those who were in relationships had agreed not to bring their partners along. Not that I had a partner.

When it was time to be seated the siblings occupied a large round table to which no outsiders were allowed access, unless that occurred fleetingly. Silently, we all somehow realized that, with this wedding, an inexorable shift was occurring for us as a collective entity. We knew that this was happening and yet no one had the courage to bring it up directly in conversation. Instead these thoughts were only detectable within certain glances that we shared during our very occasional lapses into silence, but these were barely ever for longer than the duration of a second.

"Do you like weddings Matty?" asked Gerard.

"This is the first time I've ever been to one," I said.

"Really? How old are you now?" He asked, as if I were a stranger, which in many ways I was to him.

"I'm twenty-six."

"Are you really? Well high time to attend a wedding then . . ."

He turned to Ag, who was seated to his left.

"What about you, Ag? Do you like weddings? Surely you've been to plenty of weddings?"

"Oh yes, many," she said. "All the time. My friends are the kind of people who like inventing their own ceremonies . . ."

"That's always a fun game," said Gerard.

"I think it's too profound an occasion to be called a 'Game,'" said Ag. "They're very spiritual things, highly charged events. The ceremonial union of a pair of human beings is not something that should be taken lightly . . ."

"Of course not," said Gerard, "I usually find it utterly devastating."

"You aren't happy for the couples getting married?" asked Rebecca.

"Yes, obviously I am, but I still find it emotionally devastating," he said.

Mother wandered over to our table at this point, beaming like an ecstatic worshipper. For most of the wedding she was seated with the married couple and the groom's parents. None of us had spoken to her for a couple of hours at this point. She was wearing a dress adorned with a pattern of red hibiscus flowers swirling over a dark blue background. Complimenting this was a large red chiffon hat, to which she had attached a small furry model of a yellow chick.

"Well hello there," she said to all of us, continuing to beam, a little drunkenly by now. "Is everyone having a good time?" she asked.

We gave a range of affirmative responses, our voices jostling in unison.

"Aren't all of these birds on the tables lovely," said Mother, picking up ours, which happened to be a gannet, then twirling it within her fingers.

"How are the new in-laws?" asked Lucinda.

"Oh they're delightful, an entirely delightful family for Flo to have found her way to . . ."

"What have you all been talking about?" asked Lucinda.

"Well . . . my work and theirs," said Mother. "Both of Nick's parents are radical ecologists you see . . ."

Once Mother had departed from our table and returned to her own, we all felt we could engage in slightly different kinds of conversation again.

"So, Family, what does everyone actually think about marriage?" was the question that Lucinda put to everyone at this point.

"I'm definitely not interested in it at all," said Barnaby.

Everyone around the table happened to agree with this, at least in terms of their own life decisions.

"I don't want to get married myself," said Eliza, "but of course I totally support Flo and Nick's decision to do this, as I'm sure we all do . . ."

"Well I guess this attitude to marriage does make life slightly easier for all of us," said Lucinda, "because if none us want to get married then we don't all have to dress up and buy presents and go to ceremonials every ten minutes . . ."

This struck me as a subtle way of attempting to manipulate the family's social reality through what could just about be termed 'humour'. In fact it was largely destined to work. Hardly any of us who sat around the table would ever get married. But then we did possess a Mother who had given birth to no less than ten children whilst always out of wedlock.

"The question on everyone's lips," said Gerard, "or at least on mine, is, what have you been doing to disrupt reality lately?"

There was some spirited laughter around the table at the unexpectedness of the question. It really felt like a way of returning to our shared history again.

"Well, recently," began Rebecca, "I've been trying to have a lot of lesbian sex in the bushes of parks that are ever so slightly exposed. Because that way people can get more of a glimpse of lesbian sexual relations than they normally do!"

I wasn't sure that I believed this story.

"And what about you Gerard?" Eliza enquired.

"I've been spending one month a year just telling lies," he said.

"Is that a lie?" asked Eliza.

"No."

"And that?"

"Maybe."

"Really? Only lies? All the time?" asked Eliza.

"Probably 95% of the time, but ideally it really should be always. That would be more like The True Path . . ."

This actually struck me as a more plausible story than Rebecca's somehow. Maybe it was just the different tones of voice that they had employed.

A few times during the course of the reception Flo glided over on her roller skates, her cheeks reddened with excitement. When she did she would break into animated and scattered talk:

"Hi Guys! . . . It's just so wonderful that you're all here! I really thought . . . I mean . . . honestly I expected at least one of you wouldn't make it! Of course I sort of knew Billy wouldn't, but the rest of you are here . . . !"

She hardly stayed at our table for very long, which was of course understandable given the situation she was presented with, but I think we all still felt a little sad about this. After a matter of minutes she had disappeared, moving back into the relentless orbit of her new life, moving from table to table, investigating the interconnection of people who lay beyond us.

"I'd like to hear some more grandiose talk from you Gerard," said Ag.

"I doubt that will be too difficult to achieve," said Barnaby.

"Would you like to hear about my dreams and visions?" asked Gerard

"Yes," said Ag, in a matter of fact way. I could tell she was genuinely interested.

"Lately I've been imagining cities, ones built from materials that are not usually used to build with: plastic, chromium, porcelain."

"Your mind scares me," said Eliza.

"Ah . . . don't be scared . . . so one project I would really like to enact fully is to build an entire city . . . I would put board games and climbing frames in the streets. Sculptures of giant ants . . ."

"Sounds darling," said Ag.

"Would you be the mayor?" asked Lucinda.

"Naturally, I would have a role that would be somewhat similar to that of a mayor . . ."

"Naturally," echoed Lucinda.

"Does the word 'narcissism' have any meaning for you Gerard?"

"I'm sure it's difficult being around a supreme being. I'm sorry about that," was his dubious response.

"You're a prick," said Lucinda, with some genuine fervour.

"Thank you," said Gerard.

That caused something of a lull in conversation. An awkward feeling then hung over us for some minutes afterwards.

"It's strange we're in Africa," said Rebecca.

"Is it? Why?" asked Eliza.

"Well we aren't normally here," said Rebecca.

"Yes, but we are normally on Planet Earth though . . . ," said Eliza. "Africa is on Planet Earth . . . so why shouldn't it be normal to be in Tanzania? Surely that's as normal as being in Bermondsey or Stoke Newington?"

"Alright. Good point," said Rebecca.

"Anyway 'Africa' is a false construction," continued Eliza, "can we not grant these countries actual identities? Full legitimacy? Why do they always have to be absorbed by this mythical entity of Africa?"

"I don't know guys, this is beginning to sound like an argument . . . ," said Gerard.

We all engaged in a few seconds of reflection, probably all trying to think of directions in which to steer the conversation next.

"What are people supposed to talk about at weddings?" asked Rebecca.

"I wouldn't have thought that there are any strictly designated subjects," said Lucinda.

"Maybe there are certain things that definitely shouldn't be talked about," said Eliza.

"Such as?" asked Lucinda.

"The Military, Atheism, Sloth . . . ," said Eliza, without stopping to consider this for long.

"Agreed about those," said Rebecca.

"So what are good subjects for the occasion?" asked Lucinda.

"Family? Romance? Jobs?" wondered Eliza.

"Yeah . . . ," said Lucinda.

None of us really felt like discussing any of those subjects any more than we already had, so we all silently turned our gazes over to the band, who were just beginning to warm up. These musicians had been assembled especially for the occasion and consisted of fifteen locals whose playing spiralled into twenty-minute-long jams, punctuating their music with jubilant vocal shouts and cries. Ag called their set: "Utterly Transcendent!" We all seemed to agree. For their last number the band demanded that everyone in the building "make some sort of movement". Just about everyone obeyed.

Once it got going, the dancefloor was amongst the wilder ones that I've seen. Many of the guests were acting in a way that came close to being competitive, each attempting to surpass the dancing of their neighbours in both fervour and ingenuity, if possible regaining something of their lost youth in these actions, or at least acting to deny that they were (often significantly) older than thirty.

As the evening progressed, I became so drunk that I began attempting to balance a series of objects on my head, starting with one of my shoes and ending with a plate, at which point Lucinda seized the opportunity to reprimand me as if I was still a little boy, telling me that I was behaving dangerously. Nevertheless, despite the various tensions that existed amongst us, all of the siblings made a point of huddling together in order to watch the sun rise. As we did so we were engaged in playing highly inadvisable drinking games involving numerous bottles of tequila and rum.

All through the event we were always vaguely aware of the mysterious, unseen presence of the flamingos, who we knew were surrounding us, even if they were outwardly absent. Somehow, you constantly felt besieged by swarms of thousands of extraordinary pink creatures, even if you weren't talking or directly thinking about them, a fact which felt as disconcerting as it was exciting.

Finally, on Sunday morning, the day after the wedding ceremony, everyone present who was still capable of getting out of bed toured the sanctuary, staring through binoculars at the masses of pink feathers, just about propped up by tall spindly legs. It occurred to me only then that these odd, gawky creatures were the actual reason for our presence in this place. They were a hopeful sight which no one was left unmoved by.

24.

Mother Has a Peculiar Dream

At first she was in Norway. It was not clear to her how she knew this, but somehow she did know, it was evident to her in all of the details of the suburban streets which she was wandering through, alone and in something of a daze. All of it said "Norway" somehow, in a rather dull voice. She did not particularly like the idea of Norway. There was too much money there and far too much emphasis on winter sports. She thought, "Couldn't I have appeared in a different random location?"

She then did appear elsewhere. She was now in a room inside a house which she could not identify at all. On the table there was a large pair of pliers and next to that a pot of mustard. She stared at them, thinking it was a strange combination of objects. Furthermore, she thought to herself "there is a strange air of disquiet about this room."

Suddenly the floor opened up and she fell downwards. She fell down one floor and then down another and again another. After this the chasms appeared to close up, leaving the floor wholly intact. Now she was in a room where a duck-billed platypus of altogether unusual talent was balancing a grapefruit on its nose. Suddenly a ballerina was dangling from the ceiling like a decoration, attached by a silk thread, twirling and kicking her feet into the air. Her face was blank and held no obvious expression.

All the walls fell away. There was no building left at all. That left her in a field in fact. An empty, rather large field with brambles growing around the edges. A female librarian in late middle age with hair that was by now almost entirely white, slowly walked across this field, carrying a tower of books. She ignored Mother and walked straight past her. Mother felt an urge to reach out and touch the librarian, but she controlled this urge. Somehow it did not seem to her to be a good idea after all.

Mother then walked into a neighbouring field and in that one there was a little building made out of plasterboard. Inside it there was a tiny provincial post office with only a single postal worker attending to duties. As it happened, that postal worker was made out of glass. He was an ordinary size and shape for a human being, but he was made out of glass and not flesh.

Mother felt somewhat frightened and decided to run out of the post office. Next thing she knew she was sitting on a nearly empty bus in a city which she could not identify. Across the aisle from her sat Leopold von Sacher-Masoch. At first she thought it might have been someone who was busy in the act of imitating Leopold von Sacher-Masoch, but then somehow she knew, she could tell it really was the man himself, that he had been transported all the way from 19th century Vienna to this suburban bus service somewhere in early 21st century provincial Britain. She found herself feeling even more anxious about him than she had been of the postal worker a very short time before. She did not find the courage to talk to him, which was after all a little unusual for her.

Instead she got off at the next stop and encountered a gigantic floating tongue. Perhaps that tongue is waiting for a bus, she thought. Or perhaps it is just floating about and "being a tongue". They both stood there by the bus stop for a little while, the tongue silent and passive, Mother nervy and twitching slightly.

Suddenly she found herself at the University of Surrey. That was odd, because she had never had anything to do with that particular institution. Indeed, she had barely ever thought of it before. Anyway, here she was. As she walked around it somehow it seemed one of the more aesthetically appealing campuses to her. She was, after all, something of a connoisseur of British university campuses. She really did, quite honestly, enjoy a good campus. There was a reasonably nice pond and some pleasant trees. That was enough for her.

Before she knew what she could do with herself cucumbers appeared, all over the campus! There was no escaping them unless you shut your eyes. This Mother felt inclined to do. She opened them again, but alas the cucumbers had not yet disappeared. They were there on the patches of grass and again they were there on top of buildings, lurking in the entranceways, arrayed in windows like trophies. There was just no avoiding them.

She walked through one of the open doors and then found herself, unexpectedly, rather disconcertingly, stepping into the studio of a local radio station in North Wales. They were broadcasting a live conversation about knitting. Mother sat listening to them and felt comforted by the soothing tone of the Welsh voices. She enjoyed watching a black cat traipsing across the floor of the studio and yawning.

Mother climbed into the yawning mouth of the cat because it looked comfortable there. It was. There were lots of pink arrows there indicating the direction for visitors to follow. She followed them and found herself in a room containing a swimming pool. Some people were floating around in the water, a few of them on inflatable devices, others just lolling about or diving to the bottom of the pool for fun, exploring. Mother dove into the pool and swam to the bottom, still fully clothed. On the floor of the pool she discovered a trapdoor which she prized open and clambered into, following a long ladder downwards until she finally reached another room which was entirely dry.

This room possessed mint-green walls and was full of people standing around. Various men (all of them called Gareth Powell as it happens) were chatting about the aspects of their life histories which related to the subject of surfing. All of them, without exception, were very enthusiastic about this subject and Mother absorbed some of their excitement, finding it to be really quite infectious. Then morning arrived.

25.

Dear Lilly

Dear Lilly,

It's now been some years since you disappeared. I never really expected you would do that. None of us did. It seemed a little out of character, but then maybe, I didn't really know who you were. Maybe none of us really understand each other. I wonder.

So, the fact is, I miss you. I guess that's the point of this letter. To say those words to you. I miss you. Your absence hurts me. I know you have your own life to live and need your freedom, but still, what do you expect? That's the effect your leaving was always going to have.

Certain images parade through my mind all the time and some of those include your features. I can see us hiding together when we were small. Maybe that image, above all else. I see you blushing. Or you jumping in the garden when you were trying to steal clouds from the sky. There was a time when you loved the sky more than anywhere else. It was really your favourite place. You wanted to be a pilot or at least an air hostess.

As you will be aware, not one of us has heard from you. I'm not telling you off. I know you have your reasons and they might even be ones I would approve of. Nevertheless, it is a difficult fact for us all to deal with. You must be aware of that, surely? I suppose I just want you to understand that, if you don't already.

Of course it's Mother who has been hit the hardest. She talks about you nearly every day. I'm usually the only other person staying in the house these days, so it's me she usually talks to about you. It's pretty strange being the only one left.

I just can't seem to move on somehow. The world scares me so much and I just don't know how to operate within it success-fully. That was one thing that Mother somehow never managed to teach me. I honestly think she overlooked that one. I mean, I could try and leave, try and get a job, but I'm sure I would fail at that. I really can't imagine it working out. What job would I even be able to do? Assuming that someone would trust me enough to employ me.

Still, I do find ways to occupy myself. I always do. Lately I've got really into riding around London on buses. Do you remember the thrill that was for me when I was 16? Well, I did get bored of it as an activity, so I abandoned it for years, sort of forgot about it as a possibility, but then recently I seem to have discovered it again.

So I don't mean to suggest that what I do on buses is particularly special. After all, who doesn't spend hours travelling on public transport in London? But the fact is, most people do it very differently. They do it with a definite purpose in mind. Usually to go to work, or to go home, or to go out and meet friends, or whatever. But the thing that most people miss out on is the actual *exploration* of the city via its bus routes. To spend hours drifting from one route to another, discovering thoroughfares and byways, getting to see every last part of the city. You form relationships with high street shop signs, public parks, the recurring faces of homeless people (I'm thinking of the kind that always sit in the same place and heap all of their numerous possessions on a street corner).

It's strange that it's only Mother and I in the house. After so many years of the house being so busy, it's now often silent and still. Of course frequently enough our siblings come to visit. And Mother still has lovers and academic colleagues coming to visit all the time, but I sort of learn to ignore all of the commotion of those comings and goings. The house is really so peaceful now that it only has two permanent residents. Two feels like a manageable number. It's as if the house, itself, is at rest finally. After a lifetime of hard working days it is putting its feet up.

Of course Mother does try and trouble me to leave from time to time, although nowhere near as often as she tries to convince me to look for romance, which is obviously something that I haven't managed to find (does that surprise you?!?) To be quite honest, I don't think she really wants me to leave at all. I feel like she's sort of trapped me here, maybe without even meaning to do that.

As you'd probably expect, I don't really have many friends. Most of the time there's virtually no one other than Mother to talk to. Sometimes the couple who own the corner shop down the road wants to exchange some pleasantries with me, but it doesn't usually go very far. There's nowhere to go beyond the surface with them really. I'm sure that if I tried to push one of our chats in that direction there would somehow be a disaster of some sort. I don't even know what form the disaster would take, but I do feel sure it would happen.

I always have a sense of loss these days. I'm sort of used to that though, I suppose. I lost you years ago for example didn't I? I know we never spoke about it before, but it's true isn't it? I lost you, but I learned to live with that. After a while I felt okay about that situation. I suppose that was sort of a trial run for your disappearing completely years later. Actually, I now wonder if that was your unconscious intention.

So what do I do all day? I potter about. I do a bit of this and that. When someone asks me this question, those are the sorts of answers which I give. Maybe, if I don't really want to give a direct answer, I'll just mumble "It's hard to say," or something like that. The truth is that I'm not really sure that I *know* what it is that I do all day long. But the hours do pass, that much is undeniable.

It becomes harder, at this age, to continue dreaming of "The Future." That no longer feels like some place of ecstasy and achievement, which is how I used to imagine things being. I really used to believe that one day things really would get better for me. That sort of thinking really keeps a lot of people going when they're younger I think. The movement towards an inevitable series of better days. But now I've dispensed with that kind of thinking entirely. Too much time has gone by. Basically it just feels too late now and quite simply, I'm fucked. Often I find I have very little drive left. I find myself exhausted and just lying down in the middle of the afternoon, staring out of the window for the lack of any other sort of available stimulus. I try not to pity myself, really I make an effort not to do that. Honestly, I think I've only got myself to blame for this predicament. I should have seized opportunities when they were there to be seized.

Oddly enough though, on the whole, I'm really not so unhappy living like this. I might not sound so happy all the time, but it's true. Let's face it, this is quite a comfortable way to live. It's a pleasant house and there are memories lingering everywhere. I'm at home here. I enjoy the freedom of living here, of not having to find a job, of being able to mess around. Perhaps this house is simply where I'm meant to be. As Mother gets older she probably needs someone to look after her, so perhaps it ought to be me who does that. It certainly feels that way at the moment.

I don't know if these words will even reach you Lilly. I hope that they will. Even if they do reach you I can't be certain that you'll respond or that we'll ever meet again. So I suppose that leaves me with a need to say goodbye to you, just in case this is the last chance that I get. We will all keep remembering you. I'll be waiting for you up here in the attic. Try to be brave and do what you believe in. Somehow I have the sense that you're fine, that everything is well with you. I don't know why really, but I do.

With Love,

Matty

26.

The Travelling Toucan Museum

After their honeymoon Flo and Nick decided to abandon their careers and commence a new life. Henceforth, they would travel around the country in a caravan which would act as both their home and as a mobile museum dedicated exclusively to the subject of toucans, the bird they both identified with as their favourite earthly creature. A shared enthusiasm for toucans was one of the most significant factors which had brought them together into marriage, and so they resolved to dedicate the remainder of their days to increasing public knowledge and appreciation of the birds.

Naturally, the exterior of the caravan was painted in a luminescent shade of orange. Whenever it came to a stand still, Flo and Nick would expand the caravan into a couple of further canvas display rooms which held exhibits and captions and invite any visitors inside. They would place a wooden sandwich board close by which declared "THE TRAVELLING TOUCAN MUSEUM IS OPEN TODAY". These words nestled inside a speech bubble which emerged from the gigantic orange bill of a cartoon toucan busily flapping its wings and seeming to smile amidst flurries of air.

They would charge a £3 entrance fee to all visitors and would always close the museum at 5.30 in the afternoon, pack everything up, and then drive on further down the road, either towards the next day's location, or to where they would pass the evening. Living in this way they came to feel an instinctive empathy with circus performers, gypsies and travelling salesmen, believing that they shared a similar sense of displacement with all who practiced these professions. It was the melancholy of itinerants and drifters, of everyone who could never feel at home within a single destination. Living on the road like this, they soon both believed that they really had discovered their true calling in life.

Every last available inch of space was given over to visual information which related to the story of toucans. Images of them could be seen throughout the museum emblazoned on cereal boxes, calendars, cigarette cards, examples of political party stationary, pairs of socks and illustrations taken from books written for children. These were all interspersed throughout the exhibits, resting between cabinets and displays, thrust into every last available crevice, in order to increase the quota of toucans within the cramped space of the caravan as much as was conceivable.

* * *

The museum displays conveyed many facts about toucans, including all of the following:

The notion of a "toucan" which most people have in their minds, is a bird with black plumage and a large orange bill, emerging from a white throat, but this is in fact only one of about forty different varieties of toucan, many of which possess very different colourings. This "standard" toucan is usually called a "Toco Toucan" (*Ramphastos toco*). It has individual dietary and reproductive habits which often differ wildly from other examples of the bird. There were many, carefully labelled, colourful images of the other toucans in the museum, including both photographs and paintings of, for example, Red-necked aracaris (*Pteroglossus bitorquatus*), Emerald toucanets (*Aulacorhynchus prasinus*) and the Keel-billed toucan (*Ramphastos sulfuratus*), a variety which possesses a yellowish-green bill, with bright blue swathes at its bottom and the end tipped with red.

An average toucan bill is about 20cm long. They often live in flocks of between 4 and 12. Toucans have a life expectancy of about 16 years. In their natural habitats they live exclusively in the rainforests of Central and South America, largely among treetops about 45 metres above the ground. Many toucans are frugivorous, meaning that they have a diet consisting mainly or only of fruit, particularly guavas, peppers, pindos, and oranges. Nevertheless, toucans also eat some insects, such as spiders and termites, as well as some lizards and snakes, and various smaller birds, such as doves and quails. They are threatened by various predators who are liable to eat them: eagles, hawks, ocelots, and snakes fall into this category. Toucans spit out the seeds of the fruits that they eat and these grow into new trees, which is an important practice for distributing vegetation in the rainforest.

Toucans are heavy, weighing between 115 and 860 grams, with a length of between 36 and 79 cm, so they therefore have to sit exclusively on thick branches, as thin branches might break under their weight. Their toes are in pairs with the first and fourth turned backwards, to aid them with gripping branches.

Their bills, which are made from keratin, are hollow and very light, due to the presence of many air pockets. Arteries inside the bills expand and release heat when they get hot. The bill's unwieldy form makes it impossible for toucans to crunch hard food well, but they possess small serrations resembling tiny teeth with which they can cut up and peel fruit. Their bills help them to access food and their size and brightness helps them to scare away predators.

"Bill fencing" is a mating ritual which most toucans perform, essentially a form of playfighting with their bills. Before doing this, the male toucans first fluff up their feathers to show off their colours and wave their bills up and down. Their bills in fact conceal a long, narrow grey tongue, which helps them to catch insects, lizards and frogs.

The voices of Toucans often produce irregular deep grunting notes sounding something like "grnnnkt" or "kkreekkk" or "grenggkt" or "grrr," often making a sound which resembles a rattle-like snore.

Toucans sleep with their heads turned around backwards and their bills over their backs, hidden amongst their feathers so that predators can't see them. They often roost in the cavities of trees, as well as in holes excavated by other animals, particularly those formed by woodpeckers. They have small wings and are not good at flying, only travelling short distances. However, on the occasions when they do reach the ground they are quite adept at hopping.

A number of Amazonian peoples eat toucans and their feathers have decorated the robes of chiefs and emperors there. They are sometimes seen in the Amazon as conduits between the world of the living and that of the spirits.

* * *

As you entered the museum a large map of the world showed all of the territories in which toucans live, shaded in orange. There were facilities for children to create drawings of toucans with felt tips, coloured pencils, and crayons. There were also board games involving the creatures which anyone could play. If visitors were very fortunate, then Nick might dress up in a full body toucan costume and attempt to imitate some of the noises that the birds produce, although he only did this if it seemed like the right occasion had presented itself.

Visitors to the museum tended to respond with an overwhelming positivity, mingled with a large amount of surprise and confusion. Once they had discovered the caravan, it was often difficult to lead children away from it, without them becoming upset. Adults tended to be equally enamoured by the range of materials on display and the amount of information that they learnt.

One of the principle pleasures of the museum was its sudden, unexpected appearance, always coming "as if from nowhere," and often in unlikely venues: city centre alleyways, urban wastegrounds, motorway service station car parks. This ability to appear was coupled with an ability to vanish. It hardly occurred to many of the museumgoers that they might never have an opportunity to visit the museum again. Nick and Flo never promoted themselves in any way. They relied entirely on people who had discovered the caravan at random whilst walking past it or had been given a word-of-mouth recommendation. The museum would never stay in a location for more than a few days at a time.

In the evenings, after closing time, Nick and Flo would often drive to a quiet place where they could relax, undisturbed by requests to view the museum out of hours. They would often go to a country pub and sit in silence, side by side, preferably close to a fire in winter, reading books. They might play chess, or one of various card games that they enjoyed, their favourite being pinochle. It was a simple life, which was precisely what they had hoped for.

27.

Seclusion in the Forest

Ag retreated from everyone, taking up solitary residence inside a hut that she had built for herself inside a secluded area of forest in the West Country. She felt very comfortable within its confines, more so than she had in any other place in which she had been resident during her life. Despite possessing an unassuming exterior appearance, once a visitor entered, they discovered a space which, despite its Spartan character felt like a genuine home and was filled with a number of the sorts of objects which Ag enjoyed dwelling amongst. There were wood carvings, incense holders, crystals, and candles.

She had decided to retreat from human company when she felt that all "direct human interaction," to use her own words, was interfering with any and all psychic activity which she attempted to engage in. It seemed that the voices were suddenly not speaking to her, the spiritual illuminations just would not arrive any longer. Somehow she knew that it was time for her to move on, to make some radical changes in her life.

Henceforth, she decided, her psychic illuminations would only be there to nourish her spiritually. The other uses which she had put them to in the past would be forgotten. In any case she had made so much money from her dial-a-psychic business that she did not need to worry about her finances for some time to come.

She would occasionally be visited by family or friends, but she was always somewhat resentful of their appearance when this happened, being extremely quiet, or even scowling at them (the latter being a trait that was almost entirely new to her). Members of the family were understandably worried by this and wondered quite seriously about the state of her mental health.

Ag no longer felt at all connected to the sort of life lived within cities. The longer that she stayed living outside of them, the more strongly she felt that she didn't want to set foot in a metropolis ever again. She could no longer stand the crowds, the noise, the constant movements of vehicles. She had come to hate the pollution and the way that it would always work its way towards her body, covering her skin, her hair, making her eyes sting. Within her forest seclusion she would often think back to how upsetting these sensations had become to her during her final days in London.

In this state she kept a very minimal wardrobe containing only three outfits. She liked letting her clothes get dirtied by her surroundings, a kind of dirt she enjoyed so much more than that found in the city. She would always wash her clothes by hand in the freezing water of a stream close to her hut and would love feeling the coldness of the water on her hands whilst she washed them, as she heard birds fluttering and wind ruffling the branches of trees.

Ag had never been happier than she was during this period. She enjoyed the purity of simple actions in this state, which was one in which everything came to feel elevated. Now she felt as if she possessed the space to really appreciate the action of drinking a glass of water, of washing her clothes, of breathing.

After the many chaotic years of childhood, which had

contained so many insistent, loud voices, so much hectic action of so many kinds, it was a genuine relief to her to retreat in this manner, to get away from the constant press of human life pushing up against her.

She had brought her silver cat, Esperanza, to live in the hut with her. Upon arrival, Esperanza liked to go roving and would disappear on long expeditions into the forest, presumably scouting out his new territories. At that time he vanished for three entire days. During those occasions Ag had fallen asleep each night consumed with worry and tears, feeling a desperate guilt about the fact that she had transplanted her poor creature to this new, alien terrain, a place where she was convinced he was about to get lost and die. It was therefore a great relief when his familiar form appeared out of a thicket once more, whining for food and milk. After his initial explorations Esperanza soon began to confine himself solely to the hut and its immediate environs. Their mutual seclusion made both cat and woman closer to each other than they ever had been before. She began to speak to him far more, sharing many of the thoughts which entered her mind, however ludicrous or inappropriate or banal those happened to be. These were often the only conversations which she would have with anyone for the length of a whole week.

During this time, Ag often liked to spend all day walking. Setting out at dawn, she would carry a compass in her right hand and simply walk in precisely the same direction for a few hours, before returning back to the hut later in the day. Eventually she got to be so knowledgeable about the forest surrounding her that she found a compass wasn't necessary and she could navigate her way by instinct, through glancing at trees and pathways, by following the movements of her feet as they responded to vibrations and sensory stimuli. Despite the many nearly identical landscapes that she passed through, she could always find her way home eventually.

Another way in which she passed much of her time in this

place was by drawing, something which she had done only very infrequently since she had been a child. Ag found that she often liked to spend all day drawing, perhaps repeating the same object or scene from multiple perspectives or in a variety of different shades. She didn't require any kind of audience for her creations, it was more about the meditational process of producing the work. It really didn't matter to her if the drawings were of any quality or not, the point was simply to have made them. She never felt calmer than when doing this, and to her, during these years, there was no more deeply pleasurable pursuit than this one.

At dawn every day she would meditate, forming a lotus position on the forest floor, never wearing any footwear during this ritual, whatever the weather conditions. She had got to the stage in her spiritual explorations where she was now content to invent her own form of meditation, rather than follow any prescribed method dictated by ancient texts. Attending to her breathing she would remember that she was an organic being who was seeking harmony with both herself and her surroundings. She always felt very calm and centred after doing this and would usually follow this ritual by brewing some nettle tea. This continual meditation practice made her highly aware of certain trees which surrounded the immediate vicinity of her hut, and it came to feel as if they inhabited their own personalities, with their particular patterns of sprouting branches, their individual swaying motions in the wind.

Inside her hut she gathered quite a few objects and curiosities. There were many items of interest to her from the forest: pine cones, ferns, gatherings of weeds and wild flowers, bunches of kindling ready to be set aflame. These were intermingled with objects that she had brought from the city, the vestiges of her old life. Among these there was a tiny oak side table which she ate from, used for sketching, and would examine things on top of; a dark green sleeping bag which she slept inside every night; a very minimal collection of kitchen implements bunched together inside a wooden jug and an indigo-and-cream coloured paisley shawl which hung over the doorway and acted as a portière.

Ag loved the extremity of this situation and the isolation which it involved. She loved not having to encounter the clamouring of human beings all the time. From this perspective everything looked purer, more perfectly formed. This kind of calm, clear exactitude had become exactly what she was seeking. She had come to feel that she needed it in order to live.

Whilst she had very few neighbours there was one who she came to know quite well. Michael was a farmer in his late sixties who would stop by on a fairly regular basis, always creating a little tension as he did so. On the one hand she possessed no desire to offend Michael, who did seem to her to be a pleasant enough character, but nevertheless whenever he appeared he was essentially in the business of disturbing her. Ag had to figure out how to make this known to him without ruining the cordial rapport which they had built up. There was one occasion on which she had been perhaps a little too forward with her words and subsequently Michael had not appeared for some weeks. During that time Ag had needed to admit to herself, a little grudgingly, that she actually missed Michael's occasional presence. When he finally returned she was as guarded and difficult with him as always, but after he left, she was annoyed with herself for having acted in that way with him.

Michael enjoyed talking with Ag about rural matters of all kinds, particularly subjects like pesticides, trespassers, tractor maintenance, and the kinds of people who decide to go on walking holidays. Their conversations were often largely composed of Michael's monologues, with Ag simply listening quietly, with varying degrees of curiosity. For his part, Michael was always aware of Ag's need for solitude, at least vaguely. Sometimes she would have to be quite blunt with him on this issue. At one point in their talk she might say something like: "I'm sorry, Michael, but I really would prefer to be alone right now . . ." Words like these never failed to drive him away, although sometimes she might have to repeat them as he attempted another twenty minutes of speech. He always wore a dirty green check tweed jacket and would often smell of woodsmoke. Early on in their relations Michael had told her that he was a widower and this had made Ag wary of him, as she felt certain that his interest in her was partly a carnal one. Nevertheless, over time his conduct proved to be gentlemanly.

There came a point during her stay in the forest at which Ag started to question the extent of her own sanity. For many months she felt entirely assured that she was doing the right thing by living this way. Indeed, this conviction fuelled her actions on a daily basis. However, there came a morning when she suddenly doubted the truth of all this. She suddenly began to view herself from the imagined perspective of others and no longer felt that what she saw was as agreeable as she had previously thought. Perhaps her absence was hurting other people. Perhaps it was in fact hurting her. However, she soon managed to shake off these feelings of doubt. Indeed, her conclusion to this line of thinking saw her decide, again, that this was in fact her ideal form of existence. She vowed to herself to never again depart from her hut, her forest. Even if others disagreed with her, she would persevere. It was their problem, not her own.

Fears for her personal safety led her to carry a knife on her person at all times. She kept it inside a sheath tucked against her upper thigh. Mostly this proved itself to be a useful instrument for cutting and chopping things, both in the forest and in her hut. She never told anyone, including Michael, about the existence of this knife, feeling instinctively that it might somehow possess more force if it remained a secret entity. She had decided that she was entirely willing to attack anyone who attempted either assault or even rape. She also believed, somehow, that no one would dare do this to her. All in all, the longer that she stayed living in the forest, the closer that she felt to a state that bordered on invincibility.

28.

What Happened Afterwards

Mother continued as she had always done, writing books and articles on different sexual subjects. She added copious numbers of articles to her bibliography including pieces on taboos, the pornographic iconology of air stewardesses, the unconscious sexual metaphors embedded within computer games, as well as the sexual meaning of handcuffs. However, the subject that came to fascinate her the most was that of sexuality in later life.

Lilly never returned to us. We could only speculate as to whether she was still alive or not. Some of us thought so, including me. I simply could not believe that she would ever kill herself. It just didn't seem in keeping with her character. But perhaps I had lost track of what her character had really become.

Lucinda became involved in the construction of model villages and cities. Over time she found these to be more imaginatively engaging than actual villages and cities. These she could control and perfect herself. They seemed to her some of the ultimate symbols of rationality. She would fly around the world planning and building them, constructing examples in Iceland, Japan, India, and The Bahamas.

Ag turned to herself one day and decided that she wished to abandon all of her spiritual and paranormal pursuits. She no longer believed that that she possessed any psychic abilities. She no longer thought that anyone did. Craving a form of normality she married an insurance salesman named Darren and settled into a life in suburbia.

Flo and her husband Nick remained blissfully happy in their marriage. Both of them wrote many books on ornithology. They developed something of a joint obsession with the migratory habits of swallows. Eventually they opened an aviary on the outskirts of San Francisco. Sometimes she would dress up and pretend she was an albatross.

Rebecca became a dog trainer, after a number of years specializing exclusively in the training of dogs for the deaf, teaching dogs to react to sounds such as those of doorbells, text messages and alarm clocks. This job gave her a sense of genuine fulfilment and she fully intended to stay doing this all the way up to the time of her retirement.

Billy died at the age of 36 from a heroin overdose. This was generally thought to be a deliberate act of suicide rather than any sort of accident. No one was entirely certain because he didn't leave any sort of note. On the day that he died he had apparently looked relatively happy in the squat that he was living in, taking part in a large-scale game of hide and seek and drinking a large quantity of vodka.

Gerard remained in the rural community he had established. It gradually became overtaken by a small but substantial number of people who had serious leanings towards Scientology. Gerard didn't really care about that, indeed it took him several years to even notice that this had occurred. Membership declined a little, but things just went on essentially as they had done before.

Eliza became the "secretary" to a poet who only wrote about hair. Then she took to traversing the globe inside a small sailing vessel named "Aloysius". For a time she made designs for a company that manufactured stickers. Finally she opened an ice cream parlour, in a seaside town, in Argentina, a few hundred kilometres south of Buenos Aires.

Barnaby wrote a series of children's books about a snail called Josephine. The first of these was named *Josephine and the Hidden Auditorium*. After this, he was so excited by the story he had written that he could not help but keep composing titles about this character. And so followed: *Josephine and the Hall of Mirrors*, *Josephine and the Blue Clock*, *Josephine in the Seychelles*, and *Josephine has a Wild Time*.

Out of all of us, only Ag, Flo and Eliza would ever have any children of their own.

As for me, Matty, I never left home. It looked too cruel out there. I spent years engaged in a great deal of reading and eventually did some writing. In my later years I became particularly interested in trees. These days I can genuinely say that I am At Peace.

Alex Kovacs was born and raised in the United Kingdom. His first novel, *The Currency of Paper*, was published by Dalkey Archive Press in 2013. He has studied at the University of Edinburgh, Goldsmiths College, and the University of Kent. He lives in London.